Also by the Author

The Ethan Tennant Series

The More Things Change

All Good Things

The Things That Matter Most

Highway 7: 4 Dark Tales

The Mind's
Eye

sands press

The Mind's Eye

Perry Prete

sands press

sands press

A division of 3244601 Canada Inc.
300 Central Avenue West
Brockville, Ontario
K6V 5V2

Toll Free 1-800-563-0911 or 613-345-2687
http://www.sandspress.com

ISBN 978-1-988281-30-8
Copyright © 2017 Perry Prete
All Rights Reserved

Cover concept and Design by Kristine Barker and Wendy Treverton
Edited by Katrina Geenevasen
Formatting by Renee Hare
Publisher Kristine Barker

1st Printing November 2017
To book an author for your live event, please call: 1-800-563-0911

Submissions

Sands Press is a literary publisher interested in new and established authors wishing to develop and market their product. For more information please visit our website at

www.sandspress.com.

November 13

Paige walked along the sidewalk, the heels of her high-cut boots clicking on the concrete. The weather was unseasonably warm for mid- November with the sun high in the cloudless sky. As much as she enjoyed the sun, she looked forward to the snow and the frigid temperatures. With Christmas only a month and a half away, she had always wanted to have all of her shopping done before December. It was a habit she had inherited from her mother and her grandmother before her. In every way, she was her mother's daughter. Even as a young girl, she would purchase her gifts for friends and family weeks in advance. It was difficult for her to keep them a secret sometimes, she wanted to tell family and friends before Christmas day what she had found for them. The anticipation of seeing them open their gifts was as much joy for her as it was for the person opening the package.

She stopped in front of the windows of the local shops, examined the displays and decided whether or not to enter. Like her mother, Paige loved the locally owned small boutiques for unique items that her friends and family cherished. Handcrafted gifts were so much more personal than the mass marketed items found in chain stores.

She turned and continued down the sidewalk, carrying her bags in both hands with her backpack strapped securely over both shoulders. "One more," she thought. Of course, she said that more than three stores earlier. "Only one more."

At one of the local bakers, she spotted the custom, handmade chocolates, those tiny morsels that included flavoured centers; she knew her mother would love them. She entered the boutique shop, and her senses were overwhelmed with fragrant aromas of freshly baked treats. Standing in line, Paige looked through the display glass to the delicacies beneath. The heat from the stone oven at the back of the store gave off a distinctive warmth that reminded her of an old wood stove. As she waited, she selected a white sample box of assorted chocolates for herself to make sure they would be good enough to present to her mother as a Christmas gift.

She left the shop with the sample pack in one of her bags. The boutique clerk had given Paige a free sample that she was savoring as she left. As the chocolate melted in her mouth, the bags in her hands swung freely as she felt the joy of a sunny late fall day. The sun cast tiny shadows beneath her as she walked. The chocolate and soft, creamy caramel swirled together in her mouth. She had found the last gift and pre-ordered the large gift pack of two dozen hand-dipped chocolates for pick up only days before Christmas. It wasn't even December yet, and Paige's shopping was completed.

She was feeling good, almost elated at the thought that she was free of the pressure of any more Christmas gift shopping. What she had in the bags she was carrying would be wrapped and labelled tonight then squirrelled away at the back of the hall closet.

As she strolled along the sidewalk, a man casually followed behind her from a discreet distance. With a backpack slung over his left shoulder and his ball cap pushed back far on his head with earbuds dangling from both ears, he was a man like any other, a man who would not stand out from the crowd. He carried himself as if he was just out for the day. He received nothing more than a passing glance as he passed others on the street. He had picked her out of the crowd almost an hour earlier and kept his distance as he watched her buy gifts.

Before Paige had found the bakery, she had been trying on a few clothing items for herself in the department store, he quickly ducked into the washroom and changed his clothing from the set he carried in his backpack in case she was getting suspicious.

A few blocks further down the street, Paige swung her bags by her side as she neared the parking lot. Holding the bags high, she skipped sideways between the cars instead of the taking the long way down the aisles. As Paige approached her car, she doubled up the bags in one hand then pulled the keys from her purse with her free hand and pressed the remote to unlock the doors. She opened the rear driver's side door and casually tossed the bags onto the back seat. She closed the door, opened her driver's door then felt a hand on her back push her forward, snapping her neck back, causing her to fall headlong into the roof section along the open door. Her face smashed into the rigid roof support. The cartilage at the bridge of her nose fractured, blood spurted outward and back into her throat. She tasted blood and unknowingly spit blood across the roof to the asphalt on the far side of the car. The attacker pulled her hair back, then slammed her face against the car again. She put her arms up to stop the onslaught and coughed as the blood rushed down her throat. Her eyes were already starting to swell shut and couldn't see what was about to happen. She blindly placed her arms in front of her hoping they would find the roof or door. Instead, her hands found nothing but air as her face once again hit the doorframe. Paige lost consciousness and crumpled to the asphalt.

The man opened the back door, picked her up from under the arms and tossed the helpless girl into the back seat. He felt something, something disturbing, he turned quickly and looked up. He scanned the apartment building to the one side of the parking lot, seeing nothing, he slammed the car door, found the car keys on the ground, climbed into the driver's seat and simply drove away.

December 22

"...with a high of only minus three by midday. Dress warmly. I had to spend ten minutes scraping off my car before coming to the station this morning, and it felt a lot colder than minus three. Give yourself a few extra minutes to clean the car and expect a slow drive into work. City ploughs are working hard but don't expect the roads to be clear until sometime this afternoon. Kalee has all the morning news and weather at six, coming up in ninety sec..." Paul Hammond slammed his open hand over the clock radio to silence the annoying voice of the morning deejay. He didn't care for Kalee and the news at six or how fucking cold it was going to be. Even though the room had the same darkness as a black hole in space somewhere in the galaxy, he covered his eyes with his forearm. Paul had discovered long ago he needed the room as dark as possible to sleep after working the night shift. And right now, he wanted to sleep a few more minutes but knew if there were that much snow, he would be pushing it for a time.

Paul reached down and scratched his scrotum. Instead of feeling an erection, he was flaccid again. He missed the days when he would wake up with an erection. In the last few years, the only way he could get an erection was with the help of pharmaceuticals that weren't covered by his benefit plan. Not that he needed to have an erection, Paul couldn't remember the last time he needed to take medication to help him get hard.

Paul whipped the covers off and immediately felt the cool air on his body. He hated sleeping with pajamas, T-shirts or anything for that matter. Paul hated winters, hated the cold, hated working in the cold, the snow, and freezing temperatures only made it difficult as hell to do his job. Paul walked to the bathroom with his eyes closed, the same walk he had made every morning for the past fifteen years since he purchased the house. He sat down on the toilet, eyes still closed and peed. Paul felt as if he could fall asleep if he had to pee any longer. His head kept bobbing as he attempted to remain awake. Opening his eyes, he was looking down and noticed he had a grey hair mixed in with his black pubic hair. "Damn. Seriously? I'm getting grey pubes. Great." He reached down and tried to single out the one grey hair and excise it from the rest of the mass of curly hair and pulled. Paul let out a whimper as he yanked out more than just the one grey hair. He examined the one grey hair to determine if it belongs with the rest of them or was some alien parasite. He let the hairs fall between his legs and land in the toilet bowl water. Paul blindly reached behind and flushed the toilet.

He waited a few minutes for the toilet to finish refilling before he started the shower while he waited, he looked at himself in the full-length mirror on the bathroom wall. First, he questioned why a single man needed a full-length mirror in the bathroom. Secondly, since he was never married, he didn't give a shit what he looked like. Or so he thought. Paul looked at himself in profile and grabbed his stomach. There was enough excess for both hands to grab a large roll of skin and jiggle. "Fat, middle-aged, thinning hair and grey pubes. Ladies will be lining up to be getting some of this."

Stepping into the shower, Paul washed with his eyes closed, hoping this technique would give him the extra rest he needed. He tried this method every morning, and it failed each time.

After a quick breakfast of oatmeal, Paul filled his thermos with coffee unplugged his two cell phones, one personal and the other his police-issued Blackberry, pocketed them, laced up his black running shoes (he refused to give into adulthood) he always wore with his suits, donned his parka, turned off the lights to the tiny porcelain Christmas tree in the hall and opened the front door. It was only six-forty-five, and it was still dark out. The winter blast of cold air hit him hard. "Fucking God damn fucking cold fucking winters." He swore out loud knowing full well the neighbors couldn't hear his rant over the howl of the winds. He tromped through the snow to the driver's door, dropped his thermos in the snow, walked around to the trunk and keyed the remote. The lock clicked, but the trunk failed to raise, "fuck, fuck, fuck, fuck." He swiped his arm across the trunk and pushed the snow to the ground. The snow filled his cuff and made him swear even more. He flung his arm trying to force the snow from inside his cuff. Like most of his efforts, this too was met with failure. Forcing the trunk lid open, snow from the back window slid down and into his trunk. "Fuck." Paul knew this day was starting out bad and could only get better from here. He pulled his battery- operated leaf blower from inside his trunk and slammed the lid closed. Paul squeezed the trigger and aimed it at his car and watched the snow that had accumulated on his car overnight get swept up into the blowing snow. When he was done, he popped the trunk again and tossed the leaf blower inside. Yanking the driver's door open, Paul climbed inside, slammed the door closed and sat with his eyes closed, shivering. He pushed the "Start" button bringing the engine to life. He flipped on the seat warmer and set it to high. Paul let his head fall to the steering wheel. "I hate winter." There wasn't anyone to hear him complain but he felt better for saying it.

Paul unzipped his parka and squirmed to loosen the jacket's grip around his body, so that he could drive. Paul moved the lever to "D" and pulled out of his driveway. The snow was deep, and his tires were pulled in the ruts left by cars that went down his street before him. There weren't many cars on the road at this hour. He was sure a huge percentage of the department's office staff would be late or just not show up. The weather was simply too miserable to risk the drive.

Up ahead, the light turned amber. Paul released his hold of the accelerator and touched the brakes. The pedals pulsated against the constant pressure he was applying as the anti-lock brakes prevented him from sliding through the intersection. He put his hand across the passenger seat to grab his thermos and prevent it from falling to the floor and felt nothing. He looked across the seat and remembered exactly where he left it, in the snow beside where his car was in the driveway. After he came to a stop at the light, he punched the steering wheel. The driver of the car beside him turned to look at him, and Paul gave him a friendly wave and then stared straight ahead. "Fuck." Lately, he had come to swear a lot and speak aloud when he was alone. And Paul was alone a lot. Other than work, he seldom went out or hung out with his friends or guys from work. They all had girlfriends, wives, kids and he didn't fit in anymore.

He pulled away from the intersection and made his way carefully to the station and arrived just a little after seven. Paul stomped his feet as he entered the front door and shook the snow from his jacket. He waved to the dispatchers behind the glass wall, they waved back and used his access card to gain entry to the restricted area. In the men's room, he opened his locker, retrieved his Glock handgun, made sure it was clean and loaded and affixed it to his belt. He secured the combination lock and spun the dial to the number "14". It was a habit he got into in high school when he was bullied. Paul would set the combination lock to "14" and if the lock wasn't as he left it, he knew to be wary of what may have happened if he opened his locker door. He convinced himself he wasn't paranoid. Paranoid people imagine other people are watching them, following them. Paul just wanted his privacy.

That was a long time ago, but the habit followed him his entire life. Before Paul could grab a coffee, he sat at his desk, booted up his laptop, then went to the break room where one of the dispatchers joined him. Wanda was a short, good-looking, middle-aged woman who loved to know everything about everyone. If Paul needed to know something going on at the station, he went to see Wanda. "Did you hear what one of the snow plough operators found this morning?" she stirred her coffee and never made eye contact with Paul.

"Just got in. What happened?" Paul placed a plastic lid on his disposable cup. He hated the office coffee; it always tasted weak like they used twice as much water or half the coffee grounds. That was why he brought in his thermos every day, except today.

"The guy was ploughing along McKinnon Boulevard and looked in his rearview and thought he saw a stiff leg or an arm or something mixed in with the snow bank. He stopped the plough, took a look and called it in. Uni's are on their way now. You want lead on this one? My bet is that some a-hole tossed an old mannequin in the garbage and it ended up in the snow bank." Wanda still had her headset on. It didn't matter if she was on break or lunch, that headset was never off her head.

"Sure. My workload is pretty light right now, and I haven't had a homicide in what," he paused, "maybe over a year. Christ. I'm due I guess. I'll grab a coffee, tell the Captain I'm taking a four by four. No way in hell I'm driving my car in this shit."

"I'll talk to the Captain before I assign the call and tell him you can have a lead on this."

"Thanks, Wanda. I owe you."

"Don't thank me. Like I said, I'm laying odds it's a mannequin."

Paul took a large mouthful of coffee, refilled his cup and replaced the lid. He made his way to the back of the building and signed out the keys for one of the SUV unmarked vehicles.

As Paul booked into service, his service cell phone rang. He tapped the Bluetooth button on his steering wheel and turned up the volume. Before he could answer, Wanda began to speak, and her voice filled the car through the radio speakers, "Paul, the uni's on scene said it was definitely a body. Scene's been secured; Captain said you've got lead. Oh, you've got help on this one."

"Help?"

"Workload is light all around. You'll find out when you get on scene."

The line went dead.

Paul drove the rest of the way in silence as the SUV cut through the snow. The snow hit hard towards the windshield as the wipers failed to keep the snow from piling up around the edges. Paul turned up the heat and fan in an attempt to keep his vision clear. The hidden grill lights failed to cut through the driving snow and blinded him each time the white and blue LED's flashed back against the snow. He deactivated the grill lights and slowed his speed. It didn't matter if he wasn't the first on scene so long as he arrived in one piece.

Paul kept the music off. Instead, he listened to the police radio blare out calls all over the city, mostly minor motor vehicle accidents. Regardless, the weather kept the uniformed officers busy. Paul turned the corner onto McKinnon Boulevard and saw the group of cruisers and other forensics teams standing around. He pulled in close to the other cruisers and turned his grill lights back on. As he put the SUV into park, he saw what Wanda meant by "Help".

Detectives Dan Levy and Ken Simmons were already standing outside in the cold. Their parkas pulled up high around their heads protecting them from the wind and blowing snow. They were speaking with what Paul assumed was the plough operator as he was the only one dressed in yellow and reflective tape. All three were shifting their weight back and forth and stomping their feet trying to create kinetic energy for heat.

Paul opened the door to the SUV, and the wind almost whipped the driver's door from his hand. He stepped out of the truck and had to force the door closed against the wind. He flipped the hood up and zipped the front to just under his chin. He made his way over to where Dan and Ken stood speaking with the plough operator. As he arrived, the plough driver excused himself and went to sit in the cab of his truck to get warm.

"Christ. The radio said a high of minus three, but it feels more like minus thirty." Paul stuck his hands in his pockets to stay warm. "I'm too old for this shit. I hate winter." The wispy white vapor of frozen breath escaped every time someone spoke.

Dan laughed, "You're younger than us," he motioned with his head over towards Ken, "You should be able to take the cold a little better."

"Younger. Fuck that. I found a grey hair today." Paul's face almost disappeared in the white cloud as he told the men of his discovery.

Ken broke in, "You have tons of grey."

Paul looked down, "Found the first one there."

Ken and Dan enjoyed a laugh at Paul's expense while trying not to open their mouths to the cold. Ken offered a suggestion, "My wife hated my grey and convinced me to manscape. No hair, no grey. She said she won't blow me unless I keep it hair free. Only thing is you have to be pretty fucking careful with the razor. Took out a chunk last week."

There was a chorus of "oohs" and "aahs!" from Paul and Dan at the thought.

Dan had to best them. "You thought your morning was bad. The dog wanted out at four this morning. I took him downstairs, opened up the door, and he stood there looking at the cold, and the fucking dog turned and when back to bed. When the alarm went off, I went to take a shower and stepped in pile of dog shit on the bedroom carpet. I told the wife to clean it up; I was running late because of the storm. She wasn't happy."

After the laughter calmed down, Dan led Paul to where the plough operator found the body. The three detectives kept their head low against the wind as they walked around the massive plough and Ken pointed to the top of the snow drift. Like a signpost rising from the top, a bare human arm could be seen sticking out of the snow. The flesh didn't look to be real; it was a pale, pasty white, almost plastic and the hand in an awkward position in relation to the rest of the visible arm.

"Anybody confirm its human and not a mannequin?" Paul asked.

"I climbed up myself. It's human. The wrist looked like it was fractured either before she was dumped or after the plough scooped her up with the rest of the snow and tossed her up there," Ken offered.

"Her?" Paul looked surprised.

"Her. No hair on the arm, fingernails long and some broken, frame is small. Could be a guy but my guess, it's a her. There's no blood in the snow, at least not what I could see. Most of the snow is black, dirty and there's a lot of gravel from when they sanded the roads. It's gonna be a mess to sift through for evidence."

Paul walked a few feet along the base of the snow bank. As the bank followed the road, the plough pushed the packed snow high and away from the street. Paul was five-eight, short for a cop but he guessed the snow bank to be at least seven feet high. The winter had been particularly hard, lots of snow and colder temperatures than normal. The city had already spent their entire snow removal budget for the year, so they hadn't cut the snow banks down in a few weeks. Paul looked back at the two detectives under his command, "Any fucking clue how we're going to get her outta there?"

Dan started to stomp his feet to stay warm as he spoke, "Crime techs said they'll put up a shelter and dig her out like they would as if they were unearthing a victim buried in the ground. No one is sure if it's just an arm or the whole body. The arm could've been ripped off when the plough pushed the snow. For all we know, the rest of the body could be down the street."

"Make certain they run fingerprints and DNA as soon as they can. Once you have the prints, check them against missing persons, local, national and international. I don't want us looking like amateurs. It's gonna be hard enough getting evidence outta a mound of snow almost eight feet high. Last thing I want is for some kid to find the rest of the body in the spring thaw. Got it?" Paul had that serious expression on his face his co-workers had come to recognize as his "Don't fuck with me" look.

Paul nodded to Dan and Ken then decided to walk further down the street to see for himself if any other body parts could be buried in the snowbank. He told Dan and Ken where he was going, flipped up the collar on his parka and pulled the ends in tight around his face. With his head down against the wind, one hand held the collar closed tight around his neck, the other was stuffed in his pocket, he forced his way along the sidewalk. Small orange pylons lined the one lane, directing traffic away from the crime scene. His portable radio kept squawking as his made his way along the snow bank. Every few feet, he would stop, examine the snow from base to summit and move on. It was almost impossible to see anything in the dim light within the dirty, tightly packed snow. The large chunks of packed snow piled high resembled a small mountain peak. The newly fallen snow only made it more difficult as it added a layer of white fluff covering to the mountain of snow. Paul stopped and looked back to the scene where the arm was found in the snow. He was half a block away, but in the cold and wind, it felt like he was miles away.

Buried deep within in layers of clothing, one of the phones began to buzz and vibrate. It was his phone, and not his department-issued Blackberry. He removed a glove, unzipped the main closure to his parka, felt the cold penetrate as the wind cut through, lifted his sweater and attempted to retrieve his phone from his breast pocket. The buzzing stopped. "Fuck," he screamed. He swiped up from the bottom of the screen, "one missed call" was visible on the screen. Paul saw the number and wanted to throw the phone into the snow bank. He had been waiting for this call for weeks. He spun around, wanting to vent and scream. His soft soled, black high-top running shoes hit a patch of slippery packed snow, and his leg went up, throwing his weight off, sending him flying backwards through the air. Paul landed flat on his back, his head struck the road, and the force of the impact pushed all the air from his lungs. Tiny bright lights began to pop in his eyes, his head swam from the impact, and he fought to catch his breath. By the time Paul caught his breath and his vision returned to normal, Dan and Ken stood over him, laughing.

"I think that grey pube sent you off balance," Ken had trouble getting the words out as he laughed. He extended his hand to help Paul up from the roadway. He held firm and pulled up his co-worker. Paul stood for a moment with his eyes closed to regain his balance then rubbed the back of his head and felt something wet. He looked at his hand and found a mixture of snow, blood and hair entangled in his fingers.

Ken walked around to look at the back of Paul's head, "You might need a few stitches bud."

Paul pocketed his cell phone, "It can wait until we're done here." He wiped his bloodied hand on his parka and started to walk back to the scene where the arm had been found. He lost his footing and Ken, and Dan caught him. "Whoa. You might have a concussion," Dan suggested.

"I'll be OK," Paul replied. He held his footing and slowly started making his way up the road. With Ken and Dan at his back, Paul planted each step and made his way back up the street. His mind had cleared by the time Paul was back up at the crime scene. He pulled his hood over his head to protect his wound against the blowing snow.

The crime scene technicians arrived shortly after the three detectives made their way back. The lead tech spoke to Paul, together they determined the best course of action then informed his fellow technicians. Even in the frigid temperatures, the crime techs still had an important function to complete in the investigative process. Each technician was wearing a white Tyvek suit over a snowmobile suit to protect themselves from the cold. The lead tech dispatched a female tech to the snow plough to examine the blade for blood and tissue.

Several other techs climbed the snow bank and erected a pop-up shelter which protected the arm from the environment. The shelter was balanced over both sides of the snow bank with the victim's arm centered beneath the canopy. Once the shelter was up, the technicians began to slowly excavate the snow from around the area of the arm. They placed the snow in buckets which were taken down the snow bank to a waiting truck. Inside, another technician would carefully melt the content of the buckets and examine the liquid for possible evidence. This process continued as the three detectives collected what little evidence they could from the scene.

As the slow, arduous process continued of separating snow from evidence, the three detectives each took a side street to canvas the neighborhood for any information or witnesses who may have seen the body dump. Paul carefully strolled on the icy roads, making sure each step was deliberate and planned. His rubber-soled running shoes, perfect for the summer, were now his nemesis in the freezing weather. He squinted to shield his eyes from the blowing snow that the weather channel had said would be over by noon. The storm showed no signs of letting up as Paul thanked the elderly couple he had just spoken with. He grasped the railing, took each snow-covered step slowly until he reached the path which wasn't much better than the steps.

The radio buried deep inside Paul's parka kept crackling with static that he couldn't understand through the layers of clothing. Shortly after he fell, the headache worsened. Before canvassing, he touched the back of his head and was surprised to learn the bleeding had stopped. At the road, Paul paused, closed his eyes hoping this would quell the pain. He took in a few deep breaths before continuing down the street. He made his way to the next house and knocked at the door. A young woman answered the door, pulled her sweater around herself as the wind wiped around her. "Yes."

Paul looked at her, opened his notebook and clicked his pen and stared blankly at the woman. "Yes," she repeated. Paul attempted to speak, but his mind swirled with images and then went blank. He tumbled to his knees and fell forward into the woman. She tried to grab the stranger at her door, preventing him from landing hard on the floor but she wasn't strong enough or quick enough. Paul hit the floor hard, face first rendering him unconscious.

Light broke in from all sides until all the darkness gave way. Eyelids fluttered, images came into focus until Paul Hammond realized where he was. The large stainless-steel light over his head, the constant beeping of the ECG machine that monitored his heart rate and rhythm, the clothespin device at the end of his finger that check his oxygen saturation levels were a dead give-a-away. The headache that pounded within his skull made him want to go back to sleep.

"You scared the crap outta us you know." Dan and Ken stood along the back wall of the private ED room. "I'll go get the nurse or someone and let them know you're awake." Dan left Ken with Paul to care for him.

"I have a fucking headache the size of Cleveland." Paul's eyes were closed. He rubbed the back of his head. His fingers found the plastic thread sutures that formed a straight line where his open wound had been. "How long have I been out?" Paul's mouth was dry, pasty, his tongue ran along the front of his teeth, and it felt as if sand has somehow found a way to stick to enamel.

Ken saw Paul try to moisten his mouth and poured him a glass of water. "Paramedics brought you in after you collapsed, they did a CT, found nothing, and I mean nothing. Doctors said you're the first case of any person they can find as a functioning adult without a brain." Paul finished the glass of water and held it out in the air, silently asking Ken for a refill. "Ha," was all Paul could and wanted to say. "You can go home soon."

Paul gulped down the second glass of water and put his head back and closed his eyes. "Seriously?"

"Seriously. They said you could go home as soon as you wake up and the doc clears you."

"Any more news from the scene?" Paul wiped the moisture from his lips with the back of his hand.

"Lots. You up for this?" Paul nodded. "K. The techs dug the arm outta the snow. It's female. That's all that was there. Nothing else, no more soft tissue, no blood. It was definitely a drop. She was killed, I assume she's dead, somewhere else. The arm was taken down to the station to be examined. They'll run a tox screen, check for tattoos, shit like that and see if there are any drugs in the system but the funny thing is," Ken paused, "Ready? This is pretty fucking strange."

Eyes closed, Paul shook his head again and swirled his index finger in the air, silently telling Ken to get on with it. "The arm ended at the shoulder. But the way it was severed is the strange part. You know how you pull the leg off a cooked chicken, you grab it, twist and pull then literally rip it from the carcass?" Ken had Paul's attention. He sat up on the edge of the bed and stared at Ken, waiting for him to finish. "The arm was ripped from the torso. There wasn't a single cut mark on any of the soft tissue. I mean none. The skin, muscle, tendons, ligaments, every fucking thing was torn from the body. It was as if she was, what did they call it when they tied someone's legs, and arms to four horses and they were ripped apart?"

"Quartered."

"Quartered. Right. Anyway, the crime scene tech thinks she was quartered, or some fucker is strong and pulled her apart."

"Is that even possible?" Paul hopped off the hospital bed, shook the probe from the end of his finger, pulled the leads from his chest and unwrapped the blood pressure cuff from around his arm. He stood motionless for a few moments as began looking for his clothes. Ken pointed under the bed to the plastic bag that held everything Paul had come in with. "I mean to pull someone's arm from their socket. Christ. I hope she was dead first. What if she isn't dead and that arm is just the first of four things to be ripped off the body?"

Ken suddenly had a horrified look on his face, "I never even considered that. I just assumed she would be dead. Fuck. If she was alive when that happened. Hell, I don't even wanna think about that."

Paul was pulling his pants up with his back to Ken, with one hand bracing himself against the bed in case he passed out again, "Think about it. We have one arm, no body. And until we have every single body part, the working theory is that the woman is still alive. Got it."

Paul had his back to the door as he buttoned his shirt. The door opened as Dan, and one of the ER doctors walked in. "Mr. Hammond, I'm Dr.

Hernandez. Would you mind telling me what you're doing?" The soft voice of the doctor made Paul spin around. His mind stopped, his breathing froze, Paul was looking at one of the most beautiful women he had ever met. The doctor was almost the same height as Paul and was only a few feet from him. The lab coat hung loosely over her shoulders, obviously, it was several sizes too large for her small frame, the pockets were overloaded with small manuals, a small tablet and a stethoscope. The left breast pocket held several colored pens, and there were ink streaks where either she or the previous wearer continually forgot to cap the pen or retract the tip. Her long, wavy black hair fell to her shoulders framing a delicately featured woman. Paul extended his hand silently to greet her. She shook his hand, and Paul felt just how small framed she was. Her soft hand disappeared into his. He shook it gently then released his hold. Ken and Dan recognized Paul's instant attraction to the doctor.

"Not sure if you heard but we have a case." Paul felt like a high school boy seeing the most beautiful girl in school. He knew for certain he was smiling and felt embarrassed by it. He turned and pulled the remaining items from the plastic bag that held his belongings. "We are in a bit of a hurry doc."

"You may have a severe concussion and we treat those things seriously. I'd prefer if you'd stay for a few hours longer, so we can monitor you." Dr. Hernandez gaze was one of concern for her patient.

"I have to go. We," he looked at Ken and Dan, "are working on something."

Dr. Hernandez looked at the three men knowing how stubborn they could be, "Sit for a second, let me get one more set of vitals." She patted the bed indicating she wanted Paul to sit for a moment.

Paul stopped getting dressed and did as he was told. The doctor pulled her stethoscope from her lab coat, and as she placed the ends in her ears, Paul saw the white band and large diamond on her fourth left finger. Someone has just taken out a small pin and popped his balloon. As she auscultated Paul's lungs, Dan held up his left hand then pointed to his wedding band and mouthed, "She's married." Paul nodded in agreement, and both Ken and Dan had a silent laugh behind the doctor's back. Dr. Hernandez then took his pulse and wrote them down on his chart. "If this is some he-man thing, I'm not impressed. I'd rather have you to stick around and rest for a few more hours but if you have to leave and you don't feel well, come back, and I'll check you over. Can't have our boys in blue fainting on the job."

Dr. Hernandez completed her exam, scribbled some notes on the chart, "One note of caution Mr. Hammond. If you feel anything what-so-ever out of the ordinary, I want you back here. Got it."

Dan and Ken laughed from the back of the room.

"Boys. You don't change, even when you get older, just bigger versions of children. Geez." Dr. Hernandez then turned to Paul, "Dizziness, nausea, headaches, stuff like that."

Paul shrugged his shoulders, "Hey, it wasn't me. I never said a thing."

*****

Standing alone in the autopsy room, Paul looked at the stark white walls and stainless-steel tables and instruments and wondered why the room had to look like a surgical suite. He stood over the autopsy table looking down at the Caucasian female right arm. It had warmed up to room temperature and other than not being attached to the rest of the body, it looked perfectly normal. This was the worst part of the job. He remembered the first time he watched an autopsy. The woman had been beaten to a point where the family had difficulty recognizing her. Most of her facial bones had been fractured, and she had been either kicked or punched so viciously that her internal organs had also shown signs of trauma. Her spleen had ruptured, one of her lungs had collapsed, and her aorta had torn. Paul had watched the procedure from the back of the room as the lead detective stood beside the coroner. After the autopsy was complete, Paul excused himself and went to the bathroom and vomited until his throat burnt from the acid. He rinsed his mouth several times and chewed almost an entire pack of gum before going back to his desk.

Paul examined the loose tissue around the shoulder and immediately understood the initial assessments that the arm had been ripped from the torso. The milky white head of the humerus protruded from deep within the muscle. The striated muscle fragments weren't cut but rather stretched to the point they pulled apart.

"Having fun with my patient Mr. Hammond?" The voice of the coroner came from behind but echoed in this vile room Paul came to despise. Paul didn't turn around; instead, he continued to look at the arm on the table. "Not much eh Mr. Hammond?"

The coroner stopped when she was standing to the detective's right.

Paul looked straight ahead and saw their reflection in the glass cabinet door before them. Maura was by anyone's standard, a good-looking woman, odd but a good coroner. Paul didn't associate much with any of the post-mortem staff. Maura grabbed a small stainless-steel probe from the instrument table and began to touch the ends of the muscle. "See here Paul; the muscle has literally been pulled apart." She flipped a section of the skin over, "This is the exciting part," with her gloved hand, Maura lifted the edge of the skin, "I'm not even sure how much tension it takes to rip skin apart."

Paul felt that twinge in his stomach that almost caused him to vomit right there. He clenched his teeth, held his jaw firm and hoped his stomach would calm down. Each time Maura would pull or tug or talk about ripping things, Paul felt another wave of nausea come over him.

"I'll have to research the tensile strength of skin and muscle and see if we have evidence of how much it would take to rip off an arm. Look here." Maura pointed to the wrist. "It's kind of exciting, freaky as Hell, I'm gonna have to really look, but I would've expected some type of ligature mark to show where the weight was tied or what was used to pull the arm off..." Maura was stopped short by Paul's hand swiftly coming up indicating he had had enough. "OK to do what was done. Listen, Paul, I'm not insensitive, I understand not everyone can do what I do, but I could never do what you do. This is a pretty gruesome thing that's happened, and if you can't handle it, maybe you should take yourself off this case." Maura didn't pull any punches.

"I'm fine. I fell and struck my head earlier today, and I'm just a little, well, under the weather. My stomach is flying in circles, K?" Maura nodded, she understood and let the matter drop.

Maura decided to shift the attention away from the arm and to the variety of items on the green cloth on the table to the left of the amputated arm. Using the pointer, she touched several of the items, "These were in the open wound, bits of gravel and small stones, a few bits of paper, this little bit of nylon string," she flipped a short, two-inch piece of nylon string over, "I'm not sure what this is? Nylon string from a weed whacker or something."

Paul leaned in close, "It's fishing line."

"You sure?"

"Pretty sure. Too thin to be from a weed whacker. It's clear and thinner than the line used for a weed whacker. I haven't fished since I was a kid but I'm sure it's fishing line."

Maura flipped the tiny bit of fishing line over, "Why would you end up with a short piece of fishing line?"

Paul thought about it, "Cut a piece off from the knot, not sure. This other stuff, gravel and dirt, can be found anywhere but a fishing line, not sure. When do you think I can get your idea of what this stuff is?'

"I'll send my report as soon as I'm done." With that, she flipped off her nitrile gloves, tossed them in the hazardous waste receptacle and left Paul alone with the arm. Paul heard the door close behind him, and remained there staring at the appendage.

December 25

Paul arrived at the police station just before nine. He was scheduled to be off today, he wasn't even on call but wanted to finish up some work and not be disturbed. If a call did come in, he thought he might even take it and let the guys with families stay home. He pulled out his cell phone, plugged it in to charge it, and dropped his backpack to the floor and kicked it under his desk.

It had been three days since Paul missed the call on his cell. He picked up the tethered phone to the power cord, swiped up on the screen and tapped the phone function. He looked at all the calls on his phone and saw the familiar number. His thumb hovered over the icon to call the number back. It was Christmas day; she was most definitely with her family. Bad idea. He dropped the phone to the desk, looked at it and pushed it to the back.

Paul dropped hard into the swivel chair, arched his back until he heard a sickening crack and realized this was a truly bad idea. He scanned his desk, looked inside his backpack, then cursed loudly that he had forgotten his thermos of fresh coffee. He passed several coffee shops on the way into the station, but every one of them was closed. He stood and looked over his partition wall around the room. It was eerily silent; no one else was in the small office dedicated to the detectives. He went to the coffee station and found a pot of coffee half full. He didn't want to make a fresh pot just for himself, so he decided to risk the day-old coffee. Paul added a few extra sugar packs, microwaved the Styrofoam cup for a minute. He walked from the coffee machine, through the maze of tiny desk partitions, carrying a hot, stale cup of coffee, and sat at his desk. He couldn't remember a day when the office had been this quiet. He brought the cup to his mouth; the hot liquid instantly burnt his lips. Instinctively, Paul pulled the mug back and spilt coffee over the papers on his desk and his lap.

"Fuck." The outburst would normally attract attention but today, nothing. He brushed hot liquid from his pants then touched his upper lip. "Shit that was hot." Paul realized he was talking out loud with no one to hear him. He picked up a file that coffee had pooled on, tilted it and let the coffee drain into the wastepaper basket. Still standing, it was then he saw the FedEx envelope on his desk. He let the wet file drop to the floor and picked up the plastic envelope. Again, he looked around the room, wondering when and who placed the envelope on his desk. He studied the label and noticed it had been sent on December 22 and arrived the following day. Somehow, he missed it.

Paul tore the envelope open, looked inside, then dumped the contents onto his desk. The air left his lungs and couldn't breathe. He fell back into his chair.

January 18

Paul sat at the far end of the table in the conference room as Ken Simmons and Dan Levy tinkered with the laptop connected to the overhead DLP projector. After several minutes, both men gave up and asked Paul to join them as they crowded around the laptop. Ken set the laptop in the centre of the three of them and found the picture file sent to them by the Medical Examiner.

Paul read the final report on the arm found in the snow bank. He had highlighted the areas that stuck out: "tissue was frozen" obvious he thought, the arm was discovered in a snow bank, "undetermined possible ligature mark around the wrist, with the area frozen, difficult to determine if the marks were made by a ligature or something pressing against the skin while it was being frozen". Paul knew he would never know for certain if there was something tied around the wrist. "cancerous tumor growth, size 0.5 cm in circumference, at the proximal head of the humerus".

"Poor girl."

Ken turned to look at Paul, "What?"

"The arm. The girl had cancer. Not sure if she knew or not but sad. Just reading from the autopsy report of the arm."

Ken went back to the laptop, clicked on the image file, and a series of tiny thumbnail pictures appeared on the screen. He double clicked on the first image, and it opened to show the body of deceased pig secured to a table with nylon webbing. The skin had a frostbitten appearance, white and waxy, the four legs sticking straight out to the side. Ken tapped the mouse to move to the next picture, then the next. The tests performed on the pig showed failures of dismembering the legs from the body. After several test pigs had been used, eventually, one test showed success. It showed approximately the same type of skin tearing and muscle separation as the arm. The test was repeated several times to ensure the method used was possibly the one used to remove the arm from the body discovered in the snow bank. The pig's body was frozen, one leg tied to a vehicle, the other three legs were secured to a stationary concrete pole in the parking lot. The vehicle then pulled away slowly and ripped the single appendage off the swine resulting in injuries similar to the arm found in the snow.

Ken leaned back in his chair, "So how does a guy figure out how to do this? I mean, we had to buy what, four or five pigs, let them freeze outside, hog tie them to something," the other two men chuckled, "Yeah, I said hog tied, anyway, how do you figure out this stuff without having a place to test the methodology? I mean, there has to be a reason for this. Why rip an arm off and leave it to be found?"

Paul bolted upright, "What if the arm wasn't what he wanted. What about the tumour? The poor girl had a growth on the bone in the upper arm. Do you think she even knew? Maybe we're looking at this the wrong way. What if the arm wasn't the prize but the garbage?" Puzzled, Ken and Dave looked at him. "K, serious, listen, you buy a chicken from the market, take it home and you want to make, I dunno, a chicken salad sandwich. You skin the chicken, pull the wings off, maybe pull the legs off and pull the meat from the carcass. You throw the wings away right. Some people gnaw on them, but most people throw them away. They get all hard and dried out. What if the arm was a discard, not any part the guy wanted?"

Ken suddenly understood, "I get it, for whatever reason, the guy needs to remove the arm, takes it off and doesn't need it anymore. He tosses it the way you toss the chicken skin and wings into the trash. But why does he need the rest of the body? OK, another theory, what if the arm getting ripped off was an accident?"

"Sorta like the arm got caught in something, and the body was pulled," Dave broke in, "and rip." He tugged on his own arm to prove his point.

"A total unforeseen accident. There may not have been any planning in the process, it was just a fucking accident."

Paul sat back in his chair. He was now faced with multiple scenarios that may have been the cause of the arm injury. And there was still no body, no way of knowing if the victim was even dead.

Ken studied the report, "Did you read the report on the fragments found in the wound?" Dan and Paul shook their heads that they both hadn't had an opportunity to review the findings. "Says here that the gravel was just that, gravel. Stones are no different than anything found in the area. The only odd finding was the 3.5-centimetre-long monofilament fishing line." Ken looked up from the report, "What do you guys make of the fishing line?"

Dan spoke first, "Garbage?" They all agreed.

February 28

Freezing rain battered the bedroom window, waking Nicole before the alarm went off. Still purring, her cat was sleeping on her tummy, sending gentle ultrasound waves deep into her stomach. She blindly reached down and began to stroke the cat who increased the intensity of the purr the longer she stroked her fur. She opened one eye, and from across the room, she could make out the time displayed in large red LED numbers, 5:27. She didn't have to be at work for another two and half hours, and she doubted very much that many of her co-workers would show up for today if the freezing rain continued. Nicole decided to stay in bed for as long as she could, after all, she thought, the alarm was still set to go off in another hour. She closed her eyes, enjoyed the tender cat massage on her tummy and fell back to sleep until she woke naturally almost three hours later.

Her bedroom was awash in bright light as the sound of freezing rain continued to beat against her window. Nicole sat up with a start, confused she looked around the room for the time displayed on her alarm clock on the opposite side of the bedroom. The clock wasn't working, the dim, tiny light on her cordless phone indicating the phone was charging wasn't illuminated either. She reached to her right, grabbed the TV remote and clicked the power button. Nothing. Her cell phone was downstairs in the kitchen on charge. She hopped out of bed and sprinted down the hall to the kitchen. She could feel the cool tile floor beneath her feet. She pulled the cell phone from the counter but the charging cord anchored itself to the outlet pulling the phone from her hand sending it crashing to the counter, bounced and dangled in front of the drawers by its cable. This time she made sure to hold the phone and disconnect the cord before bringing it to view.

She tapped the power button, entered her four-digit security code and saw the time. It was a little after eight. "Shit." Nicole dialed the office, and it went straight to her supervisor's voice mail. She waited for the message to finish then left a brief message about being late. She hung up and called Simone's cell who worked in the same department, Customer Service. Simone picked up on the second ring and was met with her usual musical way of speaking. "Hey, girl." When Simone spoke, she almost sang to you. It was the main reason the company put her in charge of customer service. She routinely received the highest overall scores for customer satisfaction. The two had worked side by side for years and except for the occasional spat, were as close as sisters.

"Simone, is the office closed?" There was still obvious panic in Nicole's voice.

"Haven't you heard girl? The whole city is shut down, ice everywhere. Power lines are down; traffic sucks, most of the stores are closed. I'm just sitting here having a Chai Tea and a scone." You could hear music playing in the background.

"If the power is out everywhere, how come you're drinking a Chai Tea? Is Starbucks open?"

"Honey, I have the world's best boyfriend remember. He stopped by, chained up a generator thingy to the side porch and ran a few power cords into my house. I made a Chai Tea and let a few scones thaw out on the counter. You can't have Chai Tea without a scone. It just don't happen girl." Simone laughed in her singing voice. "Do you have power at your place?" she asked.

"No. I freaked when I woke up late and tried calling the office. Are we closed today?"

"Office is closed until further notice. Why don't you come over here and spend the day with me keeping warm? I heard the power could be down for hours."

"And how would I do that darlin'? I don't have a car remember." Nicole was using her sarcastic voice.

"Pack up a few things, I'll send the BF over to pick you up in his big truck, and we can spend the day shooting the shit. You up for that?"

Nicole agreed and said she would pack up a bag and wait for Simone's boyfriend to stop by. She hung up her cell phone, found a night bag and filled it with toiletries, clean clothes, her cell phone charger and a few other odds and ends. She made sure Tabitha had a clean litter box, fresh water, a full bowl of hard kibble and a full can of moist food before she left.

Even in a four-wheel-drive pickup, the ride from Nicole's apartment to Simone's house was more treacherous than a poorly thought out roller coaster. The winter had been a mixture of heavy snow, high snow banks and the occasional mild temperatures that brought rain and flash thaws and now freezing rain. Nicole secured the seat belt tightly and held on firmly to the grab bar on the "A" pillar by the windshield. The truck would catch a frozen rut, twist itself before the wheels caught and righted itself. The wheels would slip again; the truck would slow; the tires catch a little traction and pitch forward. Nicole would let out these little shrieks, and Simone's boyfriend would laugh loudly. She could see how these two got along so well. They both had a zest for life that somehow how bypassed her.

A short time later, Nicole sat with Simone enjoying that Chai Tea she spoke of earlier and a partially thawed scone. After finishing her drink, she asked if she could steal a few moments for a quick shower then headed for the washroom. Nicole had managed a new record for a quick shower, she figured just under two minutes. She quickly toweled dried and put on fresh clothes and pulled her wet hair back. Even though there was enough power from the generator to keep the hot water tank running, Nicole wanted to make sure there was plenty for the others. Simone had plugged in a few lights, the fridge, a space heater and a power bar to keep her phone and tablet charged up. Simone surmised between music, news and some saved movies on the tablet; she was good for a few hours as long as there was gas in the generator. The two girls sat at the table, drank too much tea, partially frozen foods and laughed like eight-year-old girls on a sleepover.

"Do you know how to play Cribbage?" Simone asked as she stood to find the board even before Nicole could answer. "Of course, you do, who doesn't know how to play Crib. The playing cards are in the top drawer." Simone pointed to the bank of four drawers to the right of the stove, asking Nicole to retrieve the deck of cards. She didn't have the heart to tell her host that she has never played the game. With only one light plugged into the extension cord, the low light cast long shadows across the kitchen. Nicole decided to use her cell phone flashlight app held high over the open drawer as she rummaged through the junk Simone has collected. She pushed stuff aside and flipped papers over looking for playing cards. "Did you find the cards yet girl?" Simone said out loud. "Would kids today even know what to look for or how to play cards if they didn't have their cell phones and tablets?" The thought makes her laugh even more.

Nicole turned some papers over; a few photographs fell from the pages and without warning, she let out a blood-curdling scream. She dropped her cell phone and it landed in the drawer. She fell back against the opposite counter, covering her mouth with both hands. The light from her phone shone straight up in the air as Nicole began to cry.

"What the fuck?" Simone came running into the kitchen to find she friend shaking uncontrollably.

"There's something moving in the drawer." Nicole pointed to the drawer then covered her mouth again.

Carefully, Simone stepped closer to the open drawer and with her hand shaking, she reached in to retrieve Nicole's cell phone to use as the flashlight. She pointed the tiny beam of light into the junk scattered about in the deep drawer, "Where?" Simone asks.

"When I flipped over that stack of papers on there," Nicole points, "something fell out and moved." She noticed the finger she was using to point with was shaking and bouncing up and down.

Simone found a metal barbecue skewer and used it as a poker to turn items over in the drawer. One by one, stuff she had tossed in the drawer was turned over and moved aside. Nicole let out another scream that made Simone jump back. "There, there," she yelled.

"Christ girl. Don't yell so fucking loud. I'm right beside you." Simone held her free hand over her ear closest to Nicole. "K. What moved?"

Nicole placed both hands on Simone's shoulders and peered over to the see what was frightening her in the drawer. The light from the cell phone cast shadows as the loose items were stacked upon each other, making eerie monsters from rolls of tape, twine, plastic cutlery, papers and unused birthday cards. "There. It's moving. Don't you see it?"

Simone reached into the mess and began to pick up various items from the drawer and toss them haphazardly onto the counter. She picked up one of the items and Nicole's grip on Simone's shoulder tightened, fingers digging into the shoulder. "What girl? I don't see anything."

"You're holding it," Nicole whispered.

Simone looked down to see what she was holding. A four by six- inch photograph of Simone at an old friend's birthday party from several years earlier. She turned it over, uncertain of what her friend was scared off. Simone held it before her, "This?" she questioned.

"Don't you see it?" Nicole's voice trembled as she spoke, Simone feeling her friend's hot breath on her neck.

"I'm sorry sweetie. I don't see what you're seeing." Simone was puzzled by Nicole's reactions. Simone studied the picture, she sat at a picnic table with three other people, junk food laid out on the table, a birthday cake half eaten in the centre of the table, colorful plastic tumblers in everyone's hand, toasting her friend's birthday.

"Is that a tablet you're holding?" Nicole asked.

Simone turned the photograph over to reveal a white back, then flipped it over again. As soon as Nicole saw the picture on the front again, she gasped. "Honey, what's up?"

From around Simone, Nicole reached forward and carefully took hold of the photo. The photo shook in Nicole's hand as she moved from around her friend then held the picture firm with both hands. Nicole stared at the photo, giggled and handed it back to Simone. "You must've been drunk. Really drunk," she exclaimed.

"Ya, I was drun…" her words stopped abruptly. "How did you know?" The tone in Simone's voice went from puzzled to confused.

"You spilt your drink when you toasted then licked whatever you dropped off the plastic table cloth. And you stuck your hair in the cake icing. Your friends laughed, and you couldn't see all the white icing in your curly black hair. You kept turning around wondering what they were laughing at." Simone yanked the photo from Nicole's grasp and turned the picture over repeatedly. She took a few steps back from her friend, scared of what she had just heard. "How can you know this? This happened years ago before I moved to town and you don't know these people."

"Simone. What are you talking about? It's a video of the party. I don't know where you got this moving photo frame, but I want one. It's amazing. It's just like a photograph. Too thin for batteries, where do you plug it in to charge?"

If the room would've had better light, Nicole would've seen the color drain from Simone's dark complexion. Simone pushed past Nicole and sat down at the kitchen table where they had just been. She placed Nicole's cell phone down on the table and cradled her head in her hands. Nicole came over to comfort her friend who jumped as soon as Nicole touched her.

"What's the problem honey?" Nicole asked.

"That's not a video Nikki. That's nothing more than a picture, you know a photograph, printed on paper. It's not a video; there's no batteries, no way to charge it. And somehow, you saw everything that happened right after that picture was taken. That shit happened like; I don't know, seven maybe eight years ago. There's no way you could know any of that stuff that happened."

Nicole sat down facing Simone and even in the dim light, could make out the look of concern on her face. Nicole took Simone's hand, cupped in hers, "I'm not sure what just happened here but that picture moved. It moved like a video on YouTube or TV. I saw you lick up your drink and stick your hair in the icing and when you got up, everyone around was laughing. I saw it plain as day."

Without warning, Simone jumped from her seat and pulled the drawer from the cabinet and dumped the entire contents on the counter. She pushed most of the stuff aside until she found several photos. Simone sat back down at the table. Arranging the photos, she made sure Nicole couldn't see the image that was caught by the photographer. "K. Let's see if that was a fluke. You up for this?"

Nicole nodded, picked up her cell phone and shone the light on the stack of stills in Simone's hands. Simone looked at the image on the photo then quickly turned it over. "What's going on?"

Nicole didn't hesitate, "You and the girl with the red hair, bad dye job, by the way, are dancing." Nicole paused, laughed and remained silent for a moment longer, "You tripped. Man, you are so drunk. Little miss red hair falls on top of you then kisses you on the cheek."

Simone starts to laugh, "This one," and flips another photo.

Nicole waits for a few moments, "Same BBQ. You're setting up the table. The birthday girl hasn't arrived yet. Red hair girl is arguing with someone off in the one corner about her share of the money she still owes for the gift."

Simone continues to laugh, almost hysterically, "No fucking way. This is too cool. One more." She shuffles the photos and blindly chooses one. "Here."

"Christmas at your parent's house. You're sitting with your mom, your dad takes the picture, and I can't hear, but your dad says something. What does he say? You get up and start arguing with him. What? No. Stop. My God Simone, your dad is yelling at you about the abortion. You never told me…, wait. Stop it, stop it now. Turn it over. I don't want to see anymore." Simone turns the photo around so that Nicole can't see it.

"I'm sorry, I didn't realize what this one was."

Nicole was crying softly, wiping the tears as they ran down her cheeks. "Your dad hit you and your mom. I'm so sorry. I had no idea."

Simone wasn't as emotional as Nicole, "That was a hundred years and a million miles away. My mom is dead thank God and never has to deal with that bastard again. I left a few weeks after that picture was taken and never looked back." Simone reached across and wiped the last tear from Nicole's cheek. "How do you do that?"

"I'm…I'm…not sure. It's never happened before."

"Never? You've never had Deja vue or anything like that? It just started today? Just like that?" Simone was excited, more so than Nicole.

"I've always had the whole premonition thing. You know, don't walk there, don't touch that. I always thought it was just a bunch of crap. A feeling I get."

"Can we do more?" Simone was smiling, giddy almost. She couldn't remain still in her seat. "One more, please?"

Nicole nodded in agreement. What started as a request for one more turned into over a dozen photographs. Each time, Nicole could see images come to life, and the events in the photos begin to move as if she hit the play button. Simone was unable to see what her friend could see, but she did notice that with each "viewing" as they came to call it, Nicole seemed to become more and more exhausted.

"Honey, we have to stop. I'm really tired," Nicole asked.

Simone agreed and put the photos back on the counter. She pulled two cans of diet Dr. Pepper from the fridge, "We can't tell anyone about this. You got it. I'm not sure if the government would kidnap you or some foreign agency dissect your brain."

"You are one funny girl. It's a party trick, like reading tarot cards or palm reading." Nicole pulled the tab on the can and took a drink, "It's a party trick." She held her right up like she was taking an oath, "I promise I'll never use my gift for anything other than the good of mankind."

Simone cut in, "Or womankind."

They both laughed, "Or womankind. And I'll only use it for good, not for personal gain." She put her hand down and looked at Simone with all seriousness, "Our secret?"

"Our secret." Simone stood and kissed Nicole on the top of the head. "Our secret, pretty girl," she whispered.

April 16

Abigail Schneider hopped down the front steps of the office building, smiling, she was elated after receiving good news from her doctor. For the past few years, Abigail had been undergoing treatment for recurring cancer and today; her doctor told her that after everything she had allowed to be subjected to, she was in remission. This is the news she was waiting for. Abigail wanted nothing more than to call her mother, tell her the good news and make plans to visit her.

Abigail was close to her parents, more so with her mother. She had taken care of Abigail as a sickly child, through her teenage years and now as a young woman, the two were still inseparable.

Looking up into the clear sky, Spring has always been Abigail's favorite time of the year. Winter came to an end, the buds on the trees were already out, it wouldn't be long before the grass was green, and she would spend more time outside.

As cars continued to drive past on the street, the driver of one car slowed as Abigail caught his attention. He spun his head around to take a second look then he quickly signaled, turned at the next intersection and pulled onto a side street. He found a parking spot, killed the engine and broke into a full run onto the main road and tried to find that girl.

He found himself getting short of breath as he ran full out trying to catch up to her. He dodged people as they made every attempt to avoid getting in his way. Finally, up ahead, he saw her and stared at her. An odd blue aura shone around her. He stopped short, focusing on her as she waited at the bus stop. That same aura glowed around her. He wasn't sure what that color meant, but for a moment, he couldn't take his eyes off her.

He wasn't sure how long he stared at her, she suddenly stepped forward as the bus he failed to see, opened its' doors and the passengers began to board slowly. The bus was facing him, he looked at the bus number and raced back to his car. He would follow the bus until she disembarked.

*****

Almost all of the winter's snow had melted, the night air was still crisp, winter's bite had long since disappeared. The stars above were bright on this cloudless night as Simone drove her boyfriend's truck to a co-worker's birthday party. Nicole remained silent in the passenger seat, fidgeting with the door handle.

"What?" Simone asked.

"You know I hate these things. Besides, I only got invited because of my party trick I do at the office."

"You got invited because of who you are and what you do. Stop berating yourself. You have one bad breakup, and you think you're blackballed for life. Everyone gets dumped once or twice or in my case three times in their lives." Nicole sat in the big comfy chair in the living room, the crowd that had gathered around her laughed loudly each time she read someone's photograph. Everyone clamored to be the next person to have some story told of what happened when the picture was taken. Almost everyone had heard about Nicole's amazing ability and made sure they came with a photo or two.

Nicole held the photo before her, and on cue, the images and people in the still picture began to move. Nicole found that the more she used the talent, the better and more vivid the images would appear. One time, she swore she heard voices coming from the still image as they began to move. The picture she held was of two people standing on a sandy beach, the ocean behind them. It was evident the breeze coming from the sea was strong as their hair was blowing from behind them almost entirely covering their faces. With Simone's help, Nicole had perfected the way she told her stories. Simone looked on from the other side and coached her, guiding her when she would get the stories too accurate or didn't showboat enough.

Nicole saw the couple begin to move, the waves crashing behind them, each wave getting bigger and bigger. "This was taken in the Dominican Republic, Punta Cana if I'm not mistaken." She looked up at the couple. Using signs Simone and Nicole had researched from palm readers and fortune tellers, Nicole's had trained herself to make comments sound like questions and sometimes pretend she was reading facial cues. Often, she would make comments that were not as accurate or completely wrong on purpose to make it appear more like a trick.

In the photo, Nicole saw the couple take the cell phone back from an unknown stranger who volunteered to take their picture. The woman turned the camera around to see the screen just as a rogue wave came crashing down upon them from behind and swept them out to sea. Both of them lost their footing, their bags went flying, and they went rolling in the surf as the wave rolled back out to sea. The man quickly stood up, began to gather his effects as strangers rushed over to help and help collect their personal belongings that were now floating in the surf. The woman was on all fours; her sunglasses were gone, to be found by some snorkeler days later partially buried in the sand several feet from shore. She panicked, looking for her cell phone that fell from her hand as her feet were pulled out from under her. She eventually found the phone, covered in sand and waterlogged.

"You fell or tripped or something," Nicole looked up at the couple from the photo, they were both smiling indicating she was correct, "I can't see why, but you lost your towel, no wait, your beach bag goes into the water too." The couple began to laugh, "You used your phone to take the picture, not a camera and the phone, it's a white iPhone, goes into the water. It's ruined, but you managed to save all your pictures, but your phone is toast."

"Nikki, that's amazing. How are you doing that?" The woman reached forward and took back the photo Nicole held out for her.

"Easy. Look at the waves, that big one in the background is huge. I figured it was about to crash down and take you guys with it." Nicole tried to make it look like it was simply the power of observation.

"But you were right on all counts. How did you know it was my iPhone that we used?"

Nicole thought quickly, "I've seen you use your phone. You've always had a white iPhone. You told me you got a new one right after you got back from vacation remember (it was a lie, but it sounded convincing), and the picture is grainy, a camera usually has a better resolution, so I guessed."

"Well, you guessed pretty fucking good," the boyfriend broke in. The rest of the guests at the party broke out in applause as Nicole excused herself and went to the bathroom. Simone followed her down the hall.

Simone hip checked Nicole as they made their way to the bathroom. "You done good girl. The centre of attention and you got enough wrong and made it look convincing."

"Do you know how invasive this skill is? I'm seeing shit that I shouldn't be seeing. One of the girls who was with her boyfriend in the picture is having an affair with the married girl who took the picture. I saw what they did not long after the picture was taken."

Simone was a little shocked, "Are you being a prude about the two girls getting it on?"

Nicole laughed, "Not at all, I just don't want to know. It's sorta like reading minds. There are some things that should be kept private."

"Are you hearing more voices?"

"Sometimes, not always, and it's weird. It just happens, then it's gone. I get images, voices, things that don't make sense running through my mind. It's still all so new." Nicole stopped in front of the bathroom door, "Gotta pee," and went inside.

Over the course of the next hour, Nicole read a few more photographs, got some of them wrong on purpose, giving them the excuse she was tired and needed a drink. Simone was cozying up to her boyfriend who arrived late, and Nicole stood by the fridge in the kitchen, alone.

"Excuse me."

Nicole simply took one step to the right without turning around. The fridge door opened, she heard the clanging of glass bottles, then the door closed again. "Ahem." The male voice was deep and young, "usually when someone moves out of the way they turn around to see who asked to get by."

Nicole turned around to see a strange young man standing only a few inches away. "Hi."

"Hi. I was watching your cute stage act. I was kinda hoping you would do my picture next. That is if you're still reading them?"

"I'm beat." Nicole looked at the man, wondering why she didn't recognize him. "And you are?" She stepped back and extended her hand.

He shook her hand, "Jeff. Pleased to meet you, Nikki. I heard everyone call you Nikki. Short for..?"

"Nicole."

"I like Nicole better. Can I call you Nicole?"

"Sure. Who are you? Really?" Nicole was sure she had never met the man she was speaking with.

"I live here with my mother, Steph from accounting. It's her birthday party."

"Jeff, her son. But Jeff is supposed to be," Nicole held her hand out at waist height, "this big."

Jeff took hold of her hand and raised it just above his head which was several inches above Nicole's. "I hit my growth spurt about ten years ago. I think my mother forgets I've already graduated from university." Jeff brought Nicole's hand down but held it gently.

"Didn't I babysit you once? A long time ago." Nicole pulled her hand away, not in a way that was offensive. She took a step back and leaned up against the counter. There was only one light on in the kitchen, and it was directly over the sink behind her and lit Jeff in a glow of soft white light.

"You did. A few times I believe, a long time ago. I've had a babysitter crush on you ever since. When you walked in tonight, I remembered you right away."

Nicole placed both hands on Jeff's chest and gave herself a little more space between them, "Well Jeff, I think I'm a little too old for you, and besides, I work with your mom."

"I'm twenty-three, and you're what? Thirty-one, thirty-two?" Nicole coughed, "Thirty-six."

"So, you wouldn't go out with me if I asked nicely?" Jeff was smiling.

Nicole knew exactly what he wanted.

"Maybe." Nicole knew the answer already, NO!

"Well, you still have to read my picture, right?" Jeff was a hard man to refuse.

"K. Quickly."

Jeff pulled out his phone and leaned in low and close and took a selfie of himself with Nicole. He turned the phone over, smiled at the image then showed it to Nicole who stared at it. Nothing happened. The people in the picture failed to move. She pulled away from Jeff and stared at the phone. She swiped the image left and right to see if she could see the image begin to move. Nicole realized she had never tried to use a digital image before. She pulled away from Jeff and quickly found Simone and yanked her away from her boyfriend. After Nicole told her about the digital image, Simone walked through the party goers, found a photograph and brought it back to Nicole. One glance and the image started to morph again.

Relieved, Nicole relaxed, "I thought my gift was gone."

"I thought you would be happy if you lost the ability," Simone was caught off guard by her comment.

"I'm enjoying it now." She beamed a broad smile. "Come on; I'm tired. Let's go home."

Simone drove, Nicole sat in the passenger seat, and Simone's boyfriend fell asleep between them. Cloud cover had hidden the stars; the air had become a little crisper, so Simone cranked up the heater in the cab of the truck.

"I totally, completely freaked when I didn't see that pic of me on Jeff 's phone move."

"Jeff. That was little Jeff, Steph's little Jeff?" Simone exclaimed.

"Yeah. I just thought maybe the reason I couldn't see the future of what happened, or happens or whatever, you get it, anyway, is because it hadn't happened yet. What do you think?"

Surprised, Simone wanted to know more about Jeff, "You mean little Jeffrey was hitting on you?"

"Get over it. Yes, it was Jeff, but he isn't little Jeffrey anymore. Anyway, what do you think?"

"Well, if Jeff was hitting on me, I'd call him back. And yes, whatever the reason, it isn't that big of a deal. Like you said, it's a party trick. No one cares."

*****

It was past midnight, Paul and Ken were working late, going over the contents of the envelope they had received almost four months earlier. The envelope had over two dozen fingerprints, most of them were smudged and unusable. Inside, the photograph was printed on plain photocopy paper you could purchase at discount stores or big box office stores and yielded absolutely no fingerprints or DNA.

If it weren't for the photos that arrived by FedEx, there would be no record of the dismemberment of the female corpse. The series of eight pictures depicted a female torso placed inside an old-fashioned hard-shelled suitcase, no head, no arms, no legs. No body had ever been found, none of the missing parts were recovered. The information had been entered into CODIS and CPIC without a hit. The suitcase would be nearly impossible to trace. It appeared to be decades old, and no one even used old vinyl or leather luggage anymore. It was determined that the suitcase was either in the family for decades, purchased at a garage sale or thrift store or just found in the dump. There were no identifying marks on the suitcase.

The torso was most definitely female, no birthmarks or tattoos. She appeared young, but the skin around the arms and legs showed the skin had been cut, surgically cut. Paul instinctively knew this body was connected to the arm found in the snow bank. Was it from the same body? Was the arm torn from the body then the skin cut, without the torso, it was impossible to know for certain. But he knew it was the same person who did whatever it was to the arm found in the snow.

The lab was able to determine they were digital pictures printed on an HP model color laser jet. The resolution was low, details were difficult to make out but what each photograph portrayed was disturbing.

Almost every electronics store sold that model of HP printer, and thousands of units had been sold in the past few years. Just because the return address on the FedEx envelope was sent from a convenience store drop box in town, didn't mean the person purchased the printer from town. The store where the drop box was located didn't have video surveillance.

The printer could've been ordered online, from another town, any of the online swap sites. It wasn't like the old days when there was a limited number of stores to purchase electronics. They had pursued every possible avenue but had come to a dead end each time.

Each picture was placed in a plastic protective sleeve, and like a jigsaw puzzle where you don't have any clue what the final image is supposed to be, he and Ken kept re-arranging them in various orders to create a timeline. Regardless of what order they were in; they couldn't agree on what order they were taken in.

Paul had asked the lab techs to blow up each photo into four quadrants then enhance each section until the resolution was maxed. They spent weeks studying each of the blow-ups, asking other detectives and uniformed officers to offer their opinion but no one could provide any fresh leads.

Each grainy picture was a close-up of one section of the victim's body: back, abdomen, shoulder.

The one photo that Paul kept pinned to his cubicle wall was the one he found most disturbing.

*****

Abigail lay alone in her bed. She had taken a Lorazepam a few hours earlier to help her sleep, but she was too hyped about the news she had received earlier in the day and even with the help of pharmaceuticals, she was unable to fall asleep. She rolled over, pulled the bedspread up high, balled it tightly under her chin and curled up into the fetal position. The red numerals on the clock read "1:22". Abigail closed her eyes, took in a deep breath and slowly exhaled. She repeated this several times until she started to relax and let the pill take over.

Several hours later, Abigail awoke staring into the darkness. She had a horrible feeling that was so intense it woke her from a drug-induced sleep. She dared not budge; only her eyes moved as she scanned her bedroom. The only light that penetrated the room came from the hall, through the open bedroom door. It was impossible to discern anything in the darkness, but she felt something. A feeling that she wasn't alone.

The silence of the room scared her more than anything. There was an absence of noise, a void of sound, Abigail thought as she could hear her breathing. She looked into the darkness, straining to see or hear something in the room. Abigail stopped breathing, holding her breath for a few moments, strained her ears and listened. She was certain there was something else breathing in the room. It was a muffled sound like someone had a scarf around their mouth in the winter. Or, the thought scared her even more, someone wearing a mask. Abigail held her breath again and concentrated her hearing on each section of the bedroom. Every thirty seconds or so, she would slowly take a breath, then hold it again. She now knew for certain there was something in the room with her.

In the darkness, he saw the same blue aura that surrounded her earlier in the day. It was a color he had never seen before and confused him. She was like nothing he had seen; she was beautiful, he could barely take his eyes off her.

Abigail's mind went into warp drive. If she couldn't see whoever was in the room, could she be seen moving? Was the light coming from the hallway enough to give whoever was in the room the advantage?

Abigail moaned softly, rolled onto her side and slid her arm out from under the covers and placed her hand over her cell phone on the nightstand. She stayed in that position for several minutes then rolled back the other way, bring her cell phone with her, sliding her hand under the covers. Hundreds of times, Abigail had blindly unlocked her phone and texted friends. Now, her hands were shaking so badly; she doubted she could call 911.

Her hand fumbled about over the screen, and she pretended to sleep. Her breathing rate increased, and she fought to control her fear. Abigail held her breath again and could hear the breathing of whoever was in the room increase. She knew something was about to happen. She dialed 911 and hit send then tossed the phone towards her feet under the covers as she heard a yell from behind the bedroom door. Abigail screamed as the bed covers were pulled down and she felt the cold night air envelope her body.

Goosebumps swelled over her exposed skin as something wrapped around each one of her ankles.

"911, what is your emergency."

Abigail was pulled down to the bottom of the bed, despite her attempts to anchor herself to the cotton fitted sheet covering the mattress. She held tight to the bed sheet, her fingernails digging into her palms through the sheet, was preventing her from being pulled down any further. When the pulling motion stopped, she began to kick wildly, finally breaking free of whoever held her by the ankles. Abigail began to scream, kicking at whatever was at the end of the bed.

"911, what is your emergency?"

Neither Abigail nor the attacker heard the muffled voice of the call taker on the phone as they fought. Once again, the emergency call taker asked her question, this time with a tone that was more authoritative. As the call taker continued to attempt contact, she passed the screen to the dispatcher who would send police as she continued to try to make contact with Abigail.

Abigail let out a high-pitched scream, pulled her right leg back quickly and kicked at the hand that was holding her other leg. She kicked at her foot that was still securely held, one of her kicks found its mark to the attacker's stomach. There was a loud moan, as Abigail saw the attacker curl up in pain. Her other foot was now free. She flipped her legs under herself until she was on all fours on the bed, reached for the crumpled bedspread and tossed it over the attacker. Abigail pounced on him, swinging wildly at the form under the bedspread. Several blind strikes landed hard on something causing the attacker to double over in pain. From the bed, Abigail climbed on top of the covered form and began an onslaught of punches and kicks to whoever was under the sheet. An almost inaudible noise came from the sheet causing a burning pain to the right side of Abigail's stomach. She placed her hand over the area and felt something wet and warm. Another faint sound. The drywall in the ceiling exploded above her head. Another pop. Another burning sensation in her chest. Abigail attempted to take a deep breath but could not. She coughed and felt her throat fill with that same warm fluid she felt on her stomach. Strength left her body quickly. Abigail slid from on top of the form under the bedspread to the floor. She coughed again. The pain in the chest was unbearable. She tried to yell, but nothing happened. The form stood as the bedspread tumbled to the floor. It righted itself. All Abigail could make out was a dark figure standing before her. It moved, and the light from the hall glistened off the oily finish on the handgun now pointing at her. Another pop. A flash of white burst forth from the muzzle. Her right knee exploded sending a million pain signals to her head in a fraction of a second. Blood gurgled inside her throat, and she was unable to scream, the pain was evident in her eyes. Another pop. Another white flash. Her left knee shattered, and the pain grew exponentially. The screams welled up inside Abigail, instead of the scream, she spit blood from her mouth so that she could breathe. Abigail knew she was going to die; she wanted to die. She would die but the attacker knew what he wanted first.

*****

Nicole bolted upright in bed panting, staring into the darkness. Sweat dripped from Nicole's forehead and the tip of her nose. She could feel the perspiration covering her entire body and wondered why she felt so exhausted. Her bedsheets weren't damp; they were soaking wet. She placed a hand to her head to quell the throbbing going on at the back of her skull. She massaged her temples and thought that maybe she had too much to drink at the party earlier. Whatever the reason, her head was pounding, her eyes hurt, and she felt nauseous. Nicole used the tips of her index and middle fingers to rub her temples and soften the pressure inside her head. She closed her eyes, continued to rub her temple, but the pain failed to subside.

Nicole decided that only a couple of Advil would help. She swung her legs over the edge of the bed, stood and collapsed screaming. Her knees felt as though they were on fire, causing her unbearable pain. Nicole began to cry and gently held onto her legs wondering why she suddenly had such excruciating pain in her knees and head. She braced herself up against the bed and attempted to rub her knees, but she could barely touch them without causing more pain. Even the light material of her nightgown loosely draped over her knees caused pain.

Nicole attempted to reach for the tissues on her night stand, but the movement sent pain coursing through her and caused her headache tension to escalate. She fell onto her side and began to weep openly. She couldn't understand what was causing the pain or why it started so suddenly. Her nose began to drip and as she was about to wipe it clean with the back of her hand when a sharp stabbing pain tore through her abdomen. Waves of nausea swept over her as bile forced it way up into her throat. Nicole tried to force the vomit out, but it lingered at the back of her throat until her stomach calmed. Her eyes rolled back as the pain in her stomach intensified with a burning sensation that caused her to vomit repeatedly.

Nicole wonders if her powers to see photos move had caused a brain tumor and somehow managed to disrupt her entire body. She closed her eyes, spit out whatever sour tasting sputum was left in her mouth and knew she was about to die. Her head began to spin causing more nausea, and the pain in the knees and stomach were too much for her to tolerate any longer. She was now welcoming death and wanted the pain to end quickly. The room swirled in her mind; her memories became cloudy and unfocused as she welcomed whatever was to come next to stop the agony.

April 22

It was the type of rain that hits the cars with drops so large; it sounded like hail instead of water. The rain was coming down almost horizontal, in torrential sheets, waves of water formed within the downpour and danced in the rainfall. It didn't take long for tiny rivers along the curbs to begin washing away the last remnants of winter. The water ran dark with salt and sand used on the roads to provide traction for the cars. The storm drains had already begun to overflow, and the water rose along the curbs and flood out onto the streets. Even though it was before eight in the morning, detective Paul Hammond had his headlights on for visibility, both to see and be seen. His windshield wipers clicked each time they hit the high position as they swept the water from the glass. If he didn't get the call to attend the strange death of a woman in her bedroom, he would probably still be asleep. For as long as Paul could remember, he always loved to sleep during thunderstorms. There was something about the sound of rain, wind and thunder that comforted him and made him drowsy and helped him sleep.

Paul pulled onto the street, between two cruisers and close to the walk leading up to the house. He didn't have an umbrella or a raincoat, just his nylon jacket. He was glad he didn't take the time to shower before driving to the scene. Paul opened the car door, rain blew into the cab of the vehicle, quickly soaking him and the interior of the car. As he exited the car, his personal phone began to vibrate in his pants pocket. He looked down, almost slipped on the wet concrete, deciding to answer the phone inside the house. He quickened his pace up the steps, passed several uniformed officers as they stood outside the house. The officers didn't hold up the yellow crime scene tape as they passed under for Paul, so he could walk beneath it. He mumbled his disdain for rookies as he fumbled for the phone in his pants and moved under the tape as he entered the house. Another younger officer with a clipboard was taking the names, rank and time of who entered and exited the house. Paul stopped in front of him, handed him his badge and ID as he retrieved the phone from his pocket.

The phone stopped vibrating before Paul pulled it from his pocket. He looked at the screen and spoke out loud without realizing it, "Fuck."

"Excuse me?" the young officer asked.

Paul turned towards him, "Sorry, I was expecting a call." He took off his nylon jacket and shook it, sending droplets of water over the front foyer then started to make his way into the house. "I mean, I got a call. I've been expecting this call for some time now. Hey, how long is too long after you miss a call before you call someone back?"

Perplexed, the officer lowered his clipboard, "Depends. If it's your mother, it's never too late. One of the guys, who gives a shit. Your wife or girlfriend or someone you want to date, I'd say twenty-four hours. Max. So how long has it been?"

Paul thought for a moment, "About four months."

The officer laughed loudly, "Brother; it doesn't matter who it is at this point, you're fucked. What happened?"

"I missed the call and never called back." Paul almost seemed embarrassed to tell the man he had never met before. "And I missed it again, just now."

"Can I ask why you never called back?"

"Honestly, I have no fucking idea. Kinda hoped the missed call was a cue for her to call me back. A guy thing I guess. I've no clue when it comes to women. Or relationships for that matter." Paul shrugged as he shook the jacket again to rid it of excess water.

"You're not in a relationship with her?"

Paul shook his head side to side indicating they weren't in a relationship.

The officer leaned in close and offered some advice in a whispered voice, "Call her. Now."

"Maybe right after I look into the dead girl they called me here for." Paul smiled at the officer, tapped him on the shoulder, "Thanks for the advice pal." He pointed down the hall, "That way?"

"Yup."

As Paul walked down the hall, he followed the army of crime scene techs in Tyvek coveralls to the last doorway on the right. He entered the room to find another detective hunched over the far side of the bed. Paul knew the familiar backside, "Hey Roz. Whatcha got?"

Roz stood and turned around, "Paul. You finally made it outta bed. I like the hours you keep." "Shut it."

Roz whirled her fingers in the air, "Walk around the end of the bed and take a look."

Paul did as he was instructed and stopped short when he walked around the bed, "Jesus fucken' Christ. What the hell happened here?"

Roz stood from her hunched position and towered over Paul. She stood behind Paul, placed her hand on his back and pointed to the woman lying on the floor, "There."

"I don't see anyth…" Something caught Paul's attention, and he lowered himself until he was on all fours and saw the telltale signs of why he was called in. Paul leaned in close to the dead woman's left shoulder and looked closely. "Toss me a glove," he asked Roz without looking up. He donned a glove on his right hand only without taking his eyes off the section of the shoulder. He touched the skin and gently ran his gloved index finger back and forth over a section of skin. "What the fuck is this?" Roz stepped in closer and peered over Paul's shoulder. Paul continued to run his index finger over tiny holes in the skin, similar to a series of tiny syringe marks along a section over the acromion process, the section where the clavicle or collarbone meets the scapula at the shoulder. It was like the skin had been perforated with some type of instrument to help the skin begin to tear. "Do you think this would help the skin to rip?" he asked.

"Yup. You know those flyers you get in the mail every week, the ones where you have to bend the card stock then tear off the coupon. As soon as I saw this, I had to bring you in."

"This why I was called? The similarity to my arm case?" Again, Roz replied with, "Yup. You got lead again." Paul stood, "Techs all done?" Roz nodded.

"So why didn't the arm get taken or removed?" Paul asked.

"No clue but take a look at this." Roz pulled her phone from her jacket pocket, tapped the screen a few times and held it out beside the dead girl's arm. "I had the office email me a pic of your first vic's arm. Take a close look at the edge of the skin on her arm and then take a look at my vic on the floor." Paul squinted at the phone screen; he enlarged the picture with his thumb and index finger until he noticed something that had eluded him for months. "Fuck. I can't believe we missed this all this time." He bent low and looked at the dead girl's shoulder again. "There it is. The same circular, evenly spaced marks on the dead girl's shoulder was almost unnoticeable on the arm from the snow bank. You think the freezing and decomp affected the skin and made those tiny marks hard to find? The torn skin only shows a few sections where the small holes are. I never saw any pictures of the arm after it thawed out. I missed those marks all this time."

Roz pocketed her phone, "Whatever the reason, those same marks are on both arms. My biggest concern is if it was the same perp, why didn't he or she take the arm. And talk about overkill. This girl wasn't just killed, I mean shit, she was killed ten times over. And why start, then stop?"

"Excuse me, detectives." A masked androgynous person clad in white Tyvek coveralls from head to foot, interrupted their conversation, "I thought you should see this." He held out a plastic Ziploc bag with prescription bottles inside, "They were all opened, and the pills tossed all over the bathroom. It's like someone was pissed and scattered them all over. We're picking them all up now; we'll separate them, count them and see if the pill counts are out." As he went to leave, Paul stopped him, "Do you know what the meds were for?"

The technician looked at the meds, "Taxol, Methotrexate and a ton of vitamins, B, D and C. Methotrexate is for arthritis I think. Not sure what Taxol is for."

Roz was already tapping wildly on her phone, "How do you spell that first one you mentioned?"

"T-A-X-O-L."

Roz lowered the phone, "Taxol. Breast cancer. Our vic has had breast cancer." She looked down at the woman lying dead on the floor then up at Paul, "You think whoever did this left her because she had cancer?"

Paul shook his head back and forth, "I have no clue what goes through someone's mind when they do something like this. I thought I had a grasp of what these guys think, but this is just vicious. You think he scooped out the girl, broke into the house, found the meds, realized she had cancer then did this?" He looked up at Roz who had a puzzled look on her face.

"Any more surprises for me?" Paul asked. Before Roz could answer,

Paul continued to ramble, "Fuck. I wish I hadn't asked for lead. I've had nothing, no clues, leads, jack shit in months and the stress is killing me." Paul composed himself and continued, "Bad analogy, sorry, I'm still better than…," Paul realized he still had no information on the girl laying on the floor at his feet.

"Abigail Schneider, twenty-three, lives alone, rental house, no pets, works for some IT company as a programmer. We're calling family and friends now. We're going around the neighborhood asking if anyone saw anything."

Paul composed himself, "Security system?"

"None. And, we can't find a landline phone or her cell phone. Guess it was taken too."

"How did we get this one?"

"She was supposed to be at work at six. Apparently, she's never late, and the boss was concerned considering her health. Called 911 and here we are. Hey, did you figure out how the other girl had her arm ripped off ?"

"It takes three thousand pounds of shearing strength to rip an average arm from the torso. We think we figured out why we didn't find any ligature marks on the skin. The medical examiner thinks the body was frozen, body secured to something heavy, then a rope wrapped around the wrist or arm and a pulley or some type of hydraulic press attached to the arm. They tried it on pigs than a cadaver. But those holes punched into the skin are a new twist. We found it was easy to dislocate an arm by twisting it back really hard. If there's a will, there's a way."

Roz had a look of disgust on her face, "You had to do all that?" "Christ no. I'd toss my cookies. M.E. did the tests and sent me the results. But the tiny holes in the skin means we have to revisit the whole concept of what was done and how."

"Our M.E.? The girl? She did the test?" Roz asked. Paul smiled, "No fucking way I'd do it."

*****

Nicole opened her eyes, her mind still in a haze from the night before. It was an unfamiliar sight as she looked up from the floor. She reached up, grabbed the bedspread and pulled herself up off the floor to a seated position. Her head was pounding, she was nauseated and felt as though she would vomit any moment. A few deep breaths later, she felt well enough to stand. She stood, closed her eyes tightly shut hoping it would stop her head from spinning. One slow step after the other, she made her way to the washroom, turned on the water and pulled the plastic shower curtain closed behind her. The hot water cascaded off her back to the tub floor below. Nicole's stomach gurgled, she shrugged her shoulders and vomited whatever was left in her belly. Her throat burned from the stomach acid that was forced out. Nicole opened her mouth under the hot shower as it sprayed down upon her and spit. She repeated this several times until she couldn't taste anything anymore.

She pulled the shower head from the holder, stepped back and cleared the bottom of the tub and watched as her stomach contents swirled down the drain. She used her foot to kick the larger pieces that refused to budge under the water pressure and felt her stomach turn again. This time, there wasn't anything more to expel. She heaved a few times, hoping that if she were going to vomit, it would happen. Nothing. She replaced the shower head, adjusted the angle, sat at the back of the tub, pulled her legs in close and curled up tightly and fell asleep under the spray of the warm water.

*****

Paul leaned forward from his chair at his desk, his head resting on his forearms, eyes closed as he tried to get a few moments of rest. His head had been pounding since he left the Medical Examiner's office a few hours earlier and after seeing Abigail's body on the stainless-steel table, he had lost his appetite. He popped a few Advil, closed his eyes and waited for the meds to take effect.

The phone on his desk continued to ring, but the only phone he wanted to hear was his cell phone which was plugged in and only a few inches from his keyboard. As he sat there, he wondered if he should return the call that he missed four months earlier then again at the dead girl's house. He played several phone conversations scenarios in his head, and none of them ended in his favour. Paul kept his face buried in his folded arms as the office world continued to unfold around him. He criticized himself for not calling back so many months earlier. Paul had no one else to blame for his current situation, and he wanted there to be someone he could yell at who he thought was the root cause of his current state. Instead, the life of the office continued around him, he heard the conversations but cared little about what was being said.

Paul's stomach made noise that reminded him of a small dog growling. He didn't have an appetite, but his stomach was telling him that it still needed to be fed. Blindly, he reached across his desk, fumbled for the thermal mug of stale coffee, raised his head and chugged whatever was left at the bottom of the mug, then lowered his head again. The sounds of the small dog in his stomach stopped growling at him, for now. Paul wanted to find a way to erase any part of his mind that stored the images of the dead girl he saw this morning.

Ding. Paul's laptop made a familiar sound. He knew what that noise meant, more email. The last thing he wanted to see. Ding. Ding. Ding.

The noise continued several more times, and Paul refused to look at the screen until it stopped. That many emails at once could certainly only be one thing, photos from the autopsy completed on Abigail Schneider, grisly, disgusting pictures of indignities performed on a human body in the name of justice. It was the single most horrific part of the job that he hated the most. It didn't matter what happened to the person before they died, it was nothing compared to an autopsy. The insidious "Y" incision starting at the clavicles, across the chest and down the abdomen, the skin gets peeled back resting over the arms, the ribs are snapped with massive stainless-steel shears along both sides, midpoint between the sternum and the spine, twisted back and forth to release the attachment at the sternal notch and pulled out only to be cast aside like a section of beef ribs ready for the barbeque over a beer and football game. Each organ: heart, lungs, liver, spleen, stomach, intestines, bladder, kidneys, all removed in order, examined, weighed, cross sections taken for evidence until all that was left was a cavernous hollow. Then the scalp is cut horizontally above the ears, the skin pulled forward over the face, and a bone saw cuts through the skull until a cap is removed exposing the brain. Again, like the other organs, the brain is removed, examined and weighed. What is left is nothing of the person who was. After the autopsy was completed, the organs were placed in a large yellow biohazard tub, labeled and readied for disposal. The rib plate replaced, and the skin sewn closed with a large needle and a twine type suture. Paul shuddered at the thought of seeing those pictures of the young girl who lay on the hardwood floor this morning. Yesterday at this time, he assumed, death was the last thing on Abigail's mind.

Paul had a lot of questions about life, none that were answered by either of his parents. His mother was a nun in her previous life before she left the convent. He grew up in a religious household, God fearing, church going but lost his faith as a young man, too many questions about life and death to believe a God would allow or permit atrocities to be committed against man. Paul's head remained lowered for several minutes after the last "ding" informing him the emails had ceased. He sat upright, held the mouse with a firm grasp, like a standing person holds the overhead bar on a moving bus, and clicked on the email attachments. He printed each picture on standing paper in vivid color and without looking at them, slid them into the folder with the crime scene folders of this morning's attack. He took a deep breath and walked around the squad room, asking any of the other detectives if there had been any more leads during the canvas of the neighborhood or if Abigail's phone had been located.

"No one saw or heard anything. Sorry, bud. Wish I had better news. The guy seems to be a ghost. No one saw him enter the house or leave. No sign of her phone either." The detective rummaged through some papers, read the notes and added, "Spoke to her family doctor. She did have breast cancer, recently diagnosed. Prognosis was good. Doc said she still had a long way to go but was getting better."

*****

Simone and Nicole sat in the coffee shop sipping tea to help subdue Nicole's sour stomach. They sat at the table closest to the washroom in case Nicole had to vomit again. When Nicole tilted the white paper cup back, Simone noticed the dark circles under her eyes.

"I'm glad you called me today hon, you do look like shit. Are you sure you should be out today? Maybe you should spend a few more hours in bed?"

With shaking hands, Nicole lowered the cup to the table and wiped her mouth with a napkin. "I needed to get out of the house. Thanks for coming with me, didn't want to be alone."

"You sure you got sick from overusing your ability?" Simone finished her tea and shook the cup double-checking it was empty. "I mean, this has never happened before," she offered.

Nicole put her hand to her forehead, "It's not like this ability comes with a manual. I was fine when I got home and woke up in pain. I was super sick this morning, and then a few hours ago, I started feeling like my guts were being ripped out from my chest and this headache." She touched her forehead, running a finger just above her eyebrows. "Then, everything just stopped. I don't get it. The pain is gone, but I'm exhausted. I feel like someone beat the shit outta me and when I was down, kept kicking me."

Simone reached out and covered Nicole's hand with her own. She squeezed gently, "Honey, you know I'm here for you, but I think it's time you go see a doctor."

Nicole turned her hand over and held onto Simone's fingers, "And tell them what, I developed physic abilities and it gave me a brain tumour." They both chuckled.

"Don't be so pessimistic. How about, you started having debilitating headaches and suggest a Cat Scan or an MRI? Besides, I think once you tell him about the sudden headaches, you'll get a CT or MRI anyway."

"I'm feeling a lot better now. Really. I may not look like it, but I am. All the pain is gone. I just need rest," Nicole paused, "and company. I don't want to be alone. I can't be alone. It's too scary."

Simone stood, shook the two paper cups, making sure they were empty, tossed them in the trash, and helped Nicole to her car. Nicole was buckled in on the passenger side, she closed her eyes and tried to sleep as Simone drove. Simone glanced at her resting friend, reached across, took hold of Nicole's hand, and held it tightly. With her eyes still closed, Nicole smiled softly and squeezed Simone's hand. She interlaced her fingers with Simone's and felt at ease.

*****

The three detectives stood in the squad room, leaning against the fabric-covered partitions between desks and went over the case details with Paul Hammond. It was nothing more than a re-hash of the details they had from earlier in the day with the exception of Abigail's activities from the previous day.

"Abigail was at a party last night. Her friends took her there, sat with her, never left her side and brought her home early. They said she was weak and tired, didn't have anything to drink, didn't socialize with anyone she didn't know, didn't give out her number, take anyone's number, didn't text or call anyone while at the party. She had her fortune read or something like that by a palm reader," Ken Simmons looked at his notes, "actually, a picture reader. Whatever the fuck that is. Anyway, her friends just wanted her to get out of the house and be with other people. Abigail was still trying to hold on to some sort of routine, she still worked, even though her doctors told her to quit. She was supposed to go in today to work on some special project which is one reason why she didn't drink and went to bed early."

Paul checked his notes, "Did she meet anyone, do anything out of the ordinary?"

Dan Levy shook his head, "Nadda. Brave kid, though. Some of her friends just thought she had the flu or something, didn't even know she had cancer. She only told those closest to her she had breast cancer and was trying to just have a normal life."

Paul sighed deeply, "Did the psychic tell her about her illness or did they miss that one?" He laughed loudly.

"Never bothered to ask about that," Dan admitted. "You want me to look into it?"

Paul gave Dan a look of disdain, "Really, as if we don't have other leads to follow up than to ask a psychic what they saw in the future for our vic?"

"Ah, Paul, at this point, we don't have any more leads," he offered.

Paul realized the investigation had nowhere else to go at this point. "K. Interview as many of the guests as possible. See if anyone was paying any special attention to Abigail before she left. You know, some guy not taking "No" for an answer. Maybe an old boyfriend that didn't want to let go? Talk to that psychic too. See what he or she said."

Ken looked down at his notepad, "She, not he. Nicole Blake."

"K. Nicole Blake. Find her, interview her and find out what she and the other guests know." As the other detectives turned to leave, Paul continued, "And if you don't get a lead, see if the psychic will do a card reading to help with a few clues."

"Pictures you a-hole, pictures. Not cards."

"Whatever." Paul flipped his hand in the air, turned and went back to his desk. He was clearly on edge by the lack of process, and the stress was starting to show.

*****

Simone sat Nicole on the couch in her living room, covered her with a blanket and went to make dinner. As Simone walked away, she looked back at her friend pulling up the blanket close around her neck, and for the first time saw her as something different. Simone was worried Nicole might be sick and she decided that if these headaches continued, she would force Nicole to get that scan. Every few minutes, Simone would peek around the corner from the kitchen to check on her resting friend.

Even though Nicole did not eat much, she tried to convince Simone she was feeling better. So, well, in fact, Nicole promised Simone that she would be at work the next day. Simone countered that Nicole needed more rest.

They playfully argued back and forth, as they ate until Simone noticed her friend was almost back to herself again.

A knock at the kitchen door interrupted the two girls as they sat at the table. Simone went to the apartment door, pulled the curtain back and saw two men in suits standing before her.

"Police mam'." The men stood, stone-faced, attempting to look the part of the serious cops on the job. Simone closed the curtain, paused for a moment, wondering why they were at her house, unlocked the door and greeted them, "Can I help you?"

Dan Levy tried to be polite and smiled, it was a challenging smile, obviously forced, "We're looking for Nicole Blake. We understand you may know where her whereabouts?" Another forced fake smile. Simone thought the detective's face might crack at any moment.

"Can I ask why you want to talk to her?"

"It's nothing serious. It seems she was at a party last night, one of the guests was killed after she left the party and we are interviewing all the people who attended. Trying to get as much information as we can. That's all."

Simone thought about all the people she knew at the party and wondered who the person was that died. She mentally ran through all her friends she knew at the party, those who had posted messages on social media, couldn't recall anyone mentioning anyone missing or being hurt and felt a sense of relief that it wasn't any of her friends. Then, she had a wave of guilt sweep over her as she realized she was glad a stranger had died. She cleared her mind, "Sorry, please come in." She stepped aside and let the two men enter, "I was at the party too, Simone James," she introduced herself.

As they walked past, one of the detectives acknowledged her, "Yes, thank you. We know who you are."

Simone closed the door, offered the two men a seat, and called out for Nicole. From the kitchen, Nicole walked out and stopped short when she saw the guests. Simone was shocked at the transformation in her friend. Nicole looked as if she had just returned from a day at the spa, her skin looked refreshed, her color had returned, and the dark circles under her eyes had completely disappeared. She smiled at the two seated men, extended her hand, one of the men stood to shake her hand, "Hi." Nicole's voice was pleasant, showing no sign of stress. She sat down facing the two men, crossed her legs, "So, how can I help you two?"

Her casual demeanor didn't affect the two officers who, at this point in their respective careers, knew that a pretty woman with a good attitude usually had something to hide. Only vain or rookie cops would overlook a woman because of her looks. Nicole sat back and waited for their response. Dan flipped his notebook to the elastic band that separated the pages.

He scanned his notes, "Last night Mrs. Blake…" He was cut short. "Ms. Blake. I'm not married."

"My mistake." Dan cleared his throat, "Last night, I understand you were at a house party." He looked up to see her reaction. Nicole remained silent. "And you were there with?"

Nicole motioned to her friend, "Simone. And her boyfriend."

Dan continued, "I heard you're pretty good at some party trick. You read cards or something and tell people's fortunes." He was purposely providing false information.

Nicole laughed, "No. I don't read Tarot Cards or tea leaves, I look at photos and make up stories about them. It's more of an observational skill." She remembered what Simone had told her to say.

Dan scribbled some notes, nodded his head, "And how do you make those observations? Can you show me?"

"It's just a parlour trick."

"A party trick huh?" Dan's voice became sterner, "Some of the people we spoke with told us that you were pretty spot on. I think the term they used was," he pretended again to refer to his notes, "spooky. Spooky is the exact term they used." Nicole remained silent, unmoving. Dan decided to try a different approach. He pulled a photo from his notepad of the dead girl, Abigail Schneider, looked at it then handed it to Nicole, "Do you recognize this person?"

Nicole hesitantly took the photo and gasped when she saw the image she held. She jerked backwards, her mind filled with images of the dead girl. Events before and after the image were taken spun inside her mind like a whirlwind and made Nicole dizzy. She blinked trying to stop the images from passing before her. Pain flooded her body like a lightning strike. The photo of Abigail slipped through her fingers to the floor, and Nicole slumped backwards in the chair.

"Out!" Simone screamed at the two detectives. "Get out of my house." She rushed to Nicole's side and held her up. "She's having a seizure."

"Can we help?"

"Yeah. Get the fuck outta my house." Simone pointed at the door and didn't take her eyes off them until Dan and Ken closed the door. Simone turned her attention back to Nicole who was already starting to come around. Nicole's eyes were already red, tears rolling down her cheeks. She sniffled and wiped her nose with the back of her hand.

"I know why," pause, deep breath, "I was in pain last night," she said between sobs.

Simone sat down beside Nicole and held her hand tightly. "You saw what happened?" she asked.

Nicole was crying uncontrollably, panting, barely able to catch her breath. She rubbed her chest and knees then straightened herself up in the chair. "I saw the girl last night at the party. Remember the girl who was having an affair? She was the one. The connection must have stuck with me after she left. I felt her last night when she was murdered." She cleared her throat, "You wanna know what happened?"

"Every last detail."

Nicole asked if the detectives left the picture of Abigail. Simone retrieved it from the floor beside the chair and handed it to her. This time Nicole was ready for the gruesome images and the pain that cascaded before her. She closed her eyes and let the event flow in her mind's eye and recounted them to her friend. Nicole even saw the autopsy being performed and then Abigail lying on her back, being pushed into the refrigerated chamber and the cold, stainless steel door slam shut behind her. Then everything went black.

"You saw the guy who killed Abigail?"

"I saw what Abigail saw which wasn't much. But, I felt everything. And, that's something I wouldn't wish on anyone. It was torture. She saw a figure, male, in the bedroom. It all happened in the bedroom. I know why she was killed. She was dying of cancer. I felt the cancer inside me, burning my chest and the guy killed her because he didn't know she was sick until he was in the house. I missed the cancer last night. Not sure why but I did."

"Maybe it didn't have anything to do with the image you saw last night."

Nicole nodded in agreement. "But the autopsy was painful. For both of us."

"How the fuck did you see the autopsy?"

"I don't know. This "power" I've got didn't exactly come with an operator's manual. I even felt the pain she went through during the autopsy. I felt the scalpel cut her skin and the rib bones being broken. That's why

I was feeling like shit. I was feeling her pain."

Confused, Simone asked, "But she was dead."

"I don't know. I mean do we know what happens when someone dies? Maybe there is truth to what people say about another plane of existence. The body may be dead but the essence of who we are remains behind. I hope the pain was imagined; I can't fathom for the life of me going through that pain again after I die." Nicole placed the photo of Abigail on the coffee table. "You think we should call them and tell them what happened?"

"And tell them what? You see things that no one else can?" Simone argued. "What if they do test on you and feel more pain like you did with Abigail?"

"I'm not a freak," Nicole yelled back, "I'm not an animal to be studied and dissected."

"I'm not saying you're a freak. You're unique, and my friend and I love you and I don't want you getting hurt."

"I never should've started showing off. Maybe it's time I stop. What do ya think?"

Simone had a change of heart, "I agree you should stop, but I have one question for you. You had a connection to this Abigail girl, can you not get involved now? I mean, you felt what she felt, experienced what she went through. No one else can say that. Don't you wanna help?" Simone grabbed the coffee table, sat on the edge and looking into her friend's eyes, "Do you want the son of a bitch to get away with this?"

"I never thought of that. But I'm scared."

Simone reached forward and gave her friend a hug. "I'm not going anywhere, in fact, maybe we should take a few precautions before we go to the cops. What do you think?"

"What've you got in mind?"

"Just a few things to make sure you're OK."

*****

"Was she faking it?" Paul Hammond asked the two detectives when they briefed him on the interview they had with Nicole and Simone. The three of them stood, leaning against the office partitions, their usual way to talk over a case. Paul sipped a cold cup of coffee that he poured hours earlier. The sounds of the office went about behind them. They had become adept at filtering out noise when they worked.

"Honestly," Ken looked at Dan, "it's kinda hard to say, but I think this thing she has is not a party trick or voodoo or anything like that. I think it's legit." Dan nodded in agreement.

"We spoke to over a dozen people who told us that this Nicole girl was hitting all the guess' outta the ballpark. They didn't think anything of it until we asked if there was any way she could've known some of the stuff she spoke of. I mean even if you're observant, you can pick up some random stuff from the pictures and the people in 'em, but not like this."

"And that stroke thing?" Paul inquired.

"Seizure," Ken corrected him, "it looked real. If it was fake, she deserves a fucking Oscar. We weren't there long, but I got the impression that she knows more than she's willing to tell. I think she's scared about something."

"Any idea what she could be scared of?"

"She knows the guy who did it. Or why he did it. Or why the vic was singled out. Something we don't know yet, of that I'm certain."

Dan cut in and changed the topic, "Anything from the autopsy?"

Paul shook his head side to side. "It's gonna be some time before we get toxicology and lab results back. So, you guys think we should bring this girl in for a second talk?"

Ken looked at Dan, "I say we should. It can't hurt."

Paul flipped back his shirt cuff, looked at his watch, it was after nine, and he still hadn't had dinner. "You know what guys, it's been a long day. Let's see about bringing her in tomorrow." Ken and Dan agreed, turned and went back to their desks.

Paul fell into his chair, exhausted, ran his fingers through his hair, and took in a deep breath. He picked up his phone from the desk, dialed her number and as his thumb hovered over the button to connect the call, hesitated then discarded the call. Frustrated, he tossed the phone to the end of his desk, knocking over his coffee cup. The contents spilt over a few pages from a file he didn't care about or even worry about. He watched as the dark liquid flowed across his desk to the edge and onto the carpet below.

"You not cleaning that up?" a familiar voice from behind.

"Hadn't planned on it," Paul righted the cup, "until I got caught." He chuckled.

The man behind Paul pulled a chair from the adjoining desk and sat down facing him. He sat backwards on the chair, straddling it and rested his crossed arms on the top of the back section. It was the Captain's preferred way to sit when having a one-on-one with another detective. "Your progress reports don't offer much. Stuck?"

"Do you believe in weird shit?" Paul wiped the coffee from his phone and pocketed it. "I mean shit like Mulder and Scully, weird shit."

The Captain didn't laugh or smile but rather kept a stern look, "How long you been here?"

"Going on twelve years."

"I've been here thirty-two years, twenty-three as a detective, the last seven, no eight, as head of detectives. I've seen things that people do, to themselves, to others, things that defy logic or reason. I once investigated a scene where a car barreled through a crowd on a sidewalk, hit and killed a couple of people and in the middle of it all, leave a table untouched with the coffee cups and scones left unscathed on it. It was like the people paid their bill and just left. Except that couple sitting at that table were killed. If they had been on one side of the table instead of the other, they would've lived. Instead, they died, and their coffee cups didn't spill a drop.

I was on the force less than a year when that happened. It weirds me out to think of stuff like that, but whether it's religion or shit luck, it happens."

"Mine's not a physics lesson, I've got a girl who can see things. Like crystal ball things."

The Captain remained silent, "And? You want my advice?"

Paul didn't answer but waited for his Captain to continue. "Who gives a shit? If she helps your investigation, use her, find out what she knows. Take the information and use it to build your case. Think of it as an anonymous tip. Who gives a flying rats ass where the leads come from as long as you use the evidence and put the bad guy away. In all my years, I've found that investigative work is ten percent hard luck, ten percent bullshit and eighty percent dumb luck. Use your skill, follow up on the bullshit and don't discount the luck when it stares you in the face. You know what I mean?"

"I do. It helps."

"Clean up that mess. And call her." "Excuse me?"

"A rational man only acts like an idiot when a woman is involved. And I've watched you act like a fool for months. Do me a favour before you destroy my squad room, call her."

The Captain stood as if dismounting a horse, replaced the chair and walked away without saying another word.

Paul picked up his cell phone, wiped the coffee from the screen then patted the carpet dry. It left a slightly darker stain that Paul thought added a bit to the room.

It was late when Paul found himself back home. He put the two bags of groceries on the kitchen counter. The milk, vegetables and cheese went into the fridge; the frozen dinners went into the freezer. He dropped the grease-stained box that held the fresh Hawaiian pizza with extra pineapple and ham onto the top of the stove and went to the bedroom to change. His tie was tossed over the back of the chair, the shirt, khakis and socks went into the wash. He donned his college T-shirt and grey sweats, cracked open a beer and pulled a slice of pizza from the box and sat in front the television. His cell phone sat on the coffee table in front of him, and every few moments, he would glance down at it, unsure if he should make that call his Captain tried to persuade him to do.

Instead, he caught Die Hard with Bruce Willis about halfway in, waiting for Hans Gruber to fall from the building. Throughout the entire movie, he hoped that she would make the call. It was the same wish he had for months. Paul wasn't sure why he couldn't do it, was he scared of what she might say, or what he would say.

Hans Gruber fell from the building. Still no call. Half the pizza was gone, two beer bottles emptied. Tomorrow, he promised himself, he would call. Paul fell asleep on the couch.

*****

He cut the meat into large chunks from the long bones with the skill of a butcher and tossed everything into an old blue recycling box. All the bones were bagged and frozen for future use. A few large ones were thrown in the backyard for the dogs to chew on between meals. The raw bones would be broken down and eaten by the powerful shepherd jaws.

As he cut the meat from the host, the blade scraped against the bone, tendon, ligament and flesh were sliced away. He inhaled deeply, smelling the raw meat. As the red meat was separated from bone, it emitted colored waves like steam coming off a pot of boiling water. He knew what the vapor colors meant, the brighter the colored waves, the better the meat. If the color of the waves were dark, he was certain the meat was tainted or diseased and needed to be disposed of. He would never feed his dogs meat that gave off dark colored vapors. He separated the various colored meat parts from one another and would blend the red colored meat cuttings in the garage with an antique silver grinder he bought at a thrift store. He was drawn to the ornate metalwork of the grinder when he first saw it, the large opening that would accept large chunks of meat and the oversized handle that he would need to crank and mince up the meat for the raw diet to keep the dogs healthy. His electric grinder would bind if he placed too much into it at once. The electric motor was too weak to handle the workload and was more difficult to clean. He clamped his new thrift store purchase to the work bench to keep it from shifting as he struggled with the handle to grind the fat, eggs, meat and skin to feed his two German Shepherds. Both dogs jostled for position in the garage as he worked to prepare their food, playfully turning around against each other trying to push the other further away.

Blood and tiny particles of raw meat would often spray from the grinder as the blades cut through the fresh meat and drop the blended mixture into the white bucket below. The two dogs would lick the blood from the concrete floor and any stray particle of food that didn't find its way into the bucket. The contents of the bucket would then be separated into smaller plastic containers that each held about one pound of the food, then frozen until needed. He fed each to his two dogs, a one-pound block twice a day. He counted fifteen one-pound cubes when he was done.

He looked at the two dogs who brought so much joy to his life. The look in their eyes showed their devotion to him. Instead of freezing the two human hands that were cut from the arm at the wrist, he walked to the backyard and ordered the two dogs to sit. He tossed the appendages into the darkness, and they sat silently until he gave the command for his dogs to leave his side and find their chew toy for the night.

The dark colored portions of flesh or limbs were discarded before they contaminated the rest of the meat he carved from the cadaver.

He knew he didn't have much raw meat left for the dogs and knew he would need more raw food within a week.

April 24

Before her first coffee break, Nicole was pulled into a private office at work. She had been told little except that a few men wanted to speak with her. After the visit, she had the previous day, Nicole suspected she knew whom they were and why they wanted to talk to her. She texted Simone before leaving her desk letting her know what was happening, "called to the "bored" room??" She walked slowly to the boardroom, head down, she shuffled her feet as she walked. As Nicole sat in the office alone, worried, waiting to know for certain who wanted to see her, she fumbled with her phone, anticipating Simone's reply.

The office door opened, three men walked in, detectives, two she recognized, one she didn't. The one she hadn't met the day before wore running shoes with a suit. Her eyes locked onto his as she watched him sit directly across from her. Paul focused on the girl sitting across the table and felt something rumble in his stomach, nausea, hunger; he wasn't sure. Paul suddenly felt flush, pulled his gaze away from her and pulled out a notepad and digital voice recorder then casually stole another peek again.

Running shoes with a suit. "A rebel," she thought, inside she smiled and put her phone away. She wasn't worried anymore.

A fourth person walked in, Nicole's supervisor, pulled out a chair and sat beside her employee. "I hope you understand we are doing this as a favour. If at any point, I feel this is going too far, I'll pull the plug and ask you to leave."

Paul spoke first, "First of all, Ms. Blake, you aren't a suspect, a person of interest or anything. We are interviewing everyone who had any contact with the deceased the night she was," Paul paused, attempted to come up with a less aggressive term, failing to find any, he took a deep breath, "murdered." He tapped the recorder, "We want to record this conversation if that's OK?" Nicole and her supervisor nodded, Paul jotted some notes in his pad then began, "Today is April 24. My name is Detective Paul Hammond, here with me are Detectives Dan Levy and Ken Simmons." He pushed the recorder closer to the far end of the table toward Nicole and motioned for her to give her name.

"Nicole Blake." She looked directly at Paul. His face was now flush, and his forehead began to glow with perspiration.

Her supervisor spoke next, "Theresa Templeton."

Nicole touched Theresa's hand, "It's OK. I know you're busy and I'm fine. Really." She stressed the "really".

"I'll be in the next office if you need me." Theresa stood, the metal chair scraped across the tile floor echoing a grating sound in the small room.

Nicole watched the door close, then turned to face Paul, "I know why you're here. Can you shut down the recorder please?" A sense of calm passed over her. Nicole not only felt at ease but also instinctively trusted the man sitting across from her. She watched as tiny beads of sweat rolled down the officer's forehead, one drop made its way into Paul's eye, causing him blink uncontrollably. He rubbed his eye, held it shut for a few moments, attempting to rinse the salty solution from his eye but it only made things worse. Nicole pulled a fresh Kleenex from her purse and handed it to him.

"Thanks." Paul padded the tear duct and pocketed the tissue. He turned off the recorder.

"Do you have something personal, a picture?" she asked. "I'll show you."

Paul touched his chest, "Me?" he questioned.

Nicole held out a hand, palm up on the table, curling her fingers, waiting for Paul for oblige. Ken and Dan remained silent, watching the two.

While Paul fumbled with his wallet, Nicole turned her attention to Dan and Ken, "No notes either." They turned to Paul who agreed to Nicole's terms. Paul pulled a picture from his wallet, looked at it then slide it across the table, face side down.

"This one?" she asked before touching. Paul nodded.

Nicole turned the picture over, closed her eyes allowing the still photos to appear slowly in some region of her brain then it turned into a flood of moving images, sweeping through her. She jerked softly to one side, then back the other way. The three detectives instinctively wanted to go to her aid when they saw Nicole's movements anticipating she would have another seizure, but held back. The jerking movements began to subside; her head dropped then Nicole ceased her involuntary movements, took in a deep breath, opened her eyes and placed the photo back down on the table face down, "Why haven't you called her?" her voice was subdued, calm.

Paul sat back in his chair, amazed at the events that just transpired before him. He wanted to say something, anything that related to what just happened, but was lost for words. He pulled his hair back, feeling the dampness across his forehead. Nicole sat across from him, unmoving, her hand still covering the photo but no longer looking at it then pushed it across the table to Paul. He reached for his picture, flipped it over, looked at her face then carefully placed it back in his wallet.

"How do you... What can... There must be some sort of..." Paul squinted, refocused his gaze upon Nicole, "How?"

She shrugged her shoulders, smiled at the three men sitting across from her. "A cool parlour trick."

A knock at the door interrupted Nicole from continuing. The door squeaked open slowly, a head appeared, "You OK honey?"

"Can Simone come in?" Nicole asked of the three men.

Before they could respond, Simone took the seat vacated by Theresa. She reached for Nicole's hand, "They treating you alright?" Nicole smiled back and nodded.

Paul flipped open his notebook and clicked his pen, "You OK to talk now?"

"I'm all right."

Simone held up her hand and burned her gaze into Paul, "Before we go any further, my brother is a lawyer, and I told him about Nicole's gift. If anything happens to her, he'll have a lawsuit rammed so far up your ass that you'll need a surgeon to remove it."

Nicole chuckled, "It's OK, I think we have an understanding here. Don't we?" She scanned the three men sitting across from her. They looked at each other; Paul replied, "I believe we do." Simone settled back in her chair.

"Now, can you tell us about what happened to our vic?"

Nicole looked at the notebook still on the table; Paul stuffed it in his suit jacket pocket, then she told the detectives what she saw through Abigail's eyes. Paul, Ken and Dan sat across the table, fixated on what Nicole was saying. When she finished, the three men sat back in their chairs, stunned by what they had just heard. Was it truth, some tale of fantasy made up by the mind of a woman seeking attention or the vivid imagination of a sick mind? Whatever it was, details about the case that was never made public was just revealed in detail and new clues provided.

Paul looked across the table at Nicole, admiring this woman he just met, not only because of her ability but he was inexplicably drawn to her. With her right index finger, Nicole pulled her thick, short black hair around her ear revealing her smooth skin. Her bangs swept across her forehead in a gentle wave from left to right. Paul hadn't noticed a light hint of color streaks in her hair until now. Nicole looked back at Paul who had to force himself to pull away from staring at her. He retrieved his cell phone pretending to check his email. When Paul looked back up from his cell, she was grinning.

Sensing the tension, Dan broke the silence, "Is there anything else you can tell us?"

Nicole shook her head side to side, her bangs falling across her eyes, "This isn't something I can control. I'm just learning what is it and what it does? I'm not even sure why I was given this," she paused, "talent, gift, whatever. I just know it's scary."

Paul pulled himself together, "When did this talent of yours start?" He laced his fingers together and placed his elbows on the edge of the table and leaned in closer.

"Not long ago. It was something that just sorta turned on, like a switch. As time goes on, I'm getting a little more control over it. Just a little." She held her index and thumb close together to emphasize the amount of control she had. "Right now, it's more scary than anything else. Things pop into my head, images, scenes, people, colors I don't even know, somehow they get in here," she tapped the side of her head. "If this thing I have left tomorrow, it wouldn't bother me in the least."

"You're sure. No bump on the head, no tumor, no evil spell cast upon you, this thing just turned on one day?" Dan asked.

Nicole nodded in agreement, remaining silent, sensing some sarcasm in the way the question was posed.

There was an uncomfortable pause as everyone around the table remained silent. Simone looked at the three men on the other side of the conference table. "Well, if that's all gentlemen, I suggest we all get back to work." She pushed her chair back and stood.

"If we have any more questions Ms. Blake, can I, we, contact you?" Paul smiled coyly.

"Leave me your card, and if you have any more photos for me to look at, I'll see if I can help." Nicole stood, "I assume that this conversation is confidential. Nothing about my ability will somehow leak out to the press or the freak show?"

Dan spoke first, "I can speak for the all of us," he gestured to Paul and Ken, "anything regarding this investigation will remain, and must be kept confidential."

"If anything does get out, it could compromise our investigation. Nothing gets out," Ken offered.

The five of them gathered at the office door, hands extended and shook, smiles exchanged, confidentially re-assured. Paul and Nicole were the last two in the room; he offered his hand, she held it firmly and didn't let go. What should've been an uncomfortably long stare was anything but.

Nicole broke the silence, "You really should call her."

"Who? Oh, the picture. Right. Yeah. I'll get right on that." Paul slowly loosened his grip but didn't take his eyes off her. "Again, this stays in this room."

Nicole lowered her head, embarrassed. Her fingers slowly slipped away from Paul's.

As the three police officers walked out of the building, into the sunshine and down the front steps, Ken squinted his eyes, pulled out his sunglasses and asked Paul, "Call who?"

"No one. Forget about it." Paul stopped at the bottom of the stairs, as Ken and Dan walked to the SUV, turned, looked back into the building. He too pulled out his sunglasses and caught up to the other two in the parking lot. Paul climbed into the back seat, pulled the seatbelt over his shoulder and fastened it.

Paul remained silent during the ride back to the station, his mind shifting between Nicole, the case and the photo in his wallet. He rested his elbow on the armrest, cupped his chin in his hand and gazed out the window as the cityscape blurred past without Paul seeing any of it. Paul heard Ken and Dan talking, about what, he didn't care, his thoughts were off in the stratosphere, unable to plant his feet on the ground and come back to reality. None of his thoughts seemed to last much more than a few seconds then he would jump to another subject. His shifted in the back seat, looked at Ken and Dan chatting then let his mind drift again. Paul realized he had been doing a lot of daydreaming lately. Was it daydreaming or just getting old and unable to focus? He chuckled at himself. Ken turned to see what Paul was laughing at. Failing to notice Ken watching him, Paul continued to look out the window. "Hey," Ken spoke softly to Dan and motioned for him to look at Paul.

Dan turned to look at Paul then his attention went back to the road, "He's under a lot of stress. Let him be."

*****

Nicole went back to her desk, fell hard into her chair and wondered about the three men who just left the building. She wondered if showing them her new skill was a mistake. Had she inadvertently put herself in danger? She shook the idea from her head and decided to do a little investigating of her own.

She looked at the blank laptop screen, wondered if there were any other people in the world with this ability she had. After powering up the computer, she Googled "Psychic Abilities", over two million hits. Nicole typed "Moving Images Psychic Abilities", again, more than two million hits.

"One more try," she thought. "Type of Psychic Abilities" was typed in the search bar, almost three million hits.

Nicole spent the next thirty minutes reviewing the websites that were listed on the search. Regardless of which site she visited, none of them listed her unique abilities. She thought for certain; someone else would have the same talent to see the events unfold in a still picture. "Talent. Or curse," she thought. Nicole continued to search but failed to find any mention of anyone in the past who make any mention of the same skill set. Many of the sites described charlatans and fakes who charged for their act or conned people out of money with some slight of hand trick or mind game. Nicole didn't play mind games and wasn't good at magic or deceiving people. She wondered how people could take advantage of others.

Nicole continued her search, occasionally looking over the top of the screen to see if her supervisor would stop by and catch her. Her search still failed to locate anyone with her unique abilities. It didn't mean there wasn't anyone, just no one listed on the internet. "No one on the internet," she said aloud, "Really. How is that possible?" She pushed the chair away from her desk, letting out a deep sigh of frustration.

As Nicole sat there, her thoughts went back to the three men, the one in particular. She could still see his picture she held briefly, moving about as if it would be a video on a cell phone. She wondered about the man who handed her the picture. She knew the history behind the image. Nicole saw what happened between them. It was emotional, intense and very private. Why he chose that picture, she wasn't sure. Maybe Paul thought her skills were nothing more than a party trick, exactly as she was trying to impress upon others.

Nicole adjusted herself in the chair as she scrolled down the list of hits. She wasn't paying attention to the information on her screen as it rolled by, too fast to even read. Her mind continually drifted back to Detective Hammond.

April 29

It was just after midnight and Paul sat on the sofa, wearing mismatched socks, oversized boxer shorts and an old band T-shirt from his college days that barely fit. The photo that Paul always kept with him sat on the corner of his glass top coffee table. Not far from the picture, an open bottle of beer dripped with condensation, forming a thick water ring around the base. He had full intentions of the drinking the beer, but in the past few days, the taste and smell of beer disagreed with him. Instead, he stared at the photo, letting the beer get warm. With eyes closed, his head fell back over the top of the couch. Paul ran his hands through his thinning hair. He looked at his hand and found a few strands stuck between his fingers. He laughed at himself. In his younger days, Paul had a full head of thick dark wavy hair that he felt was his best asset. Paul's father kept his hair until the day he passed away. Paul had hoped he would be just as lucky as his father but in his thirties, his hair began to thin on top. Paul felt embarrassed that he started using Rogaine to keep what hair he had left.

Paul picked up the bottle and rolled it across his forehead. The condensation on the bottle dripped freely from his hand and left dark spots on his faded black T-shirt. He brushed off some of the water from his chest and specks of ink from the decades-old "Cheap Trick" logo broke free. "Damn." Yet another thing from his past that would soon disappear as well. He took a deep breath and blew the specks of ink and hairs from his hand. He placed the bottle back on the table and sat and watched the condensation form on the sides of the bottle again and painstakingly slow, roll down the glass to the table. As the water ring grew larger, Paul watched as it crept slowly towards the photo less than an inch away. Paul reached forward and with his index finger, pulled his treasured photo further away from the bottle of beer.

"I'm a dinosaur," he thought to himself, as he wore a decade's old T-shirt, had thinning hair, still watched a twenty-year-old CRT TV that sat in the corner of his living room and failed to embrace technology. The "It still works" justification prevented him from a purchasing a new LED TV. His most treasured possession was an old photograph taken with a camera that used film and developed the old fashion way. The corners had repeatedly been bent and broke off, the emulsion was cracked, and the image had begun to fade. He would be lost without it, and yet almost every day, he considered taking the photo down to the IT people at the police station and have them scan it, but he kept forgetting. Forgetting or too embarrassed?

From where he sat, he stared at the photo, letting his mind wander about the person smiling back at him. Feelings of guilt, despair ran through him as he tried to convince himself that she still wanted to speak with him.

He hadn't returned her call. Paul knew he should call. He retrieved his cell phone, dialed her number then his thumb hovered over the green "Call" button. He had second thoughts about calling this late at night, put the phone back on the coffee table beside the photo and stared at the two items side by side. For the first time, Paul noticed that the profile on his phone had the blue outline of a person's head on the phone. Maybe if he had the photo scanned he could add her face on his phone.

Paul placed the heel of both hands over his eyes, rubbed hard to prevent the tears from forming then the recurring thought entered his mind again. He wanted all of this to be over. He hated the feelings that kept creeping into his mind whenever he thought about the photograph or the person in it. Rage built up deep inside, and he needed a way to let it all out.

"Fuck," he screamed. Paul left his handgun secured in his locker at the station.

*****

Carl Kadner liked working nights. The offices were almost always deserted, save for the cleaning staff, and after the night cleaner left, the silence was deafening, precisely the way he liked it. His desk was illuminated by a single swing arm light he bought himself and attached to the side of his desk. To save money, all the office lights were on a timer and went out at exactly six every night. Besides, he hated the buzz generated by the fluorescent lights during the day. He used an LED bulb to keep his boss happy, so she wouldn't bitch about the cost of keeping his light on after hours. The paper was barely able to keep its doors open and print an edition every day. Cost savings were a huge priority for the paper. Carl knew the next step was to have the staff work nights and put out a morning edition as they transitioned to digital. The rationale was that the electricity savings alone of having the office and printing press run at night would go into substantial savings. It was fine by Carl; he loved the night.

Carl walked through the office, stopped at the coffee maker, poured a cup from the pot left over from the day shift. He sipped his coffee as he walked back to his desk, took his chair then held the color photocopies sent to him anonymously. They arrived a few days earlier, and he wasn't sure if they were a hoax or not. If they were fake, they were well done. If they were fake, why go through all the trouble of sending them without a note. He knew of the arm found in the snowbank last winter and the girl killed in the bedroom, but why was he sent these pictures? He hadn't reported on either one of those stories. With the eye of a skeptical journalist, he sat back in his chair, coffee cup in one hand, photocopy in the other. His elbows rested on duct-taped repaired armrests. The chair gently rocked, squeaking in each direction under his slight frame. As the newest journalist on staff, he had received the hand-me-down chair that was destined for the dumpster. He rubbed the tie that hung loosely around this neck. He hated ties, none of the other reporters wore suits and ties, but he wanted to stand out from the others. The only suit Carl could afford was second-hand seersucker from the thrift shop. It was an off-white with thin lapels, and the legs could've been an inch or two longer and was most certainly older than he was. He knew the other reporters most certainly made fun of him but that was fine, he enjoyed his new look. It made him feel the part.

He stood, sipped his coffee again as he walked over to the photocopier and placed the first of the photocopies on the scanner. Carl emailed himself each of the pictures then walked back to his desk. The night janitor was replacing the paper recycling bin back beneath Carl's desk when he returned.

"Hey, Sam. How's it going tonight?"

The old man smiled politely; it was the same opening line each night and Sam would reply with the same comment, "Any day above ground is a good day."

Carl let the original photocopies fall onto his desk as he left again to refill his coffee cup with whatever was still in the carafe. When Carl returned, Sam was sitting in his chair holding the papers he had just scanned.

"Find something interesting?"

Startled, Sam spun around in the chair causing it to give off another tone of creaks. "These pictures, disturbing, aren't they?"

Carl stood beside his desk, sipped the burnt coffee, "They are. Why the interest?"

"Just brings back memories." Sam carefully stacked the papers, "In my day, we had a full photo lab in the basement, and they would have to make copies of the originals. And they were in black and white, none of this color. Nowadays, you just copy them, and they show up on that screen," he pointed to the laptop.

Stunned, Carl asked, "You worked here?"

"Thirty-eight years retired as editor-in-chief in '98. After my wife died, retirement didn't hold anything for me, so I came back, and the paper gave me this job. Outta pity I'm sure. Minimum wage but it keeps me busy. I don't need the money, but without it, I'd be dead by now. Place is full of new people now. No one left here from the old days to remember me."

Carl squinted his eyes and tried to do the math in his head.

"Oh, for Pete's sake, ninety-eight take away thirty-eight, and that means I started here in 1960. I was twenty when I started right outta college. And yes, I'm seventy-seven now. Computers are supposed to make people smarter. No one can write in cursive anymore, and without a calculator, you can't-do the math."

Carl laughed loudly, "Sorry Sam, different era. I'm sure your parents told you all about things when they were kids." He took another sip of coffee and made a face, "You want me to get you a cup?"

"Nah, I'm good. My parents belly ached about kids the way we do now about you kids. But things have moved faster in the past twenty years than in the last hundred. Kinda hard for us old guys to keep up."

"Seventy-seven isn't that old Sam. Besides, you don't look a day over seventy-five." Carl countered.

"Funny guy. It's been a long seventy-seven years, a hard life, not a great one either." Sam stood and offered the chair to Carl. Carl politely declined and held the chair for Sam to take a seat.

"I'm sorry to hear that. Feel like sharing?" Carl was sincere in his proposition to listen to Sam.

"Rantings of an old man."

"I wouldn't have asked if I didn't want to hear your stories." He took another sip of his coffee. "Tell me, what was it like in the sixties? Were you in this building?"

"Nah, we were in the three-storey brownstone downtown on McKinnon. I think it's been converted to apartments now. Those were newspaper days let me tell ya."

Carl laughed.

"What's so funny?" Sam asked.

"You don't talk like an editor-in-chief. I expected you to speak like a socialite or aristocrat."

"The southern accent is coming back as I get older. That, and I don't give a fuck about shit anymore." The two of them chuckled. Sam continued, "I used to walk up the stairs to the third floor instead of taking the elevator and walk between the rows of desks and hear the greatest sound in the world. You ever listened to a room of typewriters clacking away and phones ringing? None of those mobile ringtones, I mean the sound of brass bells inside an old phone. That was the noise of a newsroom." Sam closed his eyes. Carl could see the image of the newsroom with dozens of desks and journalist typing away as the phones rang that Sam was re-creating in his mind.

"Newspapers were alive back then. Before TV ruined it all. I mean destroyed. TV newscasters give less than thirty seconds per spot and move on. We would give a good story half the front page and more inside. Sometimes those stories went on for weeks. We gave the public details, made them feel the story, feel compassion, or anger or whatever needed to be felt. News was an art. Now, it's boiled down, constituted, evaporated into segments, and the public has the attention span of a gnat. If they can't read the story in a few short seconds, they move on. Sure, there's more news, but the story gets lost. Have you ever sat down with a newspaper and an iced tea in the summer to read the paper, I mean actually read? None of those tabloid papers, a newspaper that takes two hands to hold up, so you can see the whole page. Feel the paper between your fingers and the smell of the ink." Sam inhaled deeply as his index finger and thumb rubbed together. Memories of ink and paper filled his mind.

"A story went out on the wire instead of the internet. No one heard of the web back then. That's how we got our stories out to the other papers. And we got their stories. Those machines were tall, about this high," Sam held his hand out about three feet off the ground, "and paper rolled out of the machines as the stories printed off."

"Like a fax machine," Carl offered.

Sam pointed a bony finger at him, "Exactly."

Carl was fixated on Sam's story, his coffee mug only inches away from his lips but never moved. He waited for Sam next words.

"I spent my whole life in that building. More years than I should've. I loved that place," Sam looked around, "it was my life. But, I shoulda spent more time at home. Had a great view of the rising sun over the mountains."

"Kids?" Carl asked.

Sam paused, shook his head, "Stayed married outta commitment, not love. Big mistake. Don't get me wrong, she was great, I'm just not sure I loved her, and the time I spent working wasn't fair to her. I let the girl of my dreams slip between my fingers because I was already married. Kept her photo hidden in my Rolodex my entire career. I imagine my wife suspected but said nothing. Commitment is a horrible thing. If I had a set of balls, I would've left my wife and gone to her. Something always gets in the way. Have you found a girl yet?" Sam paused then spoke again before Carl could reply, "Sorry, I forgot, I have to be sensitive. Let me rephrase that. Have you found someone special yet? You know, just in case."

Carl let loose with a full laugh. "No Sam, I haven't found a special someone yet. And it will be a girl. I just hope I find her soon."

"Phew. Good. In my day, political correctness hadn't been invented yet. It wasn't a problem to use the term fag or homo. In my dad's day, a fag was a cigarette. Being gay meant you were happy, not like today. Of course, every homosexual I've ever known was happier than I've ever been so maybe that's why they use the term gay." He air quoted "gay." "I was sure my boss back in the sixties dabbled a bit with a few guys on the side. He always took the new copy boys on trips with him. Today, you're weird if you aren't homosexual. Maybe I would've been happier as a gay." Sam slapped his thigh and laughed. "No fucking way, I love women too much."

Sam spun around in Carl's chair, "Tell me about this." He tapped the photocopies with his thick index finger. "Not much in the papers about these two cases. I'm guessing the cops are being tight-lipped, right?"

Carl nodded in agreement.

"So, what are you gonna do about that?" Sam queried.

"Not sure. Our current editor, Nora Tannen, chewed my ass off the other day. I'm supposed to do crime reporting, but I haven't been able to catch a break on any of these incidents. She yelled at me for ten minutes straight, and I don't think she stopped long enough to catch her breath. Each death was reported separately in the paper. No one suspected they were connected until I got the envelope in the mail. I mean why would we connect an arm in a snow bank to a dead girl in her house months apart? The city maybe has one or two homicides a year. Cops haven't commented. No one is talking. I was sent these in the mail. I haven't told Tannen about them yet. No return address on the envelope, email is too easy to trace. Pretty sure these are police evidence pics. I mean, look at this one," Carl spread the photocopies across his desk and slammed his hand down on the picture of a dead girl beside her bed. "One thing I noticed, look at the hands." He then pulled the picture of the arm in the snow bank. "This one."

"Similar, physically aren't they?" Sam noted.

"They could be the same girl, except these were months apart. And the girl beside the bed wasn't missing an arm. So why are these connected? I mean really, an arm in a snow bank, a dead girl beside her bed."

"Connect the dots."

"Dots?" Carl cast Sam a strange look. "OK. Well, both female, both have similar physical characteristics in hand anatomy. Dissimilar, one is dismembered, the other not, one in winter, one not in winter."

"So, what are you gonna do about it?" Sam questioned Carl.

Carl began to pace around behind Sam, "You sound like Tannen. What do you want me to do about it?"

Frustrated, Sam stood and forced the chair under the younger man, "Sit."

"Forget about the internet, forget about your cell phone, forget about trying to Google for leads, if you want to get leads on this case what should you do?"

Carl stared at Sam with blank eyes, "I dunno."

Sam rummaged through Carl's desk trying to find certain items, "Damn man, don't you have a notebook?"

"No. Why would we? We use voice recorders now." Carl asked.

Sam pulled a sheet of blank paper from Carl's desk. "Here, pencil and paper. Better yet, go buy a notebook then go out and start asking questions. You're a reporter, find the story and report it. You can't make sidebar notes using a voice recorder. Things that pop into your mind when you're interviewing someone. Use both."

"Where do I start?"

"Oh – my - Lord. How long have you been here? Go see the cops, find out who's in charge of the investigation. Who sent you the photocopies? What were you doing at the photocopier?"

"Well, technically, it's a scanner, copier, fax machine."

"Who the fuck cares?" Sam's look had changed, and he suddenly looked younger and had more energy. "What?"

"I scanned the photos and made digital copies and emailed them to myself," Carl acknowledged.

"To do what?"

"Examine them."

"Then let's open them and look at them."

Carl rubbed the touchpad and brought the laptop back to life. He opened the email and downloaded the attachments. He opened the best photo of the frozen arm, zoomed in until the hand was full screen. He did the same with the girl's hand from the bedroom. He rotated the image several times until they were approximately the same angle. Carl tapped the screen.

"The image is a little blurry but look at the hands. I mean if the girl in the bedroom hadn't been killed months after the arm was found, the two hands could be the same person. Look at the knuckles, the nails, no rings, no sign a ring was ever worn. I bet the girls are approximately the same age too." Carl used his index finger to run along the hand of one image then onto the next. "They look like they came from the same person."

Carl sat on the edge of the chair, "Do you think this is some kind of fetish killing? I mean some guys like feet, hair color, body type, why not hands?"

"So, what are you gonna do?" Sam placed his hand on Carl's shoulder. "Get up early and go talk to the cops."

"Good. I expect to hear some results tomorrow night when I come in. I gotta go finish my cleaning, but tomorrow night, I want a full report."

"Yes, sir." Carl stood and extended his hand, "Sam, it's been a pleasure. We should've done this a long time ago."

Sam took Carl's hand, squeezed it tightly, "Yes, we should've. It's been fun. Brought me back. Tomorrow?"

"Tomorrow."

Sam started to walk away as he pushed his cleaning cart. Without turning back, "Take my advice, don't drink the coffee. Can't remember the last time I cleaned that machine."

April 30

"Detective?"

Paul looked up to see the receptionist peaking over his desk divider. "Yeah."

"There's a reporter here to see you. Says he has some questions about some case you're working on."

"What? Here? They don't stop by anymore. They call and harass us." She leant across and played with the tiny dollar store Christmas tree on Paul's desk. "This stupid tree has been here since last Christmas. You ever gonna put it away?"

"Nope keeps me in the festive mood."

"You are so full of it Hammond. Anyway, I'm not sure why he's here.

He just showed up, no appointment and asked to see the Lead Detective on that case you're working on and if you were available. When I asked him why he said he was a reporter and had some questions."

"Why the fuck didn't he just call? Jesus Christ," Paul blurted out. "Sorry, I didn't mean that."

"Don't worry. You ever hear the shit some of these fucken' a-holes shout out when they pass my desk for processing after they get arrested. That, Paul, was tame. I told him you were busy, stupidly busy but he wanted to wait. I put him in the small conference room." With that, she left.

Paul checked his emails, went to the washroom, didn't wash his hands-on purpose then went to the conference room where Carl Kadner was waiting. Paul opened the door, propped it open and extended his hand, "Detective Hammond." They shook. Paul took a seat across the table from Carl, then hidden from sight, he wiped his hands on his pant legs.

"Carl Kadner. I'm with the Times." He slid his business card across the desk towards Paul.

Paul casually glanced at the card, "Never heard of you."

Carl smiled, "To be honest, I've never heard of you either. I guess that makes us even right. Besides, I used to do business before I started doing crime."

"Big difference between business and crime."

"Crime can be a business and business can be a crime," Carl countered. Paul cocked his head to the side, "True. So, what brings you here today?"

"Do you mind if I record the conversation?" Carl asked. Before Paul could object, he placed a small digital voice recorder in the centre of the table and pressed a button. The red light indicated it was now recording. He then pulled out a newly purchased notepad and flipped it open. "Hammond? With two "M's" or one?"

Paul held up two fingers instead of answering.

Carl wrote Detective Hammond's name in his notebook and continued, "You're investigating two cases, the arm found last year in the snow and more recently, the girl murdered in her home. These two cases are connected. Would you mind telling me how they are related and what leads you have so far?"

Shocked, Paul simply leaned back in his chair and waited for Carl to continue. There was a moment of silence as Carl waited for Paul to respond. Nothing. Carl took the detectives sudden movement as positive confirmation. He made a quick note of what the detective did.

"You aren't going to answer the question Detective?"

"Ask me a question I can give you answers to without jeopardizing any aspect of any case which may or may not be related."

Carl thought for a moment, "Are there two separate investigations into the two murders? I assume a frozen arm found in the snow would at least lead you to believe the victim is dead. Right? I mean, you haven't had someone call reporting a missing arm in the Lost and Found department?"

Paul had to think about his response without giving anything away, "We're a small department without a dedicated homicide division so any case or cases will most likely always be investigated by the same team, which may or may not be linked."

Carl smiled. It was now a game of verbal chess. "Detective, two young women were killed, OK, let me rephrase that, one killed, and one assumed killed or presumed dead. Let me start with an easy one, have you located the owner of the arm?"

"No."

Carl scribbled a few notes. "Were you able to determine if the arm was removed pre-or post-mortem? Was the arm removed by accident or by someone who knew what they were doing?"

"The arm was found frozen, and the probable damage caused by the snow plough made it difficult to determine when and how the limb was removed, even perhaps severed. So, there is no way to know for sure." Paul leaned forward and placed his elbows on the table. "Are we done?"

Carl wrote for a moment, held up a single finger to indicate he wanted a minute. "I think we are done."

Paul pushed his chair, stood and made his way to the door when Carl interrupted his departure. "One more thing Detective. Can you confirm that the two girls were killed by the same person because they were physically similar?"

Paul spun around surprised by the comments. "What the fuck are you talking about?" He felt his heart begin to race. "Where did you get that idea? Who told you that?"

Carl kept looking at the notebook before him, pretending to write, not wanting to infuriate the detective any further. He eventually looked up making eye contact with Paul. They locked stares; silence filled the room. Paul stood at the door, inviting his guest to leave. No further words were said. Carl gathered up his belongings, clicked off the voice recorder and walked through the door without saying another word. As Carl passed Paul, he forcibly stuffed the business card back into Carl's suit jacket pocket.

Carl smiled, pulled the card from his jacket and dropped it on the floor, "You may want that," and walked out.

*****

Nicole's extension rang several times before she could pick it up. She left the receiver rest on her shoulder as she continued to type, "This is Nicole."

The voice on the other end of the phone was familiar, but the tone was not, "Did you tell me everything you saw when you looked at those pictures I showed you?"

"Detective?" Nicole turned away from the keyboard and took hold of the handset.

"Yeah. Well did you?"

"Did I what?" Nicole was concerned that she had somehow missed something when she helped the police.

"Did you omit telling me something? Was there anything you saw that you didn't tell me?" Paul's voice showed signs of stress.

"Detective, I told you everything I saw. Everything. I swear. Why? Did I miss something?" There was a long pause on the line. Nicole heard Detective Hammond breathing deeply and the sound of people speaking in the background.

"Listen, I'm sorry. I just had some disturbing news, and it was something that made me look like an idiot. Something I missed, and I was deflecting my anger. Something I should have seen if I wasn't so preoccupied. My mind hasn't been on the job lately."

Nicole didn't know how to respond. She had no idea if Detective Hammond was referring to his personal life or work. "Drinks tonight?" She took the first step.

"Sure," Paul blurted out without hesitation. "Well yeah. If you have time." His attempt to sound nonchalant was met with laughter on the other end of the phone.

"I wouldn't have asked if I didn't. Are you supposed to see me, a suspect involved in an active case?"

Paul thought about what she had said, "You aren't a suspect or a person of interest. Technically, you are a consultant on the case. You helped us with the evidence we have. This is just a meeting to go over anything we might've missed."

"If I'm a consultant, do I get paid?" Nicole was kidding.

"I'll pay for the drinks, how's that?" Paul had initially called to complain and ended up with a date. He was beaming.

"In that case, I want dinner," Nicole said in her best playful voice.

Paul gave Nicole his cell number, told her that he was busy and asked if she could book reservations any time after six-thirty and text him with the time and name of the restaurant. Nicole told him she would keep the restaurant reasonable and she would spring for dessert.

"Before I book a place for reservations, is there anything you don't like?" she asked.

"If it's alright with you, no pizza, no burgers. A nice sit-down, quiet meal. I haven't been out to an expensive place in so long. I'm not trying to impress you, but since we're going out, I'd like a fancy place. Good enough?"

"I got a place. Meet you there or?"

Paul thought about it, "What works best for you?"

"I'll meet you there. You know, in case I want to ditch you between the main course and dessert," Nicole laughed softly. Paul was familiar with the "going to the bathroom" disappearing act.

"Great. See you there." He figured his odds just dropped exponentially. With that, she hung up the phone, turned around to see Simone hovering over her shoulder, causing Nicole to let out a little yelp. "Geez girl. What the fuck? You scared the shit outta me."

"What was up with all that cute talk? Dinner? Reservations? Do you have a date? Who is it?" Simone was now kneeling down, face to face with Nicole, hands firmly grasping her friend's shoulders demanding answers.

"That was Paul, Detective Hammond." Nicole blushed.

"The cop, the old guy. The guy has no fashion sense. He was wearing running shoes with a suit and tie." Simone squinted.

"He's not that old. And, he's kinda cute. In a cop sorta way."

"Fat, balding, no fashion sense but I bet he has a big gun," Simone lifted her eyebrows and sported a broad smile. "Where's he taking you? Better be someplace expensive for a first date."

"He is not fat. He has a little belly. Geez, Simone, he's not gonna wear expensive clothes to work, and as far as dinner goes, I doubt it will be over the top. I don't think cops make a lot. I doubt he could afford much. He told me to pick the place, someplace nice but I want to keep it reasonable."

Nicole looked at Simone asking if she had any recommendations. "I was thinking about "Tony's"? No wait, that's Italian. Paul said no to pizza, so Italian is out."

Simone grabbed a free chair, pulled it up close to her friend, and sat down, "My God girl, you're nervous." Simone took hold of her friend's hand and squeezed. "No need to be a wreck. How 'bout "Athenas"? Did he say anything about a steakhouse, Lebanese, Greek? You like Greek."

Nicole nodded in agreement but still appeared nervous. "Nervous Hon?" Simone asked.

Again, without speaking, Nicole nodded.

"You want me to book the reservations at Athenas?"

Nicole nodded again. She became increasingly more uncomfortable as she realized she was going on her first date in longer than she cared to remember.

Simone wheeled her chair to Nicole's desk, Googled the telephone number for Athenas to make reservations. While she was on hold, Simone cupped the phone with one hand and asked what time she wanted to reserve a table. Nicole mouthed seven-thirty. Simone booked the reservations, hung up the phone, wheeled in close to her friend and held her hand. "It's all set." Nicole still couldn't believe what she had done. She had never been so forward with a man in her life. Nicole sat in her chair, unmoving, in disbelief at her aggressive behavior, asking a man out on a date. She had never done that. Yet, she felt so at ease with Paul. Nicole looked over to Simone, "I honestly, literally have nothing to wear that's presentable. I mean, I have work clothes, but nothing to wear out, with a guy. I better text him the place and time."

*****

The days were getting longer, each day, the sun a little higher in the sky and with that, he could feel the temperature rise. He hated the winter, the way the snow covered the landscape, the barren trees, hiding everything beneath its thick coat of white. He much preferred the summer with long bright days and warmer nights.

He strolled down the sidewalk, much like he had done the past November, passing people too busy to notice who he was. But, they didn't know, no one knew. And he was all right with that, comfortable in the knowledge that he could walk down a street and not a soul knew his secret. He knew perfectly well what he was doing was wrong, so terribly wrong. His only excuse for what he did, he wanted to. And he liked it. He questioned if that was a problem. He reasoned it wasn't then thought again that if he didn't believe that it was wrong, he must have an issue. "A vicious cycle," he told himself as he strolled down the street.

His stomach loudly rumbled as he walked, a man looked at him and chuckled, "Haven't eaten since breakfast," he told him. The stranger smiled back, and they continued on their respective ways. He was hungry. Above, a sign that stuck out further than the others caught his attention. Beneath it, a patio had been set up forcing pedestrians to walk around the fenced in eating area in a narrow path. As he approached, there was an opening with a plastic figure of a butler holding a menu out for the public to read. A quick scan and his mind was made up. He entered, found a table and took a seat closest to the street with the sun at his back. Pedestrian traffic passed him just on the other side of the ornate black iron barricade. He lifted the chair and turned it, so he could watch everyone pass by. He leaned back and looked through the crowd fixating on the women that appeared to be in their late twenties. Each one was quickly mentally processed. He was so focused on the crowd that he didn't hear the server standing at this table.

"Sir?" the young man asked again.

He casually looked up at the server, "I'm terribly sorry. Just taking in the sun and the scenery."

The server was very formal, "Not a problem sir. Care to start with a beverage?"

"What's the special of the day?" He pulled the cloth napkin from the table and carefully placed it on his lap.

"We have an excellent poached salmon with dill…"

He cut the server short, "Sounds great and a beer. Imported, anything. No, make it a Heineken. You have Heineken, don't you?"

"We do sir, would you like…"

He turned his attention back to the crowd and ignored whatever the server was saying. It's not that he purposely intended to dismiss the server, there was just so much to see before him, he didn't want anything to pass him by.

Most of the crowd was a blur as they went passed, all the men, children and older women seemed to fade into the background. It was as if he had a special filter that permitted him to see only what he wanted. He likened his ability to only see a lone maple tree in a forest of evergreens. The women passed by in slow motion; their movements were almost frozen as he scanned what he wanted to observe then moved on to the next girl. He continued to look at the women's features, hands, arms, shoulders, legs. Waiting to see exactly what he wanted. His demands were precise, and he was willing to postpone any further action until the right one came along. Just beyond the sidewalk, vehicles silently rolled past, almost invisible to him. His mental filter managing again, somehow, to eliminate whatever he didn't want to see. All the sounds had been muted. He was so focused on his search; he heard nothing.

He scanned the street, continuing his search, failing to notice the server returning with his drink and placing it before him. "Your meal will be out shortly."

*****

The server stood by the table for a moment then decided not to interrupt his customer's hobby. The last thing he wanted to do was potentially upset a customer and ruin his tip.

The server returned to the kitchen, wiped his forehead free of perspiration with the towel he kept on his apron string, then tossed the soiled cloth into the linen hamper. "I've got this guy sitting in the corner of the patio just staring at the street. I've got no clue what the hell his problem is but man; he's a weirdo."

Without looking up, one of the prep cooks asked, "Why? What's he doing?"

"He's just staring out onto the street. I walked up, dropped off his beer, he didn't turn around, say "Boo", nothing. The guy is just weirding me out." The server found another towel and secured it to his apron.

"As long as he likes his meal, pays for it and leaves a tip, who the fuck cares." The chef sprinkled some seasoning into the pan and stirred vigorously.

"I know. But he's one of those customers who thinks that they are better than us."

The chef laughed, "He's the one sitting outside enjoying the weather, and we're stuck in this hot kitchen working. I think he is better than us." He lifted the pan and poured the sauce over whatever was on the plate. "You want me to drop a booger in his food?" He laughed again.

"You've never done it any other time I've asked, why start now?"

"Exactly. Get your ass out there. Play nice with the idiot customers with the money, and I'll have your order ready in a few minutes." The chef turned his back on the server and went back to work.

The server grabbed the plate, left the kitchen and delivered it to the customer who ordered it. As he left the table, he turned to the other table and found the man he was uncomfortable with, in the same position he left him. His Heineken was still untouched on the table. He kept his eye on the man as he swerved between tables, scooped up an empty glass, asked the customers if they wanted a refill and went back to the kitchen.

He overfilled a clean glass with ice, used the fountain to put in a small amount of Diet Coke for the customer and carried it back out.

The man sitting at the table hadn't moved. It was like a statue was in the man's place. The server was amazed that his customer had not even moved his arms, turned his head, he doubted the man even blinked. He set the glass on the table, asked if there was anything else he could do for them, then turned to look at his customer once again. The man sat motionless in his chair, his untouched beer still in the bottle, condensation dripping down onto the tablecloth.

The server went back to the kitchen to find the customer's lunch on a plate, surrounded by grilled seasonal vegetables and a lemon wedge centered on the salmon steak. Without saying a word, he held the plate high and walked to the patio. He stood at the doorway, and the customer who ordered the salmon special was gone. He walked to the table to find the beer bottle resting atop a fifty-dollar bill. The server looked around and failed to find his customer anywhere on the patio. At least he didn't get taken for the meal. He grabbed the bottle, passed the hostess telling her he was taking five and returned to the kitchen to eat the salmon.

*****

He quickened his pace to almost an all-out sprint to catch up to the girl who passed him as he waited for his lunch. He weaved in and out of the crowd, occasionally bumping into people who walked too slow or just failed to get out of his way. His gaze was locked on the girl who was now less than thirty feet away. He pushed his way through a group of seniors, knocking one to the ground. Several bystanders yelled at him, others stopped to help the old woman on the ground, he ignored everyone and kept his target in sight.

She slowed, turned left and stopped at a large window. She cupped her eyes and pressed her hands against the glass, raised one arm and waved at whoever was inside. She entered the coffee house and waved to her friends at the table then took her place in line to order.

He broke from his sprint to a walk, keeping pace with the rest of the foot traffic on the sidewalk. At the coffee shop, without pausing, he followed her in, stood in line directly behind her, inches away and inhaled deeply. Her scent filled his senses. There was an overwhelming calm that filled his body as he stood there, almost touching her. As the line moved forward, she kept pace. He maintained minimal space between them, acting as if it was natural for him always to invade the personal space of others. He pulled his phone from his pocket pretending to check email or texts as he looked over the phone at the woman in front of him.

The line moved forward again, the girl stepped forward to the counter, greeted the server, there were some laughs exchanged then she placed her order. The barista asked for the girl's name. "Katy, with one "T"." She scrawled the name on the cup in thick black letters. "What an idiotic thing to do," he thought. He now knew her first name, "Katy". Katy paid her bill and stepped to the side. He stepped forward, looked up at the menu board, and ordered a coffee and a chocolate scone.

"What size coffee sir?" the barista asked.

"Large is fine." His voice was pleasant, and he smiled back at the girl behind the counter. "And can you put milk and two sugar in that please?"

The barista politely pointed to the end of the counter, "You can add whatever you like at the self-service area."

He continued to smile, slid a ten-dollar bill across the counter and joined Katy in line as they waited for their orders. The barista placed the man's change before him, "Sir, your change." He turned to face her and winked. She nodded and put the change in the tip container. Another barista reached over the glass display case and handed the man his scone in a bag. He kept his distance from Katy in front of him and kept observing her. Like most of the other customers, she was busily clicking away on her smartphone. She was not only unaware of the other patrons but was completely uninterested in the man behind her.

Katy's name was called out, and she picked up her drink and joined her friends at the table. Katy sat down, removed the lid from the cup, blew across the top and took a sip. She joined in the conversation with the rest of the girls around the table. He couldn't make out what they were saying, but all he was interested in was whether or not anyone of the girls at the table would take notice of him.

He waited patiently for his name to be called, retrieved his drink, took a single table at the back of the coffee house facing the group, held his phone up high, looking beyond at Katy and her friends. Like an undercover detective, he would keep an eye on the target without giving away his presence or making himself known to the rest of the coffee house.

He sipped his coffee, thumbed the blank screen, as he watched Katy. Patrons walked past, but he never saw them. The rest of the coffee house seemed to fade away, the bustle of the crowds gave way to silence. As he watched them, the room darkened, a single light shone overhead of the table when Katy sat. He focused solely on the table, the rest of the world disappeared.

*****

Nicole strolled out of the bedroom, held her arms out to the side, "Well?" "Are you going for the Annie Hall look? My God woman, you look like you're my grandma." Simone wasn't pulling her punches. "You hafta show a little something, something. You have a nice rack, show some cleavage." "I'm not even sure if this is a date or he just wants to talk to me some more about the visions." Nicole started pulling some of her clothes off and tossing them to the ground. "And if it is a date, he must be hard up. Why me?"

Simone began picking up the clothes that Nicole was tossing to the floor, "What's wrong with you? Of course, it's a date. If it wasn't, you'd be at the police station answering questions. Other than your self-loathing, you're a hottie."

Nicole now stood before Simone only wearing her bra and panties. Simone stood, grabbed Nicole's hand and positioned her in front of the full-length mirror. Standing behind Nicole, Simone reached around and cupped her friend's breasts and pushed them up. "We have to get you another bra to show off these puppies. And, we have to find something to show off your curves. And get rid of these cotton panties. You want that cop to pat you down and feel those? Don't you have a thong or something sexy?"

Nicole slapped Simone's hands off from her breasts, "You're the first one to touch these in a long time. And I doubt Paul and I will be getting naked tonight anyway. Like I said, it'll probably just be cop talk. I can't believe I asked him out. What was I thinking?"

Simone started pulling out lingerie from the dresser drawer until she found a push-up bra and a lace purple thong. "If you were hoping to get laid, this is what you need." She tossed it to her friend. "Go put these on and let me see." While Nicole was in the washroom, Simone was sliding clothes along the rod in the closet. Simone finally found what she was looking for.

Nicole emerged from the washroom wearing what Simone had picked out, slowly turning around to see if it met her friend's approval.

"Whoa woman, you have a nice ass. And now you have some cleavage to show off too. Nice." Simone handed Nicole the black dress she found in the closet and helped her put it on. "There you go. No panty lines and it shows off your bod."

"I haven't worn this in years. It's too tight."

"It isn't tight honey; it's just right to show what you have. Pair this with some black heels and that man will want you to finish dinner early and get you outta that dress pronto." Simone had her hands around Nicole's waist to smooth out the lines. Simone patted her down, "There you go. Look in the mirror."

Nicole stood in front of the mirror again and stretched to give herself some breathing room in the dress. "Girl, my tits are gonna spill out." She was about to pull the dress up higher over her cleavage when Simone repeated what Nicole had done earlier and slapped her hands.

"You need to show off what you've got. Trust me." "Because I haven't got anything else?" Nicole questioned. "No. Because you're a woman."

Nicole nodded in agreement, placed her hands on her hips and gave herself a little pose in the mirror. "I'm not half bad."

Simone stood beside her friend, "I'd fuck you," and put her arm around Nicole's waist.

*****

He kept his distance, at least half a block, as he followed Katy down the sidewalk. It was just after six, the busy city streets were now almost deserted of car and pedestrian traffic, and he found it difficult to maintain his discreet surveillance without being obvious. Several times, he considered abandoning his prey. He felt it was easier to find another girl than to risk getting caught. He set new restrictions with this girl. If she turned around once to look at him, he would break off the pursuit. If anyone on the street even looked at him the wrong way, he would call it off.

The sun was low in the sky, casting long shadows. The afternoon heat had since retreated, and the night's chill had begun to set in. Katy had left the coffee house, done some shopping and was walking back along the sidewalk to where he had first spotted her hours earlier. Her walk was slow and casual; Katy was enjoying her walk back to wherever she was going.

As Katy's pace slowed, he found it difficult to keep his distance. The sidewalks were almost deserted, and she would almost notice any odd behavior on his part. As he decided to discontinue the pursuit, Katy did something completely unexpected, she made an abrupt turn and started walking directly towards him.

He panicked, stopped in his tracks and was about to make an about face then decided to continue his path. Katy was now walking towards him, the distance between the two of them closing fast. He watched her retrieve her phone from her purse and heard her greet the caller. They were now less than a dozen feet apart. Katy looked up, their eyes met. He stepped to his right, she to her left, there was nowhere to go, and they bumped into each other. Katy's phone fell to the sidewalk. Instinctively, he bent forward to pick up her phone. He stood and offered her the phone as she rubbed her right shoulder.

"Thanks." Katy's voice was sweet, soft and pleasant. She took the phone and held the phone up to her ear, "I'll call you back." She disconnected from the call and held out her hand, "Katy."

"Will." He shook her hand. It was the first name that came to him. For the first time, he looked at the girl he was following. Katy was slender, long wavy dark hair, perfect skin, soft features, she was a little taller than he was. He had been staring at her for hours and never really noticed how pretty she was. Her fragrance that he had become familiar with filled the air around him.

"Short for William?" she asked.

"Yup."

"What about Liam? I love the name, Liam."

He had to think fast, "My father was William Senior. My mother called him Liam. I'm William Junior. Mom called me Will to avoid any confusion."

Katy squinted her eyes, "You definitely look like a Will." They both chuckled.

Katy continued, "Listen, I'm sorry. I didn't mean to bump into you. I don't know my right from left, and when I'm on the phone, my mind is in la-la land. Hope I didn't hurt you." she said apologetically. "Did I hurt you?" Katy reached out and placed her hand on his shoulder.

Will laughed. "No, I think I have the weight advantage." He returned the gesture and gently touched her right shoulder where they made contact, "Did I hurt you?"

"Not at all. I'm stronger than I look. I work out." Again, she offered her hand. "Katy." Will shook it again.

"I know."

Katy covered her eyes, "I'm sorry," and let out a barely audible giggle.

"Don't be. Nervous?" he asked.

Katy shrugged her shoulders, "No. Just, umm, not sure." Katy cast Will an odd look. "Do we know each other? You look familiar."

Will's heart began to race, "I have the type of face that everyone seems to recognize." He quickly changed the subject. "Is your phone OK? Didn't get broken or anything?"

Katy looked at the phone, "No new scratches, screen isn't cracked. It's all good." She pocketed the phone. "Listen, if you don't have any plans, I'd like to buy you coffee for bumping into you. My way of saying "Sorry"."

"Are you hitting on me?" Will sported a wide toothy grin.

"You have a nice smile Will." Again, Katy let out a soft giggle. "And caring eyes."

"Son-of-a-bitch. You are hitting on me."

"Maybe a little." She touched his shoulder again. "Besides, I have no plans tonight now. The guy I was talking to on the phone when we bumped into each other just stood me up."

"His loss."

"Well Will, you just got yourself a free coffee."

"It's a little late for coffee. I'm being a little forward. How about grabbing a bite?" Will looked around the street. He pointed to a restaurant. "How about that place over there? You like Greek?"

*****

Nicole parked her car around the corner from Athena's and walked the short distance to the restaurant. She tossed her keys in the small clutch that Simone had told her went well with the dress. Nicole brushed the dress down on her thighs before she started the short walk to the restaurant. After the first few steps, Nicole cursed wearing heels. She hadn't worn heels in months and was having a difficult time walking with any elegance. She could already feel the blisters forming on her feet. But Simone had been right; the shoes certainly did make her outfit look better. She slowed her walk, planted each step to prevent turning her ankles. As she slowly made her way, Nicole felt her stomach flip one way, then the other, then push up her throat until she could taste the acid in the back of her throat. "Why am I doing this?" Nicole stopped in her tracks, looked at the restaurant further up the block and wondered if she was doing the right thing. She stood motionless for a moment then decided to take the risk and continue.

The night air was a little brisker that she thought and prayed they didn't have the air conditioner on in the dining room. A walk that should've taken less than a minute took several minutes because of her unbalanced gait in the high heels. As she neared the restaurant, her pulse quickened, she took a deep breath and felt better. Nicole pulled the door open, stepped inside and was relieved to feel that the AC wasn't on. A quick glance at her watch and she knew she was early. The hostess approached as Nicole walked to the entrance of the dining lounge. Nicole saw a familiar face in the dining room, sitting by himself, head down, cell phone in hand. Instead of speaking with the hostess, Nicole pointed to the man she knew already sitting alone.

The hostess led Nicole to Paul's table, pulled the chair out for her, Paul stood as she took her seat. She politely asked if they wanted a drink before they ordered. Paul quickly stuffed his BlackBerry into his jacket pocket.

"I'll have a tea please," Nicole requested as she placed her clutch bag on the table. "Milk and sugar."

The hostess nodded in agreement then turned to Paul, "Coffee please," with that, she spun around and left the two alone.

Paul turned his attention to Nicole, "You look," he took in a deep breath, "Nice."

"Not too much?" Nicole looked down at her dress.

"I would say, it's just about perfect. A significant change from your work attire."

"This is all my friend's doing. She picked everything out for me." "Please pass along my thanks, next time you see her."

Nicole glanced at her watch again, "We both got here early. I half expected you to show up as I had dessert."

"If I didn't leave early, I probably would've forgotten about the time and kept working. But seeing how great you look, I'm glad I ditched work. Was it your friend I met who helped you get dressed? Do you think she knows how great you look? Cause honestly; you do look, um, well, terrific."

"Ya, she knows. In fact, Simone got a little handsy with me as I was getting dressed." Nicole recalled how Simone adjusted her cleavage. "Sometimes I think if I let her, she would make a move on me."

"Lucky girl."

Paul and Nicole shared a small laugh; then she felt a sudden stabbing pain cutting through her skull. She dropped her head, closed her eyes and slumped forward. Nicole went to brace herself by placing her elbow on the table, missed the edge and almost fell to the floor. Paul jumped to his feet, caught Nicole and helped her back into her chair. Several other patrons came to assist Paul. The other customers all made sure Nicole was safe before going back to their seats. There were hushed tones from the others as they looked on at the disturbance.

"You OK?" Paul's voice was soft but firm.

Nicole kept her eyes closed; she felt a wave of nausea course through her and moisture forming over her entire body. She could barely keep herself sitting upright.

The hostess returned with a glass of water and stood behind Nicole, and once she had Paul's attention, she mouthed 911. Paul looked up, and past Nicole was softly shaking his head side to side. The hostess placed the glass on the table then stood back in case she was needed. Paul didn't rush Nicole and just kept quiet until she felt well enough to respond. Several minutes passed before she could raise her head and look at Paul. She cleared her throat, squared her shoulders and sat upright. Nicole skin was no longer ashen, she had stopped sweating, and she looked up at Paul with bright, clear eyes. She looked as pretty as the moment she walked into the restaurant. Nicole placed her hand on Paul's shoulder, "I'm OK."

Paul took his seat, never taking his sight off his date.

Nicole took a sip of water and placed the glass back on the table then rubbed her forehead, "I'm so sorry, I don't know what came over me. It was like someone shoved a knife into my head." She looked at Paul, squinted, raised her eyebrows, "Gone." Nicole unfolded her napkin and dabbed the moisture from her forehead and her palms.

"Gone. You mean gone as in no more pain, no nothing?" Paul questioned.

"Seriously, it's gone. The pain, the stabbing, it's all gone. I feel fine. Really. Embarrassed, but fine. And hungry."

"K, we're going to the hospital. You need a CT scan or something. The average person doesn't collapse then thirty seconds later say they're hungry."

Nicole smiled, reached across the table and grabbed Paul's hand trying to reassure him, "I'm fine. Hungry and fine. Maybe I was just super nervous about meeting you for dinner." She placed the napkin back on the edge of the table, and it fell to the floor. She bent over to pick it up and noticed Paul was wearing shoes, black polished dress shoes. "No running shoes today?"

"I wear running shoes at work because I'm on my feet all day, regular shoes kill my feet. Besides, there's less paperwork if you run after a suspect and catch him instead of just shooting the bastard in the back. The department frowns on suspects getting shot as they run away. Go figure." Paul laughed.

Nicole shared his laugh, "My friend made fun of your choice of footwear with your suit when you came to the office."

"Hey, I'm not the one squeezing my feet into tiny shoes with a three-inch heel. I watched you walk in. It looked like you haven't worn those shoes in quite some time."

"No reason to wear them until tonight." They shared a soft laugh. "I will tell you what I need. I need another tea."

*****

Sam sat across from Carl who flipped open his notebook to the first page, "You were right about the pad. It made a difference. I can't believe reporters stopped using them."

Like a student reading to a teacher, Carl read his notes aloud to Sam. When he finished, Carl waited for Sam's response. Sam reached across and took the notepad and scanned the notes.

"Well?"

Sam smiled approvingly. "I like the notes you made about the detective's reaction. Could you have done that with just the recorder and would you have remembered what he did without making notes?"

Carl laughed, knowing full well that Sam was trying to prove his point. "You're right. New is not always better."

"Besides the fact, your handwriting sucks and is barely legible, you done good kid." Sam closed the pad and slid it across the table back to Carl. "So, what now?"

Carl thought for a moment, "I know I surprised the cop with the fact we found the similarity in the physical makeup of the hands. I don't think they considered that one. I caught him completely off guard."

Sam pointed the same bony finger at Carl he used the night before, "He owes you one. Keep that in your back pocket. One of the best things you

84

can do now is cultivate the relationship with this guy. Give and take, tit for tat. You gave him something, hopefully, as time goes by, he will do the same for you."

Carl felt proud. More so than he had in a long time. "I have more stuff to go over before I can finish this story. This crime stuff is a lot more fun than writing business."

"Newbie's always get the crap stuff to write about. That's how you hone your skills. You can't play in the big leagues until you know what you're doing." Sam paused and looked at Carl in the eyes, "What do you want to do?"

"With?"

Sam laughed, "Your life, career."

Carl didn't pause and didn't have to think about his response, "Move. Move to a bigger city with a real newspaper. I love the job, I mean love this job. The pay sucks, but the challenge is incredible. Stories are always changing. It's never the same day."

Sam stood, smiled broadly, "Spoken like a future Pulitzer Prize-winning reporter." He tugged at Carl's jacket lapel, "I love your suit. I do. I think I had the same one back in the '60's. In fact, this might be my old suit." Sam laughed and pushed his cleaning cart down the aisle. "Don't ever let anyone change your style young man. You look the part. Now be the part."

Carl spun around in his chair, his smile broad. He flipped open the notepad and started to transcribe the notes into his laptop.

*****

Katy walked alongside Will down the sidewalk after leaving the restaurant. The sidewalks were almost deserted as they walked.

"Thank you for paying for dinner tonight. I didn't expect for you to pay. I asked you out remember?" Katy kept pace with her new friend, walking close enough to Will but not touching him.

"I don't mind. It's a great night, food was good, and it was nice to get out for a change."

"The place was nice. Thanks again for joining me. Weird how that lady almost passed out when we went by their table. I hope she's gonna be OK." "I'm sure she will be. I don't think they needed our help. Not like I would know what to do anyway. There were enough people there to help." Will hadn't paid attention to the events in the restaurant. His mind was trying to suppress the urges he had when he first saw Katy walk by him at lunch.

Over conversation at dinner, Will's kept his mind focused on what she was saying instead of what he wanted to do to Katy. Over the course of the night, those thoughts diminished but didn't completely disappear.

"What about you? Could you have helped? I never asked what you do," Will was genuinely interested in what Katy did for a living.

"Me. Well, I'm studying law right now. My dad is, was a cop, just retired. He wanted me to become a cop too. I always liked the courtroom part of the law; I wanted to become a prosecutor. You know, putting away the bad guy, making sure the innocent go free. All that bull shit." Katy laughed as she walked. "You're not a bad guy are you Will? I'd hate to have to put you away." Katy smiled again and hip-checked Will.

Will stumbled a bit, "A bad guy, me? Not on your life. I'm the poster child for good. Didn't I buy you dinner? Didn't I pick up your phone when I bumped into you? Doesn't that prove my goodlyness?"

"Goodlyness? Is that even a word?" Katy was laughing out loud. "Goodlyness? Please tell me you're not an English major?"

"Nope. Worse, I'm a writer," Will was laughing along with Katy.

"A writer. Really? And you come up with "Goodlyness". How interesting. Anything I would know?"

Will laughed again, "I doubt it. I ghost write."

Katy took the lead, turned and was walking backwards as they spoke, "What's a ghostwriter, Mr. Goodlyness?"

"Well, college or university students will author a paper and ask me to fix it to make it look better. You know, polish it, use the correct grammar, sentence structure, find the right goodly words to use." Will smiled at Katy. "I get paid per word and on how bad the initial paper is. If it turns out to be a lot of work, I charge more. I also write technical papers for manuals. When companies want to make instruction manual a little more user-friendly, they pay me. After paying for dinner tonight, I better pick up more work."

"Now you're just pushing it. So, I have you to blame for the "Slot A into Tab B" crap?" Katy softly shoved Will causing him to stumble slightly. He caught himself, grabbed Katy's arms and pulled her in close. She kissed him on the cheek and pushed herself away laughing.

"Not yet, Mr. Goodlyness. This is still our first date. Let's see where this goes."

Will touched his cheek where Katy had kissed him. "I'll never wash my face again," he said with a half-smile.

Katy skipped ahead, "Are you coming?"

Will was standing still, "Where are we going?" he asked. "I don't know. Maybe dessert."

*****

Paul cradled his cup of coffee in both hands and listened to every word Nicole said. He barely spoke as she told him about her job and her life. Nicole finished her second cup of tea as the server brought her a fresh pot of tea. She let the tea bag steep before pouring another cup, all the while telling Paul about her ability and how she fooled everyone at the party.

Nicole rubbed her temple and Paul bolted from his seat. She motioned for him to sit.

"Really, I'm OK. But I'm famished. I just need to eat." Nicole was still attempting to convince Paul that she wasn't injured and didn't need to go to the hospital. "Dinner will be here soon." She touched Paul's hand again, "If I have another episode tonight, we'll go to the hospital. You can drive me. In fact, it's a promise. Let's just drop this and enjoy our evening." Nicole gave Paul her best sad face, "Please."

Paul couldn't resist, "Fine. No more talk about what happened. Honestly, I'm dying for my moussaka. I haven't had it in years. So glad you decided to come here."

"I don't even know what I ordered. What was it again?" Nicole asked. Paul tried several times to pronounce the dish. Hearing Paul attempt to speak Greek, the hostess who had been by earlier with the glass of water, leaned in as she passed the table, "Pastitsio," then continued. "What she said." Paul pointed at the hostess.

Nicole sipped her tea, "Can I ask about the case?" Paul nodded.

"Is it true what they say that the police have almost no leads and that two cases may be related?"

Paul righted himself in the chair, leaned forward on the table, "I wish we had more leads. I had a reporter come by today asking if the two cases were related and talked to me about his theory that the girls were killed because they were similar physically. That's what I wanted to talk to you about."

Shocked, Nicole gave him a puzzled look.

Paul continued, "Your visions, your play-by-play review, the ability you have, did you see anything about physical characteristics that would link the two bodies?"

Nicole thought about what Paul had just asked. She went over the scenarios that played in her mind when she studied the photos and came up blank. "I can't recall anything that would've linked the two girls. Did the reporter say what the similarities were?"

For a moment, Paul questioned whether he should reveal details about the case but decided to show some of the details was worth the risk. He pulled a small manila envelope from his suit jacket pocket, searched through the contents then held them out face down for Nicole. "Are you sure you want to see these?"

She nodded in agreement.

Nicole took the photos, carefully hid them from the other patrons in the restaurant and quickly glanced at them. She then held them close to her chest and peered down looking at one then the other. One photograph was the severed arm found in the snow, now lying on a stainless-steel table. The other was a close-up of the dead girl lying beside her bed. Not knowing what Nicole was looking for, both photos showed details of the hands. She studied the picture of the severed arm and begun to see the photo come to life. She saw a man dressed in a disposable smock with black nitrile gloves pull the severed limb from the freezer and place it on the stainless-steel table. He stood aside as the photo was taken then casually picked up the arm and placed it back in the freezer. The picture stopped moving.

Nicole closed her eyes waiting for the images to clear themselves from her head, no headache, no stabbing pain, nothing. She opened to eyes, and the first thing she saw was Paul's concerned expression. "You OK?"

"Yup. On to the next one."

She held the second photograph, the image began to morph, and shadows began to move through the picture. Nicole starts to see men in white Tyvek suits and masks walking about the bedroom and camera flashes momentarily brightening the room. The camera zooms in close to the dead girl with her hand in the frame. A dark aura shone around any part of the dead girl. The flash brightened the room, the picture is taken, the technician moves on. The photo slowly freezes and then paused.

Again, no ill effects from looking at the pictures. Nicole was surprised she didn't feel the stabbing pain coursing through her skull.

"What am I looking at?" Nicole asked. "I've seen these already."

"Do the hands appear to be the same?"

Nicole didn't have to look at the photos again. With her eyes closed, she replayed the scenarios in her mind and saw the images as if she was staring at the photos themselves. In her mind's eye, she could move about the objects as if they were in three dimensions.

Startled, Nicole looked at Paul, "They could be from the same girl. The bone structure, the, the" she stuttered, "fingers, even the nails, they are identical. Even the skin looks similar. Were the girls the same age?" Before Paul could answer, she answered for him, "No of course not, we don't know how old the first girl was. Stupid question. How could I have missed this? I'm an idiot." The couple at the table next to the them turned to hear Nicole. Paul smiled politely, but in his head, he silently told them to "Fuck off."

Paul pocketed the photos to keep anyone from seeing the gruesome scenes. He tapped his pocket to make sure they were secure then turned his attention back to Nicole. "You did nothing wrong. Nothing. I missed seeing the similarities too. Actually, the whole team did."

Nicole composed herself, "Then how did the reporter know?"

Paul thought for a moment, "Somehow, he figured it out. How or why I'm not sure. I guess that's the good thing about having more people on the case. Like asking you for help. You have insight we just couldn't imagine. You haven't told anyone about any of this?"

Nicole shook her head, "No. No, of course not. I understand. I wouldn't do that to the investigation," she paused, "or you."

"I have a few more pictures to show you. I haven't shown these to you yet. This is not exactly first date material, but I have to know. Can you, I should ask, would you look at these? For me? Please."

Nicole thought for a moment, then nodded.

Paul straightened out his back, reached into his pants pocket and pulled out several wrinkled sheets of paper folded into four. He unfolded the first one and was about to hand it to Nicole, "You sure?"

"I'm sure."

Nicole took the paper and glanced at it. Her stomach turned for a moment, "Not what I expected. Sorry, I didn't..." her words trailed off. In her mind, she saw a flash of light, a camera flash maybe. It burnt her eyes. She refocused as the image began to swing back and forth. The movement caused her stomach to turn once again. The image caught a shoe then swung back into the darkness then back to the suitcase, then back to the foot. It was then she realized that she saw the events unfold through the eye of the camera.

The image raised, the torso in the suitcase reappeared, focused, and she was blinded again by the flash. Nicole waited for a few moments for her eyes to clear. The person controlling the camera moved around, framed the torso from another angle and took another shot. The flash blanketed the scene in white light. The camera dropped but hung for a moment then swung again. Nicole closed her eyes tightly and the image faded.

"How can anyone do something like this?" She folded the paper back up and slid it across the table.

"Did you want to see another?" Paul asked.

"I don't think it would do any good. I saw everything from the camera's perspective. All I saw was a shoe. And it was dark. Not sure it was a man's or a woman's shoe. Sorry." Nicole was apologetic. "Besides, any more of that," she pointed to sheets of paper held firmly in Paul's hand, "and I won't be able to eat."

"Don't be sorry. You've been a big help. Seriously." Paul reached across with his free hand and touched hers. Nicole felt the warmth of Paul's hand. It felt good. She smiled at him. He was about to pull his hand back, but Nicole quickly took hold and squeezed.

Paul looked past Nicole to the server as she carried out a tray and presented two dinners before them. She asked if there was anything more they needed. They both declined and continued their conversation while they ate.

May 1

The cell phone buzzed on the nightstand, and the tiny screen illuminated one side of the bedroom. Paul was lying on his stomach, watching the phone vibrate and bounce along the table. He closed his eyes and desperately hoped it would stop. Eventually, the light went off, the phone ceased vibrating, and he decided to fall back to sleep. He can't recall if it was only a moment or several hours later when the phone began its assault against his sleep again. It continued to buzz until Paul fumbled for the phone in the dark. He swiped at it, sending it flying to the floor. "Damn."

Paul sat up, swung his legs over the edge and reached for the phone, tapping the green button on the screen. "What?" His voice was stern and unhappy.

"Sorry to bug you. We found another body." Paul recognized Dan Levy's voice. "It's not pretty. Oh, and guess what? Remember those anonymous pictures we got in the mail months ago?"

Paul replied with an exhausted "Ya."

"It's a dismembered body in a suitcase, carbon copy of the pictures." Paul sat upright, now wide awake. "Where?"

"I'll text you the address."

Paul disconnected, put the phone down on the nightstand, rubbed his eyes and said out loud, "I have to turn on the light. Cover your eyes." He clicked the small lamp on his side of the bed.

Nicole pulled the covers over her head, "What's going on?" she said, her voice muffled.

"They found another body. On the positive side, you've got a great alibi. I guess I can remove you from my list of suspects." Paul felt a pillow hit him across the back. "You stay and sleep in. I'll be back as soon as I can. Text me when you wake up." Paul stood, walked to his dresser, stepped on something, picked it up and knew what it was. "Nice purple thong by the way."

From under the covers, Nicole explained, "Thank Simone. I was gonna wear white cotton granny panties. Never figured you were going to see me naked on the first date."

"I'll give her the details about last night next time I see her." He placed Nicole's thong on his dresser, pulled open a drawer and rummaged for clean underwear and socks. He pulled out a pair of khakis and a sweater to help keep him warm against the night air.

"What time is it?" Nicole asked.

"Just after three." Paul walked around to Nicole's side of the bed, kissed the only section of her head that wasn't under the cover. "Whatever you do, don't look in my closet."

"Why?"

"That's where I keep all my private guy stuff that girls don't ever want to know about." Paul laughed as he went back to his side of the bed, turned off the light and left the bedroom.

"Jerk," Nicole yelled, "Now I hafta look."

It was another thirty minutes before Paul arrived on scene. He stopped to pick up a coffee on the way and had it finished before he arrived. It wasn't difficult to find the address Dan had texted Paul, the red flashing lights from the cruiser light bars lit up the scene and acted as a beacon against the still night. As he drove down the residential street, Paul noticed homeowners were standing outside in their winter jackets and pajama bottoms watching the police. The Spring leaves on the trees lay motionless. A lone media truck was parked to the left side of the street, blocking someone's driveway. The camera operator was standing close to the barrier tape aiming his lens at the blue plastic barricade erected around the end of a driveway.

Paul parked his car half a block north of the scene, secured his handgun to his belt and made sure he had his police ID handy. He shook the paper coffee cup one last time, thinking there might be a few drops left inside and tilted it back. What was left in the bottom of the cup wasn't worth the effort. He released the trunk latch, dug through some junk, found his police jacket and donned it before making his way to the scene. He felt the late night crisp air bite at him.

As he neared the barrier tape, one of the reporters asked a question which Paul didn't hear or chose not to hear, then stuck a microphone in his face for a response. He ignored it and kept walking; Paul was positive he had just been called a "motherfucker" by the reporter. He ducked under the tape and made his way to where Dan was standing. Without saying a word, Dan handed Paul a Styrofoam cup of coffee. He sipped the tepid drink and grimaced.

"I think it's left over coffee from the last homicide a few months back." Dan turned and made his way to the waist-high blue tarp square barrier that was erected at the base of a driveway. Several LED lights were strategically positioned around the area to illuminate the scene. Paul peered over the edge and noticed several plastic garbage cans and a recycling bin full of paper waste and a large antique style brown leather suitcase in the centre of the barrier. The brown leather was dirty and washed-out from years of use and reminded Paul of something he would see in the old movies from the forties. The brass clasps were tarnished, and the well-worn handle hung from brass D rings. The lid of the suitcase was lined with a lime green faded material with a tiny black floral pattern giving away its age. Small spots of bright red blood dotted the material. The nude torso of a young Caucasian woman was forced into the bottom half of the suitcase. The arms had been removed at the armpit, and the portions of the collarbone were visible as they pushed against the wall of the suitcase. The legs had been removed from the groin up along the line of the pelvis. The curve of the pelvic bone was glistening white under the bright LED lights and looked oddly like that part of the chicken carcass that held the section of meat Paul liked the most. His stomach did a little flip and knew immediately; he would no longer want that particular piece of chicken anymore. The girl's body forced itself against the inside edges of the antique suitcase, making the rectangular frame bulge out along the length.

"Have you moved anything yet?" Paul asked.

Dan shook his head side to side. He instead pointed to the man sitting on the curb a dozen feet away, cradling his small dog. Two thick blankets were shouldered around him, and his tiny yorkie sat obediently on his lap. The man appeared scared and looked as if the slightest movement might make him vomit. "Guy says he couldn't sleep and took his dog out for a walk. The dog started to sniff around the garbage cans and knocked over the suitcase. I guess the body was forced in or something and the old latches couldn't hold it. The lid popped open, exposing the contents and the guy thought it was some prank Halloween body part. You know how they have the hand that sticks out the trunk sorta thing." Dan looked up at the man with the dog, "Anyway, he touched the body and pretty much pissed his pajama's right here. He called 911, and he's been sitting there ever since. We can't even get a statement until he calms down. I think we hafta get Mental Health Services down here for the poor bastard."

Paul hadn't noticed that garbage cans and recycling bins had already been placed at the end of every driveway. He decided that his lack of sleep and having a few too many drinks at dinner was the reason he missed the obvious. "I assume the homeowner," Paul pointed to the house whose garbage collection they now had scene tape protecting, "denies any knowledge of the suitcase."

Dan chuckled, "You mean Mrs. Claxton. Well, the suitcase could definitely be hers considering she probably remembers using that style of bags. She's just shy of ninety-five, still lives alone. Weighs all of eighty pounds soaking wet. Denies ever seeing the suitcase and pays the neighbors kid twenty bucks a week to mow the lawn and take out the garbage. We haven't found the kid yet."

Paul lifted the barrier tape, stepped closer and knelt beside the open suitcase. He pulled a pen from his shirt pocket and ran the tip of the pen around the edge of the suitcase. He squinted at the body inside the lower half of the suitcase. It was obvious the girl was slightly larger than the opening and was forced in to make her fit. Paul noticed areas where the decades-old material had been stressed where the end of the clavicle rubbed against it. He noticed a small puncture wound over the liver, pointed at it and asked Dan, "Liver temp?"

"31.5 C. But, the coroner says that she's never taken a temp on a body with no arms or legs or head and stuffed in a suitcase, so she has to make some calculations. Figures she died maybe around midnight. That's a rough guess."

Paul took out his phone and used the flashlight app to look inside the suitcase. "There a little blood around the bottom near where the arms and legs and head should be." Paul stood and closed his eyes, "Christ, I can't believe I'm looking at this so dispassionately. Poor kid can't be any more than what, twenty-something." He took in a deep breath, "Fuck this is sick." Paul stood, looked around at the crowd that had gathered along both sides of the street, and asked Dan, "Do they even know what happened?"

Dan look at the crowd, "Not a clue. I'm sure they're talking. The only guy that knows anything is too scared to even speak with us yet. I think he has to change his pants first. I doubt he told anyone before we got here."

A thought struck Paul, "Could she be the snow plough girl?"

Dan moved closer to Paul, "I doubt it. Coroner thought of that. She was sure the girl was killed tonight. No sign of the tissue being frozen. There was no crystallization in the tissue, and the body isn't partially frozen. So?" Dan shrugged his shoulder.

"Do we have one of those instant digital cameras? You know like the Polaroid cameras we had way back." Paul looked at the crime scene techs waiting for a response. Instead, one of the techs pulled a white camera from his bag.

"There are still Polaroid cameras. It's got a full pack of ten in it," the tech offered.

Paul held the camera and rolled it over several times. "It looks like a kids' camera."

"Those packs of sheets are expensive. So, don't be going nuts with the picture taking. And you don't have to shake the pictures when they come out of the camera." The tech made sure Paul was aware he was responsible for the equipment and wanted it back when he was finished.

Paul took a picture of the body in the suitcase standing over it. The camera spit out a small two by three undeveloped photo. Paul grabbed it and immediately began to wave it in the air. The tech looked at Paul and shook his head but remained silent. Paul continued to take several more pictures of the body and the suitcase from various angles. As each sheet spit forth from the camera, Paul instinctively shook the sheet before placing it in his pocket. Paul continued to take pictures until he felt he had enough. He handed the camera back to the tech that let him borrow it.

Paul considered showing the pictures to Nicole when he got home. He had another body, and it was too soon to link to the other two bodies, but only a fool would refuse to make the connection. From the scene, he doubted forensics would be gathering much in the way of evidence at the scene. He clenched his teeth and covered his mouth with his hand. Paul felt the moisture from his breath on his cold hand. He stood beside the barrier and waved all of the people under his command to gather around. He thought about what he wanted to say, and in his mind, he was screaming out orders. He paused and began to speak, his voice was muted but stern, "Keep this quiet. Don't give out any details to the press. Nothing and I mean nothing gets out." He pointed to everyone at the scene who was paying full attention to Paul. "I don't want any details getting leaked; I want everything to stay internal. Pack this up," he swirled his hand around the suitcase, "keep the body inside. After forensics is finished with the scene, and they take lots of pictures, and I don't mean dozens, I mean hundreds. Every angle, close-up, wide-angle, scene shots, get pictures of the houses, all these people standing around, the garbage, everything, and when they feel it's OK, close the lid, keep all the evidence inside and take it back. I'm going to talk to the guy that found the suitcase. I want the garbage schedule, which company picks it up, where it goes to. Is the schedule posted online? How would someone know to drop off the suitcase late at night to get picked up and put in the landfill? Anything and everything is important. Got it?"

There were heads nodding in agreement and a few "yeah's" from the crowd. As everyone went back to what they were doing, Dan pulled Paul aside, "You're going to show the pics to the girl aren't you?"

Paul nodded softly, "You got a better idea or any leads?"

Dan thought for a moment, said nothing and turned his attention back to the suitcase.

The tiny pang of anger that started earlier in his belly grew and spread across his shoulders and back, and he knew that if he stayed with the girl in the suitcase any longer, he would lose control. That was something he didn't want to do and something he didn't want anyone to see. He turned on his heels and headed for the man sitting on the curb clutching his tiny dog. Paul slowed his pace allowing himself to calm down. He closed his eyes, took in a deep breath and sat down next to the man with the dog.

The man still sat on the curb; blankets draped over his shoulders, his tiny dog squirming to get free. As Paul sat next to the man, the dog began to bark. The two men sat quietly, no one spoke for several minutes. Paul waited for the man to say the first word.

"It's a cold night isn't it," he said.

"Damn cold." Paul kept it simple.

"Cop?"

"Yup." Paul stared forward.

The little dog continued to bark. "You want my statement?"

"You up for it?"

The man chuckled, "No."

"You ever seen anything like this before?"

The man took in a deep breath, he was shaking his head side to side, but Paul failed to see this. The man started to cry and was barely able to get the word "No" out.

"That's OK. We don't need your statement right now."

The man spoke softly, "K".

Paul waved to one of the uniformed officers who walked over. "Is there someone at this guy's house right now?"

The man shook his head side to side. Paul stood to and spoke to the officer then sat back down. "This officer is going to take you to a hotel that will allow you to keep your dog with you. I'll see if we can have a doctor stop by and visit you and give you a little something to help you sleep. Don't worry about anything. This is on the department. Is your house locked?"

The man shook his head up and down, "It is."

"When you're ready, go with the officer, and we can chat later, OK?"

The man stood, carefully let his dog down, shook Paul's hand and even in the eerie shadows cast by the scene lights, it was evident the man was crying and would need some type of sedative to help him sleep. The officer guided him to his SUV and placed the man and his dog in the back seat.

Paul walked back to the scene as the man and his dog were driven away. His little pang of anger was gone now, replaced with extreme hunger. He pulled his cell phone and called Nicole. The phone rang only once on the other end. "Hey, did I wake you?"

"No, I've been awake since you left. I thought it was the best time to go through your closet and dresser drawers."

Paul laughed, "Did you find my stash of porn yet?"

"Must have missed it. If I would've found it, I'd probably still be looking at it," she laughed.

"You wouldn't make a good cop."

Nicole changed the subject, "What's up? You sound, well, not good."

"You hungry?" he asked.

"Famished."

"Get dressed. I'll be there shortly to pick you up, and we'll go to Denny's or something." Nicole agreed and hung up. Paul held the phone for a few moments lost in what had happened so quickly since last evening.

"...at the station. Do you want to talk to him first?" Dan caught Paul off guard. He spun around and noticed the sun was coming up over his partners' shoulder.

"Sorry. What?" Paul asked.

"I said the man who found the body is being taken to the hotel and if you wanted to talk to him before he falls asleep. That's it." Dan was surprised that Paul was looking so preoccupied. "You OK?"

Paul nodded his head, "Yeah. Lots going on right now. No. Why don't you talk to the witness, see what you can get then I'll go in? Make sure he gets some rest before we get his statement. The old man didn't look good. Just make sure a uniform stays with him in the room. No calls in or out."

"Well, we've been here almost two hours now. I'm getting tired myself. You know the chief will freak that you put the guy up in a hotel. We're supposed to talk to them first. He could be the one responsible."

Paul laughed, "Really? Do you think he's our guy?"

Dan chuckled, "I'll cover your back. Besides, we got the old man's permission to search his home before we took him away. I honestly don't think he knew what he agreed to."

Paul thanked Dan for covering him and walked to his car. He opened the door, slipped behind the wheel and let his head fall back against the rest. He closed his eyes and tried to put the image of the girl out of his mind, but regardless of what he tried to think about, the headless and limbless torso crammed into the antique suitcase filled his mind's eye. He signed deeply and thought about the picture he kept with him and wondered if now would be a good time to call her back.

Paul turned the key, and the engine roared to life, the police radio squawked with the sound of the dispatcher assigning calls. He turned the volume all the way down even though he knew it was against policy. Instead, he took out his police cell phone and placed it on the seat beside him. He grabbed the shift lever and felt his hand begin to shake. He gripped the lever tighter, but the shaking became so intense, Paul let go and held his hand in mid-air. Paul thought he had become hypoglycemic and that was what was causing his hand to shake, but he knew better. He balled his hand into a fist and swung his arm out violently landing into the passenger seat. He pulled his hand back and repeatedly punched the passenger seat over and over again until he was out of breath. His chest heaved, he felt moisture bead up on his forehead, and his heart raced. He took in a deep breath, collected his thoughts and put the image of the girl in the suitcase out of his mind.

Half an hour later, Nicole and Paul sat in a booth with crack vinyl seat cushions and two plates of super-sized breakfasts before them. Nicole dug in; Paul watched her eat in silence.

Nicole looked up from her plate, with a full mouth she asked, "You not going to eat? On the drive over here, you said you were starving. What's up?"

"I am. I was. Lost my appetite again."

"You gonna tell me what happened or make me wait?" Nicole took another bite then followed it with a sip of coffee. She then reached across the table and forked a strawberry from the side of Paul's plate.

Paul laughed, "You know I love strawberries, right?"

"Well, you're not eating and after what I did last night, you should be buying me a freaking truckload of fresh strawberries." Nicole began to laugh almost causing what she had in her mouth to spill out. She covered her face with the paper napkin and finished her mouthful. "Besides, I'm wearing the same clothes as last night except I'm going commando because I couldn't find my panties." She jabbed her fork into another strawberry.

"On my dresser." Paul was very matter of fact.

"A girl wearing a revealing black dress and tells you she's going commando and you sit there stone-faced. What's up?" Nicole placed her fork on the table, held her hand out palm up and curled her fingers, "Give 'em up."

"Not here. Not now. Besides, you're eating," Paul argued.

Nicole's hand remained open on the table waiting for Paul to give her the photos. He retrieved the stack of Polaroids, placing them face down in her palm. "Don't do this if you aren't ready. Why don't we wait until after breakfast?"

Nicole turned the stack over, and the first image, a close-up of the victim's abdomen in the suitcase struck her hard. She recoiled in her seat, dropping the photos from her hand, causing them to slide across the glossy laminate table top. Paul quickly gathered them up then looked up at Nicole. She had her eyes closed for a few moments then opened them.

Nicole looked directly ahead but didn't see Paul sitting before her. Instead, she saw the back of a man's head, he looked young, driving his car on a dark street. It was as if she was lying in the back seat, looking up at the back of the driver's head. The street lights offered no help in identifying the man behind the wheel. Nicole felt the car moving slowly; the concrete light standards passed casually across the passenger side windows. She couldn't see any houses on either side of the car. The angle was too steep to permit seeing directly out the windows.

The car slowed, she felt the car lurch slightly as he put the vehicle in park. The driver opened the door and ran around the back and opened the hatch. Nicole realized she wasn't in the back seat or the trunk, but the seats had been lowered, and she was looking up from the floor of the hatch. Nicole was tossed about as the driver dragged the suitcase to the edge and lifted her up. He had trouble hoisting the suitcase with the weight of the contents inside. He struggled to hold it steady and stepped back from the car and dropped in on the curb. She was jostled inside as the suitcase landed hard on the lawn by the roadside.

Nicole looked up through the lid of the suitcase and saw the chin of the man who had just left her there. A white man, thin chin, dark hair protruded from the ball cap he was wearing. Dark hair, it was the middle of the night in dim light, most hair colors would be dark. The man who left her there looked around and disappeared. She heard the car drive away.

Nicole rubbed her eyes and forced the images from her mind. She looked up at the man sitting across from her. Paul reached across the table and grabbed her hand. No one spoke. Paul wanted to let Nicole recover in her own time. The color had drained from Nicole's face; her pulse raced, her breathing quickened. With her free hand, she fumbled for the glass of water and drank almost half then set the glass back down.

"What the Hell did I just see?" Nicole asked. "How long was I gone for?" She spoke in hushed tones.

"You just closed your eyes for a second then opened them again. Did it feel like a long time? Tell me what you saw."

Nicole took in a deep breath, "It felt like ten or fifteen minutes." She went on to recount the vision in detail including the description of the male driver, paused then finished the last of the water. She released her grip on Paul's hand and slumped back into her seat. Nicole was physically exhausted and felt as if she could fall asleep in the booth. She sat upright, squared her shoulders and began to pick at the food on her plate. "This was the first time I've seen the events from the victim's perspective. It wasn't great. But what I don't get is the image was blurred somehow, like you had bad reception on the TV during a storm, fuzzy, you know?"

"What do you mean?" Paul looked at Nicole with a furrowed brow.

"I usually see things like I'm watching something happen from across the room like I was the one with the camera. This time I saw it like I was the victim." Nicole picked up a piece of toast, tore off a small piece and ate it. "It was weird. I could feel, well, I felt sore, my arms and legs hurt."

Paul had the photos he took of the crime scene face down on the table, "What's the first picture you saw?"

"It looked like a woman's bare stomach with some old weird material on the right side. That's all I saw before the vision hit me." Nicole rubbed her right shoulder, "It hurts for some reason, and there was that color again."

"Color?"

"It looks like some of the colors get washed out around the victims. I'm not sure why but it only happens on the dead girls."

Paul picked up the stack of photos flipped through the pictures, he paused then showed Nicole the one he thought she might have seen, "This one?"

Nicole nodded.

"Tell me more about how you feel?" Paul retrieved his cell phone, opened the app he uses to tape conversations and hit the record button. He covered the photos with his hand to make sure Nicole couldn't see the other pictures.

"Feel? Well, I feel, I don't know, exhausted, sore. Really painful." Nicole rubbed her shoulder then reached under the table and rubbed her hips, "And here."

Anyone else would have been surprised by Nicole's ability, but Paul sat across the table, expressionless, "Is that it?" he added.

Nicole rolled her neck across her shoulders, "It feels like I slept wrong. My neck is stiff. I think you need new pillows."

Paul remained silent as he searched through the pictures, finding the one he was looking for, he slid it face down across the table to Nicole but kept his hand over it, "Can you handle this?"

"I'll know after I see it." Nicole pulled the picture out from Paul's grasp and slowly moved it up her chest then held it before her. Her eyes widened, and she slammed the photo down on the table. Several people from other tables turned to see what caused the commotion then went back to their own lives.

"This is why you left this morning?"

"Yeah. Fun job huh?"

"Same guy responsible for all the other girls?"

"I think so. This is the only reason why I had to put you through this. I'm so sorry."

Nicole thought about it for a moment, "Gimme. Give them all to me."

"No. The one viewing was enough. You gave me information that we didn't have before: male, thin, white. We can work from that. You don't need to put yourself through any more of this."

Nicole stared directly across the table at Paul. Her gaze never leaving his. "I'm not sure if I'll see anything more but if I can see another detail, won't that help?"

Paul thought for a moment and stopped recording the conversation, "OK. Fine. But, would you rather do this at my place? You know, in case things don't go well."

Nicole agreed, and they had the rest of their meals put in take-out containers, left the restaurant and drove back to Paul's house. The two of them remained silent throughout the trip. Paul fought the urge to fall asleep as his stomach made vicious growling sounds at him for failing to feed it. He placed his hand on his belly, felt it move under his jacket as the sound of his cell phone ringing in his pocket shook the cobwebs from his mind. He tapped the Bluetooth button on the steering wheel, and Dan's voice played over the car's speakers.

"The old man and his dog got to the hotel and didn't need any help falling asleep. I've got two uniforms watching him, one in the bedroom and the other outside the door. The chief called me and chewed my ass when he found out. I told him that the witness was too tired to make a statement and gave us permission to search his house. It was a trade-off. He bought it. So back me up. What time are you coming down?"

Paul looked across at Nicole, "I'm just pulling into the driveway. Nicole said she would review the photos I took. I'll head out as soon as we're done here. Can you hold down the fort until I get back?"

"Take your time. I'm grabbing a little sleep at my desk then heading to the hotel."

Paul heard the line disconnect and thought that food and sleep was what he needed but felt having Nicole review the photos was more important. He pulled into his driveway, put the car in park and killed the engine.

Paul tossed his jacket over a kitchen chair as Nicole was placing the food containers on the kitchen counter, Paul was already pulling plates from the cabinets, "You want any?"

Nicole shook her head; she didn't want any more food in her stomach in case she saw too much when it came time to look at the pictures. She removed her jacket, draped it over the kitchen chair and readied herself for what was about to come.

Paul sat down with a plate of cold bacon, toast and hard scrambled eggs. He briefly thought about putting the plate in the microwave but decided against it. He placed the stack of photos face down on the table and slid them across the table until it was before Nicole. She took in a deep breath and was about to flip the first one over when Paul stopped her.

"Hang on." Paul placed his cell phone on the table, opened the app and hit the record button to record anything Nicole said. He slid his phone to the centre of the table.

Nicole smirked, took hold of the top photo, closed her eyes, flipped it over then opened her eyes. Nicole felt a wave pulsate through her and this time, she was a third-party viewer again. She was looking at the arms of a white male, lowering the limbless torso in the suitcase. The torso was heavier than the man thought for a young girl. She could see he was having problems holding it up. Nicole turned her attention to the man's arms. There wasn't a lot of hair on his arms, and they were thin as if he was younger or not very fit. He wasn't wearing gloves. How could he touch a body like that and not wear gloves? The torso almost slipped from his grasp, but he hoisted the body up and grabbed hold around the waist. He lowered it into the antique suitcase, but it didn't fit properly. He twisted the body to the right, forced the left part of the torso against the wall of the suitcase and then stood back. It was the first time Nicole saw the complete torso. It was the body of a very young woman. The body was that of a girl in her late teens or early twenties. The skin was pure, no blemishes, small breasts, Nicole could see the ribs on the left side. A sparkle caught her eye. She looked down to see a navel ring, a tiny gold loop with a purple stone, an amethyst perhaps, a birthstone. The man reached down and unlocked the loop, gently pulling it out from the girl's navel. The arms disappeared, and the image went blank.

Nicole opened her eyes, sighed deeply and wanted to cry. The sight of the limbless torso was a horrifying sight, but she was upset with herself that she had become almost immune to these things now. She had seen so much in such a short time. Nicole reached across the table, took a piece of cold bacon from Paul's plate and ate it. The bacon crunched, and a few fractured pieces fell to the table. She looked down to wipe them from the table and saw the image on the photograph that forced the vision into her mind. A wave of nausea overtook her, and she ran to the kitchen sink and vomited.

As Nicole felt her stomach contract and force its contents up and out, she was happy that she hadn't lost all compassion for the victims and that she was still sickened by what she had seen. As the second wave of nausea hit her, a gentle hand was placed on her back. She opened her eyes as she was bending over the sink and saw Paul's feet standing beside hers. This man she went out to dinner with the night before and had sex with after was comforting her as she vomited in his sink. She was oddly happy.

Blindly, Nicole reached above her head and turned on the tap and washed the vomit down the drain then rinsed her mouth several times. "I hope this won't clog the sink. I'm so sorry."

She heard Paul laugh out loud as she was still leaning over the sink, "That's why they invented Draino. Don't worry about it." He placed a tea towel over her shoulder as she stood.

"I must look just lovely."

Paul took the tea towel from her shoulder and wiped the corners of her mouth, "I'd kiss you right now but honestly, your breath is fucking bad."

Nicole laughed and fell into Paul's arms and hugged him. She held him tightly, then pulled back, and cleared her throat, "Let's finish this. What do you want to know?" Nicole took her seat.

Paul sat across from her. He made sure his phone was still recording, "Tell me everything you saw."

Nicole began to tell Paul every detail of the vision she had of the man stuffing the torso into the suitcase. When she was done, Paul pat himself down, realized he didn't have a pen or his notebook, found his jacket and got what he needed.

"Tell me again where he grabbed the body?" he asked. "What did his arms look like?" He scribbled notes and continued to bombard Nicole with questions. "You said there was a belly button stud. I don't recall any. What color did you say?"

"Around the waist. There was a stud, purple I think. Is that the birthstone for February? Anyway, I'm not sure what type of stone it was, but it was purple."

"Where did you say he grabbed her?" Paul asked again.

"Waist." They were almost talking over each other to get everything out.

"Was it a stud or a ring?"

"What?"

"The belly button ring, was it a captive or barbell?"

"Barbell."

"His arms. Tell me about his arms, tattoos, hair, skin color? Anything special or different?"

"Light skin, pale almost, thin, not a lot of hair, no tattoos, no moles. I think but…"

Paul interrupted, "His nails, what about his nails?"

"What about his nails?"

"Did he bite his nails?" Paul never took his eyes off his notepad.

"No. Wait, I think so. Is that important?"

"It is. It tells something about his habits, grooming, and it's a dead giveaway, especially since we don't know what he looks like. Yet."

The barrage of questions continued for several minutes until Paul was satisfied he had every last detail documented. Paul slouched in his chair. "It was unbelievable. We know more now than we ever have before."

Nicole was surprised, "From that? I doubt I gave you much information."

Paul tapped his notebook, "For starters, we had suspected the unsub was white, but now we know, you told us he was thin, dark hair, doesn't have a lot of hair on his arms, a nail biter, and where he touched the body. I'm texting Dan to tell him where we can attempt to lift prints from the body. Chances are we won't get anything off the body, but at least it's an opportunity that we didn't have before. And now we know where to look."

Nicole was stunned, "You can get someone's fingerprints off of human skin?"

Paul knew a little about forensic science from spending time with the techs at crime scenes, "We can if we can figure out where to look and it's done soon enough after contact. I seriously doubt in this case we'll get lucky, but at least we know where to look and keep our fingers crossed."

He took a bite from a piece of dried toast and tapped his notepad with the end of his pen. He forced down the piece of bread, coughed, got up and went to the sink to get a glass of water to clear his throat. He stood, leaning against the counter, "You up for another vision?"

Nicole shook her head, sighed deeply and grabbed the next photo on the pile.

Paul was still standing, "You sure? If this is too much, you don't have to do this, you know." Paul's voice showed concern for Nicole. There was silence as they looked at each other. Nicole turned away, picked up the next photograph, flipped it over but didn't look at it.

"Whenever you're ready."

Paul took his seat across from Nicole, pushed his plate to the side and had his pen handy to take notes. They looked at each for a few moments, then Nicole stared down at the photograph and closed her eyes.

*****

The thin man sat at the table, a coffee cup to his right, the newspaper spread across the table before him. He flipped the pages back and forth, looking for headlines, for stories about what he had done. He was oddly concerned that the details of his deeds went unreported. He enjoyed reading about what he had done and seeing if the details were correct. So far, little of what he had done made the papers.

He reached for his cup of coffee, his hand fell forward and past the cup. The back of his hand striking the cup, knocking it over, spilling coffee across the smooth surface of the table, as his vision went blurry, his head swimming in imagery. Flashes of things he had never seen, a place he had never been blinded him. He was in his kitchen, but he was somehow now seeing a place strange to him. He closed his eyes, opened them again but the same strange kitchen was in his mind. He turned his head, but the scene didn't move with him. He rubbed his eyes, opened them again, but nothing changed. He stood, his head swimming with images and a stranger before him. He yelled out loudly, spun around blindly, the image never changing perspective. He struck the counter, lost his balance and fell to the floor, but as he fell, the image didn't fall with him. He was on the floor, blind with a vision in his head that wouldn't leave him.

The image turned, and he was now facing a strange man with dark hair who was talking, his mouth moving, but he couldn't hear the words. He reached for the man, but his hands never appeared in his vision. He waved his arms like a man flagging down a passing car. It did no good. Nothing changed. His sight remained on the strange man. The image began to blur, the orientation slowly drifted down and went to black. His eyes were open, yet he saw black. He thought he had gone blind.

Light slowly filtered in from the sides until the familiar sight of his kitchen cabinet replaced the strange image of what he had been seeing. His vision returned, seeing things that belonged, things he knew, things he understood.

He grabbed hold of the counter and pulled himself up. Standing in his kitchen now, he suddenly felt nauseous and bent over the sink and vomited. He felt a hand on his back, someone comforting him, he looked down and thought he saw a man standing beside him. He stood up, spun around to confront the stranger, but he was alone. He turned around in the kitchen, thinking the stranger moved faster than he could react. He turned back the other way, still nothing. He ran to the living room, down the hall, nothing. Adrenaline spilt from kidneys, a rush went through him and raced to the front door. He grabbed the handle and twisted; it was locked, the deadbolt still firmly latched from the inside.

For the first time in his life, regardless of anything he had done, he was now questioning his sanity. He placed his thumbnail under teeth and began to bite hard. Tiny shards of nail broke off, he spit them out, but he continued to chew, he could taste blood, but that didn't stop his compulsion.

*****

Almost two hours later, Nicole sat at the table, exhausted, barely able to stay awake. She had examined all the photographs Paul brought and described the visions that filled her head. The images frightened her, but she persevered through each horrific scene. Each photo brought another image of the dead girl and the man behind the wheel, but none of them revealed any new information about the identity of the thin man or the dismembered girl in the suitcase.

Nicole rubbed and closed her eyes against the bright overhead light sending a dull ache flowing across her forehead, "Can I take a nap?"

Without saying a word, Paul stood and took Nicole by the arm, helping her stand. With her eyes still closed, she blindly reached around, took hold of Paul's hand, squeezed it tightly as he led her to the bedroom. He sat her on the edge of the bed, removed her shoes, laid her down as she instinctively curled up in the fetal position for comfort. Paul pulled the comforter over her, kissed the top of her head, shut off the lights and closed the door as he walked out.

Paul went to the living room, laid down on the couch, rubbed his eyes, then placed both arms behind his head, deciding an hour of sleep was well deserved. Paul could feel his mind drifting, images of the dead girl in the suitcase began to slip in and out of his thoughts as he began to fall asleep. He shifted his position on the couch hoping his mind would release it's hold of the murder scene. Instead, his mind filled with the various photographs he had taken and the sight of the milky white pelvic bone pushing against the old green lining of the suitcase, sent waves of nausea through him. Paul squirmed as he thought about what it would take to dismember a young girl and hoped she was dead long before the killer decided to remove her limbs. And her head. Paul clenched his teeth and felt the pressure of his jaw biting hard as he thought about how she died. The room was white, sterile white. A bright light came from all directions eliminating all the shadows. Paul saw the thin armed man place his hand on the girl's forehead and with a sharp curved knife, cut into her skin just above where the collar bones meet the sternum. The blade sunk into the skin and began to separate the tissue. Blood oozed out from the incision. No, he thought. If the wound bled, she would be alive; she was dead, she had to be dead. Paul hoped the girl was dead before she was dismembered. His mind went into reverse, the knife cut into the skin, but this time, there was no blood. The knife plunged deeper into the wound cutting through the esophagus and trachea, the arteries and when the thin man reached the spine, he sawed at the neck, cutting between the vertebrae, separating the neck from the body. The thin man pulled the head back and cut the skin at the back of the neck. He grasped the girl's hair and lifted the head up high. The eyes were open, looking forward, seeing nothing. As the thin man held the head up, he looked down to see the headless body at his feet.

The body would have to be cleaned somehow, placed in a shower, hosed down, even in death, there would be fluids dripping, leaking from the areas where the limbs and head were removed. Blood and other body fluids would drain. How long would it take to drain a body of all it's fluids? Otherwise, the body would lose any fluids from the core and fill the suitcase. Paul imagined a side of beef hung from a hook in a cooler as it bled out. Was the victim killed days before and hung to let the fluids drain before being disposed of like garbage? That was a question for the coroner.

Paul pulled one arm out from behind his head and looked at his watch. He stretched out, yawned and sat on the end of the couch. He went to the bedroom, cracked the door open to see Nicole still sleeping in his bed. Twenty-four hours ago, he couldn't imagine having a girl in his bed again; now he was letting her sleep while he went back to work.

*****

Paul stood alone in the medical examiner's office, looking over the autopsy table. The girl's torso found in the suitcase lay on the stainless-steel table, with nothing to rest on the black rubber head block. The open sections around each armpit, the neck and legs were now apparent. Normally, fluids would leak from the body and drain through the tiny holes in the table and disappear somewhere below. Paul never questioned where the fluid went, and he didn't want to know.

Paul hunched low, slowly walked around the table and peered into the sections of the body where the limbs and head were removed. He kept his hands behind his back, fingers interlaced, to quell the urge to reach inside and touch the soft tissue around the openings. He examined the skin around the openings and was amazed how clean the edges of the wounds were. The skin was cut cleanly, no hesitation marks, no sign skinny arms, if it was skinny arms who did this, thought twice about what he was doing. He was oddly impressed at the skill involved to surgically cut through a body without hacking at it.

"Nice job, huh?"

Paul knew the voice of the medical examiner. He remained bent forward; his focus remained on the body and wounds.

"This guy is a surgeon or should be. He has skill."

Paul stood, turned to see the medical examiner. She was young and beautiful, unlike the cliché coroners on TV that are usually grumpy old men with total disregard for the living.

"I bet she was a looker. I mean look at that alabaster skin," she ran her gloved finger along the side of the torso, "smooth, no blemishes. I doubt this girl had a zit anywhere on her body in her entire life."

Paul grimaced at the thought of touching the body with such a sensual touch. "Maura, that is disgusting."

Maura laughed off Paul's comments, "I appreciate the human body in all forms, alive or dead. The body is a marvelous machine, complex yet simplistic in its design, strong and often delicate. This is one delicate girl. I hate seeing victims on my tables; it makes me wonder how one person could possibly hurt another."

"You picked an odd choice of careers," Paul offered.

Maura walked around the table, her gaze never leaving the torso on the table. "On the contrary. I've always found it fascinating why we simply can't keep someone alive when an organ fails or is invaded by mutated cells? What causes the body to change and turn on itself? What causes the cascade of system failures as one organ is damaged, or malfunctions and the body compensates to keep it alive? Why can't we take the brain from one person, put it into another body and retain the essence of who that person was alive?"

Paul began to chuckle as Maura ranted about the anatomy and physiology of life, never once taking her eyes off the torso. "If memory serves, there was another doctor who thought the same as you."

Maura slowly pulled her stare away from the body to look at Paul, "And who might that be?"

"I believe they called him Dr. Victor Frankenstein." They both laughed.

"That's so funny you mention that. That was my favorite book as a kid. Mary Shelley, the author, was a visionary. It is an original story. There was nothing like it at the time. Do you know the history behind Frankenstein?" Paul didn't want to get into this conversation but shook his head indicating he hadn't. He realized shortly after that he had made a mistake. He placed his hand on the cold stainless-steel autopsy table to support himself then quickly pulled his hand away and wiped imaginary germs on his jacket while Maura went on one of her famous long rants.

"Did you know that the book was written because of a bet?" Paul shook his head again.

"It's true. Three authors made a bet who could write the scariest story or something about two-hundred years ago, well maybe not that long ago, but it was a fuck of a long time ago. Anyway, Mary Shelly wrote this thing when she was in her twenties, I think. Pretty original for the time when the thought of transplants didn't even exist. Frankenstein is not the name of the monster you know but the man who created him. The monster was referred to "it" or "thing" but never had a name. It was only after that the public started to associate the monster as Frankenstein. Can you imagine the ideas floating around in that young girl's head at a time when women didn't even have the right to vote?"

"Yeah." Paul was trying not to show how annoyed he was.

"Now my favorite movie about Frankenstein had to be "Young Frankenstein". Have you seen it?" Paul nodded hoping Maura would stop talking. "Wasn't that a great movie? I mean, you take something as scary as the original story and turn it into one of the funniest movies of all time." Maura hunched over and let one arm swing loosely, and with a lisp, she attempted to imitate the actor who played Igor or I-Gor as it was pronounced in the movie, "Walk this way," and proceeded to walk around the autopsy table laughing. Paul had a faint smile on his face in case she looked up to see him. He didn't want Maura to think he didn't enjoy her performance, which he didn't.

As Maura performed her best Igor impersonation, Paul wondered how Maura ever graduated from medical school. She made one full lap around the table, stood before Paul and began to laugh so hard she started to cry. "I'm so sorry." Maura wiped away a tear from laughing so hard. "I just love that movie."

"I can see that." Paul stood in front of Maura as she composed herself after her performance. "Anyway, can I go over the body with you?"

Maura wiped her eyes, walked around to the opposite side of the table, donned a fresh pair of nitrile gloves and placed both hands on the girl's belly, "Young, early twenties, cause of death is indeterminate at the moment. She may have died from a variety of things: drug overdose, decapitation, could be suicide by a variety of means. She may have ingested something, cut her wrists, until we run toxicology, check her stomach contents, blood work, if there's any blood left, do some X-rays, maybe a CT-scan, we won't know a thing. All I can tell you at this very moment is that there is no way to determine C.O.D. without more tests. She could've died from natural causes and then she was cut up. There isn't a mark on this body other than she's missing a few parts." Maura stood back and glared at Paul. "We don't have fingerprints, and without the head, we have no idea what she looks like, or teeth to run dental."

Paul shook his head. His gaze never left the body on the table, "DNA?" "Already took a sample. I'll send it off but it's gonna be a few months before we get a result and unless she's already in the system, we won't get a hit. Once I cut her open, I'll know a lot more than I do now. Hey, did you ever get a DNA hit on that arm?"

Paul simply shook his head. He had always hated it when the medical examiners used that term, "Cut her/him open" like a roast at Sunday dinner. "Keep me posted," he asked.

"I'll post results and email them to you," Maura yelled at Paul as he left the room.

Maura turned back to the torso on her table, "OK. Let's find out what secrets you're hiding."

Maura picked up a scalpel and held it just above the right clavicle, "I'm sorry honey." The blade sunk deep into the skin, and as Maura pulled the blade across to the sternum, the skin slowly spread apart. There was no blood; the body was void of most or all of its fluids. Maura reached the centre of the sternum, then reached across to the left clavicle and made the same cut across the chest until the two incisions met then she continued down to the navel.

"I hate this part honey, but I'm hoping you can tell me something." Maura placed the scalpel down on the stainless-steel side table, took in a breath and continued with the autopsy.

Behind her, the door slowly squeaked open, Maura didn't hear any footfalls entering her room, "If you need anything, Paul, I told you I'd send anything I found after I'm done. If you forgot something, just come and get it. No icky stuff yet."

"Hey, Maura."

She recognized the voice but couldn't place it. She turned to find Carl Kadner leaning in the open door.

"I'd never think of bothering you while there's icky stuff on the table," Carl snickered.

"You." Maura exclaimed, "Out. Get out. The last time I saw you, you broke my sister's heart. She cried for days when you never called her back."

"You and I both know, it wasn't going to work. Let's be honest Maura, your sister, well, she's special. And not in a good way." Carl slowly walked into the room. It was a strategic move, calculated, in case Maura threw a scalpel at him. He stopped within a few feet of the table. He casually glanced at the torso of the girl that lay on the table; a "Y" incision already cut into the chest with one side of the skin pulled over the right breast. Pale red muscle and white bone were visible. Carl felt his stomach turn, but he maintained his composure.

Maura stepped between Carl and the table, "What do you want?"

"Well, frankly, that." Carl pointed to the table behind Maura.

"Well Carl, you aren't getting any of that or anything else for that matter." Maura firmly planted her gloved fists against her waist to prove her point. "And how did you get down here anyway? This area is restricted."

Carl smiled coyly.

"No, no, no you didn't. Did you say," Maura pointed at Carl then back at herself then back to Carl, "that you and me." Maura's face became red with rage.

"No. I said I was almost family. That I was serious with your sister and wanted to talk to you about some very personal stuff." Carl moved to one side to get a better look at the torso.

Maura repositioned herself between Carl and the table, "That's pretty much the same. You and my sister are never gonna happen, never did happen." Maura flung her hand in the air and pointed towards the door, "Out. Now. Out."

"Maura, I just need some information. Please."

"That's it. That's the reason you're here." Tiny balls of spit hit Carl in the face. He didn't attempt to wipe his face clean. He thought that might only enrage her further. "You're still a reporter. You? They haven't fired you yet?" "This is my first crime story. Please, Maura. I'll call your sister. I promise." Maura let out a loud laugh, "I don't want you to ever call my sister. Again. Ever."

Carl took one step back, the barrage of wet balls spitballs continued. "Fine. I'll never call her again. How's that? Just give me some info, and I'll never see or talk to your sister again."

"Never?" Maura's voice lowered. Carl crossed his heart.

"You don't have a heart," Maura told him.

"I won't use your name, take any pictures, you'll just be a confidential informant." Carl flicked his eyebrows up and down.

Maura turned to the autopsy table and pointed, "You see that thing dangling from the ceiling? Do you?"

Carl nodded so rapidly he thought he would give himself a headache.

"That thing is recording everything we say. I'll edit out this part of the conversation and keep it on my system only as proof of our conversation. If, for any reason what-so-ever, my name gets used or suggested or anything," Maura stepped towards Carl, "so help me God, I will practice my scalpel technic on your scrotum, cut out your balls, drop them on the floor and stomp on them until you see your testicles flattened into tiny mounds of goop."

Carl had a sudden urge to vomit.

"Got it?"

Carl nodded, "Got it."

"Good." Maura stepped aside, "And never call my sister again. Come here."

Carl stepped around Maura to get a better view of the torso on the table. She looked Carl up and down, noticed the antique suit he was wearing and wondered what her sister saw in him.

*****

Upstairs, Paul was sitting at his desk, he cradled a cup of coffee in two hands and blew across the top. He took a sip and placed the cup on his desk beside the phone. He opened the new three-ringed binder labeled "JANE DOE" in bold black marker down the spine. It was empty. There wasn't a single piece of paper inside yet. Most of the files were computerized, and the case hadn't generated any reports yet. The scene notes still had to be transcribed and would then be placed in the binder.

Paul took another sip of the coffee as he wondered how many binders would be filled with evidence on this case. On the floor, he had six more binders filled with evidence on the cases he oversaw, the arm found in the snow, Abigail Schneider and now the torso in the suitcase would be added to his list of cases. Paul shifted in his chair; something was digging into his thigh.

Paul emptied his pockets and tossed the offending object onto his desk. His personal cell phone landed on top of the new "Jane Doe" binder. He picked it up, tapped the corner of the phone on the desk and thought now was the time to call her back. He didn't have to look up her name in the contacts, Paul knew the number. Paul dialed the number as he was about to tap the green button to connect the line, he felt a hand on his shoulder.

"Hey, bud. Any luck?"

Paul didn't have to look up and recognized Ken's voice.

Paul breathed in deeply and sighed. "Maura likes Young Frankenstein, does a horrible Igor impression. She is also one fucking scary woman." He spun around in his chair and propped both feet on the corner of his desk, "Nicole went over the crime scene photos and we got something on the unsub. Problem is we can't legally use it, but it gives us something to go on." "What did we get?" Ken firmly planted his ass on the desk opposite Paul's and crossed his arms. He looked down and noticed a new dark stain on the carpet by the corner of Paul's desk.

"White male, thin, not much hair on the arms and bites his nails." "Actually, that's a helluva lot more than we had before. We can work with that." Ken changed the topic of conversation, "Scuttlebutt around the office is that you had a date last night. Any truth to that? I think the last time you went on a date, we were still using VHS tapes."

Paul enjoyed being the subject of ridicule by his co-workers, after all, he gave as good as he got. "I think it goes further back. My dates are as rare as 8 track tapes."

"Do we know her?" Ken asked.

"I'll post all the details on the bathroom walls as they develop."

Ken stood, "Just glad you broke your slump," and walked back to his desk.

It was another few hours before Paul had scanned all the crime scene photos in the log, notes below each and all his notations included. He knew he would have to wait for the uniformed officers on scene to enter their notes and Maura to document her findings.

In black permanent marker, he wrote the date and case number on the white stripe beneath the image of each photo and placed all the photos in protective sleeves. Each sleeve then went into the binder. The Chief was big on electronic documentation but mandated all physical evidence and notes still be kept as a backup just like in the old days. The Chief made it a habit of sporadically reviewing case notes on the system without the detective knowing it.

Paul had created a small case board that hung by the side of his desk. It was supposed to show the progress of the case, pictures of the victims to keep their faces current, photos of suspects, of persons of interest and pertinent details. Instead, it had little more than an arm on an autopsy table, a blow-up of the photo from the drivers license of Abigail Schneider and now the torso from the suitcase. He sat back, placed his arms behind his head and stared. The images, already frozen in his mind, remained motionless. He wished he had Nicole's ability to have the dead speak to him. All three pictures declined Paul's request to tell their story.

Paul gathered his jacket, pocketed his two cell phones and realized he hadn't called Nicole and wasn't even sure if she was still at his house. He thought about calling her to see where she was but didn't want to seem needy. It was Saturday, he was supposed to be off this weekend, but circumstances often prevent him from having a normal life.

He picked up his office phone, then slowly placed it down on the cradle and left for the day.

*****

Katy was at home, thinking about her date she had the previous night. Will was a little odd but cute and something about him stuck with her. They had exchanged cell numbers and promised to stay in touch. She wondered if one day was too soon before calling. She picked up her cell phone, swiped up to bring the screen to life and found Will's number. She paused for a moment, "Fuck it." She dialed the number and paced around the apartment until he picked up. After quite a few rings, the call went directly to voicemail. Unfortunately, Will hadn't set up his voice mail and the system wasn't able to record her message.

Disappointed, Katy disconnected and hoped that he would still see that she had called. She thought about calling again and fought the urge to redial. Instead, she put the phone down on the kitchen counter and hoped he would call her soon.

*****

Saturday at the newspaper office was always quiet. Most of the staff were gone by five. Carl and a few others remained behind as they finished a story or used the company phones to make long distance calls while the boss was gone.

Carl sat at his desk, frantically typing away. He flipped his notepad pages over then back again to make sure he had every last detail for the story. As agreed, he would omit any reference to where he got the information or how he happened to come across privileged information. He had a promise to keep, and if he wanted to continue using Maura for more information, he had to keep his word.

"The sound of a real typewriter is so much better than the plastic sound of keys from a computer keypad."

Carl spun around in his chair to see Sam standing behind him. "How long have you been there?" he asked.

"A few minutes. Long enough to read over your shoulder. Isn't some of that a little over the top? You certainly have a flair for the sensationalism."

"It's a sensational case." Carl never looked up from the monitor.

"You're sure the body was drained of all fluids before they found it?"

"Torso. No legs, no arms, no head, just the torso. And yes. No fluid. It was drained." The plastic clicking continued as Carl spoke. "The killer managed to drain the body of all fluids. Whatever method was used was ingenious or barbaric."

Sam grimaced and shook his head side to side. "You're making it sound like whoever did this was some freak."

Carl looked up from the keyboard, "He kills a girl, dismembers the body and stuffs it in a suitcase. Isn't that the quintessential definition of a freak?"

"You're supposed to be impartial. Not judgmental. It would sound so much better if you were on a real typewriter." Sam reached down under the yellow vinyl bag that held the trash and pulled out a small case. He casually pushed Carl aside and placed it beside his keyboard. "Anybody can write. This," Sam tapped the case, "is how you become a journalist kid." Without saying another word, he began to push the cleaning cart down the aisle.

Carl looked down at the case on his desk and considered what Sam had just said and realized he was writing an article for the tabloids, not a newspaper.

He pushed his keyboard to the back of his desk, placed the case before him, opened it to find a portable typewriter inside. He removed the lid from the case, put it on the floor and positioned the typewriter at the edge of his desk in front of him. The word "UNDERWOOD" was embossed in gold on the gloss black finish beneath the space bar. He pulled a sheet of paper from the printer tray and fed it through the roller. The gears made a sound like no other machine he had heard.

Never having used an actual typewriter, Carl looked at the machine, played with the arms and buttons and knobs before figuring out the basic functions of the machine. He looked at the keys, held down the shift key and pushed hard on the first letter and watched as the metal arm swung upwards, the ink ribbon moved to place itself between the page and the arm before it struck the paper. He looked at the brilliant black letter "C" on the page. Carl turned and looked over his shoulder to see Sam cleaning some of the other desks further down the aisle. He smiled and went back to his work. He slowly struck the rest of the keys to put his name at the top of the page. Sam was right. There is no other sound than that of a typewriter.

*****

Paul backed his SUV into the driveway just before seven. He had spent most of his day off at the station working. Not his favorite place to be but until recently, he hadn't had much of a life. He hoped that Nicole was still inside but understood if she wasn't. He unlocked the side door, as he entered the foyer, the smell of, he wasn't sure what, but it smelled good. Paul called out to Nicole, no answer. He went directly to the kitchen.

On the kitchen table, an inverted plastic bowl kept Paul's dinner warm. Beside the bowl, a short note, "Wasn't sure what time you would be back. Enjoy". Paul lifted the plastic bowl to reveal a large plate of fresh jambalaya. He never had jambalaya, but it looked good and smelled even better. He sat down, started to eat and texted a quick message to Nicole thanking her for dinner.

He finished his meal, cleaned the dishes and sat on the couch in front of the television. It was on, but Paul wasn't watching. His eyes became heavy, and he thought about calling Nicole, but he wanted to wait until she texted him back first. He fought to stay awake as his eyes continued to close. Eventually, sleep overtook him, his eyes shut, his mind was blank, no dreams, no images, nothing but restful, tranquil sleep. Something that Paul had not had in a long time.

*****

Katy ran for her phone. The phone displayed the icon of a shadowy male figure and the name "Will" beneath it. She swiped the button to the left to answer the call, "Hello."

There was only silence on the other end, "Hello," she repeated.

"There must be a lag on the line. I can hear an echo." The voice was hollow and distant.

"Will?" Katy asked.

"I must be in a dead zone. I was just asking if you wanted to meet for a drink?"

"Sure. Where?" she yelled back.

"How about the sports bar on Franklin Street in an hour?"

She knew it would be a late night, but Katy was looking forward to seeing Will again. "Sure. An hour. See you then."

Katy ran to the bathroom, ran the shower, disrobed and stepped in.

Will was already at the bar when he called, found a table near the front where he could watch the girls arrive and see if they were there to meet anyone or were alone. He held onto his beer with two hands, the condensation formed between his palms and glass and flowed through his fingers. He didn't drink from the bottle; the contents became warmer with each passing minute. He was concentrating on the girls as they passed his table. He studied whether they were alone, their features, their skin, their bone structure, admiring or dismissing them.

A group of girls walked passed his table, stopped and they gathered in front of him. They stood in a group, talking, laughing. Of all the girls in the group, Will focused his attention on one girl, a young redhead, her skin pale, smooth and flawless. His gaze followed her bare left arm down from the end of her short sleeve shirt, down her slender forearm to her hand. Will's attention focused all the way down to her hand and fingers. Her hand was curled, fingers hidden under her jacket she had removed when she walked into the bar. He never removed his eyes from her hand, waiting in anticipation for her to reveal her fingers. She was only a few feet away, the bar crowded and noisy, but Will heard nothing, saw nothing other than the smooth skin of her hand and the fingers that remained hidden.

As he waited, his grip around the bottle tightened, had he found her, everything was perfect, Will just needed to see her fingers. The group turned, the redhead slipped her jacket from the left hand to her right, she raised her left hand to pull her hair around her ear. Will recoiled in disgust at the sight of the false nails glued over the tips of her fingers. The black aura swirled around her hand, obscuring her face and hair. He turned away, infuriated at wasting his time on the redhead. He could feel himself getting upset, his teeth clenched, his desire burned inside to reach out and strike her. It was taking more and more restraint to quell those feelings.

The group of girls were assigned a table; they laughed as they walked deeper into the bar and disappeared behind a wall. Will felt his temper cool. He closed his eyes, forgetting about the girl that upset him.

Will hadn't noticed the time pass until Katy walked in and took a seat next to him. "Hey, stranger. Thanks for the call."

Will didn't seem startled, didn't react, he simply turned, smiled at Katy, "You want a beer?"

She smiled and nodded, "Wine please."

Will raised his hand to catch the server's attention. He stopped by the table, took their order and left. Will placed his hand on hers, "I'm so glad you decided to come."

Katy laughed, "Your hand is soaking wet."

Will handed her a napkin, "Sorry, I was holding onto my beer. Makes me look more manly holding a beer than drinking iced tea all night."

Surprised, Katy asked Will if he drank.

"No. Never did. I always order a drink, but I never drink it. Just out of habit. I was bugged a lot in school. A habit I picked up."

"There's nothing wrong with not drinking. A lot of people don't drink anymore. Same goes for smoking." Katy returned the gesture and placed her hand atop of Will's. "In fact, it's nice to meet someone who doesn't drink. You don't smoke, do you? Cause that is a deal breaker."

Will smiled, "No." He squeezed Katy's hand then pulled his hand and locked his fingers around the bottle again. He looked at Katy's hand and felt nothing. He was glad she didn't have what he wanted.

The server returned with Katy's glass of wine and a fresh bottle of beer. Before he could place the drinks on the table, Katy slipped a twenty-dollar bill on the tray, told the server to take the glasses back and bring back two large iced teas, regular iced tea, not Long Island iced teas. "It'll be fun to be out and not have a drink."

*****

The two girls sat in the living room apartment and shared a bottle of whisky that Simone had purchased earlier in the day. Nicole was sitting with her legs tucked under her, giddy like a high school girl ready to tell her best friend all her secrets Simone poured a shot glass of the expensive whisky and handed it to Nicole, "This stuff is old and supposed to be good. Well, according to the guy at the liquor store. Here."

Nicole took a sniff and grimaced, "This is a little out of my comfort zone. You know me, I'm not a big drinker."

"Sugar, I'm trying to get you drunk, so you tell me all the lurid details from last night." Simone fell hard into her chair, but she balanced the small glass in her hand and didn't spill a drop. "Tell."

Nicole sniffed the drink, grimaced once again, "Never had whisky before," and tossed back the drink. "Wow. That is good." She held her glass out for a refill.

Simone put her glass down, grabbed the bottle and refilled Nicole's glass. Nicole downed the refill with the same enthusiasm as she did the first. "Whoa." She blew out. "That's warm."

Simone took her seat, decided enough was enough, "So, did he rock your world?"

Nicole smiled coyly, "More than once actually."

Simone cocked her head to one side, "More than once?"

"It was unbelievable. You know how it can take more than a few times before you get a rhythm going, you know what he likes, he knows what you like?" Simone nodded and swallowed her drink in one gulp. "Well, it was awesome the first time. I just hope that things don't go downhill from here. I don't think Paul's been with anyone in quite some time. He was possessed. A man on a mission. A point to prove. He knew which button to rub, where to touch, everything. And does he know how to use his tongue? Wowzers. I mean, life is too short to be with someone if they don't know or care about how to get you off or take the time to learn how to please you. Remember I had that problem with the ex. That asshole couldn't find his way around even after I showed him a chart to tell him where all my good parts were located."

The two girls shared a laugh.

"Oh, oh." Nicole jumped in her seat, "You'll never guess."

"What?" Simone almost yelled.

"He's a moaner."

Simone let out a loud, "Nooooooo."

"And a talker. I think it was the first time in a long time someone other than himself got him off. He thanked me at least a dozen times." Nicole started to blush. "Gimme another shot of that stuff." She held out her shot glass. "If I'm gonna tell you all this shit, I better be drunk, so I have an excuse."

May 3

"You're kidding me. You're flipping kidding me. What is this?" Nora Watson threw the stack of papers on her desk; it slid off the end landing on the floor by Carl's feet. "Who types out stories today on a typewriter?"

Nora stood behind her desk, beads of sweat dripping down her forehead. The heat from the sun breaking through the window behind her desk combined with her mood, caused her to perspire. She looked out the glass partition to see the office staff staring at her questioning Carl after reading his story.

Carl picked up his story and threw it back on Nora's desk. "Are you pissed because it was done on a typewriter or the content? Because it's a damn good story."

"Why can't you write a story like the rest of the reporters on staff? Every time I give you an assignment for the simplest of things, you turn it into a conspiracy, a hidden treasure or some creature terrorizing some town."

"Hey, I never once wrote about a hidden treasure."

"Last month you almost got arrested for impersonating a police officer to get interviews from witnesses. Before that, you stole a car. I asked for a briefing of the murders that have gone on in the city in the last few months, and you tell me we have a serial killer on the loose. How do you figure we have a serial killer? Huh? Tell me that? The police don't even think it's a serial killer. Why can't you please, for once, keep it simple and just do as I ask?"

To emphasize his frustration, Carl picked up his story and slammed it down on her desk again, "I never said I was a cop, I just didn't deny it. It's called commandeering a car, not stealing. Big difference. And did you read the story? If you read it, you wouldn't be asking me why I came to that conclusion. And I'm pretty sure they know it's the same person who killed all three girls."

"Really? And why is that?" Nora sat down in her chair. It creaked under her weight.

"Again, did you read my story?"

"Why don't you enlighten me?"

"If you read my story, I wouldn't have to," he yelled in frustration.

Nora stood and went to the small table beside her desk and poured herself a cup from the coffee machine, didn't offer one to Carl, and sat back down. "If you wrote something worth reading, I'd read it."

"Funny." Carl flipped through a few pages, found what he wanted and began to read, "...the skin was cut with surgical precision. The joints, shoulder and hip joints, where the limbs were removed, were carefully separated. For what reason, the police do not yet know."

Carl proudly stood as if he had made his case. This time, he held onto his story instead of throwing it back on Nora's desk.

Nora sipped her coffee and tilted back in her chair, "That's two of the three girls. What about the one left behind in her bedroom?"

"Again, if you bothered to read my story you'd know. The similarity between the girls, their physical characteristics were identical. They think the second girl was left untouched because she had terminal cancer." Exasperated at having to explain himself, Carl continued, "Next time you decide to toss my story in the trash, perhaps you'd read it first."

"Where did you get this information anyway?" Nora asked.

"A friend."

Nora laughed, "Can you confirm what you've written?"

Carl nodded.

"Edit the story, cut out the superfluous crap and put it on the computer."

"Superfluous? I'm surprised you can pronounce that word and even more surprised you used it correctly in a sentence," Carl screamed.

"You'd be more surprised if I used "fired" in a sentence. Just have it ready for today's edition. And if you insist on using that typewriter, use it for your drafts only. Send me the e-version." Nora pulled the keyboard tray out from beneath her desk and began to work.

Carl turned to walk out, smiling, "Hey, Nora, be happy. I'm saving you money using that typewriter. It's manual, no electricity and I'm not using any toner for the printer."

"Maybe I'll buy you a new suit with the money I save. Now get back to work."

Carl slammed the door to Nora's office and walked back to his desk. He sat down, pushed the typewriter to the side and pulled out the keyboard and placed it at the edge of the desk. He flipped through his story, refusing to remove the "superfluous" content and typed it out as he had shown Nora then sent it to the content editor to be placed in the day's edition. He didn't bother to copy Nora when he emailed the story.

Carl knew he would get yelled at by Nora or worse after she read the day's edition, but the story had to be told. He pushed his chair away from his desk wondering if he would have a job waiting. Regardless of whether or not he had a job, there was still something he had to do.

*****

The two adult German Shepherds ran freely in the backyard. They were hungry, waiting for Will to feed them. Between feedings, the dogs were lucky if they managed to catch a slow squirrel running along the grass or a groundhog between feedings. Will liked to keep them hungry. He felt it kept them angry.

Will opened the door to the basement, walked down the carpeted stairs, flipped the light to the rec room. The recessed LED illuminated the large room where he kept his antique pinball machines and jukebox. He favorite toys were lined up along the far wall, plugged in and powered up, ready for a quick game whenever the need struck him.

Will found that the rhythmic sound of the bells and music and the concentration required as he followed the steel ball around the mazes help keep his mind busy. He ran his fingers along the games as he passed them on the way to the freezer room. He opened another door where he kept his cold storage, canned foods, preserves and a large commercial grade walk-in freezer.

He grabbed the silver handle and pulled hard, releasing the lever and swung the door open. The blast of frigid air hit him; he shivered then walked into the right side where wire shelves held the frozen meat for the dogs. To the left, he kept his prize. He found two sections of frozen thighs he had removed and portioned from the girl before placing her in the suitcase.

Will removed the two large sections, closed the freezer door and walked upstairs to the back of the house. Will slid the patio door open, whistled and the two dogs came running from the far end of the yard. As they approached, he raised his hand; the dogs sat on command. He tossed the heavy portion of the girl's thigh one by one into the grass. Each piece hit the ground with a loud, dull thud, then rolled for a bit. The dogs never moved. They stared at their master, waiting for his permission for them to feed.

Will waited for a few moments, then yelled "Eten", the Dutch word for "eat". The dogs turned and ran to find their food in the long grass.

The dogs each found their piece of the meal. The larger alpha male had the choice of the two pieces of flesh, taking the slightly bigger chunk leaving the other portion for his sibling. The dogs bit hard, their teeth sinking deep into the frozen flesh. Each dog was taking off into different directions with its prize. It would take more than a full day for both dogs to gnaw through the frozen skin, flesh to the bone. The dogs would eventually devour everything, including the raw bones and would be satisfied for a few days before needing another feeding. Any uneaten portion would be buried deep in the ground, perhaps dug up again later to be finished off.

*****

The department phone rang on Paul's desk. He reached over his keyboard and his coffee to answer.

"Ya." His usual response when he knew the call was internal.

"You're cheerful first thing in the morning." Paul recognized Maura's voice.

Paul deflected the direction he knew the conversation was going, "What's up?" His voice hadn't changed tone. Paul could hear Maura shuffling papers about, waiting for her to say something, "Maura," he called out.

"Hang on. I got an email today and printed it out. I wanna read it to you." Paul heard Maura swearing as she continued to search for the missing email. "Got it."

"What's it about?" asked Paul.

"We finally got the DNA results back on the arm found in the snow last year. You'll never guess who it was." Maura expected Paul to respond. Instead, the line went dead. "Hello. Hello." Not getting a response, Maura hung up the phone as Paul burst through the swinging door to the lab.

"What do you have?" He was panting as he spoke.

"What did you do, fly down the stairs?"

Paul was in no mood for an idle chat, "Come on." He put both hands down on his knees and took in a deep breath. "Whoa. I'm in bad shape."

"Do you remember the missing case from last November, a few weeks before Christmas, the girl that just disappeared when she was out shopping?" Maura hopped up onto the stainless-steel counter, swinging her feet.

Paul was out of breath and couldn't answer; he shook his head.

"The arm belongs to her." Maura handed Paul a sheet of paper that confirmed the DNA match. He looked at it, not certain he understood the meaning of the explanation but found the word "MATCH" and the person's name, Paige Kirkby.

"That's your CODIS copy by the way," Maura said.

Paul studied the sheet, then looked at Maura, "If she had DNA taken, why didn't we get a match on her fingerprints?"

Maura returned to her desk, opened the case file, found the documents she was looking for, then handed them to Paul.

"What's this?" He turned the paper over as if the answer was on the back of the sheet.

"That Mr. Hammond," Maura paused, "is Paige Kirkby's school fingerprint and DNA sample taken when she started school twenty some odd years ago. When I got her DNA match, I noticed there were no priors, so I checked with the lab, and they sent her school info."

Paul squinted his eyes, puzzled.

"Did you ever have kids, nieces, nephews?" Maura asked. Paul shook his head.

Maura continued, "God. OK. In some school districts, when a child starts school, the school board encourages the parents to get all the children under a certain age fingerprinted, DNA swabs and photos were done. In this case, if you recall, the fingerprints from the arm that was recovered were badly scarred. That's probably why we didn't get a hit by AFIS or CPIC. DNA is the gold standard, not fingerprints. You can't alter DNA."

"So, the scarring on the fingertips is why we didn't get a hit on them?"

"It was probably done intentionally to slow down the identification of the arm. Or dragging the arm through the snow by the plough damaged the prints. Most people don't have their DNA on file. The killer probably took a chance that the vic wasn't in the system or didn't even think about DNA. He or she was wrong. Dead wrong."

Paul contemplated what he was hearing. It was luck that Paige Kirkby had her DNA taken as a child. He was finally standing upright and had caught his breath.

"Shit," Paul exclaimed. "What?"

"If I recall that case, it's considered a missing persons case. I think she was here to go to school or started a new job or something. The parents don't live here in the city. I'm gonna have to go notify her parents that we suspect her daughter is dead or missing. Oh man. I just thought of something. What if her arm was surgically removed for some valid reason and it just got, I don't know, lost and ended up in the snow bank."

Stunned, Maura looked distraught, "Christ. I'd rather just get the news that my daughter is dead rather than hear that we found her arm. What do you tell them?" Maura's tone changed, "Hi Mr. and Mrs. Kirkby, we found your daughter's arm. We don't know where she is or if she is still missing or perhaps dead?"

"I'm going upstairs to check missing persons, then check with all the state hospitals for surgical procedures and see if she did have an, what would you call it, an "armectomy"," Paul air quoted as he chuckled, "before I even contact the parents."

"It's just a regular amputation you jerk," Maura told Paul. He laughed back. "Just checking to see if you knew."

Maura looked invigorated. She ran to the cold storage drawer that held the arm, placed her hand on the handle, then paused, "Well, you do your thing, looking up whether or not Paige Kirkby is still missing or if she's been found or had surgery, and I'm going to look at the arm again to check for medical reasons why or if the arm needed to be amputated for medical reasons."

As Paul turned to leave, Maura shouted at him, "Check with all the hospitals and medical schools."

Paul stopped at the door. "Medical schools?" He looked confused.

Maura released her grip on the handle, "It just hit me, Paige could have died of natural causes and donated her body for medical reasons, and the arm was removed as surgical practice for medical students. Or the students could've removed it and did something stupid as a practical joke that got out hand. No pun intended."

"Christ. Really? A joke?" Paul had a look of disgust on his face.

"You don't want to know what we did as medical students to the medical cadavers. It's one thing to donate your organs for transplant; it's another to donate your body for medical research. Oh my God, I just, what a great way to get rid of a body."

Paul walked back into the autopsy room, "What?"

Maura joined Paul, "Think of it. You want to kill someone, right? Well, the DMV makes it mandatory that you list your wishes when you renew or get a new driver's license. You have to register if you want to donate your organs and or tissue or body for medical research." Maura held out her hand, "Gimme your license."

Paul obliged and pulled his driver's license from his wallet and handed it to her. Maura flipped it over and pointed out the section to prove her point. "On the back, it has a code for what you want to donate at the time of death. If someone is computer savvy, you can hack the system and change your wishes. When you die, the hospital has an obligation to expedite the organ retrieval. After that, if you donate your body to research as well, it gets shipped to the nearest school or lab or whatever. Gross. I know you're dead, but you're lying there naked with people prodding and poking at your body. Not for me. Believe me; I know what we have to do. I hope when I die, I hope it's by natural causes and never have to have an autopsy done." Maura handed Paul his license back.

"You can hack into the government site and change the code?" Paul asked.

"Have you seen the sites that have been hacked in the last few years?

So, I doubt that the government site that controls organ donations is that secure. A halfway intelligent kid on his or her smartphone could probably hack the system in no time at all."

As Paul replaced the card back in his wallet, he didn't want to think of those things that were done on the silver table a few feet away from him. He promised himself he would check to see what he had promised to donate at the time of his death.

He took the stairs one at a time going back up to his office, thinking about all the ways a person's arm could end up in a snow bank. He had a lot to check on before contacting the parents. Paul secretly wished that he would find that Paige died of natural causes, whatever it was, and donated her body for medical research to help find a cure for the disease that ended her life and some immature medical students decided to do something stupid with her body. If only. Nothing was ever that simple. Paul hoped against the odds that this one time, things would turn out to be that easy.

Paul fell hard into his chair causing it to creak and strain under his weight. Sitting forward with his elbows on the edge of the desk, he mentally went over his conversation with Maura. Paul quickly jotted down all the ways he and Maura had determined Paige's arm could've ended up in the snow bank. He then wrote numbers beside each line in the order of probability. He studied the list, crossed out a few of the rankings then re-assigned them. When he finished, he studied the list and hoped he had picked the correct number one reason why Paige's arm was found in the snowbank, she had died of natural causes, and some misguided, idiotic medical students decided to play a prank. Without any evidence to substantiate his feelings, deep down, Paul knew Paige hadn't died from natural causes, and it wasn't a bunch of college kids that took her arm from the cadaver room.

Paul pulled up the internal department file folders, found the missing persons file for Paige Kirkby. He read the file; nothing stood out. The file still hadn't been updated to show that Paige Kirkby was connected to the amputated arm. He opened a browser, went to Facebook and went to the Missing Persons page. Paul scrolled down for several minutes until he found what he was looking for, the name Paige Kirkby. He clicked on the picture and read the report that was posted beside her face. The picture of Paige was obviously cropped from a larger photo, possibly when she was with a group of friends, Paige was young, beautiful, happy. The contact name was Detective J.C. Haines. Paul recognized the name. J.C worked down the hall in missing persons. He then went to Paige's personal Facebook profile.

At the very top, the banner across her page showed her parents and friends standing in front of a banner displaying the reward money for the safe return of their daughter and friend. He scrolled further down, clicked on the "Photos" to pull up all her the pictures she had posted before she disappeared. In every picture, Paul could see the person Paige was, smiling with friends or family, with animals, her graduation photos from high school and in her first apartment away from home.

Paul printed the Facebook contact photo for Paige and selected a few sheets for the missing persons file and sent them to the printer then waited for the laser printer to finish spitting out the report. He grabbed the sheets then walked to down the hall to the west side of the building to J.C.'s office.

Paul peered into the office through the open door, knocking softly on the metal door frame. A bald head popped up from behind the fabric wall unit separating the only two desks in the small room.

"Hey man. What brings you down in the bowels of the cop shop?"

J.C stood and extended his hand. Paul walked in and shook J.C.'s hand. Paul pulled a chair from behind the empty second desk and sat facing J.C.

Paul asked J.C. if he had heard they had located Paige's arm.

"I just opened the email from Maura. CODIS found a DNA hit on the arm you found in the snowbank, huh."

"You wanna bring me up to speed on what you have?"

J.C. turned to face Paul, leaned back in his chair and sighed deeply. "We have a lot of nothing, piled high on top of zilch. The girl went missing while doing some Christmas shopping. Found some blood in the parking lot, not much else. We checked all the downtown cameras that we could find that were working, checked for anybody that was following her, got nothing. The kid parked her car in a backlot area, no lights, no cameras, no attendant, no witnesses." J.C. sighed deeply again, "We looked everywhere, checked all the people that knew her, boyfriends, ex-boyfriends, girlfriends, casual friends, work, family, everyone checked out. No one had a grudge against her; we couldn't find any weird guys that had a crush on her. I worked with the family, had three or four searches organized. I always figured she was abducted; it just didn't seem like a girl who just wanted to get away and walked away from life. There were just too many unknowns."

Paul nodded, "You have the case file on her?"

"I do. Why?"

"I want the case. Now that we know she's probably dead, I'd like to take charge of it."

J.C. stood from behind his desk, "You know the policy, it's not yours until we know for certain the vic is dead. We have an arm, that's it. She's still classified as a missing person."

Paul could feel his heart begin to race, he clenched his teeth then cast J.C. a look that made him shiver. Paul was not one to hide his emotions when he wanted something; not much stood in his way. After years of working together, J.C. knew better than to argue department policy with Paul, he rose, went to the back of his office and lifted a banker's box from the floor and placed it on his desk.

"Is that it?" Paul asked as he lifted the lid from the box.

J.C. retrieved the second box and dropped it on his desk beside the first one.

"Done?"

J.C. grimaced, turned and picked up the third and last box, placing it on top of the second. "Now I'm done." He wiped his hands on his trousers. "I'll have you sign the transfer papers. You'll have the case files and lead on this one." J.C. pointed a finger at Paul, his voice was stern and direct, "I kid you not, you fuck this one up, and I'll make sure the Chief knows you pressured me to take lead. And, I want in on the investigation when you close."

Paul didn't answer. Instead, he stacked one box on top of the other and carried them to his office. He dropped them on his desk, lifted the lid of the box marked with a large "1" and let it fall to the floor. He looked inside and found several binders; each spine was labeled "1" through "5".

Paul quietly said to himself, "One. A great place to start," and pulled the first binder out and opened it to the first page. He grabbed the arms to his chair, pulled it in close and sat down. Paul knew he had a lot of reading to do. He uncapped a highlighter and started to read.

Paul's personal phone began to vibrate in his shirt pocket. He pulled it out, swiped up to reveal a text from Nicole.

*****

Carl parked his car a few blocks away from the parking lot where Paige Kirkby had been abducted almost six months earlier. He walked along the sidewalks, examining the shops and stores along the street and imagined the young girl walking in front of him as she stopped, looked into the shop windows, deciding what would be a good Christmas gift, then moving on. Carl turned around and looked behind him. The sidewalk crowd was sparse as he looked through them, in his mind, he saw a shadowy figure, a ball cap pulled down low, wearing clothing that any guy on the street would wear. As Carl stood in the middle of the sidewalk, people parted way and walked passed him on either side, staring at him as he stood motionless looking at imaginary figures from the past. The man with the ball cap pulled down low walked towards him, then passed through him. Carl turned to see the back of the mysterious man blend into the crowd as he followed Paige. His pace slowed each time Paige stopped to window shop. Carl watched as Paige turned to see face the man as he approached, smile at him then turn her attention back to the items behind the glass.

The man walked into a small store, stood at the window, his eyes never left his target. When Paige passed, he waited a few moments then exited the store and began to follow her again. Carl, in turn, followed the two imaginary figures from the past as they walked down the sidewalk.

Paige turned down the alley towards the parking lot, the predator never pausing, turned to track his prey. Carl could see the young girl up ahead, happy, swinging her bags as she walked towards her car. He imagined the man was twenty or so feet behind her, turn right at the opening of the parking lot and made it look as if he was attempting to locate his car. The man with the ballcap pulled down low knew this is where he would strike. He glanced behind him, to the left then to the right. Walked between cars, he stealthily made his way towards where Paige fumbled for her keys.

A few feet from the girl, the man, broke out into a full out run and pounced on the girl.

Carl found himself in the centre of the parking lot, uncertain exactly how he ended up there. He looked around to see if anyone had noticed his odd behavior. He knew he was acting strangely and wouldn't be surprised if someone called the police on him. He shook the thought aside, closed his eyes, in his mind, this is the way the abduction of Paige Kirkby occurred.

Carl spent a few minutes looking around the paved lot for clues, shards of glass, anything. He was confident that the police investigators had done an excellent job of collecting evidence immediately after she had been taken and in the six months or so since the abduction, anything found on the ground was undoubtedly not from the crime scene.

Instead, Carl looked up, something he was certain the attacker would have done. There were office buildings on two sides, the north and west, and an apartment building to the east. Behind him to the south was the alley. The abductions took place in the middle of the day, and given the time of year Paige was taken; he speculated the office buildings would be full and the staff working and not looking out the windows. He turned his attention to the apartment building. He extended his right index and pretended to touch each floor as he counted. Six floors, eight balconies across each floor, forty-eight potential witnesses who may have been looking out from their apartment during the abduction.

Carl walked across the parking lot, to the north side of the entrance and exit. The lot was unmanned, a silver box on a steel pillar dispensed your ticket as you arrived and charged your debit or credit card as you exited. Carl walked up to it and wondered if the machine kept a record of the times cars that came and went. Even if they did, it wouldn't provide a description of the vehicles. Carl thought of his used typewriter, sometimes progress isn't always better. Would Paige have been abducted if there was a person sitting in a booth who took your money instead of a machine? She probably would have been taken somewhere else he rationalized.

He walked around the block to the front entrance of the building that backed onto the lot. In the front foyer, Carl's heart sank when he looked at the call panel. An old-style black Bakelite handset on a hook with a long list of surnames behind glass. There was no way to tell which apartments faced the parking lot. At the very bottom of the list, one name stuck out. He picked up the handset and pushed "0".

A soft, pleasant voice answered the phone, "Can I help you?"

"My name is Carl Kadner; I'm a reporter. I'm here to talk to someone about the girl that was taken from the parking lot last Christmas."

There was no response on the other end of the phone and Carl wondered if the Superintendent just dismissed him when a loud "Thunk" echoed in the vestibule. He hung up the phone and pulled on the silver handle of the glass door. Not knowing where to go or who to ask for, Carl stood in the middle of the foyer waiting for the voice to make herself known. The foyer had four black leather chairs, placed in a circle around a marble table. A vase of fresh flowers was positioned perfectly in the centre. The lobby was spotless and had a strong fake floral scent. He paced around the chairs then walked to the elevator directly in front of him and looked down the hallway to his left and right. He wondered how long it would take for the voice to come up and meet him, but he thought maybe she had hit the buzzer accidentally and granted him access to her building.

Carl was about to take a seat when the soft voice spoke from down the hall. Carl shot back up and stood until the person behind the voice appeared from around the corner. A middle-aged woman, stunningly beautiful, impeccably dressed in casual black slacks and a white shirt stood before him. Carl's preconceived notion of what a landlady should look like was tossed aside forever.

He smiled, extended his hand, she took it softly, then covered their hands with her left. She gently shook his hand, and as she did, Carl looked down, "No ring," he thought.

"Sophie."

"Carl. You're the landlord?" he asked surprised. Sophie looked nothing like his landlady.

Sophie smiled, "Well, my husband's company owns this building and a few others. I was here just checking on a few things and covering for the landlord while he's off."

Carl hopes were quickly deflated. "Ah."

Sophie smiled politely knowing what the "Ah" meant. She had it said to her more than once. "Anyway, you wanted to know about the girl that was kidnapped?"

Carl composed himself, "Yeah, there's been some new leads, and I wanted to follow up on them. I was outside in the parking lot and looked up to the back apartments to your building..."

Sophie interjected, "My husband's building."

Carl smirked and corrected himself, "Your husband's building. Yes. The back apartments look out onto the lot. I was wondering if the I could knock on a few doors and see if any of the tenants happened to remember seeing anything that day?"

Sophie thought for a moment, "I'm pretty sure that the police did that. The landlord that works for my husband," Sophie smiled coyly, "said that he escorted a few police officers around to all the apartments."

Dejected, Carl persisted, "Would it hurt if I asked them again?"

Sophie thought for a moment, "Sure." She turned and led him to the elevators. "Do you want to start at the top and work our way down?"

Carl shrugged, "Owner's wife's discretion."

She chuckled, "At the top, it is," and pushed the up button. As they waited, she turned to Carl, "I should've asked, you do have ID, right?"

Carl reached into his pocket and pulled out a plastic identification card and casually held it in front of her. "That's a credit card."

Carl turned the card to see the newspapers' name and his picture and the word "REPORTER" in bold black letters across the bottom. He couldn't believe he fell for that. He pocketed his ID card and stood in the corner of the elevator looking at the numerical floor display as Sophie snickered.

"Nice building," Carl said almost softly.

"Better be for the rent my husband charges. He's a fanatic for top of the line everything. He hates a dirty building, or anything broken that needs to be fixed."

"Oh, well do you have a security system?"

"Top of the line. Front door has shatterproof glass, all the doors have a key pass and card swipe like a hotel, and there are multiple cameras hidden in the foyer and stairwells and the parking garage."

"So, you have cameras pointing outside overlooking the parking lot." "Nope, my husband has the cameras pointed towards the side of the building. That's a public lot, and he didn't want to infringe on anyone's right of privacy in the parking lot. He was pretty mad at himself after that girl was taken. If the cameras were pointed at the lot, it might have caught something. The cops asked the same thing by the way."

"Did he change the angle of the cameras after the abduction?"

Sophie shook her head side to side, "Nope, he kept saying people should have the expectation of privacy in a public lot and if the city wants to have cameras on the lot, they should pay for it. He did increase the number of cameras in the garage. You can't hide a cat down there without the landlord having eyes on it."

The elevator let out a low "ding" to indicate they had arrived. The doors opened on the sixth floor, and Sophie exited, turned to the right and swiftly walked to the end of the hall. At the last door on the left, the side facing the parking lot, Sophie stood waiting for Carl to catch up.

"Unfortunately, I only know a few of the tenants, but I'll introduce you and wait outside."

"Actually, I'd prefer if you'd join me. I just don't want there to be any misunderstanding of what I'm doing."

Sophie reached for the lanyard around her neck and pulled out her ID and pass card from inside her shirt, "You better keep your credit card out too in case anyone asks."

Carl retrieved his press ID, confirmed it was indeed his press ID then held it tightly in his closed hand as Sophie knocked at the door. No one answered. She knocked again. Still no response.

"Most of our tenants are professionals. They work during the day. You know we have a few units for rent if you're interested."

Carl was almost embarrassed to tell Sophie he couldn't afford half the rent they were probably asking, "I have a great place now thanks."

Sophie knocked once again. Still no answer, "On to the next."

*****

Paul pulled into Nicole's driveway, killed the engine and walked to the front door. Simone answered the door almost immediately and invited Paul in.

"What's up?" When Paul received the cryptic text from Nicole earlier about another vision, he rushed to her apartment. Simone didn't answer his question. Instead, she quietly led Paul to the living room where Nicole was sitting on the sofa. She was sloughing back with her forearm across her eyes. Paul carefully sat next to Nicole, leaned in close and whispered, "You OK?"

Without moving, Nicole mumbled something unintelligible to both Simone and Paul. He sat down beside her and whispered something to her. She mumbled something back. Again, Paul couldn't understand what she said. Nicole dropped her arm, sat upright and kissed Paul on the cheek as Simone blew a party favour, "Happy Birthday," they both bellowed. Simone quickly disappeared into the kitchen and returned with a frozen cake still in the foil container it came in.

"Sorry officer. We didn't have time to bake you a real cake."

Paul began to laugh loudly, stood up and looked at Nicole and Simone, "Who told you it was my birthday?"

"Ken."

Paul laughed even louder, "This is my third birthday this year. It's his favorite thing to do. What a bastard. Well, he got you guys good."

Simone placed the cake on the living room table, "You mean I spent three bucks on this cake for nothing?" she said jokingly.

Paul reached over and hugged Simone, "Thank you. This is sweet. It is. It means a lot that you would spend three whole dollars on me when the last thing I need is more sugar and fat. But really, thank you." He then bent over and kissed Nicole.

Nicole stood, "Well, to be honest, I don't know Ken at all. He just called me and told me it was your birthday today, and you were feeling depressed. So, I, we," she motioned to Simone, "came up with this at the last minute."

"It's sweet. Really. Listen, I have to get back to work, but I have time for a piece and cup of coffee."

Without saying a word, Simone disappeared into the kitchen and returned with plates and cutlery. She cut the small cake into six equal pieces, placed one piece on a plate and handed it to Paul, "For the birthday boy." She scooped up the second piece and gave it to Nicole, "For the sucker who fell for the gag, and one for me." Simone was transferring the third piece to the plate when it slipped from the knife and landed on the living room table. "Oops," she laughed, picked the piece of cake up and placed it back in the foil container. "Sorry about that birthday boy, you can give that piece to Ken when you take the rest of the cake back to the station." Simone noticed the swirls on the top of the cake didn't match so she took the knife and blended the chocolate icing in a vain attempt to make it appear as if the mismatched piece belonged.

Paul stared at the cake as Simone continued to play with the cake. He placed his plate down on the table and couldn't take his eyes from what Simone was doing.

Nicole looked at Paul, said something that Paul didn't hear or ignored. Simone noticed Paul's odd behavior, stopped what she was doing and put the knife down, "Sorry. Do you not like people playing with their food?"

Paul stare didn't leave the top of the cake. He picked up the knife Simone was using and started to duplicate the motions she was doing to make the icing swirls match. "Gotta go." He picked up the foil container of cake and ran from the house without saying another word.

As Paul raced out, Simone looked at Nicole, "Girl, you have one fucking weird boyfriend."

*****

Several hours later, Carl and Sophie had only interviewed five of the tenants when they stood at the second to last unit on the third floor. Carl was quickly losing interest in the process while Sophie appeared to enjoy the break from her routine.

Sophie knocked at the door, waited a few moments and rapped on the door once again.

"You know the person who lives here?" Carl asked.

"I hardly know any of the tenants. It's…" Sophie was cut off. "my husband's building. I know, I know." Carl said teasingly.

Shuffling could be heard coming from behind the door as the homeowner made his way to the apartment entrance. It took a minute or so before the door creaked open slightly, an eye peered from between the frame and the door. A security chain was pulled taunt and pressed against the man's cheek. He glanced at them, casting an inquisitive look to Carl and Sophie. Carl studied the eye between the crack; his long grey unkempt eyebrow hair grew wildly in all directions, deep crows' feet drew out of the corner of the eye, an eye that appeared to have seen more than a life full of events. "What can I do for you?" The old man's voice was young sounding and musical. The old man refused to open the door any further. Neither Carl or Sophie answered the old man's question.

"Well?" He asked again.

Carl posted a fake smile then pulled out his press ID and held it before the eye behind the door for only a moment then pocketed it as he had done so often. Both Sophie and Carl waited while the man behind the door made the decision to close the door, release the chain and invite them in.

The old man shuffled from the hall to the living room, grabbed hold of the recliner arm for balance, turned and fell into the chair. He motioned for them to take a seat. Carl looked at the room with the zeal of a reporter, Sophie, the eye of a landlord. He looked at the furniture, the lack of clutter; she studied the apartment for damage.

Carl took a seat directly across from the old man, Sophie chose to stand. Carl and the old man stared at each other for a few moments before they both began to speak at almost the same time. Carl stopped abruptly; the old man continued to speak as if nothing had happened.

"…been at least eighteen years since I've been living here. The Mrs. passed away, must be at least fifteen years ago now. The ungrateful kids never stop by anymore, not going to be leaving them any money. If I can't see my grandkids, I'm not gonna leave my children anything. Bastards."

Inside, Carl was laughing at the old man that reminded him of his grandfather, "I couldn't agree more. Now, Mr., er?"

The old man, studied Carl, looking him up and down, "Chermak."

Carl continued, "Mr. Chermak. I'm here to find out if you had seen anything a few months back, before Christmas, a girl was abducted. Do you remember anything about that Mr. Chermak?"

"I'm not a senile man you young snot. I'm old, not stupid."

Carl leaned back in his chair, laughing, "You're right Mr. Chermak. My poor choice of words."

"I'd say. You're not much of a reporter are you."

"I'm new."

"And poor. Look at that suit. I've got newer suits in my closet. You get that at a thrift store or some garage sale?" Mr. Chermak pointed a thick finger at Carl and waved it up and down.

"To be honest, I got it at a thrift store. It reminded me of one my grandfather used to wear. It may very well be his old suit." Carl grabbed his jacket lapel and looked at it, "I think it might be at that."

Mr. Chermak laughed, "Honest and funny. I like you." He turned his attention to Sophie, "Her, she's too quiet, I don't trust quiet people." He pulled himself to the edge of the chair and leaned in close to Carl, "You and her?"

Carl broke into another laugh, "No sir, she has a husband. And besides, we just met today."

"Don't make no matter if she has a husband. If she likes ya, that's all that counts." Mr. Chermak pushed himself back into his chair, "Besides, she's too skinny. I like my women with a little," he put his hand in the air and partially opened and closed his fingers, "you know, meat on them bones."

Sophie interjected, "Mr. Chermak, I'm right here. And just so you know, I agree, I like my men with a little, you know, too. And I don't have a husband; I have an ex-husband. I work for him."

Mr. Chermak winked at Carl, "There you go, young man."

Carl smiled again, thinking this was another waste of time. As he was about to get up and leave, Mr. Chermak's expression changed, "Shame what happened to that girl isn't it." Carl relaxed back into his chair.

"Tell me about it." Carl pulled out his phone and started the recording app and placed it on the table before Mr. Chermak.

"I remember the day. I was watching TV, Price is Right, still like the old host better than the new guy. He tries too hard to be funny. Anyway, I got up to take a pee, just happened to look out the window and I see this guy push this girl into the roof of the car. Her head bounced off that roof like a basketball off the backboard. I wasn't sure what happened, so I keep looking. The guy just picks her up and tosses her in the back seat and drives off."

"Did you tell the police about this?"

"No, why should I? I thought it was some lovers fight. At the time, I didn't believe it was what it turned out to be. I didn't know the girl was kidnapped until I read it in the paper when I got back."

"Back? Back from where?" Sophie interest peaked, and she pulled up a seat and sat beside Carl.

"Right after I took a pee and finished watching the Price is Right, I had to go to the hospital and have my prostrate removed."

"Prostate," Carl corrected the old man.

"Whatever. Anyway, this skinny guy had some strength, he just picked her up and tossed her into the back seat like she was nothing."

"How long were you in the hospital?" Sophie asked.

"Must be a week or more. I got a nasty infection, had to stay in isolation with a tube in my arm the whole time. They kept taking blood until they said the infection was gone."

Carl turned to Sophie, "That explains why the police never spoke to Mr. Chermak. He wasn't home when they came by to talk to the tenants in the building." He turned his attention back to the old man, "Did you see anything else?"

"When the guy tossed the girl into the car, he stopped for a second, then like he knew I was looking at him, he turned and looked right at me. He was scary. Skinny face, weird eyes. He just didn't look at me; he looked into me."

"Skinny, weird eyes, how weird? You saw that from here?"

"Even from here, you could see them, dark, evil eyes." Mr. Chermak shivered slightly.

Carl reached out and touched Mr. Chermak hand as it rested on the arm of the chair, "Think back Mr. Chermak, close your eyes, look at the man in the parking lot, did you see anything else?"

Mr. Chermak closed his eyes tightly; his bushy eyebrows moved like white caterpillars along his forehead, let his mind go back to that day, "Skinny white man, eyes that could burn the crucifix. He wasn't tall, wasn't short either, average, but skinny. Nothing. Sorry." He turned his head like he was attempting to see things from a different angle then opened his eyes, "Did that help?"

"It did. Thank you, Mr. Chermak." Carl and Sophie stood. "Is there anything I can get you before we leave?"

Mr. Chermak chuckled, "Yeah, a new set of legs so I can walk more than a few feet without pain, and a girlfriend." He laughed loudly at himself, "Nothing. I'm good."

Sophie stood over the old man, "Can't help you with the new legs sir but if I could recommend that the next time you see something like what happened to the girl, you call the cops. You don't have to give your name."

As Carl and Sophie made their way to the apartment door, Mr. Chermak yelled out, "Did that skinny man kill the girl?"

Without turning around, Carl yelled back, "He did."

"It's my fault isn't it, you know, for not calling the cops when I saw him take her."

Carl sighed deeply, fearing he made the old man feel guilty, "No sir, you aren't responsible. Skinny man is the one who killed her."

"You gonna catch him?" "Count on it."

Sophie closed the door as the two of them entered the hall. She stood at the door as Carl was making his way to the elevator. "You want to hit up a few more apartments? I've got more time to spare."

Carl pressed the down button, turned, and walked back to where Sophie stood. He pulled a business card from his suit jacket and presented it to her. She took it and pocketed it without looking at it. "I have to get back. I appreciate your help. I couldn't have done it without you. If you hear of anything around the building, call. That's my cell number." He went back to the elevator door, looked up at the display and realized the lift hadn't moved yet and decided to take the stairs.

*****

Paul walked into the coroners' suite, placed the foil container with what was left of the cake on the stainless-steel table and called out for Maura. He walked to the back office, peered in and saw only an empty chair. He went back to the hall, looked right then left, no one in sight. Turning around, Paul saw Maura standing over the cake, running her finger along the edge of the foil, scooping up icing, then licking her finger.

"Where the Hell did you come from?"

With her finger still in her mouth, Maura turned her head to the bathroom. She licked her finger clean and was about to go in for another swipe of icing when Paul pulled the cake away from her and slid it further down the table.

"Hey. I washed my hands after I used the loo."

"Teaching tool." Paul pulled up a silver stool and offered one to Maura.

"I have some questions. Sorta fill in the blanks if you will."

Maura looked at the finger she ran through the icing, seeing that some remained, she stuck her finger in her mouth to get whatever frosting remained. "Whaddya got?"

Paul spun slightly on the stool, "You said something the other day, something about the Young Frankenstein movie."

Maura squinted, cast Paul a puzzled look, "You bring me cake and ask about Young Frankenstein. You wanna come over tonight and watch it? I have it on Blu-ray."

"No. Tell me about the Frankenstein story."

"What does the cake have to do with Frankenstein?"

Frustrated, Paul pulled the foil container close to him, pulled a pen from his suit jacket and point it at Maura, "This is a bit far-fetched but stay with me." He took in a deep breath, "I haven't exactly thought this through myself, but I have a theory, it's out there, like way, way, out there." Paul symbolically pulled his brain from his skull and threw it high in the air.

He settled down and continued with the story, "Girls are going missing, two so far, a third dead, parts are missing. We have one arm from one girl, a torso from another and we might have more girls missing from other jurisdictions, but that's all we have right now."

Maura was eyeing the cake, "Tell me something I don't know. We gonna eat that cake or not?"

"Not. I need it to make a point."

Paul paused for a moment to organize his thoughts, "OK, so, arms, legs, heads, go missing from different girls, right? What if we have a Frankenstein?" "Well, technically, Frankenstein was the doctor, the monster was called "IT" or Frankenstein's monster. Remember I told you all this?"

"Maura, you're missing the point." Paul placed the cake between them, "My friend was serving cake, dropped a piece and put it back in the container."

"Which piece? Is it still clean?"

"Stop fucking with me. Concentrate Maura." Paul was quickly losing patience, "She put the piece back in the container in the wrong spot. The little swirls in the icing didn't match up, so she tried to make it match by taking the knife and blending the icing." He pointed to the area with the blended icing.

Paul looked up and saw the Maura was now caught up in what he had to say. "We know the piece of cake went someplace else, but she tried to make the cake look complete. Now, I'm just saying, what if the body parts are coming back because they don't match. What if the unsub is trying to make a whole cake. You know, building his own Frankenstein's monster?"

Maura stood up, "Holy fuck." She reached down, ran her finger through the icing and licked her finger clean. "The sicko is blending the body parts to make a new girl. Swirling the icing to make it look like one big piece of cake. Holy fuck." She ran her finger through the icing again, "This guy is building his own monster. But why?"

Paul looked at Maura, "The perfect girl. All the best parts. That's my guess. The best legs, the best arms, the best hands, the best of everything or shit, I just thought, what if he was dumped, and he has a particular plan in mind, a specific girl and he wants a real-life version." Paul caught himself, "Well, dead version."

"Maybe he has a plan, a vision of what the perfect woman is. And that could be a dead girl. Maybe he wants her that way. Maybe he has a thing for dead people; they don't talk back, argue, they do have a certain benefit over the living."

Paul chuckled, "I'm not a psychologist, but the guy could just be fucking nuts."

Maura grabbed a chunk of cake with her hand and started to nibble on the edge.

"Really? We're talking about building a person from different body parts, and you're eating."

Maura took another bite, "I missed lunch."

Paul composed himself, "Am I way off base, is this even possible? Sewing someone together?"

Maura finished the piece of cake, "Of course, with the dead it's easy. Line up the parts and sew them together. Did you know the Nazis used to do that to live patients in the concentration camps? They would experiment on twins, cut off their legs or arms and switch them and see if they rejected the body parts. They didn't live long thank God, but it did lead to a lot of what we know today about rejection. The Nazi doctors butchered the patients, but essentially, it's the same process and much easier with a dead person. Anyone with basic anatomy could do it."

"Cutting the limbs off, making sure you don't hack the bones, you want the skin to match and the bones to fit into the joints right, that would take some skill wouldn't it?"

"If you want the suture lines to look good and the arms and legs to articulate, you bet that would take some skill."

Paul looked around, he pointed at the freezers, "Those things, the freezers, he would need a freezer, I mean, the body would start to decompose quickly, get pretty ripe. He would need a freezer, wouldn't he?"

Maura nodded, "Of course. And if it were a chest freezer, it would have to be long enough. No wait that wouldn't work unless he had a winch. It would be next to impossible to lift a frozen body out of a freezer by yourself unless you were really fucking strong. Even then, it would be difficult. My guess, a drawer like what we have here. That way you could pull out the body and work on it. Or..."

Paul waited for Maura to continue. She was thinking, not saying a word. "A walk-in freezer. She would be on a table, like my table or a wooden table or you could use a freaking dining room table. He could walk all around her, do whatever he had to do and not have to lift her or pull her out. He wants to admire her. See what he created. Yup, that's my guess."

*****

Sam pushed his cart between the rows of desks. He heard the familiar sound of a typewriter further down the aisle and saw a single light illuminating the desk. As he cleaned each workstation, wiping down the desk and emptying the paper into the recycling blue bin, he looked over each partition and to check on Carl. The typewriter kept clacking away as Sam worked his way closer. With each strike of the keys on the platen, the sound brought him back to the day when he was still the publisher of the paper. A few feet from Carl's desk, he stopped, the unique sound had a cathartic effect on the janitor as he closed his eyes and remembered what it was like forty years earlier when he was younger.

Sam released himself from the trance, poked his head around the partition. Carl looked up, took in a deep breath and pushed his chair back, "Take a seat, Sam." Carl turned around, used his foot to hook the chair in the cubicle behind him and pushed it towards him. He grabbed the chair, spun it around and took a seat.

"That was some article today." Sam reached into his trolley and pulled out the edition released earlier in the day, unfolded the paper to the article and placed it before Carl.

Carl pushed the paper to the edge of the desk, "I had to tell the story."

"Your job young man, whether you like it or not, is to write the story. It's your publisher's job to decide if it deserves to be told. Can you prove what you wrote?"

Carl snatched the paper, unfolded it to his article, scanned it, then read aloud, "...the physical similarities between the deceased body parts are surely not coincidental. The ages of all three victims are under the age of twenty-five. If placed side by side, it would be difficult to identify one victim's body part from another.

A source within the police department confirmed that the physical characteristics are so similar that one could mistake them as being from the same victim. It is for that reason that the police are looking for a single suspect in all three slayings that they believe are connected. The reason why someone would attack three women of similar appearance has eluded the investigative team.

The suspect is described as male, Caucasian, between the ages of 20 to 35, of average intelligence working in a position that gives him freedom to move about without bringing attention to himself."

Carl closed the paper, "I can prove it all. This is what Nora is pissed about. The fact that I've connected all three of the murders in a way that no one suspected or would say. I think it's the whole creep factor that's wigging everyone out."

"And everything you said can be confirmed?" Sam asked. "I can't give my confidential source away but yeah."

"Don't ever make anyone force you to give up your source. That's sometimes the only thing that keeps people honest; the fear that someone may rat them out." Sam spun around in his chair. "What did Nora say?"

Carl unfolded the paper again, found a pair of scissors in the drawer and began to cut the article out, "Nora won't stand up to the owners. The owners don't want to piss people off because they need the subscriptions and paper sales are down. Even our online edition is barely scraping by. Everyone is afraid of lawsuits, pissing off the readers. No one wants news anymore. They want fluff, not reality."

Sam continued to spin while sitting in the office chair as Carl spoke. "It's hard to deal with life. Sometimes I get overwhelmed myself. A little fluff never hurt anyone." Sam reached out, grabbed the end of Carl's desk to stop his spin. He looked at Carl as his head continued to swim. "Whoa. I'm too old to be doing that." He placed a hand to his head, "Anyway, listen, write your story, tell the truth, don't be so, I don't know, melodramatic. Tell the truth without making it sound so macabre. Do you have any more leads?"

Excited, Carl pulled his notepad from his jacket pocket, he flipped through the pages, stopped and told Sam all the details of the visit to the apartment building.

Sam stood, smiled, placed his hand on the young man's shoulder, "Tell the story," took hold of his cart and walked away.

Carl watched as the old man sauntered down the aisle, realizing that Sam was teaching him what a reporter was in the early days. He continued to watch as Sam pushed the cart. Carl admired the old man, wishing he had been his editor. Carl turned his attention back to the notebook, scanned the notes and began to type. As Carl pounded out his story, the sound of the old typewriter echoed in the newsroom.

*****

Ken, Paul and Dan were sitting in the only boardroom of the police department. They had brought all the case files into the room, the whiteboard was taken from Paul's desk and placed at the end of the table, and all three of them typed feverishly searching for any information on amputations and transplantation. Paul had invited Maura to join them in case she had something to add as he presented his theory to his friends.

Dan pushed Ken's shoulder, "Hey, did you guys know they're doing limb transplants on amputees. Arms more than legs but it says here they will be trying a full head transplant soon. It's one thing to get a heart, liver, kidney from someone. You never see the organ; it's inside you. Those face transplants are just, well, gross. But if they can get everything worked out, imagine looking down, and one hand is yours, and the other is a transplant. Two different hands on the same person. Two different sets of fingerprints." Dan thought about the ramifications, "Our job is going to be a whole lot harder in the future.'

Ken leaned over to see Dan's laptop screen, "Seriously. They can do all that shit?"

"That's what it says here. Hey, if it's on the internet it has to true right," Dan chuckled.

Maura weighed in, "The advancements on limb transplants are probably further ahead than anyone really knows. A lot of science is conducted behind closed doors and isn't presented until after they know if the procedure is successful. I don't think the public wants to know what kind of animal cruelty actually exists in the name of science."

Paul considered what Maura had said, "If the advancement is further along than we know, would our guy have to have access to those studies?"

Dan and Ken turned to Maura. "Not really. If this guy is doing what you think, the vic's are dead. The procedures are easy. No real risk. Other than having to kill the vic first that is."

Paul left his laptop and stood behind Ken and Dan, peering over their shoulders, "I'm just spit balling guys. Do you think the girl could be alive while these surgeries are being done?"

Dan didn't look back at Paul, "I doubt it. The article talks about teams of surgeons and physiotherapists and months or years of rehab. And that's for one arm. I can only image the team behind the scenes to make this work. The facility alone would be massive and the cost extreme. There would be no way a lone person or even two or three could pull together something this complex. Not to mention the cost, it would be in the hundreds of thousands or more."

Paul thought about what Dan had just said, "We all in agreement that the girl would be dead?"

Ken, Maura and Dan shook their heads.

Ken turned and looked up at Paul, "What makes you think the unsub is doing this, what did you call it, this theory of yours?"

"I called it the Frankenstein theory. You make one new girl outta many. You saw the pictures, the arms, hands, fingers, nails, body shape, they all coulda been from one girl, right?"

Ken still looked puzzled.

Paul walked around the table to face Ken and Dan, "If you want to brick your house, you use the same type of bricks. Otherwise, the house looks odd, different colors, different styles, things just don't fit. Am I making sense Maura?"

She nodded in agreement.

Paul continued, "I'm thinking this guy is a perfectionist. He has a goal."

"Which is?" Dan asked.

"To have the perfect woman. Whatever is in his mind, whatever he sees as the perfect woman. It would certainly be different than what you and I think, but in his mind, he knows exactly what he wants. And if it takes three or four girls with all the parts from them to build the one single perfect woman, in his mind, she will be the perfect woman. Hear me out. One: two torsos, no arms, no legs, no head. Two: one arm found. Three: we found fishing line in the arm. He may be using fishing line as sutures. I asked Maura, sutures eventually dissolve or breakdown. Fishing line can potentially last forever. If he was sewing the parts together, why not use fishing line. Somehow, this guy knows when a body part is faulty. They found a tumour in Paige Kirkby's arm and Abigail Schneider had cancer too. You've heard of dogs that can sniff out people with cancer, what if this guy has a dog that can do that or maybe he can do that? What if he can tell when someone has cancer?" Paul was excited. He felt like he finally understood exactly what the unsub was doing. "My Frankenstein theory. This guy is a modern-day Dr. Frankenstein. At least, I think so. But my theory is sound."

Ken and Dan considered what Paul had just explained. "Do you think the guy is sick enough to try and bring her back to life? Like they did in the movies," Ken had a disgusted look on his face.

Paul paced around the room, trying to contain his excitement, "We all know you can't do that. But even if he tried, what harm can he do, she's already dead. The worst you can do is bring her back to life."

Dan had a horrible thought, "What's he doing with the parts he doesn't want?"

Ken reminded Dan, "Two torsos and an arm so far. What haven't we found?"

Paul picked up a can of Dr. Pepper, took a drink, "At this point, I'm more concerned about what happens next. What if he isn't finished? What if he needs more body parts? What if he doesn't have all the parts to make a whole?" Paul felt his personal phone vibrate in his pocket. He pulled it out, saw the name on the screen, without excusing himself, ran from the room. Paul's pulse quickened, his palms moist, he swiped the icon to answer the call, "Hi. I've been waiting months for your call."

*****

The room was cold, below freezing, and with each breath, he could see the vapors rise and disappear above him. The room was large enough to work around the stainless-steel table placed in the centre. The table wheels were locked to prevent it from rolling as he worked. LED lights were set in the ceiling, evenly spaced to avoid even the tiniest of shadow, providing Will with a perfectly lit workspace. The LED lights were chosen so that they could remain on and not create any heat in the room.

Will had purchased all the components for a walk-in freezer and insulated

146

the floors, walls and ceiling and placed the evaporator unit inside the freezer and outside the house hidden beneath the back deck. The walls, ceiling and floor had been strapped, and urethane foam sprayed between the studs and the walls lined with rigid foam insulation. The fans blew freezing air into the room to keep it a constant minus ten. It meant that he had to wear a winter jacket, toque, gloves and insulated pants to work, but it was worth it.

On the table, a woman's body lay uncovered on the cold stainless steel. The body rigid, not from rigour but from being frozen. Her eyes were open, staring up at the ceiling, seeing nothing, void of emotion, unable to comprehend the events that went on in the room around her. She stopped caring long ago. The skin was a pasty pale white, hard to the touch. All the blood had been carefully drained out when she first arrived, and the various body parts preserved in one of the many freezers in the basement.

He removed a glove and ran his fingers lightly across the frozen skin of her cheek. He felt something stir within him. Unable to pull his gaze from her eyes, his fingers ran down her neck, across her breast, slid over her stomach, passing by the vagina instead veering off to her left outer thigh. He stopped at her knee and made tiny circles around her patella. He traced her knee cap and took in a deep breath then continued to her feet. He admired his work. The sutures were even spaced where he added the appendages, the arm where it attached to the shoulder, the hand at the wrist. He had used a Wartenburg wheel to run along the skin, piercing evenly spaced marks along the skin before the monofilament fishing line to sew the parts together. He had practiced his suturing technique and perfected the method of joining the two body parts, making the suture and hiding the knot inside the skin. His method was almost perfect.

The right leg had been carefully removed from one body along the natural fold from the groin to the hip. The incision had been precise and exact. He made sure the muscles, ligaments and tendons, and the femoral artery was undamaged during the amputation. The head of the femur was aligned with the socket in the pelvis of the main torso, and he moved the leg around to ensure a proper fit. The last two sets he had weren't a fit, and regardless of what the pieces looked like, they had to be perfect.

With his eyes closed, he remembered how she had looked, every curve, the angle of her jaw, her raven black hair, how her body felt. Soon, he thought. But only when she was ready. He covered the body on the table with a white cotton sheet, turned off the lights and closed the door. He removed his heavy jacket, hung it up on a hook beside the door, stuffed the gloves into the jacket pockets and went upstairs.

*****

Will heated his soup, grabbed a large whole wheat bun, placed his dinner on the table with the newspaper laid out beside the bowl, sat down, ready to eat a late dinner. He sank his spoon into the soup, blew across the hot liquid then sipped it. He repeated this many times until he found the article written by Carl Kadner. Will tore a chunk from the roll and ate it as he read the article, smiled broadly, laughing at times as the article described the events and who the reporter thought might be behind the murders. He was amazed at the conclusions Carl had come to, "He's good, wrong but good," he thought to himself.

Will dipped his spoon and took another mouthful as he continued to read. "This guy is pretty smart." He tore another piece of bread and this time ran it around the edge of the bowl. He bit into the moist crust as he finished the article.

He brought the bowl to the sink, washed the dishes, dried them and put them away. Will wiped down the counter, folded the cloth and draped it over the tap and brought the moist towel to the laundry. He smirked as he thought about the article and what the reporter thought of him, even his own actions sickened him at times, but it was a means to an end.

In the distance, Will heard his cell phone chime. He went to the hall table, retrieved his phone and saw that Katy had texted him. He read her message, typed a reply, grabbed his jacket and car keys and headed out the door.

He walked past the dogs as they slept in the yard. Will called out to them. They raised their heads and broke into a full run to the edge of the yard and stopped at the chain link fence. Will walked over, extended his hand, they sniffed it. He scratched their heads, told them he wouldn't be long, got in the car and drove away.

Katy was waiting at the coffee shop. She had both hands wrapped around the paper cup, warming her hands. She had just received the text from Will informing her he would join her shortly. She was looking forward to seeing Will again. They didn't have plans to meet, but she was feeling special, hoping things would move forward with Will and thought a cup of coffee, some small talk, would lead to something more. She anxiously waited for him to show up, shuffled her feet under the table and couldn't keep still. Each time the door opened, her eyes would dart up to see who had arrived. She smiled broadly, only to be disappointed when she didn't see Will. Katy took another sip of her coffee; the drink was cooling down quickly. She removed the lid, looked in to see that the cup was almost empty. Katy couldn't believe she had almost finished her drink. With one large gulp, she downed the last of her coffee, left her jacket on the chair and went to stand in line for another. She rationalized that she must be really nervous if she finished her drink that quickly.

Katy tossed her empty cup in the trash, stood in line and waited her turn at the counter. One by one, she moved closer until she was at the counter. As she was about to place her order, she jumped as she felt someone grab her waist. Katy spun around to see Will standing behind her. She wrapped her arms around him, hugged him and kissed his cheek.

"Glad you could make it."

Will simply smiled, told her to take her seat and he would bring the coffee to the table.

May 4

It was just before midnight, the office building was empty, even Sam had already completed his office cleaning and left for the night. Carl rubbed his right eye where it struck the desk. Sleep deprived one moment, pain the next. He stood, pulled his jacket from the back of the chair, donned it as the phone rang. He picked it up answering with "Yeah" forgetting where he was.

"Is that the way you answer the phone?"

"Sorry, I'm working on a few hours' sleep for the last few days. Who is this?" Carl was too tired to recognize the voice.

"Do you want the latest from PD central or not?"

"Maura?" Carl felt a burst of energy, took his seat and fumbled for a pen. "Why didn't you call my cell?"

"I figured it would be harder to trace a call to a general number than a cell. Maybe I'm just full of shit or paranoid but what the fuck."

"Whatcha got?" Carl knew this had to be good if Maura was calling him.

"Go stream Young Frankenstein and read up on limb transplants." Maura figured being cryptic was more fun. "Had a chat with the detectives."

"What the fuck are you talking about? I don't have time to watch movies." Carl was more than a little frustrated.

"Watch the movie then do your research, Carl." Maura hung up the phone.

He leaned back in his chair, rubbed his eyes, "Young Frankenstein and limb transplants. Huh." Removing his jacket, he pulled his laptop closer and clicked on the Netflix icon. "I'm going to need another energy drink," he said out loud for no one to hear.

*****

At that moment, Paul stood before Nicole's house, wondered if what he was about to do was right and knocked at her door. He waited for a few moments, knocked again, still no answer. He waited, was about to call her when the overhead light came on, and he heard the door creak open. An eye peered between the crack then swung wide open.

"What's going on?" Nicole was wearing flannel pajamas and Croc sandals.

"Can we talk?" Paul looked as though he had been up for days, his hair askew, bags under his eyes, he looked physically and emotionally exhausted. Nicole opened the door wide inviting Paul inside. Without saying a word, Paul stepped past Nicole and went directly to the couch and fell into it. Nicole didn't detect a scent of alcohol as he brushed past on the way to the living room. She followed and took a seat directly across from him. "Coffee?" she offered.

Paul didn't answer. Instead, he asked Nicole a question, "Do you remember when you read my picture that I carry?"

Nicole nodded. "Did you call?"

"Called me." He reached down, untied his running shoes and pulled them off. He squirmed out of his suit jacket and let it fall to the floor beside his shoes. "Can I crash here on the couch?" It wasn't so much a request as telling Nicole he was going to do what he was asking. He fell to the side, curled up and before she could answer, he had fallen asleep.

Nicole picked up the jacket and laid it over his shoulders. She stood over him, looking at Paul wondering what had happened and went back to bed.

*****

Katy and Will sat across from each other in the nearly deserted coffee shop. It was almost one and more customers were leaving than entering. Canned music played overhead; the baristas were cleaning up the coffee machines, readying them for another busy day.

Will sat back in his chair, Katy was fidgeting with her jacket and constantly playing with her cell phone. He noticed Katy avoiding eye contact and her inability to focus on the conversation. Will smiled politely, often looking past Katy towards one of the workers. She was cute and young with shoulder length thick dark hair. He would watch the young girl for a moment when Katy was looking away, then glance back at Katy. Will would sneak a peek at the young girl, waiting to see if she had an aura, nothing.

"So, tell me, you asked me here, and now you're playing shy. What's going on?" He laughed, "You're acting like a fourteen-year-old." He looked past her to the young girl.

Katy reached across, gently touched Will's hand that held his coffee cup, "It's just that, well, I was wondering if things were going to go anywhere from here?"

Will let out a loud belly laugh, "From here," he pointed to the table, "like from right here?"

Katy slapped his hand, "Not from here, here," she pointed to the spot on the table Will touched. She pushed back in her chair, "I mean for us, you know, from this point forward."

"I'm just shitting with ya. I see what you mean. I've been thinking a lot about you too, us too." Will liked Katy, considering what he was thinking of doing to her the first day they met, he realized he must truly like this girl. "You're kind of special, and pretty. What do you have in mind?"

Katy felt slightly embarrassed to broach the subject, "I don't know, it's our third date. We get along well. I like you; I think you're cute and funny. I like you."

"Me too."

"So, what do you want to do?" Katy asked coyly.

"Let's finish our coffee and see how things go from there. Deal?"

"Deal." Under the table, Katy tapped Will's foot with her boot and gave him a look. Will replied with the same look.

Will stood, "Let me get us some fresh drinks. Large black?" Katy nodded and smiled at him. "Anything else?"

"I would love a scone. Nothing with raisins or cheese. Plain or something sweet."

"Got it."

"Oh, don't go to that one," Katy pointed to the large barista behind the counter.

Will looked at the pleasant girl serving customers with a broad smile, "What's wrong with her?"

Katy shivered, "Fat people creep me out. She probably tastes half the food before it's brought out."

Instead, he pointed to the one girl he had been watching all night, "That one meet with your approval?"

She nodded softly, "Thank you."

Will timed his approach to the counter to make sure the girl he was eyeing would be the one taking his order. As she walked by the register, Will jumped in to place his order. The girl smiled at Will; he smiled back.

"May I take your order?" she asked.

"You certainly may," Will looked at her name badge, "Kerry." He placed his order for two more coffees and two scones.

"Take-out or are you having them here?" Kerry asked.

"Make that take-out; it's getting late. Thanks."

*****

Carl finished watching "Young Frankenstein" and Googling limb transplants. He shook several empty cans of Red Bull scattered on his desk that he had consumed to help keep himself awake. Carl understood why he was researching transplants and why Maura had asked him to watch the movie beforehand. He printed several articles relating to the limb transplants, many were decades old some newer, and he even found a few that mentioned the German concentration camps of the Second World War.

Carl now had a goal for the article he was working on and what he had to do first thing in the morning. He was too tired to go home, looked across the newsroom to Nora's office and decided to stay put. He did his zombie walk into the office, fell hard into the sofa, stretched out, balled up his second-hand suit jacket as a pillow and fell asleep.

*****

As Kerry left for the night, Will had readied himself for a sudden onset of nausea and kept the take-out bag the scones were placed in at the ready when Kerry served him Katy's coffee.

Kerry opened the door to leave, as Will grabbed his stomach and expelled a mouthful of coffee into the bag to make his fake illness seem legitimate. Katy reached over the table, touched Will softly on the shoulder as he hunched over and heaved again. Will looked up, gave Katy his best tired, sudden illness look, "I don't feel well," he said softly.

"I'll take you home." Katy was quickly donning her jacket and standing to take care of Will.

He held out his hand, "The last thing I want is you in a confined space with me, breathing in my germs and getting sick. I'm sorry. You were looking forward to this evening, but I don't think you want to get anywhere near me right now." He grabbed his stomach for effect and moaned. "I promise, if I'm not better tomorrow, you can come over and take care of me. If I'm better, dinner tomorrow night. K?"

Katy smiled, disappointed that her plans had fallen through, "All right. You gonna be OK driving home?"

Will shook his head side to side, "No, but I don't want to puke in your car, and I think our relationship is too new to have to hold my hair back while I throw up." He laughed then let out a soft moan. He excused himself, apologized again, bent low to give to kiss Katy on the cheek then pulled back, "Sorry, I don't want to get you sick in case it's contagious."

He made his way to the door, moaned then exited the restaurant. He continued his sickly walk, holding his stomach, giving an Oscar-winning performance, looked back to make sure Katy wasn't watching from the door, dropped the bag of coffee vomit to the ground and scanned the parking lot for Kerry. Will found her as she slammed her car door, and pulled out of a spot at the back of the lot. He ran for his vehicle, keyed the engine to life and followed her at a distance. He knew what he was going to do and powered off his cell phone.

*****

It was the time between night and day. The people who worked during the day were long asleep, soon to be woken by their alarm clocks or cell phones. Only the few who worked the night shifts wouldn't have any reason be out in this section of town at this time of the morning.

Kerry drove her car down the street to her apartment building. It certainly wasn't her first choice to live, she wanted something newer, modern, but her budget overruled and this place won by default.

Kerry pulled into the parking lot. If there was a security system in place, it had long fallen into disrepair, and the owner never bothered to have it fixed. She found an open spot, kept the vehicle idling and the headlights on to provide some light until she was ready for the short walk to the back door. She grabbed her purse, killed the engine then made her way to the entrance. If Kerry had turned the car off earlier, she might have heard the car follow her into the parking lot and park not far from hers. The driver made his way along the unkempt bushes and hid among them knowing she would have to pass close by to make her way to the back door. Will crouched in the woods, waiting for her to walk past his location and he would make his move. As she neared, he got down on all fours, and crawled between the parked cars and stopped close to the back bumper.

Kerry's pace was steady and grew slightly louder in the stillness. Will pressed himself against the vehicle and felt the cool metal through his jacket. Evenings were still cold for May, and he realized that he could see the wisp of steam when he exhaled. He held his breath as Kerry approached.

Will kept his head down, staring at the parking lot when her first shoe appeared, he reached up, grabbed Kerry from behind, threw her to the ground between the two cars and straddled her. Both knees held her arms down, his hands placed around her neck, Kerry looked up and saw the man wearing the ball cap. She recognized him as fear took over. She was powerless to fight against her attacker. She began to randomly kick her legs out attempting to get some leverage to force the man off her.

Kerry tried to take in a breath, but nothing happened. It was only then she knew what was happening; it wasn't rape, the man wanted her dead. She bent her knees, brought her feet to her bum, planted them, then quickly bucked her pelvis up high. Will, caught off guard, released his grip and was sent flying over Kerry. She knew she had seconds to react, took in a deep breath, felt the fresh air enter her lungs, had renewed energy, noticed the SUV beside her and rolled beneath it. Kerry looked out from under the SUV and saw that her purse with her cell phone was still between the two vehicles. Her attacker was still on his side facing away from her, Kerry took the risk. She reached out and took hold of the purse handle and pulled it in. She yanked hard then felt a jerk pulling the bag back. Kerry looked out to see her attacker had a hold of the bottom of the purse. With her free hand, she reached inside the purse, fumbled for her cell phone as the two of them fought for control. Kerry felt the plastic shell of the phone with the tips of her fingers as she clawed at it in an attempt to gain possession of the device. Kerry's fingers caught the edge of the phone case and pulled in close. She palmed the phone then let go of the purse handle. The attacker rolled backwards as Kerry relinquished her hold. With her hands quivering, she unlocked the phone and dialed 911.

The attacker rolled towards the SUV and blindly swept his arm, grabbing at Kerry, trying to take hold of anything he could to take control of his victim.

Kerry began yelling loudly at her phone, asking for help, even before she knew if the line had connected. The attacker found her jacket and took hold of her collar. As he began to draw her out, she reached up beneath the SUV and took hold of anything to keep from being pulled out. Kerry reached up and began to scratch and dig her nails into the attackers' hand then turned her head sunk her teeth into the skin between the thumb and index finger. The man screamed in pain, released his grip on the collar, but Kerry's teeth had a firm hold of the skin. Kerry felt his hold release on her jacket and knew she had the upper hand. She tasted blood, and it only drove her desire to inflict more pain. With everything she had, she bit harder and growled like a rabid dog killing its prey. The attacker pulled against her teeth, tearing the skin, eventually ripping free of her grip. Kerry spit out the chunk of skin and blood to the pavement. He pulled his hand back, screamed in pain and held it close. He rolled away, stood up and ran from the parking lot.

*****

Will fell into the driver's seat holding his hand. Blood flowed between his fingers as he held his injured left hand. The pain was so intense; he felt tears welling up. He wanted to look at the wound to see the damage, but he knew he had to leave. He turned the key, the engine caught, and he slowly drove away to avoid attention.

He stuffed his injured hand in his pocket to prevent getting blood on the car's interior. Will could feel his mind getting cloudy with pain but fought against the sensation to pass out. He steered his car home, travelling only slightly faster than the posted speed limit and obeying all the traffic laws to avoid being stopped. As he drove, he passed a strip plaza, pulled in, removed his ball cap and jacket that could identify him from the witness statements and tossed the clothing into the dumpster. He found a rag in the trunk and wrapped his injured hand until he got home.

Will pulled the car into the driveway, killed the engine and almost passed out in the front seat. The dogs barking in the backyard kept him from losing consciousness. He sat up, exited the car, stumbling his way into his house, knowing he would need a good excuse for his injury and knew exactly what he would do. Will bandaged his hand before crawling into bed, turned his cell phone back on, texted Katy and told her he was feeling much better and asked if they could meet for lunch. He put his phone on the nightstand and fell into a deep sleep.

*****

The morning sun was above the tree line as Paul Hammond exited Nicole's apartment. He double checked the door as he left. His SUV was still on the street where he'd left it the night before.

Nicole was already gone when he woke to find himself alone. She had left a short note telling him to make himself at home. He decided to accept her offer and threw his clothes in the dryer for a quick spin while he had a shower. After the shower, he cleaned the tub, sink and toilet, failing to find a hook to hang the wet towel, decided the shower curtain bar was the next best thing. Paul let his clothes cool before getting dressed, left a short "Thank you" on the same sheet of paper Nicole left for him and thought it would be best to pick up take-out on the way to the station.

Paul walked down to his SUV, feeling a little ashamed, although he had nothing to be anxious about. He scanned the neighborhood; no one was out on the sidewalk or in their yards, quickly unlocked the door and drove away. He tapped the phone button on the steering wheel, flicked the down button until he found the number and hit dial. When the automated voice answered, Paul, asked for Ken Simmons, his extension rang, "Hello."

"Ken. Paul."

"What the Hell happened yesterday? We were in the middle of the bull session, and you just flew outta here. You OK?"

"Got some bad family news. Sorry about leaving and not telling anyone. I'm on my way in. I haven't eaten yet, so I'm stopping at Starbucks. Coffee's on me. Text me the order."

Paul knew Ken spent most of his after-tax food budget at Starbucks and wouldn't say no to a free drink. It was Paul's way of ensuring that Ken couldn't be upset with him leaving so abruptly. He disconnected the call and drove to the closest location a few blocks from the station.

He felt his phone buzz in the parking lot, checked the order before entering the restaurant and was happy to see the lineup relatively short. Almost all the tables were occupied with guests abusing the free Wi-Fi offered at every location. As he made his way through the line, he approached the counter as he was about to place his order, Paul overheard a young couple talking about the recent unexplained deaths in town. He suddenly felt ashamed and embarrassed by the fact he had been working the case since November and in seven months, he was no closer than he was the very first day.

The couple began to ridicule the police departments efforts in finding the person responsible. Paul didn't turn around but focused on their conversation and ignored the young girl behind the counter who asked him several times if she could take his order. He stood at the counter; his head partial turned to better hear what they were saying, Paul, felt the anger rise inside him. They only knew what they had read in the papers, social media or online and Paul knew, it was only a fraction of the true story.

The anger inside began to swell. Paul turned towards the table, took a few steps, stopped and walked out of the coffee shop without placing his order. He pushed the glass door open, striking the stop, snapping back hitting him on the shoulder.

He raced back to his car, jumped in, slammed the door, sat behind the steering wheel and slammed his fist into the horn. The blaring sound startled a woman as she walked by and turned to see the man in the car yelling to himself. She paused for a moment, though briefly about asking if she could help then decided to walk on.

Paul raged against the feeling of incompetence that he felt for not being able to solve the case. He was taking the circumstances personally and hearing the conversation in the coffee cemented his justification of inadequacy.

He keyed the engine to life, slammed the gear selector "D" and squealed the tires as he drove away. Paul remembered little of the short drive to the station; his mind flooded with self-loathing and realization of his limitations as a detective. He pulled into the parking lot, the front wheels bumped hard against the parking curb, jostling Paul in his seat. He put the car in park then sat there. It seemed to Paul that he remained in the driver's seat few only a few moments, but when he broke from the trance, he looked at the display on the dash and realized almost fifteen minutes had passed.

He leaned to the right, pulled his wallet from his back pocket and retrieved the picture he carried for so many years. Paul looked at it, recalling what was said last night and how he felt after he hung up the phone. He placed the photo against the dash cluster and stared at the image through the spokes in the steering wheeling. Thoughts raced through his mind, scattered scenes from his life, a collection of snapshots of times in his life that had no relevance other than they formed what was the life of Paul Hammond. There weren't many times that Paul could remember when he was truly happy. Then he asked himself what did he want out of life to be happy. He quickly shook that thought from his mind. Happiness is not for people like him; he didn't deserve happiness. At least, not the kind he dreamt about.

He left the photograph where it was on the dash, slammed the door and locked it. Paul sauntered to the back entrance of the station and swiped his card. He went to his locker, found a few old granola bars and an energy drink and went back to his desk.

Ken saw Paul arrive and was about to ask where his order was when he noticed his friend staring down at the can of Red Bull and bars. Ken went to the coffee machine, made a cup for Paul, walked over, stood on the far side of the desk and placed the mug in front of his friend and walked away. He had seen Paul in this state before, and it was always caused by the same thing. He instinctively knew who it was that had called Paul last night and decided to leave well enough alone. Paul either didn't notice Ken placing the coffee cup on his desk or didn't react.

Paul pulled back the tab on the Red Bull and guzzled the drink down without stopping. He ripped open a granola bar package, broke it in halves, ate one-half, sipped the coffee, then ate the second half. As he crumpled up the bar wrapper, he noticed the best before date was almost a year ago. He took another gulp of coffee, checked the date on the second bar which was the same as the first but ate it anyway.

With his mouth still full, he went over to Ken's desk, tried to ask him to find Dan and meet him in the conference room without spitting out too much food as he spoke. Paul went directly to the squad room, pulled out his notes and began to review everything they had. Not long after, Ken and Dan arrived with their coffee and took a seat.

The two detectives stood watching their friend mull over case reports. These were the same reports they had all gone over several times in the previous months. They both took seats facing Paul and waited for him to pause long enough for him to pay attention to them. Paul ignored them while he flipped through the reports and statements.

"Did we double check the surveillance tapes from the stores from back in November after we got the description of the guy?" Paul asked without looking up.

Ken and Dan glared at each other. "We did take a second look and a third at all recordings we got from the stores in the area. We looked for a skinny guy. It was November; people wear jackets. Kinda hard to see how skinny they are," Dan said sarcastically.

Paul looked up, his tone angry, "Well maybe you should be looking harder. Look at the faces, see if the guy had on gloves, a hat."

Ken got defensive, "We looked. Not once, not twice but three times. If you're having problems, take it up with the person giving you shit. Don't take it out on us. We're doing our best, but we don't have much to go on." Ken stepped in closer and lowered his tone, "Maybe it's time we realized we don't have a handle on this and hand it over to the feds."

Paul stood, prepared to defend his position, then slowly sat back down, "Maybe you're right. We've had this for half a year now and other than a far-out theory, we haven't got jack shit."

Dan knew Paul wasn't upset at either one of them, his frustration had been building for weeks, his finger swirled in the air, "I'm, we, all of us, we're gonna go over every single statement, every piece of evidence, review each photo, talk to Maura, talk to anyone and everyone who may have seen something. If we don't find a new lead, something to go on, we call in the feds. Agreed?"

Paul didn't have to think about the offer; it was the best he was going to get, he nodded in agreement. "How about we go for that coffee run, relax, not talk shop then come back and take a fresh look at everything. Nothing is too far-fetched, too wild to consider. Since I forgot to pick up the coffee, it's on me." Paul had calmed down, his voice back to his normal tone.

*****

Will sat in the emergency department, his left hand wrapped in a towel by the triage nurse. He waited his turn as those patients with more serious injuries or illness went before him.

The lady got up from the chair, and the triage nurse waved Will over. He walked over and sat in the large, high-backed vinyl-covered chair. He cradled his arm while the triage nurse set up the new registration form on her computer system.

"Well, let's see what happened to you today?" Her voice was musical and light, a tone that would make the more severe patient feel at ease. With a gloved hand, she slowly pulled back the white towel she had given him as he walked into the ER earlier. She peeled back a fold, then another, slowly exposing the injury to Will's left hand. When she finally revealed the injury, the experienced nurse didn't even seem surprised by his wounds. The skin between the thumb was torn and there were visible puncture marks across the back of his hand and inside the palm.

"Hmmm. Dog bite you say?"

Will was in extreme pain from the new injury, "Yeah."

"OK then, let's get you registered and get this looked at. Do you have your health card and insurance?"

Will kept his injured hand immobile, reached back to retrieve his wallet, "Shit. I forgot my wallet at home. I left in a hurry and didn't realize I forgot it. I've got cash. Do you know how much it will be?"

The triage nurse thought for a moment, "That depends on the work being done. You might need x-rays, lab work and whatever else the doctor thinks might be necessary."

"I can put down a deposit and either get a refund or pay the balance after."

The nurse pulled up a chart on the computer, reviewed the charges on the hospital pricing policy and wrote down the amount she thought was appropriate.

Will didn't hesitate, pulled out his wallet and paid the entire amount to the nurse.

"In detail sir, can you tell me what happened?"

Will had thought about how he could hide the bite he received from the girl in the parking lot, and after he woke when he got home, he covered his injured hand in a thin piece of raw meat and began to play and tease his German Shephards in the backyard. The dogs smelled the flesh, but Will kept his left hand behind his back. He got the two dogs jumping and excited then stuck his left hand in the one dog's mouth. The dog bit down on the meat, sinking his teeth through the raw meat deep into Will's hand. As the dog tried to pull the food off Will's hand, he forced his hand further into the dog's mouth. He could feel the dog's teeth dig deep into his hand. The pain was more than he imagined when he conceived this plan to cover the first injury with the dog bite.

"I was out back with my two dogs when a stray dog showed up. It was a big dog, black, came running up the driveway and when he got close, he started to growl at my dogs. I have an electric fence that keeps my dogs from getting out but this stray was big and in a bad mood, something was pissing him off. He ran up, changed direction and came at me instead. When he jumped on me, I defended myself by sticking my hand in his mouth. Probably not the smartest thing to do. Anyway, I kicked him off, and he ran away."

"Have you seen this dog before?"

Will shook his head.

"Is your tetanus up to date?" she asked.

"Yeah. I think so."

"We may have to start rabies shots and see if you need a tetanus booster. The doc will make that decision after she examines you. You'll need some stitches. You've got a nasty bite there. Do you want anything for pain?"

"Please." Will had taken several pain pills before he went out and forced his dog to take a chunk of his already injured hand.

The nurse finished typing the incident history then took a set of vitals. She completed her assessment on Will, gave him two extra-strength Tylenol and a small glass of water, then asked him to take a seat and told him that due to the severity of the injury, he would be seen relatively quickly.

Will waited only a few minutes before his name was called. He carefully cradled his injured hand as he stood, walking through the security doors. He was led to a small treatment room and sat on the edge of the bed. Again, he sat waiting for someone to come and treat his wounds.

Upstairs in the same hospital, Kerry was resting comfortably with the help of heavy sedation. The cardiac monitor had been silenced but continued to record her vitals. Kerry rolled back and forth in bed in spite of the medication. She had been brought to the hospital by ambulance hours earlier after calling 911 following the attack. Her injuries had been treated, and she was now admitted in the security wing following her rape attempt. She had severe bruising around the neck where Will had taken hold of her.

The door to Kerry's private room remained open in full view of the nurses' station. Several uniformed police officers continued to take notes while the detectives spoke with the physician in charge of Kerry's case. Detective Liz Cummings who initially talked to Kerry, was focused on note-taking as she spoke to the physician, "She told us there wasn't a sexual attack, she fought him off before he could do anything. Is that your opinion doc?"

The doctor spoke in hushed tones attempting to get the detectives to follow her lead, "I agree. There was no sign of any injury to the victim other than the neck. Whoever did this is very strong. Her larynx is bruised, and I doubt she'll be able to eat solid food for a few days. She still has trouble speaking. Other than that, physically, she's fine. Emotionally, she's doing better than I would. That young girl is very strong. The counsellors will be speaking to her as soon as she wakes up. Right now, that girl needs to sleep. She's been through a terrible ordeal."

"You're sure there were no other injuries than the neck?" Detective

Cummings asked in a way that questioned the doctor's ability to perform a physical exam.

The doctor stepped back and placed her hands on her hips, "You might want to adjust your tone detective or the next time something like this happens, I won't be so cooperative. I know my job. I suggest you curb your attitude. Your team took all the pictures. Perhaps you want to take a look at them and come back and apologize to me after you see there weren't any other injuries than those I've noted."

The detective's eyes never left her notepad and were not at all apologetic for her tone, "It seems a little odd that a rape suspect would try to just choke the vic and not try something else."

"Like?"

"It's not common for a suspect to want to choke his vic to the point of being unconscious. One of the aspects of rape is fear. They want the girl awake and to be afraid. Usually, they try to force the legs open when they're on top."

"Listen, I didn't say it was rape. Those guys over there," the doctor pointed to the two uniformed officers who stood guard over Kerry's room, "are the ones who told me it was rape. Maybe they assumed it was rape, maybe my patient thought it was rape, I don't care whether it was rape or not. We treat the physical injuries the same and assign counsellors to deal with the emotional trauma. Why don't you do your job, instead of telling me how to do mine, and find out who it was that cried rape. Maybe it wasn't rape, and it was a purse snatching gone wrong or maybe an assault or worst. If it wasn't rape, the ordeal you put her through with the rape kit and exam was possibly as traumatic as the attack."

For the first time, the Detective Cummings looked up from her notepad and stared at the doctor's back as she walked away. She turned to her partner, "Who the fuck said this was rape then?"

Her partner shrugged his shoulders, "No fucking clue. I was with you when we got the call at the station that we had an attempted rape."

The first detective walked over the two uniformed officers standing guard at Kerry's door. She separated them and asked the younger looking officer, "Who said this was an attempted rape?"

"We were pulled from patrol. Dispatch told us to come here and secure the room as per protocol for a suspected rape. That's all I know. We," he pointed to his partner then back at himself, "just got here after the ambulance dropped her off. We stayed outside the ER room, followed her up here. We didn't even get a chance to talk to the Paramedics. Maybe they thought it was rape."

"So, who the fuck said this was rape?" The female detective's voice was showing signs of stress and frustration, and her voice was getting louder.

"Ask the guys on the scene. Don't start getting in our face because you can't figure who did what." the officer turned his back to her and walked down the hall, opened the door to the guest bathroom and went inside to avoid further questions by the female detective.

Her partner understood what he had to do and went to the far end of the hall, pulled his cell phone from his pocket and called dispatch. He asked for the names of the responding officers and if they could call him. He left his cell number with the dispatcher and waited patiently for a return call. He wasn't in the mood to deal with his partner's attitude and thought it best to put some distance between her while he waited.

It wasn't long before his cell phone vibrated. He turned away from his partner, swiped the screen icon to answer the phone and spoke quietly. After a short conversation, he hung up, pocketed his phone and re-joined his partner.

"It was a bystander who told the responding officers it was rape. The victim was hysterical at the scene, they tried to keep her calm, she had problems talking because of her throat injury and they went with the rape call. On their report, they said they indicated rape, assault and possible abduction to cover all the bases."

"Fuck." Detective Cummings was annoyed. "Call what's his face and get his fat ass down here."

"Could you be a little more specific?" he chuckled.

"Hammond," she barked as she walked away. "His team covers assaults and shit."

*****

Will watched, fixated, on how Dr. Hernandez was suturing his hand wound. He was hoping to pick up some technique on how to suture. He watched as she carefully found the perfect spot to anchor the curved needle into the skin, pull it with the needle drivers as the thread followed through the skin. She then found the opposite side of the wound, tapped the area of the skin with the end of the needle until she was satisfied she had found the best match.

She had injected the wound with an anesthetic to numb the area, prepped the suture tray and tested the area to make sure her patient couldn't feel anything. She used a forcep to bring the skin edges together to see how the edges would meet before she began to close the large open bite wound. She pulled one side of the skin edges tight, inserted the curved needle with the suture attached then adding stitches along the laceration until one section of the wound was closed.

"We really should have plastics doing this. You have a nasty wound there. There's also a small piece missing, and I'm not sure I can close this wound and make it look right." Dr. Hernandez never took her focus off the wound.

"I'm not too concerned about how it looks." Will chuckled. "I don't have any scars. This is my first battle wound."

"You already signed the paperwork saying you understood the procedure and gave me permission to do this. As long as you know that it won't look pretty."

Will laughed, "I know."

Dr. Hernandez was leaning in close to the wound, her head directly under Will's face. He stared at her long, dark hair, inhaling deeply. He admired her slight frame and tried to imagine what she looked like without the oversized lab coat she wore.

She pulled on a section of skin that hadn't been numbed by the anesthetic. Will let out a soft yelp like a puppy would do if you yanked on its tail. Dr. Hernandez chuckled, "Cute laugh," never looking up from her task. "Do you want a little more freezing? This is going to take a little longer than I thought. The piece of flesh that's missing is little larger than I thought. You may have some difficulty opening your hand completely while this heals until the skin begins to stretch out again."

"I'm fine."

"You don't have to impress me. If it hurts, I've got lots of drugs here to freeze the area." Dr. Hernandez never lost her focus from the task. She attempted to piece together the sections of skin that were now missing. The wound was more than half sutured when she realized that it would be too difficult to hold the skin and attempt to repair the area by herself. Dr. Hernandez removed her gloves, pushed the tray to the far side of the room and excused herself. She pulled back the curtain and left the treatment area.

*****

Carl slammed on the brakes causing the car to lurch forward as he came to a stop on an angle, taking up a spot and a half close to the main entrance of the hospital. He ran from the car, forgetting to lock his vehicle and kept his pace until he arrived at the ER. He slowed to a frenzied walk, went through the Ambulance entrance and not the general entrance for walk-in patients, passed the security desk that was left unattended and made his way to the main patient care section of the ER. Grabbing a patient chart from the corner of a stainless-steel stand, he carried it like he was reviewing the patient's medical history or treatment.

His pace and demeanor were that of someone who belonged in the ER. The department was chaotic; the PA voice above belted out requests every few seconds, few people cared or seemed to notice. There were patients in every bed, staff mauled about, walking passed without question. Carl's mission was to find the girl who had been attacked earlier that morning. When he woke that morning, his scanner was still full of chatter from the on-scene officers and crime scene technicians who were still scouring the scenes for any clue of the incident.

Carl had heard it was an attempted rape, but he knew, everyone in town knew that there hadn't been a sexual assault in years. Instinctively, he felt there was a connection between the murders and this event. He wanted to see if he could speak with the assault victim before any other reporter or the police told her to keep silent.

He walked through the halls, peering into rooms and around curtains. Staff went about their work with little regard to someone who looked like they worked in the hospital. None of the patients matched the description of a young girl who had been attacked. Frustrated, at the end of the hall, he stopped short, causing the person behind to bump into him.

He turned quickly, "I'm so sorry, I'm lost."

"Obviously. Otherwise, you wouldn't have stopped in the middle of the hall," Dr. Hernandez looked frustrated. "Are you just going to stand there or get out of my way?"

Carl stepped aside, "Sorry."

"What are you doing anyway?" She now stood in front of Carl, despite being quite small, there wasn't that much difference in size between her and the man standing before her.

"I work upstairs. I was looking for a friend I heard was here."

"You work here. Where?" she asked suspiciously.

"In the lab." It was the only part of the hospital he could come up with quickly.

"Good. You're with me." Dr. Hernandez took hold of Carl's jacket sleeve and pulled him into the room behind the curtain. "We are so swamped, and I need help with a patient. You can handle a little blood, right?"

Stunned, Carl shook his head and shrugged his shoulders, "Yeah, 'course."

As Dr. Hernandez pulled the curtain back, she told Carl he was about to assist suturing a hand injury.

Carl walked to the side, placed the metal clipboard on the counter and stood behind the patient as Dr. Hernandez donned a fresh pair of gloves.

"You can't help me from over there. Come 'er," she pointed to the exact spot on the floor she wanted Carl to stand. He walked over and planted his feet exactly where the doctor had told him to.

"Well?" she looked at him. "Put on a pair of gloves."

Carl looked around the room, saw the glove dispenser mounted on the wall, walked over and pulled from the box marked small. As he did, a bundle of gloves fell from the table to the floor. Embarrassed, he kicked the fallen gloves to the corner. He held the gloves before him, then attempted to put on nitrile gloves for the first time. Carl struggled to fit his hand in the glove, his fingers found a corresponding part of the glove, but the thumb section of the glove was on the wrong side of his hand. "I must be putting a left glove on my right hand." He looked apologetic.

"They're ambidextrous." Dr. Hernandez pulled the suture tray close and pulled back the sterile towel from the equipment. "Grab another pair of gloves. Oh, there's no way you're a small. Try a medium."

Carl did as instructed, and finally had a pair of white gloves on that fit and all five fingers had found a hole. He walked around and stood where he had been told to stand.

"I thought you said you worked in the lab?" she asked.

Carl again made up a quick lie, "I do. Purchasing."

"Well, you're too late to back out now. You're getting a crash course in suturing."

Carl looked up at Will with raised eyebrows, gave his best "I'm sorry" look without saying a word and stood beside Dr. Hernandez waiting for further direction.

Dr. Hernandez poked Will with a needle, he grimaced. She injected more anesthetic into the wound and told Will it would be another few moments before the medication took effect. Without looking up, she used the needle driver to point back and forth to the Will and Carl, "Patient, meet lab guy. Lab guy, patient."

The two men head bobbed to one another then ignored each other. The doctor used the needle held firmly in the jaw of the driver to poke at the wound. Will didn't react, so she went back to repairing the damage she thought was caused by a dog.

"Forceps please," Dr. Hernandez asked Carl.

He looked at the tray of instruments, confused at what he was looking at. This was the first time he had seen most of these tools in real life.

She pointed, "The ones with the gold ends."

He picked up the forceps, dragged another tool along with it, sending it crashing to the floor. It made a hollow metallic sound as it bounced off the floor.

Will laughed, Dr. Hernandez grimaced.

*****

Paul and Dan exited the elevator, looked right then left down the hall and noticed the officers sitting outside the room. They both turned right and walked silently down the hall. In the hospital room where Kerry lay sleeping, they stopped, introduced themselves, were asked by the officers to show identification before they were permitted into the room.

Kerry lay sleeping, a nasal cannula provided oxygen, the bruising around her neck evidence of the attack. Paul looked at the monitor, unsure what he was looking at, pulled out his notepad and jotted down her vitals in case it was relevant. He was shocked at how young she looked, "a baby" he thought, barely old enough to be in high school. Paul had a difficult time pulling his eyes away from the young girl, feeling sorry she had to endure this horrific event.

He quickly turned on his heels, his running shoes squeaking on the polished hospital floor, exited the room, Dan followed then asked the two officers who remained seated where the initial investigating detectives were. Paul and Dan were told their fellow detectives were in the cafeteria waiting for them.

They made their way once again to the elevators, went down to the main floor where the cafeteria was located. Paul scanned the room and found the two people he was looking for. Both Paul and Dan grabbed a coffee, paid for it and joined the other two officers.

"Thanks for the referral," Paul was sarcastic. "Now you want me to do your work too?"

Detective Cummings was not impressed with Paul's comments, "You want us to do your work too? You've been working on your case for what, half a year and I hear your amazing investigative skills have gotten you exactly nowhere. Maybe you should go back to wearing a uniform if you can ever fit into one again."

Paul shifted in his chair, Dan took hold of Paul's arm and held him back. Paul was about to speak, but Dan interrupted him, "Funny Liz, coming from someone who's been stuck in the same job for the last seven years investigating petty crime and the what, one sexual assault we get every ten years. Maybe one day, you can join our team and find out what real police work is all about, so you can speak from experience." Dan raised his eyebrows and cast Liz a look, "Lose the attitude. Girl or not, I'll fucking punch you in the throat if you ever talk down to us again."

Liz bolted upright knocking over her cup sending coffee across the table. She wanted to say something, but she feared that Dan might follow through on his threat. Instead, she looked at her notepad, then tossed it into Paul's chest. She left her spilled coffee and walked away, partner in tow.

Quietly, Paul leaned closer to Dan and whispered "Thanks." He used a napkin on the table to clean up the spill.

"Actually, if I didn't think I would get fired or charged, I'd fucking kick her arrogant ass. Christ, she bugs the living shit outta me. She's nothing but a fucking loud mouth."

Paul laughed, "I've felt the same way."

He laid the notebook that was tossed at him with such disdain down on the table and began to leaf through her notes. He found the notes Liz had taken at the scene, in the ER and at her room. He scanned the pages one by one, looking for anything that might stand out. There wasn't anything in her notes that indicated her team had found any evidence on scene other than a small piece of skin that the victim had off from her attacker. Her notes stated the evidence had been taken the police station for blood testing and DNA. Paul knew from previous DNA sampling that the results wouldn't be back for months.

Paul opened his notebook and began copying anything of relevance. He didn't find much. Paul passed Liz's pad to Dan and had him review the notes to see if he had missed anything. He used the opportunity to excuse himself and use the washroom.

Paul felt his phone vibrate in his jacket pocket as he stood in front of the urinal. He quickly finished, zipped up, pulled his phone from his pocket, smiled when he saw the caller and answered.

"Hi. This is a nice surprise. What's up?"

Nicole was sitting at her desk at work, leaning back in her chair, "It's a slow day. I asked the manager if I could leave early and she gave me the OK. Are you busy?"

Paul shrugged his shoulder holding the phone against his cheek as he washed his hands. "I'm at the hospital. There's a young girl here who was attacked last night. At first, it was thought it was a rape until they dug a little deeper. Turns out, it may be related to our case."

"Do you have pictures?" Nicole asked with excitement. "Yeah. They're at the station. Why? You wanna do a read?"

Nicole sat upright, "It's almost lunch. If you buy, I'll do my shtick."

Paul laughed loudly, his voice echoing in the industrial washroom, "I'll buy. But it's hospital food."

"Deal."

"I'll have the photos brought here. How long before you get here?"

"If I rush, I can be there in fifteen. But you pay my traffic tickets."

Paul guessed that would give an officer enough time to bring the photos to him, "I'm great at fixing tickets. Meet me in the cafeteria."

Nicole disconnected, stuffed the phone in her purse, pulled the jacket from the back of her chair and bolted from her office. She ran to her car and drove to the hospital.

Paul had ordered three identical lunches and waited for Nicole to arrive. Not long after, Nicole walked into the cafeteria, took a chair and placed it close to Paul's, their legs touching. A large manila envelope lay on the table before them, unopened. The three of them picked at their salad as the envelope lay untouched. Halfway through her meal, Nicole reached for the envelope and with a single finger, slid it towards the edge of the table. She pushed her lunch to the side and turned the envelope over to open the flap. Paul placed his hand over the envelope, "It's not as bad as some of the other stuff you've seen, but I want to make sure this is something you want to do."

"I offered to come down, didn't I? Besides, do you have any leads that I haven't provided?"

Paul hung his head in embarrassment, "No."

Dan interjected, "Nicole, you've been kind, but I don't think that either one of us expects you to put yourself through anything traumatic for the department."

Nicole smiled softly, "I'm not doing this for the department or you Dan." She placed her hand on top of Paul's and squeezed gently. "It's self-explanatory, isn't it?"

*****

After the procedure was completed, Carl noticed a few drops of blood on his shirt. He found a lab coat on a hook in the treatment room and donned it as he yanked the curtain to the side and stepped out of the room. He was thanked by Dr. Hernandez for his assistance suturing up Will's hand wound. He just nodded, not wanting to open his mouth. Carl had never done anything like that before, and although he felt like vomiting several times, he kept his stomach quiet, and its contents down.

Dr. Hernandez went back to her patient, swapped the area around the wound clean, checked the sutures and turned Will's hand over several times to appreciate her handy work. "It's not perfect, but it's the best I could do under the circumstances. How's your thumb? Do you feel the restricted movement?"

Will looked down at his hand, the tiny pieces of black plastic suture sticking out from the skin. He ran his finger along the sutures; the edges felt sharp and the tickle under his skin. He felt he had done a better job on the sutures in his cold room. He tried to move his thumb, feeling the tension in the skin, he stopped when he saw the skin stretch tight.

"Does it hurt?" she inquired.

"Tight." Will turned his hand over, "Nice job suturing. Will these be in long or dissolve?"

"Not long at all. A week to ten days. These won't dissolve. Your skin will eventually stretch out, but you'll have a scar. Nasty scar I'm afraid. You lost a chunk of skin that plastic could've done a better job of repairing."

"I don't have insurance, and besides, it's not that bad of a scar." He brought his thumb up tight against his hand, "See, you won't even be able to see the scar when I do this." Will put his hand in front of the doctor.

She held his hand, admired her work again, "I'm glad you're happy." Dr. Hernandez covered the wound with a gauze pad then taped it in place. "I'm going to have you lay down for a few minutes. I worked on your hand a lot longer than I should have. I want you to put your head down, relax for half an hour or so and I'll come back and check on the sutures before I release you. Some of those sutures are a little tight, and too much movement can tear the skin."

Will didn't move. Dr. Hernandez tapped the pillow, "Down mister. That's an order." She gave her patient her best fake smile and was about to leave the room, "I'll be back shortly with the papers to release you and some instructions on how to care for your injury at home."

Will did as he was told, slowly lowered himself to the pillow, brought his hand up over his head and looked at the sutures. "Not bad," he thought. He could feel his eyes getting heavy quickly, his eyes closed, he opened them again, they closed again, and this time they stayed closed.

*****

Now looking the part, Carl walked down the halls of the emergency department figuring any patient of a rape case would have security guarding the room. All of the rooms were left unguarded, so he made his way to the main section of the hospital. There, he scanned the signs directing him to the elevators. Carl asked a middle-aged lady pushing a cleaning cart which floor the new patients would be admitted to. She laughed and asked if Carl was new. He apologized, claiming to be a new medical student.

She told him all patients are on floors two to five, but it depended on why they were in the hospital and all the other floors are administration. He thanked her and made his way to the stairwell to avoid as many people as possible.

Carl slowly walked up the stairs, pulled open the door to the second floor and casually walked down the hall towards the nurses' station, glancing into each room as he passed. Seeing nothing, he continued to the far end of the corridor and took the stairs to the next level. The second floor revealed nothing. He walked across to the stairs knowing the girl who was attacked was most likely there. Until now, he hadn't devised a story in case he got caught. He wondered what the penalty was if he got caught posing as a doctor.

If she was admitted, she had to be on this floor. The door opened slowly, Carl made his way onto the floor and immediately noticed the two uniformed officers outside a room, her room no doubt. He continued down the hall, avoiding making eye contact or even looking at the officers standing guard. A few rooms before the one he wanted to visit, Carl entered and stopped short. He pushed himself close to the edge of the door and peered across at his target destination.

*****

Nicole opened the envelope, tilted it and let the photos slide out onto the table. They landed on the table face down. She took in a deep breath, took hold of the first photo and was about to flip it over when images began to flash in her mind. Whatever Nicole was seeing was moving so quickly, she couldn't focus on a single image. She closed her eyes, trying to focus on anything but her mind was flooded with so much information at once, she couldn't process anything. Her mind began to spin wildly causing her stomach to turn.

Seeing Nicole sway in her seat, Paul placed his arm around her. In an instant, she looked as if she had aged ten years. She lurched forward, put her hands on the table's edge, turned her head and threw up on the floor.

Paul and Dan jumped from their seats and came to Nicole's side. She began to slump to the side, Paul took hold of her jacket and pulled her back. Her head snapped back, then forward as she vomited again. Paul was about to call for help when he heard footsteps come running from behind. A nurse grabbed hold of Nicole, leaning her forward in her chair then pulled the chair back all in a single move. The nurse held her head and calmly asked another hospital worker to get a wheelchair or a stretcher.

Nicole woke up momentarily, found Paul in the growing crowd, she whispered something inaudible. Paul leaned in closer; she whispered again, "He's here. He's here right now."

In shock, Paul stared at Nicole; she whispered again, "Go."

Paul looked at the medical crowd who had gathered around Nicole, knowing she was well cared for, he broke away and headed for the hospital's main lobby. Dan looked at Nicole, then Paul and broke into a run to catch up to his friend. Paul didn't let up, carrying his large girth, ducking and swerving between hospital staff and visitors until he reached the lobby.

*****

There were two security guards standing at the main entrance. Paul stopped quickly, almost knocking one of them over. He was already out of breath, sweat beading on his forehead. He fumbled for his police identification in his jacket, presented it then replaced it. Paul wanted to speak, but he found it difficult to catch his breath. He placed his hands on his knees, leaned forward and forced himself to breathe.

"Lock down the hospital," Dan spoke with authority to the security

172

staff.

The two security guards looked at Dan with bewilderment. The older of the two guards, who appeared to be retired from an executive's job, stood and questioned the police order, "On who's authority?"

Paul, who finally caught his breath, stood upright and was as tall as the guard, "Mine. Problem?"

"Major problem. We can't lock down some twenty odd entrances and garage doors and shipping bays. We don't have the manpower and it's a fire hazard. We can't lock the entrances down in case of fire. People have to get out."

Frustrated, Dan spun around looking at the lobby and tried to comprise, "Can we post security guards at the entrances?"

"You can. But who are you going to get to guard the doors? We have a total of four guards on duty, us, one in the ER and one who walks the floors and grounds. That's it. Besides, do you even know who you're looking for?"

Other than a skinny male, Dan and Paul realized they had no complete description of the person they wanted stopped from leaving the building.

Dejected, Paul and Dan stood beside the security guards wondering what to do next.

"K. Can you let us know if you spot a young skinny Caucasian guy," Paul instructed. "That's all we got."

The two guards looked at each other, "Really? A young skinny guy."

"Just let us know if you spot someone matching that description. If you do, try and detain him and call us. Got it?" Paul's voice was authoritative and direct.

Paul turned and began to run back into the hospital with Dan fast on his heels. Dan wasn't sure where Paul was headed but kept pace. Paul took in deep breaths as he made his way to the ER.

Paul turned to Dan and asked him to radio for additional officers to help with the search for the suspect.

*****

Carl watched the two officers from his perch. He wondered how he could get the officers distracted and leave their post. It would have to be a great ruse. Maybe, he thought, he could pretend to be a doctor or nurse and go in to exam the patient. He still had his lab coat, he had misled the doctor in the ER and helped suture a patient, why not go in and pretend to examine the patient?

173

As Carl was refining his plan, he heard the officers' portable radio squawk. He pressed his ear to the edge of the door and heard the person on the radio asking for more officers to respond to the emergency department to assist in the search of a murder suspect. Carl's plans just changed.

One of the two officers broke away from his assignment, leaving one officer to guard Kerry and made his way to the elevator. Carl casually exited the room and joined the officer as he waited for the elevator to arrive.

"Busy day?" Carl asked as he watched the LED numbers change on the display.

"Kinda." The officer also kept looking at the display.

The elevator dinged to indicate its arrival, the doors parted, and the two men entered. They each turned to face the door and remained silent. Carl reached forward, pushed the button for the main floor then stood back. The two men remained silent until the doors opened and the both exited. Carl let the officer lead, he decided to stay a few feet behind and follow the officer to the ER.

*****

Will bolted upright in bed. Confused, it took a few moments before he finally recognized his surroundings. His stomach growled at him; his mouth tasted sour and dry as if he had just vomited. Will looked around the hospital room, he couldn't find any vomit on the floor or in a basin. His head spun, images had filled his mind while he slept. Images that didn't make sense. Images that didn't belong to him. Will tossed the cover sheet to the floor and felt the sting of pain in his hand. He had forgotten about his injury; the sudden movement caused a few stitches to rip through the skin. He looked down; the wound began to ooze blood from the open section. Will froze as he watched tiny drops of blood fall to the bed sheet. Blood continued to slowly flow down his fingers then pool on the cot. The muddled events of the day began to fall into place until Will finally knew what was happening.

What didn't make sense were the images of people sitting around a table that he didn't recognize. He recalled two men, dressed in suits, looking directly at him. As the men stared at him with concern, the image panned down, seeing his legs but those legs were not his but those of a woman. Now, standing in the hospital room, looking down at his legs, he saw his own, not those of a woman. Not only didn't he know these two men, or seeing women's legs, he couldn't remember ever being in that situation.

The horrible feeling that he had to flee immediately wouldn't leave him.

Will hopped from the bed, stumbled, took hold of the bed, his head still fuzzy from the strange images he had been seeing. He placed both hands on his head, squeezing tightly, attempting to stem his mind from flowing side to side. Will felt his mind clear enough to make good his escape. He slowly pulled the curtain back, looked to the left then right, and adrenaline surged through his body. Two men, two men he didn't know but recognized from the images in his mind, were running down the hall towards his room.

Shocked, Will couldn't comprehend what he was seeing or believing. Will went back to his room, grabbed the cotton sheet from the floor and draped it over his shoulders and pulled his ball cap down low. Hunched over and limping like an old man, he slowly exited the treatment room, making his way towards the front entrance past staff and other patients. He felt the pain from the open wound on his hand.

The two men from his dream ran past Will, turning at the corner and stopping at the reception desk. He continued limping towards the glass doors, glanced backwards at the two men then disappeared outside.

Carl walked past the room where he assisted the doctor, peeked inside and found the room empty. Still wearing his lab coat, he had now been seen by the ER staff for hours, and no one questioned his presence.

As Carl walked past a room, the patient inside called for him. He continued with little regard for the wants of the person inside the room. She called for him again. Carl felt a sense of false responsibility, stopped, leaned back, and looked in.

"Can you help me, doctor?" A large elderly woman was sitting on a commode, her feet dangling inches from the floor, her gown on backwards.

Carl entered the room and stood before her, "I'm not a doctor."

"I don't care if you're a doctor or not. I need off this stupid thing. I've been on here so long; I think it's now a part of my ass now."

Carl stiffed a laugh, smiled coyly and told her he wasn't sure if he knew how to get her off. "I'm not sure if I should be doing this or not. I don't work here."

"You're wearing a lab coat aren't you. You work here. Help me get my ass off this fucking thing."

Carl let out a belly laugh and nodded. He stood close in front of her, put his forearms under her armpits, hugged her and lifted. He hoisted her up, and the commode remained fixed to her backside. He softly let her back down and released his hold.

"Well, you are stuck to this thing." He stood back, hands on his hips and wondered what his next move would be. "How long have you been here?"

"Almost an hour. They forgot about me."

Carl took a different approach, moved around behind her, placed one foot on the metal bar between the wheels, hands under her armpits once again then lifted, his foot holding the commode in place. The commode refused to release its grip on the old lady's buttocks.

Dr. Hernandez went past the room, then returned. She watched as Carl fought to separate the commode from the patient. She quietly walked in, took hold of the lady's hand and pulled. With the sound of suction suddenly losing its grip, she popped off the commode, and her feet landed softly on the floor.

Carl and Dr. Hernandez put the lady back to bed. "Look at you helping out."

"I've no clue what the hell I'm doing. I couldn't just walk by and not help. She's so grandmotherly."

"Grandmotherly? Is that a word?"

Carl shrugged his shoulders, "No clue. But it sounded good."

"What are you doing back down here? I thought you worked in the lab?"

"Looking for someone." It wasn't a lie.

"Everyone's looking for someone."

"Really?" Carl was surprised. "Who?" There was excitement in his voice. He stepped in close. "Do you know anything more?"

"The police are all over the ER right now. I heard they went to security to look at the tapes and see if they can find someone."

"Someone? Is there any way to find out who they're looking for?"

"I'm still here you know," the old lady went to sit on the bed, ignored by Carl and Dr. Hernandez.

"They said it's a suspect. Must be someone nasty. I counted at least a dozen uniformed officers and some detectives. They're all over the department right now. Asking everyone for their ID's, checking everyone out."

"Shit." Carl had a concerned look on his face. "You busy right now?" He asked of Dr. Hernandez.

"I was just going on a break. Why? You asking me out?" She smiled at him.

Carl peered outside the room, left then right then back to Dr. Hernandez.

"I sorta need you to help me out."

She stepped back, a sudden look of fright overtook her. "You're the guy they're looking for."

He laughed loudly, "No. I'm looking for the same guy. I don't work here." He realized he had to trust the doctor with his secret. "I'm a reporter. I'm looking for the same guy they are."

"A reporter," she exclaimed. "I let a reporter help me suture a patient." Dr. Hernandez was visibly upset. "I could get into a lot of trouble for what I did. Now you want me to help you?"

The old lady broke into the conversation, "I let a reporter get me off the toilet?"

Carl looked at the lady, "Hey, if I didn't help you off the toilet, you'd still be stuck on it, so shush up." He gave her a nasty look then turned back to the doctor. "I need you to help me find out who they're looking for."

"Why should I help you? Why? One good reason why I should help you?"

Carl looked confused, his eyes darted back and forth, "Shit. Shit. Shit. OK. I can't think of a single reason why you should help me. I just need your help. Please. That's all I got."

She thought about it for a moment, "What do you need? If I'm gonna get in trouble, I'll turn you in."

"I don't have any ID. I need you to take me around the hospital, so I can see if I can find who they're looking for. I want the story before they put this guy away. That's it."

"Where to first?" she asked.

"The security office. Good place as any to start."

Dr. Hernandez shifted from one foot to the other, "Fine." She stepped out of the room, "Follow me."

*****

Nicole sat alone on a cot in a private ER room, the nausea that caused her violent vomiting earlier had disappeared as rapidly as it had come on. She had been seen earlier and assured the nurse; she was feeling much better.

Nicole heard the commotion outside her room, knowing full well what Paul and Dan were doing. The feeling of helplessness and frustration only increased as she sat waiting to hear the results of the search. She had been told to remain in the room until Paul came to get her.

After an hour, she fidgeted about the room, playing with the medical equipment and dressings and texting Simone about work. After repeated texts, the battery indicator on her phone flashed red, Nicole reached into her purse to retrieve her charger and felt the envelope that contained the photographs she had come down to see. She forgot about the charger and instead, pulled the envelope out and held it before her. She held her breath, unable to take her eyes off the package.

Nicole inverted the envelope, about a dozen sheets of paper came into her hand. She felt a sense of relief as all the sheets were face down. She sighed, closed her eyes, flipped the first sheet of paper over, then opened her eyes. Instantaneously, the scene on the paper began to move. The picture showed a close-up of the bruising around Kerry's neck. The photo timeline began to rewind, slowly at first then faster and faster until Kerry was on the ground in the parking lot and Nicole saw the hands around the girl's neck. He squeezed, his fingers dug deep into her neck. Kerry's eyes began to bulge as the pressure increased. Kerry struggled but failed to get her attacker to release his grip. Even without any audio, Nicole could imagine the sounds of the fight, the victim gasping for air.

Nicole hoped that by turning the picture she would get a different vantage point, but she realized it didn't work that way. She spun the sheet of paper around and flipped it over, again, no result. This photo didn't reveal any new information or clues. She placed the paper on the cot to her side and turned the second one over. This photo depicted the side view of the SUV Kerry hid under. Nicole held the photo up high, focused on the vehicle, then felt the impact of the images flooding her senses in one horrific moment. From the point of the view of the camera, the image reversed in time until she saw Kerry hiding under the truck fighting off her attacker. Kerry flailed and fought for her life against the man reaching under the vehicle, trying to grab hold of her. She saw Kerry bite his hand. The attacker's face was covered by a ball cap; he stood holding his hand. Nicole saw the man's face reflected in the rear-view mirror. She gasped. The man was in pain, the look on his face undeniable. He stared directly into the glass, and she studied his face. In the reflection, the man turned and ran away. The image stopped moving. "I know this man," she said aloud to herself.

*****

In a small, dark room, there was one desk with a bank of monitors along the wall and a lone guard sitting at the controls. Paul and Dan stood behind the security guard as he used the mouse to scroll through the video files.

"Do you even know who you're looking for?" the guard asked without looking up.

"Someone who doesn't belong," Paul offered.

"Someone who doesn't belong. Well, that helps a lot," the guard said sarcastically.

Paul made a motion like he slapped the guard in the back of the head but stopped short before he made contact, "We're looking a male, white, young. Someone who's keeping his head down, most likely wearing a ball cap to help cover his face, he might have a hoodie up over his head too. He most likely has his hands in his pockets. He won't have his phone out. Someone who is looking straight ahead, not looking around like a person should. This guy doesn't want to attract attention but stands out. He won't make eye contact with anyone. The definition of someone who doesn't belong."

"Got it. Oh, and I saw your reflection of you pretending to hit me in the monitor."

Instead of trying to hide what he did, Paul explained his actions, "Next time don't be such a dick, or I won't pretend to hit you. Got it." He used the same words to make his point.

The guard went through the tapes at regular speed, "You realize we have like sixty or seventy cameras throughout the hospital. If we narrow it down to a one-hour time frame, that's still sixty to seventy hours just to get through all the cameras."

"Eliminate the floors, the OR, maintenance and laundry and services. Let's stay focused on the main areas, let's say, the main entrance, ER waiting room, the ER itself, the stairwells." Paul looked at Dan, "If he wanted to come back for whatever reason, let's say it was to finish off the girl upstairs, he would take the stairs, right? Not the elevators?"

"I wouldn't," Dan offered.

"K. Let's look at the stairs and the elevators." He looked to Dan, "Better safe than sorry."

"What do you want first?"

"Wait. You said you have sixty to seventy cameras throughout the hospital. What about outside the hospital looking at the grounds and the doors?"

The guard thought for a moment, "That includes the outside cameras."

"Would it help if we look at the public doors instead?" Paul turned to the guard, "Do employees need to swipe in to get into any non-public entrance?"

"Of course."

Paul looked at his partner, "What do you think? Wanna take a chance and look at the footage of everyone coming and going first?"

Dan placed his hand on the guard's shoulder, "Select your best camera, the one that would show the best angle, show the faces if possible of everyone as they come or leave the public doors. Let's start with the main entrance."

The guard cued up the video file of the main entrance for the past hour. He typed in the time stamp, and the video began to play. They watched as people came and went through the large glass doors. No one seemed to match the description that Paul had described.

After several minutes, a knock at the door interrupted them. Dan opened it and saw Nicole standing before him. She had a serious look about her; he motioned for her to enter. Paul turned to see Nicole pressed into a corner in the cramped room. She stood, motionless, hugging herself, her eyes filled with fright.

"What's the matter?"

She shook her head side to side, saying nothing. "What?" he asked again.

She motioned Paul to approach. He leaned in close. "What?" he whispered again softly.

Slowly, barely audible, she said, "I know him."

He pulled back, looked deeply into her eyes, Nicole nodded and whispered again, "I know him."

*****

For almost twenty minutes, Carl and the doctor walked about the ER, chatting to one another, as if he belonged. They had been approached by one of the uniformed officers, Dr. Hernandez had been pulled aside to speak with the officer alone. When she returned, she told Carl she had vouched for him. Carl knew he could trust her because if she had told the officer the truth, he would've been escorted out or arrested.

"We checked all the ER rooms and ICU. We would have to go upstairs now, but I'm not sure if it would do any good. We still don't have any clue who we're looking for."

Carl stopped and hung his head low, "You're right. The thing is, I know the guy we're looking for is here, was here, might still be here. With all these cops, if I don't have you with me, I know I'll get stopped. The problem is…"

His words were cut short as he felt a hand placed firmly on his shoulder.

Carl turned to see the detective he interviewed at the police station. The detective had a scowl on his face, clenching his jaw. A woman and another detective stood beside him.

"Detective Hampstead, right?" he asked.

"Hammond," he growled. "What are you doing here impersonating a doctor?"

Carl looked at Dr. Hernandez, "It's not a crime to wear a lab coat? Is it?" He looked at the doctor. "Did I say I was a doctor?" She shook her head.

"What are you doing here?" Paul released his grip on Carl's shoulder. "Same as you, I imagine. Looking for the guy who attacked the girl last night."

Paul looked back at Dan, "That was a suspected sexual assault. Not your usual beat is it?"

Carl took a step back, placing some distance between himself and the police. "You might be telling the public that was a sexual assault, I know better."

"Listen, don't be talking about shit you don't know anything about. Right now, we don't even know for sure." Paul was looking upset.

Carl moved in closer to Dr. Hernandez, standing beside her, almost touching shoulder to shoulder, "I can't imagine you know much at all."

Paul laughed, "K. Stay out of our way. Don't do anything stupid but for you, ah, ah," he snapped his fingers trying to remember the reporter's name.

"Kadner, Carl Kadner."

"Kadner, Carl Kadner. Doing stupid shit is a daily occurrence for you, isn't it? And get a new suit. Weren't you wearing that suit when I first had the unpleasant task of meeting you?" Paul smirked and began to walk away.

Carl exhaled forcefully through his nose and shook his head, "Taking fashion advice from a cop."

Dr. Hernandez turned to Carl, "It was nice meeting you, but I have to get back to work. I've got to finish the paperwork on that guy's hand injury we sutured up earlier. He left before we could discharge him."

Nicole turned around and quickly walked back to face the doctor, "Hand injury?" Paul and Dan joined her.

Excited, Paul looked at the doctor, "Can you describe the injury? Who came in with the hand injury?"

"Skinny guy. Polite, very nice man. A little shy. Why?"

Nicole took the doctor by the arm, gently turned her until they faced each other, "Tell me, his arms." She rubbed her sleeves, "Hair, did he have any hair on his arms."

Carl interjected, "None, no hair at all."

"A hand injury? Not a crush or anything like that. But more of a bite?" Dr. Hernandez replied by simply nodding.

Nicole continued, "Skinny guy, not sickly thin, just thin. Smooth complexion, dark hair, good looking."

"I guess. Why?"

Nicole looked at Paul, "It could be him."

Paul took over the conversation, "You treated him?"

"We treated him," Carl added.

"He had a nasty dog bite. I, we, had to suture it closed."

Nicole was excited, "Here. She grabbed the skin between the thumb and index finger. Here. That's where he was hurt."

"How did you know?"

Paul was convinced they were speaking of the same person, "Show me his room."

The five of them walked back down the hall towards the ER. Dr. Hernandez walked into the room and stood at the back, "This is where we sutured his hand."

On the tray were blood-soaked gauze pads, an open package of sutures, a small stainless-steel cup with yellow fluid in it, and an assortment of other surgical tools. "This is his room. For certain?"

Dan knew exactly what Paul was referring to, "I'll get the security tapes to confirm no one else was treated in this room, and we should be able to get a few still images of him entering and leaving the room. I can check the time logs when he left then follow him outside the building. Be nice if we can get him walking to his car and get a tag. Either way, I'm hoping we can get a good pic of him."

Paul pointed at the doctor and Carl, "I'm gonna need statements from both you."

"After my shift. I've got to get back to work."

Carl started to walk away as well, "And I've gotta go track down this guy and write my story."

As Carl turned to walk away, Dan told him quite frankly, "Leave now and I'll put out a warrant for your arrest as a material witness and hold you indefinitely. I'm just saying."

Carl stopped, slowly turned to face the trio and walked back to join them.

*****

The barking dogs greeted Will as he pulled into the driveway. They ran up the fence, tails wagging, jumping up to meet him. The tires slid in the gravel until the car came to a complete stop. He ignored the dogs as he went inside, poured himself a glass of water and sat at the kitchen table.

He went through the events at the hospital. Having only the one hospital in the county, he had no choice where to go. Travelling to another hospital certainly, would've raised suspicion. What was more disconcerting were the images that ran through his mind, strange images that he couldn't explain or even hope to understand. He rested his head in his uninjured hand. Looking down, he saw the bleeding had finally stopped, but the skin had torn where the suture pulled through.

Will's mind raced with more questions than he had answers for. Regardless of how he tried to rationalize things, everything was spiraling out of control. He could feel the tension rise inside; his stomach knotted up, his chest felt tight. He finished the glass of water, refilled it and drank that with some pain meds. To clear his mind, Will went downstairs, pulled two frozen chunks of meat from the freezer. They had once been part of some girl's thigh. He couldn't remember which girl but that was something long passed, and it didn't matter anymore. In the kitchen, he pulled each piece from the protective plastic bag, felt the burn of the frozen meat on his bare hands then walked out to the backyard. The dogs came bounding up to the house, happy to see him, running around in circles as he approached.

"Zitten," he yelled with a stern voice, the Dutch word for sit. Both dogs dropped and sat for their master mid-stride. Both tails continue to wag uncontrollably as he approached. He loved both dogs, they loved him and seeing them made his worries seem less important.

Will stood before them, holding the meat, the dogs trained not to move until given the order. With all his strength, he tossed the meat into the backyard over the dogs heads. The dogs turned, watched the chunks of flesh land and roll in the grass then turned their attention back to Will.

"Eten."

The dogs turned, ran, found their prize in the tall grass and went their separate ways to gnaw on the frozen chunks of human flesh.

Will went back inside, turned on the taps and washed his hands thoroughly, careful of the open wound. He patted his hands dry using the tea towel, placing it back over the stove handle, went to the fridge and pulled out the egg carton and laid it on the counter. Standing silently at the sink, he began to slowly inhale and exhale methodically to calm the tension. He held each breath in for the count of five then exhaled for the count of five. When he felt more at ease, he picked up the carton of eggs, walked to the basement and entered his freezer.

He stared at the body on the table, almost complete, almost ready. She was nearing completion, and he promised himself he would refrain until that time, but he had to vent, he had to quell the feelings inside that were tearing him apart.

Will pushed some of the instruments aside on the wheeled table, placed the egg carton upon it, opened the lid, picked one up, turned and with all his might, threw it at the frozen body on the table.

"You fucking bitch." He yelled. The egg missed the body and hit the wall on the far side of the room, shattering against the frozen wall. The shell exploded, sending its yellow and white contents out in a haphazard pattern. The room was so cold; it took only seconds for the yolk mixture to freeze in place.

Mist rose from his mouth with each breath and spit spewed forth as he screamed. "You cheating cock sucking whore." Will picked up another egg and threw it at her again, this time hitting her in the face, the shell and yolk burst open, covering her face in a sticky mixture. It too froze quickly. The frozen body lay still, helpless, no way to protect itself from the onslaught of degradation.

He threw another egg, then another, some hitting their mark, others hitting the wall behind her. He didn't aim, he just picked up each egg and threw it with every ounce of built up anger inside him. With each hit, the eggshell would shatter sending shards flying and goo dripping slowing down until it froze somewhere on the body. Will continued to yell and demean the body on the table until he was out of ammunition. He wanted to continue hurling eggs at the body, but the carton was empty. He picked that up and threw it. The floppy, compressed paper carton floundered in the air and landed on the opposite side of the table. Panting, he fell back against the wall and slid to the floor. He continued to breath heavy, the cold taking more out of him then he thought.

Will could feel the cold against his back and buttocks as he sat on the floor. He stood, still angry, still wanting to insult the body with something but fought against the urge. Instead, he locked the door behind him as he went back upstairs.

*****

"One more time Carl. Tell us how you ended up helping the doctor suture up the suspect." Paul was firm and direct.

"One more time, one more time. Come on, guys. Seriously. How many times are you gonna say "One more time?" Carl asked. "I tell you the same story, and you keep asking me to tell you the same story over again. Trying to see if I slip up? Am I a suspect?"

"One more time will last as long as it takes until we are convinced you told us the whole story. And everyone is a suspect."

Carl laughed, "Guys. We can be here all day. I told you everything. I was there to look into the sexual assault that I knew wasn't an assault."

"And how did you know it wasn't a sexual assault?" This time Dan broke in.

"I suspected. OK? Maybe I'm better at my job than you guys are at yours."

Dan continued, "Yeah, I'm sure it takes a lot of intelligence to become a second-rate reporter at a rag paper. We have you dead to rights on impersonating a hospital worker, practicing medicine without a license, obstruction of an official police investigation,…"

Carl started to laugh out loud, "Impersonating a hospital worker? Since when is that a crime? I was hauled in to that room by a doctor to assist; she did the work, I helped. I did nothing. And as far as obstruction, you guys better go back to Law 101. I'm a reporter; I was following my leads, our paths crossed, I did nothing to hinder your investigation. You wanna charge me, go ahead and charge me."

Nora walked into the police department with the air and authority of someone who knew their station in life. Once through security, she made her way to the room where they were interviewing Carl. She found the door, chose not to knock and burst in. In the small interview room, Carl was sitting on one side of the table, Paul and Dan on the other.

Nora propped the door open, "Carl. Out now. You haven't said anything?"

"I kept the words simple and limited them to one or two syllables, so they could understand." He stood up, grabbed his jacket from the back of his chair, "Thanks, guys, it's been fun. We really should do this again over beer and wings." Under his breath, he whispered, "Fucking cops." He left the room.

"I assume since you let him leave, he isn't under arrest?" Nora said defiantly.

Both Dan and Paul remained silent.

"Good. I would think that you guys would know better than to trample on the rights of the press." Nora was visibly upset.

"We were only attempting to get all the facts on what happened at the hospital," Paul admitted.

"Find another way."

As Nora was about to leave, Paul spoke out, "He is a bit of a dick you know."

"Yeah, well leave him alone, he's my dick."

"Really? He's your dick?" questioned Paul laughing.

Embarrassed, Nora stormed out of the room slamming the door behind her.

*****

Katy called Will several times without success. She sent him text after text and received no reply. She sat alone in her apartment wondering why he hadn't taken her call. She pulled her jacket from the hanger in the closet, her keys from the hall table and decided to drive to Will's place.

*****

Carl sat at his desk, tapping his pen to his notepad. The constant tapping created tiny indentations in the paper. He stared into space, not seeing what his compulsive habit was doing to the notepad. His mind was full of the scattered events that occurred at the hospital, but each time he wanted to write something down, something new jumped to the forefront, pushing all else aside. He opened a drawer, tossed the notepad inside and slammed it shut. Pulling the typewriter forward and squaring it before him, he fed a sheet of paper into the roller and turned the knob to advance it. The sound it made stirred something inside, and he was now ready to write his story.

He placed his fingers on the home row of keys; one key struck the roller, then two, then a flurry of keys being pressed and the sound of the typewriter creating a story filled the newsroom.

Nora was on the phone with her lawyer discussing Carl's interrogation when she heard the unique sound of Carl's typing. She stood, walked to her door and looked out into the newsroom. There were phones ringing, people talking but the sound that stood out was the one coming from Carl's desk. It was the sound of a real newsroom, the sound of a writer creating a story.

*****

Nicole drove home after leaving the police station. She called Simone from her car asking if she could stop by after work. She suggested Simone bring a bottle of wine, maybe two. It was a good time to get drunk. Simone said she would see about leaving work early and would bring a pizza as well. Nicole parked her car, locked it and entered her apartment. She went straight to the shower, drew a bath, dropped in a bath bomb and let the suds fill the tub. She tested the water and stripped, letting her clothes fall to the bathroom floor in a heap and stepped in. She slid under the water until her chin touched the water. She left her phone on the edge of the sink, music playing from the favorites list. It was still light out but the seizure she experienced in the cafeteria exhausted her.

She thought it was time to take Simone's suggestion and get a CT scan or MRI to see if there was something wrong with her. What started as seeing pictures move had developed into so much more. Nicole wondered if she had a tumour, a lesion, some type of an aneurysm, something that was causing her ability to become so much stronger than she ever anticipated. The thought that there could be something wrong scared her; she would give it up in a moment if she could. The only good thing that had come of it was meeting the slightly overweight detective who wore running shoes with his suits. Nicole smiled thinking of his running shoes. He was a kind man, caring, she liked him and wondered if there could be something more.

She thought that maybe a future with Paul was possible then thought about her ability and began to cry. Was this something that was slowly killing her? Now that she had finally found someone she could have feelings for, dare she think it, fall in love with. The thought that someone could love her frightened her more than the possibility that she could have a tumor. With a bubble covered hand, she wiped away the tears, *"Grow up,"* she thought. *"This isn't something worth crying over."*

The tears stopped, she wiped her nose with the back of her hand "My new ability is making me sentimental," she said aloud to herself. Nicole closed her eyes, let her mind go blank and felt sleep take over. Her head bobbed, her mind cleared itself, and she slowly drifted to sleep.

Nicole snapped her head upright. The sound of her door creaking open broke her sleep. She slowly lifted herself from the tub, strained to reach for a towel on the far side of the bathroom as the bathroom door opened.

Simone walked in, seeing her friend standing in the tub covered in bubbles. "You do realize those bubbles don't cover all that much. If that tub were a little bigger, I'd be tempted to join you." She raised and lowered her eyebrows quickly.

"You know sweetie, I believe you." Nicole slowly lowered herself back into the water. "Maybe I should just invite you in and see if you have the guts to follow through with your threats."

"Promises, promises. I'll get the glasses and the pizza." Simone left the bathroom and went to retrieve dinner.

Nicole let a little water out of the tub then ran more hot water. Simone returned, placed a full glass of red on the edge of the tub and handed her a slice of pizza then sat on the toilet. Nicole shook the bubbles from her hand, accepted the slice and took a big bite.

"Wanna tell me about it?" Simone had a mouth full of thick crust pizza with pineapple and bacon.

"You know my little party trick?" Nicole twirled a finger around her head. Simone nodded in agreement, her mouth too full to speak. "It's weird; I don't understand what's going on with it."

Simone took another bite, remained silent, waiting for Nicole to continue. "It's, I don't know, getting stronger, I'm seeing more and more and different things now too." She sipped the wine, her hand covered in bubbles, her clean hand held the pizza. She took a small bite, with a mouth half full, she continued, "I'm connected to the guy. It's like he has the same power I think. We're, I don't know, like conjoined twins. I feel when he's close."

Simone had already finished her first piece and reached for another. "Connected? You get inside this guy's head and read his thoughts?"

Nicole shifted in the tub, "No, not that much but I can sense him, and it's scary. I mean scary. This feeling just takes hold of me, and I feel this rush of pure evil course through me and makes me wanna puke. In fact, it did. I puked up a ton. Is this making any sense?" She downed the last of her glass.

"Honey, none of what you do makes sense. I mean you can see things that no one else can. How or why is a mystery." She took a bite, then a sip of wine.

"I just hope you aren't burning out your brain or something."

"I saw him today you know. I saw his face." Nicole held her glass out for a refill.

"You bumped into him?" Simone shrieked.

Nicole tapped her head, "In here. I saw him. Paul took me down to the station, and I had to help some tech create a sketch of the guy. Paul was busy, so I left. It was so nerve-wracking to see his face."

"What does he look like?" Simone leaned in close.

"Like an average kid. I mean we would pass him on the street and never give him a second look. Normal, thin, good-looking, sweet looking. I almost feel sorry for him."

Simone sat up straight on the toilet, "Sorry? Are you fucking kidding me? You saw what he did. He cuts up girls. He could've killed someone we know."

"I mean I always figured bad guys look like bad guys, mean with skull tattoos and guns. He looks like a nice young kid. Just a young kid. For some reason, some stupid reason," Nicole began to cry, "I see him, and feel him, and I feel his rage or the evil inside him that goes through me. It scares me, and I don't like it." She began to sob openly and put her hands up to cover her face, knocking the glass of wine off the edge of the tub, spilling its contents on the floor. "I'm scared this thing, this thing inside my head, is going to kill me." The tears continued to stream down her face, "I don't want to die."

Simone stood, stepped into the tub behind her friend forcing Nicole to the middle of the tub. Simone sat in the water then wrapped her arms around Nicole. She continued to cry, placing her head on Simone's shoulder. They stayed that way until there were no more tears to cry.

*****

Katy sat naked on the edge of the bed, panting, holding Will's hand, "Well, that was fun."

Will wasn't sure how to respond, he felt embarrassed, "Sarcasm doesn't make me feel better."

She was still looking away, unsure she could face Will with what she was about to ask, "Can I ask you a question?" Her question was met with silence. She asked anyway, "Are you a virgin?"

Embarrassed, he laughed loudly, "No, but you're only the second."

Relieved, Katy let out a small sigh. "If you're willing to learn, let me teach you?"

"I am."

"K then, rule one, don't be so God damned rough. Not every woman likes that. Some want to be treated like a woman."

"Speaking of treating someone like a woman, what was that comment you made about that large girl working at the coffee shop?"

Katy kept looking away from him, surprised he had to ask, "She was no woman. She was a fucking cow. Did you not see that fucking cunt, cut her up, and she would feed a family of four for a month."

Her comment was followed by an awkward silence that lasted longer than either one of them was comfortable with. Inside, Will was laughing at the irony of the situation and put the matter aside and decided the conversation needed to take a different direction.

Will rubbed her back, "Let's get back to my problem. I'm not that experienced but tell me exactly what to do and how to do it. I can take direction, just let me know exactly what you like and how you like it," he laughed.

Katy spun around on the bed, "I know what I like and who I like." She leaned in close and kissed Will hard. "I got my breath back. Wanna go again? This time, I'll give you some pointers, some ideas of what to do and see where your imagination takes you. I hope you have an open mind because I have some freaky kinks."

Katy crawled on top of Will then shimmied her body back and forth, "I can't wait to find out," he whispered.

*****

Paul inserted the key into the door handle, wiggled it, attempted to get the key to fit then realized it was the wrong key. He fumbled with the key ring, found the correct key, unlocked the door and sauntered into the kitchen. His head hurt, a tired headache after working a seventeen-hour shift with only two meals and too much coffee. He flipped his running shoes off, dropped his trousers on the floor as he left the kitchen, his suit jacket fell to the floor in the hall, as he was about to enter the bedroom, he heard his cell phone ring.

His head dropped, thinking of ignoring the phone, he continued to the bedroom, changed his mind, found his pants, pulled the cell phone from the pocket, swiped to answer without looking at the caller ID. "What?" he didn't hide his anger.

The voice on the other end was quiet and taken aback by Paul's tone, "Hey."

He recognized the voice immediately, "Nic. I'm sorry. I'm just getting home. It's late. Everything OK with you?"

"Bad day. Can I come over?" Nicole's voice was stressed.

"Sure. What's going on?"

"I'll tell you when I get there." The line went dead.

Paul picked his pants up from the floor, went for the jacket when he heard a soft knock at the kitchen door. He knew exactly who it was. He opened the door to see Nicole, disheveled, eyes red from crying, still wearing a bathrobe.

"I was in your driveway when I called," her voice barely audible.

"Wanna talk?"

"Can I sleep first?"

He reached forward, put his arm around her and guided Nicole to the bedroom. He removed her bathrobe and shoes and laid her down, then sat in the corner of the room, saying nothing and let her drift off. He used her robe as a blanket, bundled it up high under his chin. It wasn't long before he too was fast asleep.

*****

Carl slept at his desk as he had done many times. Still seated, his head resting on nested arms, a small amount of drool dripped to the blotter. His right leg cramped, twitched, sending his chair rolling backwards. He slowly slipped off the edge of the desk, waking him just as he was about to fall to the floor. He stretched, felt the muscle cramps in his back, yawned loudly then looked around. The entire room was dark, no sound, nobody around to make any noise. He coiled his arms under his head, as he was closing his eyes, he noticed some scribbling across his story he had written earlier.

He pulled the paper from the top of the pile, turned it sideways so he could read it with his head still resting on his one arm. Carl read it, sat upright, shocked at what was on the paper. Standing, he knew who he was looking for but saw no one. He waited, hoping someone would stir, make a noise, but nothing happened.

Carl stuffed the paper into his pocket, grabbed his suit jacket and raced to his car.

Sam watched Carl leave from the far corner of the room, hiding behind a bank of unused filing cabinets. He had a sinking feeling in his stomach and immediately regretted giving Carl that information and knew it would be the last time he would see him.

*****

A low dense mist hung across the country road as Carl checked his phone for directions. He wasn't familiar with the road or this area outside of town. The mist left a small amount of moisture on the asphalt that glistened under the glare of the car's headlights. The moonlight barely broke through the young leaves on the trees and offered little help to brighten the area. The roads were tree-lined, almost to the edge of the pavement. His eyes seldom left the base of the trees, he was concerned a raccoon, or a deer would jump out at any time.

Raising his phone to eye level, he checked his location in relation to the destination. The arrow indicated his direction; he was only a few miles from where he wanted to be. His eyes never left the road as he let the phone fall to the passenger seat.

A chill went through him as he drove along the road. He knew it wouldn't be long before he arrived at the address. Up ahead, the road went into a slow meandering curve that disappeared beyond the trees. He slowed the car, followed the bend until it was straight again. Carl could see a break in the tree line along the right side, he slowed, picked up his phone and saw that this was the driveway he was looking for.

He turned off his headlights, hoping the moon would illuminate enough of the road to help him make his way to the house undetected. Carl was wrong; the overhead growth canopy was so thick; the moonlight couldn't penetrate to help guide him. He pulled his car to the side of the driveway, put the car in park and killed the engine.

He pocketed the phone and exited the car. He gulped, unsure what he was getting himself into, he slowly walked up the gravel driveway. Carl stepped softly heal to toe, attempting to limit the noise he made as he approached the house. Eventually, the trees opened to a clearing, the moonlight casting an eerie glow around a modern home set up high on the rise, surrounded by the woods on all sides. He stopped in his tracks, wondering if this was such a good idea after all.

He checked his watch; it was almost four, the sun would be up before six. He debated waiting for daylight or going in now. There wasn't much of a choice. He hurried his pace to the house scanning the area for security cameras or motion sensor lights. Two cars were parked in the driveway, he carefully moved in, placed his hand on the car's hood that was at the base of the driveway, cold and moist. It hadn't moved in hours. He cupped his hands on the driver's window and looked inside: the interior was clean, a single

Starbucks cup in the holder, dangling from a USB slot in the radio, it is hard to see in the dim light, but Carl thought it was either a pink or purple mobile phone power cord. "A girl's car," he thought.

He did the same to the second car, parked closest to the house. Inside he saw another clean interior. There wasn't anything inside the car, no loose receipts, no papers, no CDs. It was immaculately clean. "No clue. Damn," he thought.

He turned his attention to the house, and as he was about to walk around the back, he noticed a four-foot-high chain link fence. "Small dog?" He stopped, strained to see beyond the fence for anything that would give away what was on the other side. Carl followed the fence to the east; it disappeared into the darkness of the night. He had no idea how far the fence went. Looking west, most of the fence was obscured by the house. He took in a deep breath, feeling the cooling night air, he debated whether or not to continue. If it was a dog beyond the fence, it couldn't be too large. The fence couldn't hold back a large dog. If it were a small dog, it would probably still be inside the house. His mind raced with options. None of the options involved leaving and coming back during daylight, so he decided to press forward.

Following the right side of the house, he moved slowly, hoping there wasn't any motion sensors to activate the lights. The moon overhead only provided enough light to maneuver to the house. Rounding the corner, he scanned the surrounding backyard which was a solid blanket of darkness. He assumed the trees must be blocking any light from above. He decided to move forward, heard something, paused then heard it again. Footfalls on the grass moved closer to the fence, soft, steadily advancing from beyond the other side of the fence. His heart stopped, blood froze in his veins, Carl heard the growl of a large dog in the darkness. The snarling continued and grew closer. Slowly emerging from the night, he made out white fangs surrounded by curled lips. The full head of a Shephard appeared and pressed its muzzle against the fence. Saliva dripped from the dog's fangs onto the fence links, hung for a moment then trickled to the ground. The growling intensified and echoed in the night as Carl realized there was now a second dog emerging behind the fence. Something came up in the back of his throat that didn't taste very good. He forced it back down. "That's no small dog," he thought.

Carl slowly backed up along the wall, the dogs followed him along the fence. He needed a distraction. Moving at a snail's pace, he pulled his cell phone from his jacket, opened the camera app and pointed it at the dog and pressed the shutter. The camera clicked, the flash failed to go off. "Fuck." He set the flash, pointed it at the dogs and pressed the shutter. The bright light temporarily blinded the dogs; they turned away from him giving Carl an escape. He bounded down the driveway, sliding on the loose gravel, not daring to look behind him. He figured the dogs would give chase and be on his tail. Running as if the dogs would pounce on him any moment, he slid and continuously lost his footing.

Ahead of him, the end of the driveway was completely shrouded in darkness. The upper part of the driveway was partially lit in the moonlight. A different type of fear overtook him. He couldn't remember from which direction he came; does he turn left or right? Ahead of him was nothing but the darkness. His heart raced, so many thoughts ran through his mind in a split second: Why did he go? Why didn't he wait for daylight? Why didn't he research the address before going out? Which way should he go, left or right? Carl made up his mind, he went right, for better or worse. He still couldn't make himself look back to see if the dogs were following. That's when the person being chased always stumbles and falls and the person or thing giving chase catches up. He was frightened, scared for his life, adrenaline coursed through his body. His legs found new energy to propel him faster. He entered the tree-covered section of the driveway, felt his head snap back, and fell to the driveway unconscious.

Will stood over Carl holding a large branch he had picked up when he first woke up when Carl set off his alarm. He had watched Carl from the window and made his way to the end of the driveway knowing the house was secure and Carl would eventually have to leave when he couldn't gain access to the house.

Blood flowed freely from Carl's nose and upper lip and dripped onto the gravel driveway. Will stood over the unconscious body, looking down on the man he had just attacked. He knew the man, recognized him from the day before at the hospital. He raised the large tree branch over his head to deliver another blow to Carl's head when a light came on in the house. Katy was up. He lowered the branch, tossed it into the woods, then stood there and waited for the light to go out. Waiting another few minutes, he grabbed Carl by the hair and dragged him off up to the house.

Will entered the combination and unlocked the outside door to the basement. He dragged Carl down the stairs, through the basement to the back, opened the freezer where he kept his prize and rolled him inside. Carl moaned, moved his hand up to his face to check his injury. Will casually stepped closer, raised his foot and stomped on Carl's head. His head bounced off the frozen concrete floor with a dull thud. Carl was now unconscious.

Upstairs in the bedroom, Will placed his hand on Katy's shoulder, rocking it gently, rousing her. She stretched, turned over and smiled when she saw him.

"What time is it?" she asked as she covered her mouth with her hand. "My breath must be horrid."

He smiled, "Nonsense. I want to show you something." He took her hand softly. "Come on."

She slid out from under the covers, slightly embarrassed, still naked from the night before. She pulled the sheet to cover herself, but it fell back to the bed as he guided her out of the bedroom. They walked down the hall towards the back of the house.

"Where are you taking me?" she asked. "I should put some clothes on."

"You don't need clothes. You look perfect."

He turned right from the hall into a small room with a window that ran the expanse from one wall to the next, floor to ceiling. Two large recliners faced the window, along the back wall, a bookshelf ran from end to end holding hundreds of books. The second-floor window overlooked a vast canopy of treetops and a mountain range far off in the distance. "My father had this put in when my mother was still alive. They used to have their morning coffee and watch the sun come up almost every morning."

Katy stood in front of the window, her arms spread, palms flat on the glass, looking out onto the forest. The sun hadn't come up yet, but its faint glow of whites and yellows and oranges bounced off the sky and blended with the Spring leaves on the trees.

"They must've sat up here a lot." Her eyes never left the sky.

"My mother got bored with it after a while. She stopped coming up. Dad never did though. I would catch him up here all the time when he wasn't working." Will walked over and stood beside Katy, both looking out, waiting for the sun to come up. "Funny thing is, he said this was his favorite place to be. He liked being alone. My mom and dad didn't get along all that great. He tried, he really tried. She just had no, I don't know, zest for life. She was content just being a wife. I always figured dad settled."

Katy reached down and took his hand, "Never settle. Worse thing you can do. Marriage isn't like a car that you grow tired of then trade it in for a new model. You don't have to keep the car if you don't want to. I wouldn't want to be stuck with someone who doesn't appreciate me. And I wouldn't want to be with the wrong person either."

The edge of the sun broke over the top of the mountain, the light became brighter, stronger, replacing the colors with pure, crisp white daylight across the sky.

Katy got excited, "Look," she pointed, "The sun is coming up."

Will had seen that very moment hundreds, perhaps thousands of times since childhood, instead he stared at Katy as she marveled at something that happens every single morning and few people take the time to witness it. The sun rose a little higher over the mountain, the beam of light cut over the treetops, hitting the house, bathing Katy's naked body in pure white light.

*****

The morning light cut through a crack in the curtains of the bedroom window and across Paul's face causing him to shut his eyelids tighter. He moaned, turned away from the window and curled up on the chair under Nicole's bathrobe. His back hurt, his neck ached, his bladder was full. He let the robe fall to the floor, tip-toed across the floor to the washroom. He pulled his underwear down and sat on the toilet. His head bobbed as he tried to stay awake. He had fallen asleep once before and still bears the scar on his forehead where he hit the toilet paper holder on the opposite wall.

When he finished, he contemplated flushing or not. He closed the door and flushed just as his cell phone began to ring in the living room. He sprung up, ran for the phone, looked at the screen, "Caller ID Blocked", he swiped to answer the call anyway before Nicole woke up.

"Paul Hammond."

There was silence on the other end; Paul thought he had missed the call when he heard a faint noise on the other end. "You called me," he told the caller.

"You're still investigating the missing girls, aren't you?"

Paul couldn't place the voice, thought long and hard about his response and settled for, "Yes." Was it a tip or the unsub?

"I saw a picture of the guy you're looking for."

Paul's mind began to race. The police hadn't released the composite sketch of the suspect or any details of the previous day's events at the hospital. "Yes."

A long pause, "I know where he lives. I know who he is." The voice was monotone, quiet, painful to hear.

"Who is he?"

"What will happen to him?" The voice was still difficult to hear.

Paul thought carefully before answering, "My job is to make the arrest. That's it." Best to keep the answers truthful and short, he thought.

There was a long pause on the other end of the line, no noise. Paul pulled the phone away and checked to see if the line was still connected. The phone timer continued to run.

"Did you want to tell me something?"

Still silence. Breathing could be heard on the other end. Paul decided it was best to wait, not to pressure the caller. Was the caller debating whether to say anything or under pressure to make the call from someone else? Either way, Paul would stay on the phone until the called disconnected.

Several minutes went by with nothing but silence on the phone. Paul kept the phone to his ear until, "1971 East Parkway. It's on the other side of the ravine, way off the main road." The line went dead.

Having nothing to write on, Paul repeated the address over and over, "1971 East Parkway. 1971 East Parkway. 1971 East Parkway." He found his notepad and jotted down the address. Rushing, he put on yesterday's clothes, silently walked back to the bedroom, kissed Nicole softly on the forehead, left her a note on the kitchen table and left.

*****

Carl woke up, confused, unaware of his surroundings. He looked around, seeing nothing but darkness. The room was beyond black; there wasn't a crack of light penetrating the thickness around him. He took in a deep breath, felt the bitterness in the air, his lungs immediately hurt from breathing in the freezing air. He was cold from lying on the concrete floor. The type of cold that digs deep into your body sending shivering tremors through the body. He placed his hand on the frozen floor and pulled his hand back. Unable to see, he wasn't sure at first if he was blind. He slowly swung his arms around himself to gauge the size of the room and what was around him. His right arm hit something hard. He began to pat the air until he found whatever it was he hit and grabbed it. His hand started to burn and pulled away. The metal bar was so cold; he couldn't sense the difference between heat and cold. He brought his hand to his mouth and blew warm air into the closed fist. For the first time, he tasted the blood in his mouth. It must have frozen while he was unconscious on the floor. He spat a small amount of blood out and heard it hit the floor.

Sitting on the concrete was too cold to bear. He slowly stood, unsure if he would hit his head on something. It was difficult with his stiff leg muscles, but Carl was able to stand. He was still cold, shivering, desperately wanting to feel something warm but getting off the cold floor was a good start he reasoned.

Now that he was standing, he could feel the cold air being blown in from multiple directions. He lifted his arms and let the breeze cut across his hands. One source from the front, the other from the back. "Good," he said aloud.

He wasn't sure how he got into, whatever it was he was in, but he knew that he couldn't survive too much longer. He needed light. He padded himself down, looking for his cell phone. Gone. Whoever had brought him here, took it, or it was on the floor. Not knowing where he was, or how large the room was another problem. "Tackle one at a time," he whispered to himself.

He knew the cold was the first problem. Scared, wondering if he was alone in the room, he had no choice but to create a mental inventory of the items available and try to stem the flow of cold air blowing in the room.

Carl took one step forward. Nothing. "Good." He stepped back. He took one step to the left. Same result. Back to the starting point. One step to the right. His thigh struck something. He closed his eyes, unsure why, but he wanted to be able to imagine what he was doing. Placing his arms directly in front of him, he felt nothing. He felt the cold metal against his legs and knew it was part of the same device that burnt his hand. He pulled his jacket sleeve down, covered his hands and found the edge. It was a table, metal, tubes or rounded edges. He lifted his leg and swung it forward, nothing beneath it.

Taking a deep breath of frozen air, he slowly, methodically moved his hands forward on the table. His fingers found something, hard, frozen. Pausing for a few moments, his mind ran the variables and couldn't place what he was touching. He decided against what his better judgment was telling him. He moved his hands forward, over the frozen object then across. His hands were trembling or shivering. Whatever was frozen on the table had curves. He followed one and found something he immediately recognized. He pulled back, falling backwards, crashing into the counter behind him. The items on the counter went flying and came crashing to the concrete floor with a distinctive hollow metal sound he remembered from the day before. He knew what was on the table and what had just been sent crashing to the floor. Carl was no longer cold.

*****

Paul tried calling Ken and Dan repeatedly without success as he followed his vehicles navigation system to 1971 East Parkway. Instead, he called dispatch and told them where he was going, asked the dispatcher to continue calling Ken and Dan and send at least two uniformed officers to join him. Satisfied, Paul dropped the phone to the seat and steered his way through the country road guided by the female voice of the nav system.

A few hundred feet from his destination, Paul pulled the car over on the gravel shoulder, put it in park and waited for the uniformed officers to arrive. He had no warrant; he just wanted to speak with the owner of the house and see if he matched the sketch. But there was no way, he told himself, he was going to the house alone.

Paul found the phone on the seat and was about the call Nicole when a raccoon crossed the road directly in front of him. He lowered the phone and watched as the animal lumbered across the road, taking its time, not caring that a car was only a few feet away. It stopped in front of the car, cast Paul a look of indifference then casually walked into the woods. He realized that he hadn't seen a raccoon in years let alone watch one walk passed.

He picked up the phone, decided to text Nicole instead of calling. He left a short text, telling her exactly where he was, just in case. That feeling that he always got when things were about to go bad had been brewing inside since he received that cryptic call. As he continued to type the message, he heard a car approach, glanced up then went back to his phone. He did a double take, looked over his shoulder, got out of the car and watched as the car continued down the road. An uneasy feeling came over him that he couldn't shake.

Closing the car door, he settled in behind the wheel, finished the text and waited for the other cruisers to arrive. As he waited, that feeling wouldn't let go of him, it started in the back of his neck and moved through him like ants crawling under his clothing. He squirmed in his seat, shifting back and forth, trying to scratch that itch, even the top of his head felt itchy.

Paul got out of the car, walked to the driveway, did some recon to see the layout of the path leading up the house. No cars in the driveway, double bay garage. "One way in, one way out," he said to himself. He planned his introduction as he made his way back to the car, leaning on the hood, waiting for backup to arrive.

It wasn't long after that the two cruisers arrived with one officer in each. The two uniformed officers parked behind the detective's unmarked car, exited their vehicles, walked over the detective and introduced themselves. Handshakes exchanged, Paul, detailed how he wanted to approach the house.

He pointed to the smaller of the two officers, "You," "Officer Taylor sir."

"Officer Taylor, you go around back. When I scoped the house earlier, I swear I heard dogs barking, but I can't be sure. You," he pointed to the other officer, looked at his embroidered name tag, "Officer Belanger, use your cruiser and block the end of the driveway. Stand 'bout halfway down the drive. If he tries to get out, stop him. I want to bring this guy in."

The two officers looked at each other, "Don't you have a warrant?" they asked Paul.

"I didn't have time to ask, and frankly, I have no evidence other than an anonymous call. So, this is nothing other than a friendly chat at this point. I'm kinda hoping he does something stupid so we can arrest him. Remember, we can't enter the residence without his permission; he doesn't have to answer any questions, he doesn't have to do a fucking thing. Let me do the talking; you guys are the muscle and intimidation. Got it?"

They both nodded.

The sun was well over the trees; the shadows were long across the driveway as Paul began to walk towards the house accompanied by Officer Taylor. The officer walked around to the back of the house, paused when he saw the fence and stopped at the corner. Officer Belanger pulled his car to the end of the driveway as instructed and stationed himself halfway up the driveway. Once everyone was in place, Paul knocked at the front door as that odd feeling came over him once again. His stomach did tiny somersaults sending waves of nausea through him. Between the itchy skin he had and the nausea, he thought about taking a Benadryl. Instead, he swallowed hard, refocused and knocked again. No answer. Knocked again. No answer. Turning towards the officer standing in the driveway, he shrugged his shoulders. The officer responded in kind.

As Paul walked around the right side of the house, he heard the dogs growl as they ran towards the fence. Startled, he fell backwards landing against the house. The two dogs stopped at the small fence and snarled at the stranger before them. Paul froze, his movements deliberate and methodical. Slowly, he pulled himself up, attempting to be as non-threatening as possible. Halfway up, the dogs jumped up, their front paws resting on the top edge of the fence. He fell backwards again, in the same position he was only moments earlier. Every time he moved, the two dogs followed his every move and countered with their own along the fence line and forced their dominance over their territory. Looking across the length of the fence, he realized the dogs could easily jump over and attack him at any moment. He raised his arm, slowly, slid back his jacket and placed his hand on the butt of his handgun.

*****

Nicole bolted upright in bed. She was confused; her surroundings were not her own. It took a few moments before she recognized where she was. She looked around the room for Paul. Getting out of bed, she walked around the bedroom picked up her bathrobe off the floor then went out into the kitchen. A small piece of paper on the counter caught her attention. She read Paul's note, went back to the bedroom, got dressed and left his house.

*****

Even in the stark blackness of the room, Carl hoped his eyes would've adjusted, and he would finally see what he was certain was on the table. He was still leaning against what he thought was a table or counter attached to the wall motionless, not wanting to move in case he bumped into something else that might be in the room. The shock of what he thought might be on the table had worn off, but the chill of the room was quickly overtaking him. His toes and fingers were numb, each breath burnt as the cold air filled his lungs, his skin was beginning to feel hard, and his mind was getting foggy.

Carl knew he had only minutes before he passed out and would most likely die from exposure unless he escaped from the freezer. He pulled his hands from his pants pocket, stretched out, turned to his right and began to map out the room.

His fingers found instruments or tools hanging from hooks on the wall. They too make that familiar sound. He was careful not to touch or bump into the tools for fear a sharp edge might slice his finger or hand.

Continuing, he found a corner, five paces from where he started. The back-wall surface was metallic and bitterly cold to the touch. His fingers barely touched the surface because the extreme cold was too much. He pursed his lips and blew warm air into his cupped hands, but his breath wasn't much better than the air inside the room.

He stomped his feet hoping the motion would speed up the circulation. It did little good. A feeling of fatigue rushed over him; his eyes grew heavy, he wanted to sleep. If he let himself, he could've fallen asleep standing up.

One step to the right and a blast of cold air whipped across his face. He quickly moved to the right several paces to get out of the frigid cold. Carl stopped, he wanted it to end. The sudden blast of cold air that he inhaled filled his lungs and made his core that much colder. He was done. He was ready to give up and sit down and let the cold take over.

Carl stood motionless, but it felt as if the room was moving inside his head. He knew he would lose consciousness any moment. Stumbling backwards, he bumped the table in the centre of the room causing it to move back slightly. He braced himself against the cold edge of the table, got an idea and decided one last attempt at living was worth the effort. He made his way down, found the rubber wheel and casters, no locks, his hand found the wheel to the left, no lock. He then ran his hand along the bottom rails to the front wheel and casters, found a lock, released it, went to the other side and did the same. All four wheels were now free. He stood, pulled his suit jacket sleeves down to cover his hands before he took hold of the top metal platform, summoned all the strength he had left and ran the stretcher into the wall ahead of him. He hoped whoever set up the room, placed the cot in the centre of the room. The back wall had cold air blowing from the compressors, it made sense to Carl, that the door would be on the opposite side.

The stretcher hit the wall or door, stopped suddenly, jostling Carl, sending him to the floor. He found new energy, stood, grabbed the stretcher, rolled it a few paces back until he hit the back wall and took another run at the opposite wall. With a thundering crash, the stretcher crashed against something and Carl could swear for a moment, he saw a sliver of light break through the darkness. With newfound hope, he pulled the stretcher back a third time, closed his eyes and pushed with every reserved once of strength, sending the wheeled stretcher into the far wall. The door he was certain was there, gave way. Carl lost his footing and fell to the floor and was hit with something frozen then rolled to the floor. The door had given way, allowing light and heat in, and cold to escape.

He let his eyes adjust to the new light, looked to his left and saw the frozen body of a naked woman on the floor next to him. He let out a scream, loud and long. Kicking at the body, he could not get away from it soon enough.

Carl scrambled to his feet, slipping on the floor, pushing the stretcher out of the way and attempted to squeeze his way through the crack in the door. He pulled and ripped at wood and insulation, taking off chunks with his bare hands in his bid to escape. Finally, the hole was large enough, and he forced his way out of the room and fell to the floor. The heat was a welcomed relief. Cold air was still blowing through the broken door, but no longer was the deadly menace it once was when he was trapped. With his heels, his pushed himself a few feet away from the cold air, put his head on the concrete floor and lost consciousness.

*****

As Paul thumbed the release on his holster, he heard a scream coming from inside the house. The scream caught the attention of the dogs, who for a moment, lost all interest in the stranger on the ground before them. As fast as the dogs turned away from Paul, they turned their focus back on him. By this time, he had pulled his gun from the holster and methodically brought it up and fired two shots into the air. The dogs whimpered, spun around and ran off to the far end of the yard.

Paul heard squawking on his portable radio as the two uniformed officers called to confirm he wasn't in danger. He ignored the radio calls as he stood, holstered his gun then answered their calls.

"Everything is 10-4," he calmly said as if he had angry dogs confront him daily.

Officer Taylor came running from the left, the other from the right. Paul brushed the dirt from his pants, embarrassed he had been frightened by the dogs. He repeatedly told the officers he was fine, that the only thing hurt was his pride.

"I'd have pissed my pants if those two dogs came at me," Officer Belanger said as he pointed to the dogs. "Those are big fucking dogs." "Yeah. Listen, did you hear a scream from inside the house?"

"I thought it was you."

Paul turned to face the house, "I was standing right here, well sitting," he pointed to the spot where he had just been. "But you heard it?"

"I did."

Officer Belanger shrugged his shoulders, "I was too far down the driveway."

"Doesn't matter. We have two to confirm we heard a scream. Probable cause to enter the house. No warrant needed now." Paul walked to the back door with the two officers in tow. He jiggled the locked handset. Looking around, he had trouble finding anything loose lying about the pristine yard. Instead, he put his hand out, "Can I borrow your flashlight?"

It was a metal door with a half-moon shape glass insert near the top of the door. Reaching up, he used the head of the flashlight to smash the glass then ran the metal flashlight around the edge of the frame to clear any broken pieces of glass that remained. Paul stood high, reached through the open pane and was unable to reach the lock on the inside of the door.

"Sir." Officer Belanger casually brushed Paul aside, "Let me." With a forceful kick, the door buckled, the lock released its grip and swung wide open, crashing against the inside wall, then slowly creaking back. The officer caught the door before it closed again.

"Thanks. You're handy to have around." Paul stepped in front of the two officers, drew his gun and announced himself. No answer. He indicated one officer go right, the other left as he walked straight into the kitchen. The room lit with the early morning sun, casting shadows in corners and further down the halls. The counters were clean, spotless, "Showroom clean," he thought, "Can anyone actually live without a little clutter?" Pausing at the fridge, he looked down the barrel of the gun, further down the hall then behind before opening the fridge door. He had to take a double look, everything inside was arranged by category then height, the orange juice beside the apple juice, then beside the milk. All the fruit were neatly arranged in their respective bins, the fresh vegetables arranged similarly in the next bin. "This is just sick," he said aloud.

Paul closed the door and softly stepped towards the hall. He stopped in his tracks; a barely audible noise caught his attention. He paused, heard nothing but that feeling he got was back. Spinning around, he pointed his gun in the face of Carl Kadner.

Too weak to move, Carl stood there, exhausted, skin pale, ready to collapse. "'Bout time you guys get here. I've been waiting most of the night." He attempted a fake smile, but all he could manage was to curl the corners of his mouth. "I'm just gonna sit for a bit." He steadied himself on the kitchen counter, then slowly slid down to the floor. "I feel like shit."

Paul knelt beside Carl and asked if he needed an ambulance. By this time, the two other officers had returned and stood in the kitchen.

"I just need a little time to warm up for a week on some tropical beach. I bet that frozen popsicle of a corpse in the freezer at the back of the basement is gonna take a lot longer to thaw out."

Paul nodded at the two officers who made their way to the basement.

"Corpse?"

"Stiff. Hard. Frozen. Immobile. Solid. I'm trying to run through the synonyms in my mind. Mine's still a little fuzzy too. She was dead, naked, suture marks all over the body and gunk everywhere, frozen on her body." Carl rubbed his head, "I collapsed for a few seconds after I escaped. When I woke, I looked back in the room to see what I was trapped with then heard you guys come in. I thought the owner was back. I was trying to get out of the house and saw your fat ass from the top of the stairs."

Paul cast him a look.

"Lose weight if you're offended."

Paul sighed deeply, "Did you see who did this?"

Carl laughed, tried to work the kinks out in his neck, "Yup. The guy we sewed up in the emerg the other day. I saw his face before he cold-cocked me with something. Put me out cold." He ran his fingers along the bridge of his nose, "Not broken, but I have a fuck of a headache. You have any Advil?"

Paul stood, "Yeah. Don't move. I'm going to check downstairs. If the homeowner comes back, arrest him."

"And how do I do that?"

"Talk to him. You put me to sleep every time I have to listen to you."

"Funny. Hey, what about my Advil? You said you had some."

Paul disappeared around the corner, "I do."

Carl tried to stand, found it too difficult, sat back down, "Fuck I hate cops."

*****

Paul joined the two officers who stood outside the broken freezer door. Officer Belanger pointed his flashlight inside the room through the fractured door. Tiny wisps of frozen stream rolled out onto the floor around their feet. Cold air, still being pushed into the room by the compressors, spilt into the open area outside the room.

"Did you get a look inside," he asked.

"Yeah. There's a body in the room. Female from the looks of it, naked and dead."

Paul waved his arm around the area, "You, Taylor, keep this place secure. Got it? Belanger, come with me."

The two of them walked upstairs to find Carl rummaging through the kitchen cabinets. He didn't stop as they approached.

"Would you mind telling me what you're doing?" Paul yelled.

"I have a fucking bad headache. I'm looking for an Advil OK. Is that OK with you?" He slammed one cabinet door and opened another.

"This is a crime scene. You can't be looking through shit for an aspirin."

Carl turned to Paul and screamed, "I told you, I'm looking for an Advil, not a fucking aspirin."

Paul reached into his jacket, pulled a bottle from the inside pocket and tossed it at Carl. He caught the bottle mid-flight, "Thanks. Was that so hard?"

Walking over to the kitchen table, Paul pulled out a chair, motioning for Carl to take a seat. Carl opened the bottle, let a few pills roll out into his palm, popped them into his mouth and drank straight from the kitchen faucet. He then joined Paul at the table. He fell into the chair and defiantly crossed his arms.

Paul took a seat across from him, pulled his cell phone and notepad, laying them on the table, "Tell me everything. Don't leave anything out, nothing." He clicked his pen, opened his notebook and waited for Carl to start telling his story.

*****

Will drove as Katy sat in the passenger seat, still content from the night before and finally bedding her new boyfriend. He looked across, saw her smiling at him, smiled back. Inside, he was concerned about the man he had left in the freezer. Rushed, he should have killed him before leaving. While dragging him back to the house, he recognized the stranger as the man who helped the doctor. Inside, his stomach was sour as he tried to remain calm. How did this man somehow track him down? He was careful not to provide any information that would give him away. Were things beginning to unravel?

As they sat in the car, Will wondered if Katy was getting too close. Was this relationship a mistake?

*****

Paul continued to interview Carl, who for the most part was still annoyed with the police, but was too weak to argue. His headache had subsided slightly but was still pounding in his temples. Closing his eyes, he would rub the sides of his head every few minutes, if only to prolong the interview and antagonize the detective. Carl provided a few new details and asked when he could leave. He desperately wanted to get back to the paper, so he could write his story.

*****

Back at her house, Nicole stood under the shower head looking straight up, the water streaming down over her face. Brushing her wet hair back, she wondered about the dream she had seen Paul being attacked by two dogs. In the past, her dreams had always been vague, blurry images of scattered scenes. This time, it was as if she was watching a television program, clear, in focus and she remembered all of it. Why this time she wondered. When she closed her eyes and thought about it, the images came flooding back in full vivid detail. She saw Paul sitting, scared, with two growling dogs bearing down on him.

The note said not to worry. He would be okay and would call shortly. She looked out onto the kitchen sink to make sure her phone hadn't gone off when her face was under the water. Nothing. She looked down and watched as the water swirled around her toes and flowed down the drain. Closing her eyes, Nicole felt as if she could fall asleep, her body void of energy.

As her mind drifted in and out of consciousness, images of the things she had seen in the photographs swirled around melding into one another, nausea overcame her; she was suddenly propelled out of the shower and was now sitting in the back seat of a car. She stumbled, put her arms out to stop from falling but instead of touching wet tile; she was feeling cloth. Looking up, she recognized the car. It was the same car she saw in the images of the girl found in the suitcase. It appeared as if the same skinny man was driving. Nicole shrunk down, fearing the skinny man might see or hear her.

Curling up, she realized she was naked and wet in the back seat of the car. A woman's voice caught her attention. She looked over the back of the front passenger seat to see a beautiful young woman chat with the man driving the car. The conversation went back and forth, casual, funny, not about anything dire or evil; they were talking about breakfast, where to go, what they wanted.

Hiding on the floor behind the driver's seat, she needed to move to make herself comfortable, her foot got caught under the seat, and she let out a soft squeal. Covering her mouth, she feared the driver would hear her. Instead, they continued to talk. Nicole made another soft noise. They didn't hear. A little louder, again, nothing.

Nicole sat upright and was now only inches from the skinny man. He didn't see her, and neither did the female passenger. She tried to look at herself in the rear-view mirror only to discover that she didn't have a reflection. Water continued to stream down her face as if she was still in the shower. Maybe she was. Reaching forward, she waved her hand between the two occupants of the car. No reaction. She thought for a moment she was a ghost, but she was most likely still in the shower. Feeling more relaxed, Nicole realized it wasn't a dream, she was safe, or she hoped she was. The skinny man continued to talk, Nicole listened to their conversation. As they spoke, Nicole noticed the bow tie symbol on the steering wheel horn and dark blue paint on the hood.

The conversation went on about the view out the window, the house, his parents, "...nice you love my house. What about your parents?" Will asked Katy.

"My parents are both still alive, still married. Typical catholic couple. They would rather be miserable than divorce," she laughed. "I love them both. They just don't love each other anymore."

Looking between them, Nicole watched as the female passenger reached across the centre console and took hold of Will's hand. He continued to drive with one hand, squeezing her hand, relaxing then squeezing it again.

"Where did you want to go for breakfast?" she asked. "I'm famished. You?"

Nicole continued to listen as they talked. Looking outside the car, she recognized the shops and restaurants on Rose Street. Traffic was light, few pedestrians on the sidewalk. The sun was still casting long morning shadows. She made a mental note of the surroundings.

As the skinny man and the girl spoke, she wondered how this new power came to be, being able to view live conversations outside of a photograph. Concerned about possibly being stuck between where she thought she was in the shower and in the car, she closed her eyes tightly, letting her mind go blank, she shut out all external stimuli, then opened her eyes, and she was back in the shower. The water continued to run down her body to the bathtub drain. Feeling a bit easier with her ability, she concentrated on being with the skinny man in the car. Placing her head under the shower, she felt relaxed, comfortable, no longer threatened. Her mind swirled with images, none of them making any sense, she was unable to reconnect with the skinny man. She made the attempt again. Nothing.

Turning off the taps, she didn't bother to dry off, she went straight to her cell, saw the text from Paul and instead of replying, she dialed his number. The phone rang, once, twice, three times before it went to voicemail.

"Shit."

*****

Paul walked around the house, his hands protected by black nitrile gloves. He opened drawers, used the end of his pen to rummage through the contents. He was looking for envelopes, medications, papers, bills, anything that would bear the name of the man who lived at the house. Where ever he went in the house, he was greeted with the same organizational marvel that astounded him. He would constantly repeat to himself that no one could live this way. There wasn't so much as a rubber band out of place; there wasn't any dust on the shelves, all the food in the fridge was within the best before dates. Even the clothes closets were organized with military precision.

Alone, he walked upstairs checked the bedrooms and closets. Only the master bedroom was disturbed, the bed unmade, bed sheet crumpled, and the pillows piled one on top of the other on one side of the bed. Everything else in the room was immaculate. Pulling open dresser drawers, the contents displayed the same organizational marvel as the rest of the house: socks, underwear and T-shirts folded and stacked neatly. He was unable to find any reference to the homeowner, the walls barren of any photos, landscape, family, wife or girlfriends. Leaving the master bedroom, he turned right down the hall and discovered the room with the vista expanse over the trees. Paul stood in the centre of the room, admiring the view, feeling rather insignificant with such a wondrous view over the mountain. He turned to see the wall of books behind him, walked over to admire the collection. Looking up to leather bound books, paperbacks, Paul was astounded at the small library collection. In the centre of the bookshelf was a carefully stacked pile of newspapers, the fold yellowed by the sunshine. He thumbed the edges of the stack then picked up the top copy from 1998. He smirked when he saw a picture of President Bill Clinton with the caption "Clinton Impeached". He placed the paper back on the stack and heard someone from behind but ignored it. The person spoke out again.

"We've got the SPCA coming to take the dogs."

"What? Oh sure. Yeah, that's good." Paul paused, "Some view huh?" Dan walked in and stood beside him, looking out over the treetops.

"Man, imagine waking up to this every morning? I wouldn't have to take my fucking blood pressure meds."

They both stood in silence, looking at the rising sun. The room was awash in yellow light. Paul could feel the heat against his skin. "Well, the guy who lives here certainly needed a bit more than the view to keep his blood pressure down. Did you see that girl downstairs found in the freezer? She looks like a jigsaw puzzle."

Dan shook his head, "Did you find anything yet with the homeowner's name?"

"No, but I texted the station to look up the registration for the house with the country. We should hear back shortly."

"Okay. You say you got a tip leading you here?"

"Outta the blue. A guy phoned and gave me the address. I don't have luck like that very often."

"Well today's your lucky day," Dan snickered.

Paul didn't say a word and left the room with Dan in tow. They walked through the kitchen, Carl still sat at the kitchen table and watched as they walked passed him. Carl was about to say something; instead, he stood and followed the two detectives to the basement. Paul heard him join them as they descended the stairs.

Paul turned to Dan, "Did you see the stack of old newspapers in that room? They go back almost twenty years. Looks like they just came off the press."

"Sounds like my in-law's house. They never throw anything away," Dan chuckled.

At the foot of the stairs, Officer Taylor stood in front of Carl, stopping him. Paul eyed the officer, silently granting Carl permission to pass. At the back of the finished basement, crime scene technicians muddled about, as they went through to the freezer. The temperature was noticeably cooler the closer they got to the broken door.

"Say anything," Paul pointed his finger only inches away from Carl's face, "I'll have you arrested. Touch anything; I'll shoot you on the spot. Got it?"

He just nodded in agreement knowing full well; Paul meant every word.

The three donned Tyvek shoe covers, and gloves then squeezed through the broken door which was not covered by a heavy sheet of clear plastic. The room was now lit, illuminating every gory detail Carl had lived through. They stood side by side, each one taking in every macabre detail of the room. Nothing was said, no one moved.

It was several minutes before Dan spoke, "The guys were already in, went through as much as they could."

"Geez it's cold in here," Paul exclaimed. "I hate the cold. Christ, after this I'm moving to the Florida Keys."

Dan knelt beside the body. He gently touched the body, the skin was still frozen solid, "They said even with the door broken, the temp is still below freezing in here."

Without turning to face Carl, Paul posed one more question, "You wanna go over in detail what you did in here?"

Once again, Carl was scared. He was now glad that when he was trapped inside, the lights were off so that he didn't have to see what was in the room with him. He looked at the walls, some of the instruments were still suspended by their hooks, others were carefully arranged in some order he didn't understand, other pieces had fallen to the floor. He resisted looking at the girl on the floor, but after going over the entire room, he had no choice but to look at her. Once he did, emotions overwhelmed him, and tears welled up inside. He felt them roll down his cold cheek, wiping them away before anyone could see he was crying. Everything inside him told him to run but wanted to help catch the man responsible was more powerful than his fear. Carl either refused to answer the question or couldn't.

Paul and Dan knelt beside the body. The body was now supine, looking up at the ceiling. Her face expressionless, showing neither sadness or joy or fear. The girl's eyes were open, staring into nothing with a blank gaze. The eyes appeared to have some crystallization on them. Her mouth was closed, the jaw frozen in place. With a gloved hand, Paul touched the frozen skin, ran his finger to the shoulder area where the sutures were still in place. He titled his head to get a better view of how the suture line ran around the axillary area up along the scapula and met in the front.

Even frozen, Paul could see that the body was assembled from more half a dozen different parts: the torso, the head, the arms, legs and feet, both hands were still missing. Even frozen, the skin tones were noticeably different from one another. He placed his hands on the floor of the freezer and squatted down to see inside the wrist. It was a clean-cut, surgical.

"We found a picture of a girl in that cabinet over there," Dan pointed to a small metallic cabinet on the same wall as the door, "She's a dead ringer for..." His words trailed off. "Sorry, poor choice of words. The girl in the picture looks identical to the body on the floor."

Paul stood, walked to the cabinet and used his pen to open the door. Inside, a color photo of a young girl, black hair, delicate features, smooth skin. It was a sunny day when the picture was taken; her head was slightly tilted to one side, a soft smile on the face, wearing a light teal dress. She was beautiful, but it was her eyes that caught his attention. With a gloved hand, he carefully removed the photo from the cabinet and held it beside the body on the floor, comparing the two girls. There wasn't much of a difference, but he did notice some small variations. Paul placed the photo on the counter and used his department phone to take a picture of the mysterious woman.

"What do you figure?" he asked. "Unrequited love? Bad breakup?"

"Who knows." Dan pointed to some frozen residue on the body, "See here, this hardened substance. I'm betting its raw egg. Look over there." He pointed to the far wall, "There's more of the same, and we found eggshell pieces in the corner."

"Not like him to leave the body dirty or this room a mess," Paul observed.

"My best guess, this was a fit of rage. Either at her or at someone else that set him off and time didn't allow for a cleanup. Things got in the way and prevented him from following a routine. Based on what I've seen and by no means am I a shrink, this guy is either ex-military or had a military or strict upbringing. Or, he's a complete whack job. I'm betting on the whack job."

Carl hadn't said anything or moved the entire time. He continued to cry but was dry; tears stopped flowing quite a while ago. There wasn't anything left inside. There were times he wanted to say something but couldn't. He couldn't find the right words. He was lost.

Dan stepped over the body on the floor, walked to a small chest freezer and opened it. "The funny thing is, well, the total opposite of funny, the SPCA team took the two dogs away. They said the dogs were as docile as puppies. Very well trained, well cared for, healthy, overall good dogs. We escorted the SPCA guys through the compound, the house and we couldn't find any dog food, none, no dry, no moist." He paused for a moment, "This is what we think he was feeding the dogs." He held the lid to the freezer open and stepped aside so Paul could look inside. "These were the unused parts he discarded. Not sure why some parts were given to the dogs, and some were thrown away. We found a meat grinder; we're testing it for blood and DNA. He may have fed the parts whole or ground them up. Not sure yet."

*****

At the bottom of the freezer were small frozen sections of human legs, arms, feet and hands and sections of the torso and organs, all wrapped in clear plastic. Paul took a few steps, peered inside, then ran out of the room. Carl didn't move from his spot; he didn't want to see what was inside the freezer. He has surmised as much, but if he didn't look, he would never know for sure, and that suited him just fine.

Carl finally spoke up offering his opinion to Dan, "The body parts he threw away had cancer cells or tumors in them. That was the common thread between all the parts that were found," his voice soft, sullen. "He wouldn't even feed them to the dogs. Instead, they ended up in the trash." He was shivering again. The cold bit through his clothes but he felt nothing. He wanted to leave in the worst way possible, but his legs had gone numb.

*****

Paul hung his head in the toilet and vomited several times. He thought he had seen the worst that life had to offer but to see body parts wrapped up like food put him over the edge. Eyes closed, mouth open, the rubble in his stomach was persistent, and he felt as if another wave would come over him any moment. Blindly reaching up, he flushed the toilet, sending the contents of his stomach down the drain. Pulling himself up, he sat on the toilet and hung his head. He desperately wanted to vomit again, but his stomach overrode his head.

He went to the sink, ran the water for a few moments, rinsed his mouth several times then splashed water on his face. He repeated this several times before he felt better. He patted himself down to ensure that nothing found its way to his suit jacket. He suddenly went into panic mode. His cell phone was missing. He looked in the toilet, around the base, the wastepaper basket then realized he left it on the kitchen table. Rushing upstairs, Paul paused momentarily in the doorway when he saw his cell phone. Breathing a sigh of relief, he reached for his phone as it began to vibrate. Answering the phone, he spoke in hushed tones; his eyes widened until he hung up and rushed from the table.

Paul didn't know Ken had arrived and saw him in the driveway as he was looking at electronic images on the crime scene techs camera. Paul came running over, already out of breath, "We got," breath, "a 20 on," breath, "the guy."

"What?" Ken was stunned. "Where?" He replaced the camera. Winded, Paul was only able to speak in two-word sentences, "Rose Street. Dan's still inside. I'll drive, you call him and tell him where we're going."

Paul slammed the driver's door, keyed the ignition and floored the accelerator. Ken barely had time to close his door as the tires kicked back small stones from the gravel driveway. Paul turned right hard on the street, activating the lights and siren.

"Can you call dispatch, tell them we want the patrol cars to be on the lookout for a dark blue Chevy, four-door sedan, possibly with two people inside, one male, one female. The male is Caucasian, slender built, the female is also Caucasian and young. The car may be parked at a restaurant. Do not engage if the vehicle is located."

Ken looked surprised, "How did you get all this information?"

"Nicole told me."

Stunned, Ken turned to his partner, "Would you mind explaining how she knew? We haven't shown her any photos, and that info is pretty specific."

He stared out the windshield, "Didn't ask. She didn't tell. You got a problem with that?"

Paul took a sharp turn a little wide, the tires hit the dirt shoulder, he corrected, and the car righted itself.

"Nope." Ken applied his seatbelt, tightened it then picked up the mike and radioed dispatch to relay the newest information.

Paul kept the speed well above the posted limit but avoided the shoulders. He would hit the siren when cars were a little slow to yield. He was under twenty minutes out driving the limit; he hoped to be there in ten.

*****

The restaurant was almost full of early morning customers. Will and Katy sat in the far booth of the dinner, half-finished plates still on the table but pushed to the side. Coffee cups continued to be refilled by the server as she passed by the tables and pulled creamers from her apron laying them on the table without paying attention to the customers.

Katy rested her chin in cupped hands on tented elbows that rested on the table's edge. She listened to everything Will had to say, her eyes staring at this young man that captivated her. Even though he carried the conversation, Will was concerned about the stranger he left in the house and felt uneasy. His words began to slur and suddenly stopped speaking. The noise in the restaurant added to his anxiety; he kept rubbing his temples as he spoke.

"You Okay?" Katy seemed concerned about Will. He began to look tired and had quickly developed bags under his eyes since they left the house. "You're not looking well."

Looking down, his head filled with images, swirling around, making little sense, sending him off balance. He put his hand out as if to tell Katy he was all right. She stood, walked around and placed her arm around him, "Let's go." Katy signaled the server for the check.

He slid out of the booth, attempted to stand, his knees buckled and almost fell to the floor. He braced himself on the table's edge and pulled himself upright.

The same girl who refilled their coffee arrived and helped Will to stand, "Is he alright? You want I call you an ambulance or something?"

Will shook his head adamantly refusing anyone be called, "I'm all right." His voice was aggressive and stern, something Katy had never heard before. She pulled more than enough cash from her purse and laid it on the table then helped Paul to the car. He became weaker as they made their way to the car outside in the parking lot. Opening the passenger door, she helped Will inside, fastened his seatbelt then went to the driver's side.

"You doing OK?"

Will turned and looked at her, his eyes now completely bloodshot, welling up with tears.

"Oh my God. What's happening to you? You look horrible," she said worriedly. "I've got to get you to a hospital."

Barely able to whisper, or keep himself sitting upright, "No. Home." Will wasn't able to understand what was going on either. He was fighting this feeling inside that his mind was being pulled apart in every possible direction at once. Sitting back in his seat, he placed both hands on his head, closed his eyes and tried to force his mind to stop spinning.

*****

Nicole lay in bed on top of the covers, her head resting on the pillow, she dreamt about the skinny man with the hairless arms. She saw him at a table eating breakfast, the same beautiful girl that was in the car earlier, was now sitting across from him. They spoke, their lips moved, but their voices were silent. Instead of the clear vision she had when she was in the backseat of his car, now the image was blurry, like television with poor reception. The vision floated around the table, around their heads, below table level then back up again. Nicole focused her attention on the eyes of the skinny man.

The image fluttered, re-focused then moved in close the skinny man then disappeared into the blackness. She saw nothing, no color; there wasn't any sound. She was lost, not knowing where she was, she concentrated and felt a violent jolt. Her whole body shook violently. Fighting back, she righted herself and saw a crack of light, then a little more until she was looking at the face of the beautiful girl from the car. She had a look of concern on her face and was staring directly at Nicole but not at Nicole. It was then she realized, she was inside the skinny man's head, seeing what he was seeing but she wasn't able to hear anything. Nicole turned to look around inside the skinny man's head. Each time she turned to look at a memory or thought, the skinny man attempted to fight back.

Nicole began to pull at threads of memories and saw him following a girl to a parking lot then attack her pushing her head into the roof of the car. Nicole recoiled at the anger inside the skinny man. He tossed her into the back seat then drove away.

She could feel the skinny man fight her; he tried to block the memories, the images that she was making him relive. She was able to fight him off, pull at those thoughts that made him feel uneasy. Nicole opened as many memories as she could, opening a flood of images all at once, she just kept at it, grabbing at whatever she could. In bed, Nicole also saw the same pictures and was sickened by what this man had done.

The girl stood and walked around to the man's side, tossed some cash onto the table and helped him stand and assisted him to the car.

With her mind, Nicole reached out and pulled at a memory and stopped. She saw the skinny man watch his dogs pull violently, snarling and growling at whatever they had their teeth sunk into and pull. They pulled in opposite directions until they each had a chunk of flesh they were fighting over. She woke up, sitting upright in her bed. Nicole was drenched in sweat and exhausted. She reached for her cell phone and collapsed rolling off the bed to the floor.

Will opened his eyes, the nausea and feeling that his head was about to explode were gone in an instant. He was himself again. Confused, he looked at Katy and smiled, "How did we get here?" he laughed.

"Will? What the fuck happened? I was taking you to the hospital. I thought you were having a stroke or an aneurysm or something." She looked across at him. "You, you look amazing now. Like nothing happened."

Will shook the cobwebs from his head, "I was having breakfast with you right?" he questioned her.

Katy nodded in agreement as she slowed her speed, "Yeah, you wanted to go home, but I was taking you to the hospital."

He laughed, "I'm not sure what happened but all of sudden, my head was, I don't know how to describe it, pulled apart, like something on the inside was ripping my brain apart all at once." His hands whirled about his head helping to explain what he was feeling.

"I still think we should get to a hospital." Katy was still worried about him.

Traffic was heavier than it was before they stopped for breakfast and Katy failed to notice a car pulling out of the restaurant parking lot remaining several lengths behind. A second car joined the slow and quiet pursuit. One car would move in closer, break away from the chase and make a left or right turn, keeping in contact with dispatch and rejoin several blocks later.

Neither one of the police cars following Will and Katy notice a fourth vehicle following further behind. Carl overheard Paul telling Ken at the house that the suspect had been spotted and began his pursuit. Carl recognized the two unmarked police cars but was unsure which car they were following. He kept his distance, observing their tactics of deception and as more cars pulled off the road. As cars tuned left or right, other vehicles entered traffic; Carl was finally able to determine which car they were following.

Paul was in the lead car almost a full block behind the car driven by Katy. Carl maneuvered his car closer to the unmarked cars until he was within a few car lengths behind them. He changed lanes attempting to see if there was anyone else in the car they were following. Trying to gain a little distance on the car, he almost pulled up alongside the second unmarked police vehicle. His attention had been on the skinny man's car that he didn't realize what he had done. Letting off the gas, his vehicle slowly retreated to the rest of traffic. He cursed at himself for pulling such a dumb move.

He rubbed his head, his headache was still pounding in his temples, but he wasn't letting this story go. In the back of his mind, he wouldn't mind a little revenge for being tossed in a freezer and being left for dead.

He struggled with the two reasons for being where he was. In the end, he thought, he decided the story won out.

He reached inside his jacket, unlocked the phone and started the camera app. A few action pictures of the chase couldn't hurt, he thought. He held the phone low on the dash and clicked the shutter several times. The phone was tossed in the centre console in case he needed more photos. Taking his attention off the chase to take pictures caused him to fall further back than he had wanted. The traffic light up ahead was amber, the lead car and the two police cars had already made it through the intersection and Carl was too far behind to make it through without running a red. He slammed on the brakes, the tires of his old car bit the asphalt coming to a stop just over the thick white line.

"Fuck," he punched the centre of the steering wheel, the horn blew startling the driver to his left.

Carl looked at the road ahead and watched as the three cars increased their distance from him. Looking left then right, he decided on a calculated gamble. The road they were on went directly to the highway, to the left was an industrial zone, right took them back to Will's house. He didn't bother to signal, cranked the wheel hard and floored the accelerator. He navigated his way through the city streets, weaving between cars, driving faster than he should. He was taking a huge risk turning away from the group, but they had pulled so far ahead at the light, they could be anywhere. At least this way, moving was better than remaining motionless at the light. Going through the city streets in his head, he imagined where the skinny man would go. As far as Carl knew, the skinny man was unaware he had escaped or that the police were at the house.

Without warning, Carl slammed on the brakes and stopped in the middle of the street. Behind him, cars swerved around him to avoid crashing into the rear of this car. "Fuck, fuck, fuck," he screamed at himself. He looked behind, made sure there were no cars behind him and floored the accelerator.

*****

In the lead car, Paul and Ken remained silent as they kept their distance. Paul drove as Ken entered the vehicles license plate into the vehicle laptop. Almost immediately, the computer brought up the owner of the car, Katherine Tilley. They now suspected who the female driver was. As they followed the car, their erratic maneuvers indicated that they were aware they were being followed or were lost. Several times, the car took a turn, pulled over, after a few moments signaled and pulled into traffic again. Each time, the lead surveillance car would pass, slow as the rear car would assume the chase. Paul was certain they had been discovered.

*****

Will rubbed his temples trying to stem the pressure inside his head. He kept his eyes closed opening them momentarily to get his barring's, give directions, then close his eyes again.

"I should take you to the hospital. You're being stubborn. Let me help," Katy begged.

Will could barely open his eyes, the pressure increasing with each passing second. He felt his stomach content rise in his throat, and he fought hard to keep from vomiting in the car. "Quiet, please. My dad will help."

*****

Carl ran upstairs to Nora's office and burst through the office door. She was on the phone, listening to whoever was on the other end, gave Carl a look that could kill and went back to the conversation. He walked over to her desk, placed his finger on the disconnect button and ended the call.

"What the fuck?" Nora stood and screamed. "Do you know who that was?"

"Couldn't give a shit." He sat on the corner of her desk, "I need information. I need it now. This isn't a request."

"You can't come in and start demanding things." Nora stood and came nose to nose with her reporter. "I've been looking for an excuse to fire y…"

Carl spoke over her, "Sam, the cleaning guy. HR won't give me his last name or address. I need it. I need it now."

"Sam, what guy Sam?" Nora was confused; she honestly didn't know the name of the night cleaner.

"The guy who used to be you, like twenty years ago. He used to run this place."

"You mean Smitty Frischmann. His name is Sam, but they called him Smitty back then, way before my time. I didn't know he worked here cleaning. I've never taken the opportunity to notice." Nora retook her seat, "Why do you need his address?"

Carl was excited and started to pace around Nora's office. He placed his hand over his mouth, thought for a moment, "I'm spit balling here. This is gonna go way off track, like way out in left field." His hand went up in the air and spun to the left. "I was almost killed this morning before…"

219

"What! Killed?" she screamed at the top of her lungs. Several of the staff stood and looked at them through the glass.

He wasn't phased by Nora's outburst and continued, "before I could talk to the skinny man who owns the house. So, when I helped suture up the guy in the ER…"

"You sutured some guy?"

"You keep interrupting me, and this is going to take a long time."

Nora sat back and decided to let Carl finish. He babbled, Nora had a difficult time understanding every word, "Turns out this guy was the one responsible for the all the girls going missing. I was told last night where to look. I was clubbed when I got to the house then put in a freezer with a dead body made up of several different girls' body parts. I managed to escape the freezer and was rescued by the police. When they went through the house, they found a stock of pristine old newspapers going back twenty some odd years. Sam said he retired about two decades ago. It's a long shot but something Sam told me about his house, it sounded just like the house I was at."

There was silence in the room as the two stared at each other. She reached for the receiver, dialed an extension, spoke to the person on the other end, scribbled some notes then hung up. She left the sheet of paper on her desk, stood and walked out of the office. Carl scooped up the sheet, stuffed it in his pocket and walked out of the building.

*****

Katy pulled into the driveway of a modest home. She noticed the grounds were immaculate; the grass cut short, the shrubs manicured, even the flowers were of the same height along the front of the house. She killed the engine, waiting for the owner of the house to come out and greet them. Instead, there was silence save for the slight moans coming from Will in the passenger seat. She ran around to the passenger door, Will almost fell out and vomited onto the driveway.

Katy knelt, held Will as he wretched and vomited again. He reached for the door handle, missed falling to the asphalt almost landing in the vomit. He rolled onto his back, still holding his head, moaning. Katy failed to notice the elderly man who exited the house standing behind her. "Quick. Get him inside the house," he barked.

They helped Will to stand, leading him to the side door. They led him to the living room and laid him gently on the couch. He continued to hold his end and roll side to side.

"How did you find me?" the old man whispered.

"Will gave me directions." Katy removed her jacket and placed it under Will's head. She stroked his damp hair from his forehead. "He's burning up. Can you get me some Tylenol? It'll help with the fever."

The old man returned with a glass of water and two pills, handing them to her. Katy helped Will swallow the pills then laid him back down.

"Thank you... I don't know your name."

"Sam. He's going by Will now."

Katy spun around to look at him, "Now?" she questioned him. "What do you mean by that?"

Sam took the chair facing Katy, "He's always changing his name, ever since he was a kid. His birth name is Ariel Frischmann. He always hated his Jewish heritage. That's my fault; I was never there for him. You know, to help him find himself."

Katy sat on the edge of the couch holding Will's hand, "His name is Will, as long as he wants me to call him Will, we're going to call him Will."

Sam shook his head in agreement, "Will it is." He watched how she cared for his son, "You care for him?"

"I do. He's special." She looked at Will's face, tiny beads of perspiration rolled down his forehead to her jacket. "He's sick. Really sick."

"How well do you know him?" Sam adjusted himself in the chair bracing himself for what he was about to tell her.

"I know him well enough to know I care." Katy's eyes never left Will. "He's not well."

"That's obvious."

Sam shifted again, "I need to tell you something about him. You won't like it."

Katy turned and faced Sam, "Did you give him up for adoption?" "No, just the opposite. He never told you about his mother then."

Katy shook her head, "She was beautiful. In every way possible, the most beautiful woman in the world. I loved her more than you could ever love someone. His mother was the love of my life, but I was married to someone that I couldn't ever leave. I was a failure as a man, weak. Instead, I spend as much time with Will's mother as I could, got her pregnant. I bought her this house," he looked around, "and gave the two of them everything they needed except for a father and husband. The older he got, the more he hated me. When his mother died, I gave him my house, money, every opportunity to be whatever his wanted."

"Instead, he disappointed you."

Sam lowered his head, "I disappointed myself. I was a failure. He grew angry over the years, wanted his mother back, wanted a life that I denied him. He wanted a family." Sam's voice began to crack. "There was so much hatred towards me for what I had done. Maybe adoption would've been better. He would've had a family, a mother and a father."

"You were what, a weak father if that? Of course, there was resentment. Right now, I'm not worried about what you did wrong to Will; I want to find out why he's sick. Has he ever been sick like this before?"

"No, not that I know of." Sam looked at his son with worry.

"Not that you know of? What do you know about your son?" Katy screamed at Sam.

Sam stood, paced around the room, "I know things about him that no one knows about. I'm sure I know more about him than you do. I don't recall him ever mentioning you before. You've been around for what, a few weeks. Believe me, when I tell you, you don't want to know what I know."

Infuriated, Katy spun around, fire in her eyes, stepped in close to Sam,

"You mean his little playroom in the basement. Yeah, I know about that."

Stunned, Sam fell back into his chair. He stared at her wide-eyed, unable to breathe or comprehend what he just heard. "How?"

"Late last night when he was sleeping, I couldn't, so I wandered around the house, found his hobby. I was shocked at first but not surprised. Actually, I was fascinated by what he had collected."

Will moaned on the sofa, he appeared to be sleeping; his arms had fallen loosely to the sides.

Sam looked at his son, then back at Katy, "Fascinated? Not repulsed?" She smiled, "You sound surprised that I wouldn't be shocked. I've always been fascinated with death. I've never shied away from it, but rather I've embraced it. I've always wondered what it would be like to kill someone, now maybe, I'll get the chance."

"Get the chance? To take someone's life? Seriously you need to re-evaluate your life choices. You can't be like my son. What he's doing is wrong."

Katy stood defiantly before Sam, "You don't need to protect me, old man."

Sam's voice quivered and shook, "My whole life I've tried to protect my son. But what he's done in the past year goes above what I can cover up. He needs to be stopped. I was scared for him the last time I went to the house and saw what he had done. I sent police pictures and tips, but they were too fucking stupid to put the clues together. If the police couldn't stop him, I thought I better try. I tried reasoning with him, explaining to him what he's done has no excuse."

Katy came to Will's defense, "Why would you stop your son? He's caring, compassionate, thoughtful and intelligent."

Sam was dumbfounded, unable to respond, "He can't go on like this. And you shouldn't try to be like him."

As she was about to defend her position, Will let out a whimper. They both turned to see him roll over.

"He needs a doctor," argued Sam. "Then we need to call the police. This has to stop here and now. The two of you need to be stopped."

Katy went to Will's side, touched his forehead, then looked around, "I'll get him a glass of water. He's burning up."

She walked past Sam to the kitchen, poured a glass of water and returned to the living room. She stood behind Sam, swung her arm and plunged the knife through the chair into his back. Sam stiffened, eyes widened, he felt the blade twist inside him. Katy retracted the knife, swung her arm and plunged the knife into Sam over and over again. The material began to stain red as blood flowed from the wounds as life left the old man's body.

Katy walked around to face Sam as he drew his last breaths. With blood dripping from the blade, she held onto the knife, gripping it tightly. She watched as Sam stared at her, he tried to take in a breath but couldn't. He coughed, blood bubbled in the corner of his mouth then slowly flowed from his chin. His chest stopped heaving, his eyes closed as his head slumped forward.

She gripped the knife handle firmly, feeling the blood between her fingers. Her pulse quickened, her chest heaved with deep breaths. Katy thought she would be more heartbroken about taking a life. She wasn't. Will moaned, she turned to see him roll over on the couch.

*****

Outside of Sam's house, Paul and Dan sat in the car, waiting, watching the house where Katy's car was parked. As Dan kept an eye on the house,

Paul kept texting Nicole without any success. His anxiety mounted with each text that went unanswered.

"What?" Dan asked.

Paul remained silent for a moment, "Trying to get in touch with Nic. I'm getting worried."

"Send a uniform over to check on her. Once our backups arrive, we're gonna be busy for quite some time."

Paul exhaled, thought about Dan's suggestion and without saying, picked up the mic and requested dispatch to send a car to Nicole's house to check on her well-being. He seemed to relax slightly and sloughed in the driver's seat. He began to fidget with the switches on the dash as he waited for a response from dispatch and the backup crews to arrive.

As he played with the radio, a car drove past them, into the driveway and parked behind Katy's car. The door swung open, and Carl rushed to the front door.

*****

Nicole woke up on the floor beside her bed, weak, barely able to push herself up. She reached up, pulled on the bedspread for leverage and sat on the edge. Feeling like she had just run a marathon, she had nothing left. She felt the moisture on her brow and used the bedsheet to wipe her face. Looking down, she noticed a small amount of blood on the sheet. Rubbing her nose left a trace of blood on the back of her hand. She rested for a few moments, never letting Will's presence leave her mind. She wanted that man stopped at all costs. Resting, she wanted her strength back in case Paul needed her again. Needing sleep, wanting sleep but couldn't let herself drift off. She decided the best way to ensure she didn't fall asleep was to get up. She was tired and hungry but more tired than anything else. Sitting on the bed, she pulled herself up, went to the bathroom, splashed some water on her face, then made a quick cup of coffee to feel a bit more energized. At the table, she cradled the cup in both hands; the headache pounded with each pulse through her temples. She considered taking something for her the pain but decided against it. After all, it was the body's way of saying when it's had enough.

Picking up her cell phone, she noticed the battery had gone dead. It took what little energy she had left to go to the living room and plug the power cord into the phone, waited until the screen lit up then walked back to the kitchen. Her eyes felt heavy as she tried to drink, but all she wanted was sleep. She sipped her coffee, then heard the phone chime that she had unseen texts. She ran to the living room, picked up her phone, entered her password, scrolled down then tapped the icon. She snapped her fingers hoping this would make the message come up quicker. When they opened, she read them and quickly typed back a response. She stood at the phone waiting to hear back from Paul.

*****

"What the fuck is that asshole doing?" Paul exited the car, slammed the driver's door and ran towards Carl. As he did, Carl turned to see Paul then Dan gave chase. Carl picked up the pace and made it to the side door, yanked it open and entered the house. Paul didn't let up even though his size prevented him from closing the gap between them. He burst into the house and stopped; Dan almost bumped into him just beyond the kitchen.

Katy was behind Carl, holding him tightly, a knife at his throat. Paul saw this small framed woman, holding an already bloody knife close to Carl's neck. He remained silent, a look of fear in his eyes, his arms hanging loosely at his side. He offered no resistance to Katy's hold.

To Paul's right, Sam was slumped forward in a chair; blood dripped from his open mouth creating a small stain on his shirt. Behind Katy and Carl, Will lay motionless and silent on the couch. Paul thought that he was dead until he noticed the chest rise and fall.

"You must be Katherine Tilley." Paul's voice was calm and direct.

Katy held her composure, the knife continued to press deeply into Carl's skin. Her hand was steady, her voice never wavered, "Katy, please," she politely said as she smiled.

"Pleased to meet you, Katy. I'm Paul; this is Dan." He blindly motioned to Dan standing behind, and as he did, he rested his hand on his handgun. "Did you want to put the knife down? No reason to involve this little shit," Paul smiled back. "Why don't you let him go, and we can discuss what you want." He could see Carl silently mouth the word "Little shit?"

Katy smiled again, "No that's fine. I'm good."

Carl finally spoke, "Well, if anyone's interested, I'm not all that comfortable. I could use a seat."

Katy laughed. Her hand held the knife tightly against Carl's neck. "I didn't know how things were going to go when I woke up today. It's not exactly how I had envisioned it, but I'll tell you, it's been a hell of a ride so far."

Paul looked to Sam in the chair, then back to Katy. "I'll say. I'm sure no one thought the day was going to be like this." Paul slowly moved behind Sam's chair. "I'd really like to go home tonight Katy. I'm sure everyone else would too. Since we already know he…"

"Will," Katy broke in.

"Will over there is the guy responsible for all the girls' disappearances and from what I can tell, no one saw what happened to this guy," he pointed to Sam, "maybe it was you, maybe it was Will. However, we can all assume a good lawyer would say Will did it and gets you off. It's not like he can defend himself after what he's done. And the dead guy isn't telling any tales. Am I right?"

Katy nodded in agreement.

Paul continued, "Then this little shit," again Carl raised his eyebrows, "burst in, and you grabbed the knife not knowing what was happening and defended yourself. Then we came charging in. One major fuck up if you ask me. You're just a victim here, like the guy you're holding. See, easy as pie."

Katy's hold on the knife relaxed, and she lowered it slightly from Carl's neck.

Behind her, Will let out a soft moan, rolled and almost fell to the floor. Katy turned, relaxing her hold on Carl. He bolted from her grip and ran to the other side of the living room. Without warning, Sam leapt from the chair and went head first into Katy's stomach, knocking her off balance, sending her sprawling on top of Will.

Sam fell, screaming in pain as his injured back smashed to the floor. He arched his back then went limp.

Katy stumbled momentarily, regained her balance as Paul reached for her and the knife. She blindly swung the knife, the edge of the blade ripping across Paul's stomach. He doubled over as the pain tore through him. He went down, holding his stomach and instinctively curled up in the fetal position.

Dan pulled his gun, aimed, pulled the trigger twice, paused then twice more. The sound in the tiny living room was deafening as bullets tore through Katy. The first bullet went through her right bicep into the wall behind them causing her to drop the knife, as the second round hit her in the chest, the third went into her neck from one side and out the opposite end, blood sprayed outward, the fourth missed her entirely, hitting the large picture window sending the entire pane crashing to the living room floor.

Katy hit the edge of the couch, then rolled to the floor beside Sam. She gasped for air, her mouth open, trying to suck in as much air as possible. She looked like a fish out of water trying to breathe. The bullet left a large wound on her neck when it exited. Blood squirted from the torn carotid artery in the neck; it would be only a matter of moments before she died. Smoke billowed from the end of the gun barrel as Dan lowered it. The smell of burnt gunpowder hung in the air. He paused, waiting to see if Katy attempted to stand then walked cautiously over to her, raising his gun and pointing it directly at her chest. He reached back, pressed and held the red button on the portable radio attached to his belt. The tone sent out a distress call to police dispatch notifying them that officers were in need of assistance.

His steps were slow and calculated as he approached her. Looking down, he noticed Sam's breathing was shallow but still breathing. Holding the gun with two hands, he stiffened his grip, finger on the trigger, he pointed the gun at Katy's head and called out to his partner, "Hey buddy. You still with me?"

Paul's voice cracked, "I think if I let go, my stomach is going to spill out all over this nice carpet," and let out a soft chuckle.

"Hey. You. Reporter guy. A little help here." Dan's stare never left the sight at the end of the barrel.

Carl had already run to the bathroom and pulled a large towel from the closet and was now holding it to Paul's stomach. "I'm on it." He applied pressure to the wound as his stomach decided to turn on him. He felt tiny rubbles and tasted something sour at the back of his throat as he held the towel to the wound.

Dan kicked Katy hard in the side. She didn't move. He kicked her again, harder this time. Again, she didn't move. The gun was still pointed at her head as he reached for a carotid pulse. None was found. Her eyes were wide open; she didn't blink. "Pretty sure she's dead."

He looked at Will on the couch, he was breathing, but didn't move. Dan reached out and poked him; he remained motionless on his side. Reaching for the cuffs that usually hung over the back of his belt, he couldn't find them. "Shit." He turned to his injured partner, "Do you have your cuffs?"

In a barely audible voice, Paul answered, "Car."

Dan turned his attention to Carl, "You got this? I've gotta go to the car for the cuffs."

"Go." Dan ran past him before he got the word out.

Carl held pressure with both hands against the massive open wound. The blood-soaked towel was already saturated and couldn't hold anymore. He looked up to Paul whose color was ashen, his eyes looked tired, "You hanging in there?"

"Yeah, just feel like I got hit by a train. A really big fucking ugly train with attitude." Paul reached into his pocket with a bloody hand and took hold of the photo he always kept with him. He squeezed it tightly, knowing full well he was probably destroying it.

Carl laughed, "You OK if I go get another towel?"

He just nodded. Carl looked back at Will who remained immobile on the couch. He ran to the bathroom closet, found another clean towel, then raced back. He wasn't sure if the extra towel would fit over the blood-soaked one, so he quickly removed it, saw the open wound, gagged, a wave of light-headedness overtook him, but he fought through it. He stuffed the towel into the wound and applied as much pressure as he could.

"That was totally gross by the way," he said as he heard Dan run into the living room.

"Where the fuck is Will?" Dan screamed.

Carl spun his head around, the man that was on the couch only moments ago was now gone.

*****

Will ran between houses, keeping low and in the shadows to avoid being seen. The headache and vertigo he was suffering had subsided, but his head still pounded. He stumbled a bit, regained his footing as he kept the pace to get as far away from his father's house as possible.

Running along a backyard fence, his foot caught some overgrowth sending him sprawling to the ground. Landing on the grass, he slid for several feet before coming to a stop. He lay there, panting, trying to catch his breath. Eyes closed, he could feel his mind spinning like he was in a small boat on rough seas. He raised himself on all fours, paused, let the spinning settle before standing and racing away once again.

He realized that if the police tracked him to his father's house, they must surely know where he was living. Shocked that Katy knew his secret, he was sorry she had been killed but better her than him. As he ran, he wondered where he could hide, where he could go without being discovered. He paused where the fence ended, looked down the path between the two houses. He noticed a garden shed in the backyard directly across from him. He jumped the small fence into the backyard, stayed quiet, waiting for any sign that the homeowners or a dog would have discovered him. He carefully made his way to the shed, found it unlocked, slowly opened the door, entered then closed the door tightly.

Will found a section of open space on the floor, carefully lowered himself, curled up on the floor and quickly fell asleep.

*****

Dan stood outside with a dozen or more uniformed officers, coordinating the search for Will Fleischmann. He assigned duties to several of the officers, expecting they would search the entire dozen or so blocks surrounding the whole house. Several officers were already going over every single piece of paper in the house looking for a possible clue as to where Will might be headed. They combed their way through neatly packed boxes, organized in military fashion, easily referenced and catalogued.

Parked in the driveway and along the street were several marked police vehicles, unmarked cars and two ambulances. When the paramedics arrived, Dan couldn't remain with his friend. He had become too emotional, and the only way to deal with his anger was to work. The other paramedic crew was working feverishly to save Sam's life.

Carl sat on the curb between two of the cruisers and spoke into his cell phone. He was recounting the events that had just transpired in the living room and his heroic deeds that helped save the life of the injured detective. At least that's how the story would read. As he held the phone inches away from his face, in the excitement, it was only then that he noticed his hands were blood soaked. Placing the phone in his pocket, he realized he had nothing to clean his hands. He walked to the back of the first ambulance, on one of the open back doors was a hand sanitizer dispenser. Pressing the lever, a tiny drop of sanitizer squirted into his palm. He looked at the amount in his hand and pressed the lever a second time, then a third. Something snapped, and he continued to push the lever over and over again until the fluid spilt out over his palm.

Looking at his hand, the hand sanitizer fluid penetrated the dried blood on his palm and fingers and slowly changed color from clear to a soft pink then dripped onto the asphalt by his shoes. He stared at his hands for several minutes, the voices behind him going unnoticed. Eventually, a soft tap on the shoulder broke his trance.

"You okay bud?"

Carl turned to see one of the paramedics standing behind him at the foot end of a stretcher with Paul secured to it. He was sitting up, his knees bend up, held in place by two large pillows. An IV of normal saline was inserted into his right arm, a nasal cannula provided some much-needed oxygen, the vital signs monitor displayed his readings, each one in a different color. Carl looked at the screen, not understanding any of the numbers but the steady beeping made him feel confident the detective would survive.

"Yeah. I'm okay. Just a little freaked out." Carl shook the remaining fluid from his hands.

In a weak voice, Paul thanked him, "You did good in there. Thanks for saving my life. I owe you big time. Was that my blood on your hands?"

Carl just nodded.

"Does that make us blood brothers or something?" he smiled.

Carl offered a fake laugh, "If it does make us brothers, I'll be hitting you up for inside information one day as payback."

Paul smiled back. "Deal."

He watched as the paramedics loaded Paul in the ambulance and drove off with lights flashing as they made their way beyond the parameter. After the rig disappeared at the end of the street, he turned to see the other crew wheeling Sam out of the house. Each of the paramedics had a look of concern on their face as they made their way to the second rig. The same equipment was connected to Sam that he saw on Paul. Carl made his way over to the back doors. If Sam wasn't dead, he certainly looked it. Carl assumed Sam was still alive because if he wasn't, the paramedics would be performing CPR.

"How's he holding up? He saved us in there," Carl barked at the medics.

The paramedic at the foot end of the cot gave Carl the death stare, "I don't tell you how to do your job, don't tell me how to do mine."

The stretcher was loaded, the other medic hoped into the back and quietly offered, "I'm doing all I can." The gruff medic closed the dual doors and walked to the driver's door. He drove off, lights flashing, but as soon as the rig cleared the barrier tape, he heard the ambulance engine accelerate hard, and the siren blared to clear the bystanders who had gathered on the street.

*****

Nicole and Simone sat at the kitchen table, silently drinking coffee, the box of doughnuts Simone picked up on the way over, remained untouched. Nicole kept her eyes focused on the cell phone before her, waiting for it to ring.

Simone was about to speak, looked up then went silent again.

"What? You've done that like ten times now. If you have something to say, just say it," Nicole exclaimed.

Simone put her cup down carefully on the table, "Stop brooding. You're being a child waiting for him to call."

"What can I do if he won't call?" she questioned.

Simone thought for a moment, "Didn't you say that you're getting better control of your, whatever you call it, ability? If you can direct your spirit or your mojo, send it to Paul and connect with him."

"That's a huge personal invasion. They don't know I'm doing it. And I don't know if I'm hurting them or giving them cancer or turning their brain to week-old oatmeal." She tapped the table with her fingers. Her anxiety was evident, but now she was seriously considering Simone's suggestion.

"Why don't you call the police station first? If that doesn't get you an answer, then try your voodoo."

Without saying a word, Nicole picked up the phone, dialed the station and asked to speak with any detective currently working. It took several minutes before she was connected, "Hi. My name is Nicole Blake. I'm a friend of Detective Paul Hammond. I've been trying for several hours to reach him on his cell phone, but it keeps going to voicemail. I was wondering if you could help me?"

There was a short pause on the other end of the line, "We aren't permitted to give that information out," said the female detective. "I'm truly sorry, but unless you're on the detective's emergency contact list, I can't tell you anything. What's your name again?"

Exasperated, she attempted to remain calm, "Nicole Blake."

"Nicole Blake," the detective repeated back, "I'll check his file and see if," there was a pause, "one moment please."

Ken took the handset from the other detective, "Nicole, it's Ken. Paul's OK; he's been hurt. I just got back from the scene. He wanted me to call you anyway. They've already taken him to the hospital. Are you at home? I can have a car pick you up."

Nicole's voice was panicked and cracking, "I'll drive."

Ken sternly interjected, "You're not driving. Paul told me how bad you drive."

"Okay. Not the time for jokes Ken. Seriously, is Paul alright?"

There was a pause from Ken that only added to Nicole's concern, "He's stable, but he has a serious injury. He was taken to surgery; I assume he'll be in recovery by the time you get there. Now, I want to send a car to pick you up. You shouldn't drive."

"Can you tell me what happened?"

"The suspect attacked him with a knife, cut him bad. He'll be fine but he needed to have a surgeon close the wound."

"Skinny man?"

Ken thought for a moment, and he realized Will and the skinny man were one and the same, "Will Fleischmann, the skinny man. Yes."

Rage welled up inside Nicole as she thought what Paul had gone through.

"Let me send that car for you."

She thought about his offer, "I have a friend here. She can drive me," she barked back and hung up.

*****

Will woke up feeling refreshed, all traces of dizziness and the headache was gone. He stood and looked around the dimly lit shed. He spotted what he thought was a bicycle and pulled it from the pile of junk on top of it. With a quick check to see if was ridable, he opened the door a crack, peered outside, sensing everything was clear, he carried the bike out of the shed to the path between the houses. Mounting the bike, he casually rode away as if nothing had happened.

*****

Ken walked through the hospital with an army of uniformed officers behind him. He spoke as he walked, "Two officers at each entrance, loading bays, doors, windows, I don't care if it's a locked door that never gets used, guard it. Nobody gets by you unless they have ID confirmed by the head of the hospital and me. You all have a picture of the suspect?" They all agreed. He stopped and turned to face the officers, randomly pointed at them, "You two, inside Paul's room, you two outside the room. You four, the same thing with the father. He's still in surgery. Park outside the surgical suite, and if he makes it, sit beside him in the ICU. Understand?"

They all agreed, and the four officers appointed to stand guard left to their respective assignments, the rest went to their assigned location.

Ken walked alone and slowly to the recovery room feeling guilty he had not been with them when the incident occurred. He knew the guilt he was feeling was misplaced but couldn't shake the feeling. He checked in with the two officers standing outside the room, found a seat and waited for Nicole to arrive.

*****

Carl sat in his car, wiping his hands clean even though all residue of blood had been cleaned. Rubbing his palm with the end of his thumb, he pressed hard to wash away the imaginary blood. The stains were long gone, but he wanted to make sure there was absolutely nothing left. Knowing full well his actions were the signs of someone with anxiety issues, he laughed at himself, hoping this would alleviate his feelings of guilt and fear. Not once in his life had he ever been one to act irrationally. He was often impulsive, but rarely irrational. Today was certainly different; he was lost, things had happened that were so far out of his control he didn't know where to turn. He had no leads, no clues, no one left to rely on. He keyed the engine to life and went back to the only place he could think of.

By the time he arrived, the police had completed their search of Will's house. Yellow barricade tape strung across the entrance to the driveway, flapped and twisted in the wind. Carl pulled his car to the shoulder, walked to the tape, ripped it from the tree on the one side then drove up the house, parking out of sight from the roadway.

As he made his way up the drive, there was an eerie silence about the place. The dogs had been taken away, all the wildlife in the area were silent, nothing made a sound. Walking up the driveway, the only sound was the gravel crunching under his shoes. Looking up at the house, there was nothing special about it other than what had happened there earlier in the day. He went to the back door, bright yellow police tape warning the reader it was illegal to entre, ran across the door frame onto the door. He used a credit card to cut the tape; the door was locked, so he raised his foot and kicked. The door didn't budge; he kicked again and again and again until the wood fractured, and the door finally relented. The door swung wide open as Carl entered the house. He didn't bother to announce himself; he knew he was alone.

He thought momentarily about going back to the freezer room, but he didn't think he could handle the stress. Instead, he went upstairs, walked down the hall and found himself standing at the door to the room with a view. The noonday sun was above the house, shadows cut deep into corners of the room and considering the events earlier in the day, a horrible feeling came over Carl. He had trouble entering the room but knew he had to. One foot followed the other, slowly making his way towards the large window. He placed his hand on the back of one of the chairs. With his eyes closed, he inhaled deeply, attempting to calm his nerves, it didn't work. His heart pounded in his chest, his stomach growled at him, his legs became weak. He hadn't eaten since the day before, and he wasn't sure if the weakness was fright or hypoglycemia. He chuckled at his stupidity for not eating and made a mental note to steal something from the fridge before he left. Then again, he thought, considering what Will did in the house, Carl decided to check for something pre-packaged.

He began to rummage through the room, looking for something, anything that might give him an idea where Will would go after escaping his father's house.

*****

At the hospital, Nicole and Simone went to recovery to see Paul. They were granted access through police security and were escorted into the room by one of the officers. The officer stood back allowing the two women to get closer to Paul's bed.

Paul's eyes were closed, the monitor overhead attached to him, beeped with each heartbeat. He sensed as Nicole approached. With tired eyes, he looked at her, still feeling the effects of the anesthetics from surgery. His right-hand slide across the bed for Nicole. She had already begun to cry, hand trembling, she took hold of his hand and squeezed tightly. He gave her a faint smile; his mouth was dry, his lips stuck together.

"You OK?" she asked softly.

He nodded, "A little pain."

"They told me what happened. Maybe someone is telling you to lose a little weight." She squeezed his hand tighter. "When you get out, we can both lose a few pounds. We'll do it together."

"Deal." Paul was finding it difficult to keep his eyes open and slowly drifted back to sleep.

*****

Carl sat on the floor, newspapers scattered on the floor, books open, the two chairs overturned. He was exhausted, hungry and close to collapsing. Looking around the room, he wondered what he had missed. Everything had been opened, examined and scrutinized. There was nothing left in the room that hadn't been inspected. He was certain the police would arrest him, detain him or something worse for breaking into the house. He fell flat on the floor, eyes staring up at the ceiling. Sleep, he thought, should come easy. The ceiling was a pale shade of white, no texture, allowing the shadows of the sun to run unobstructed across the top of the room. His eyes felt heavy; his mind could no longer concentrate as he began to nod off. For a while, he fought the body's need for sleep, but in the end, he gave in.

He wasn't sure how long he laid there, but when he opened his eyes, the room was entirely cast in shadows. The sun was high in the sky, over the house, he had been asleep for at least a few hours. Carl stood, stretched, relieved he hadn't yet been discovered. Looking around the room, he felt a sense of disappointment that his only lead had not yielded any results. He thought about cleaning up then decided against it. Walking towards the hallway, he cast the room one last glance, frowned and closed the door. The door immediately swung open as Carl entered and found the item that caught his eye. He had looked at the framed photograph on the wall a dozen times as he ransacked the room, but it wasn't until now he realized it was what he was looking for.

He stood in front of the photographs in a beautifully ornate wooden frame. Studying the images, he realized how passionate Will was. The mat was cut to showcase two different pictures; one was a larger, black and white, version of the colored photo found in the freezer. The second was taken at a gravesite on a sunny day. The headstone was centered, fleshly cut violets laid carefully at the base, the grass lovingly manicured, the name and dates clearly visible: Evelyn Fleischmann, Born June 14, 1952, Died August 3, 2015. An oval porcelain picture of his mother was affixed to the headstone between the dates. It was hard to see, but Carl moved in closer, squinted and saw that the picture on the headstone was the same as the picture above and from the freezer. The woman in the freezer was meant to look like Will's mother.

*****

Will sat against the headstone, knees curled up; his arms wrapped his legs. He scanned the area; he was certain no one had followed him, he was alone with his mother. He always felt at ease, comfortable speaking with her. There was so much to say, thinking about what he wanted to tell her, how he needed to tell her.

He spoke to himself in a soft voice, barely audible, "You probably already know, Dad is dead, or at least I think he's dead. This girl I was seeing killed him." He laughed, "Or tried to anyway. He always was a stubborn 'ol fart. That was something I never would've seen coming. Like holy shit Mom. Right outta the blue. You would've liked her too, Mom. She was a lot like me," he laughed out loud, "Maybe too much like me."

He adjusted his position on the ground to face his mother's headstone. Will stroked the side of the stone, a sad smile came to his face realizing he missed his mother. It had been years since he had seen his mother and missed her more each time he thought of her. His hand slid across the headstone to the centre ceramic picture of his mother, his finger circling its rim. "I miss you, Mom."

Will heard the grass crunch as a group walked passed and settle around another headstone. They stood in rank, facing the stone, heads down, mumbling a prayer in unison. He watched as they prayed to their God, a prayer to help keep their deceased loved one at peace. "A waste of time," he mumbled to himself. "Idiots."

As the group finished saying their goodbyes, Will turned back to his mother, jumping back when he came face to face with Carl. He stood motionless over Will, hands in his jacket pocket, staring directly at him.

Carl's voice was calm and soft, "Don't worry, I'm here alone." He paused, then laughed. "Not the most intelligent thing to say, is it?" He cast a coy smile, "How's the stitches?"

Will looked down at his injury, rolling his hand over. He had forgotten about the wound, "Fine. You and the doc did a great job. Thanks, by the way."

Carl squatted low, reached for the injured hand. Will didn't resist as Carl took hold and examined the stitches. "A few let go. You should put a bandage on it. Keep it clean." An obvious observation but he was nervous coming face to face with the man who earlier in the day tried to freeze him to death.

"Why did you come to my house?" Will kept his injured hand close to his body.

"A story. Plain and simple, I wanted your story. THE story." Carl held his hand out as if to say everything was alright, that he had forgiven him, as he lowered himself to the ground. Crossing his legs, the two men were about four feet apart. "I'm a reporter," his hand still outstretched.

Will laughed loudly, "Seriously?"

Carl pulled his hand as he shook his head, laughing, "Yup. Seriously, I'm a reporter. I'd like to think I'm better than I actually am but that's up for debate." He raised his eyebrows. "Your dad was sorta my mentor," realizing that in another universe, another time, quite possibly, the man before him could've been a friend. "Carl Kadner," he extended his hand again.

They shook.

Carl slowly reached into his pocket and pulled out his phone, showing it to Will. "I'd like to record your story if you'd permit me?" He nodded.

Carl opened the recording app and placed the phone on the grass between them.

"Why?" Carl asked.

"Why, what?" Will seemed surprised by the question, not expecting to be asked such a direct question.

"I think it's a good starting question, an honest question. Why do you do it?"

Will thought for a moment, the reason that the reporter wanted to hear didn't come easily. The answer should've rolled off his tongue. Thinking about the first life he took, the reasons why, maybe it was only one reason. "I missed her." It seemed as if that was the only reason.

"Who?"

"My mother." He looked at Carl as if the answer was self-evident. "I didn't know my father. I mean I knew who he was, what he was, what he made me. I was the bastard child of his affair with my mother."

"Your father told me about a woman he loved more than anything. But he was married, he also said that he could never be with her. Was your mother that woman?"

Carl could see how Will was affected. The man who killed for the sake of his mother, had tears welling up, his lower lip quivered, he rung his hands, too embarrassed to face the man across from him. With his head low, he whispered, "My mother was the only person in the world to my father. I was, I don't know, an inconvenience I guess. An excuse for him to stop by. If things happen in this world for a reason, he got my mother pregnant so that he had an excuse to stop by and see her and pretend he cared about me. He would bring me a gift each time he stopped by but never spent any time with me, never came to my school, never treated me like a son."

Even with his head hung low, Carl could see the tears streaming down Will's face.

"He paid for everything, our house, food, education, everything, gave me everything but what a young man always wants from his father." He wiped his face with the back of his hand then faced Carl, "Do you know my mother never dated another man, never so much as looked at another man, and she cried each and every time that man left. And I hated her for that. She was weak. I hated him, and I wanted my mother to have someone who would be there for her the way she was there for me. I wanted her to leave my father behind."

"Did she?"

"No," his answer was barely audible. "She died alone, I came home, found her on the kitchen floor. She had cancer and didn't tell anyone. Kept it a secret until the day she died. She was good at keeping secrets." He sniffled. "If you can love someone your whole life and then suddenly hate that person, well, I hated her. I hated her for a long time until I realized she kept that secret to keep me from worrying about her." Will paused, he was deep in thought, gone far away.

"What happened to you?"

Will snapped out of it, "What happened to me?" he laughed. "I missed her. I missed her so much. I had a handful of photographs, old ones, the way I remembered her when I was growing up. I wanted her back. I wanted something back. Something tactile," he held his hand in the air, palm side up, fingers wiggling back and forth. "I needed to feel her, touch her, hold her. So, I started to make her alive, well to me anyway. I needed to be with her again. Does that sound crazy? I'm not mad; I know what I did was wrong. But, if you do something out of love, is it still wrong?" Will looked at him, expecting an answer.

Carl thought carefully before saying anything, "I'm the wrong person to ask. I'm not in charge of determining what's right and what's wrong. I'm not entirely innocent myself." He waited to see if Will would respond, he didn't. He sat there, head down, a runny nose, a look of guilt on his face. "I was in the freezer with her. I saw her. Well, you put me there, so you know that. When the police were going over the room, they found what looks like egg on the body."

Will laughed, "I get mad at my mother. I get so mad at her for leaving, for not telling me, for not getting treatment. Maybe she would've lived. I lost my temper," his words trembled as he spoke. "I think God is getting back at me. He knows what I've done is wrong, to those girls and to my mother. I believe he gave me an aneurysm and it might burst today. Maybe today is my day."

Carl looked at him confused, "Your little episode on the sofa. That was real?"

He just nodded, "My head felt like it was going to explode. Felt like it anyway."

"Please don't take this the wrong way, I have a hard time believing that your headache came on at just the right time."

*****

Nicole held Paul's hand as he slept. Simone had also fallen asleep as she sat in the corner of the room, a police guard standing beside her and another outside the room. Nicole had no more tears to shed; she was all cried out. She released her hold, stood, carefully pulled the sheet down to reveal the large dressing across Paul's stomach. She knew he had been slashed, but until then, she didn't comprehend the severity of the injury. Her concern disappeared, replaced with rage at the person who attempted to kill him. She felt something new grow inside her, something she had never felt before. Teeth clenched, she stood over the bed watching over Paul. The pulse pounded in her temples, her fists tight, she had a new mission. Katy was dead, but the skinny man was still alive and on the run. And she knew exactly how to find him.

She excused herself and left the room, walked to the end of the hall, entered the bathroom, locked the door, turned off the light then sat on the toilet seat. Closing her eyes, she cleared her mind of anything except the skinny man with the hairless arms. Her mind went blank, thinking about nothing other than the goal at hand. The darkness in her mind slowly began to swirl with bright light, spinning, circling around her head, the darkness giving way to greens and browns and blues. The images in her mind began to form; stones emerged from the ground in rows, some covered in the shade by the trees above, others brightly lit by the sun. The stones eventually formed, and she knew where she was. Two men sat on the ground facing each other. One man she recognized, the other she didn't.

Nicole focused on the skinny man and entered his thoughts.

*****

"I'm telling you, it's like every single image, every experience is being ripped from your mind and examined. Memories I've long forgotten are replayed in my head, all at the same time." He closed his eyes and rubbed his temples as a new headache stuck him again like a bullet to the brain. With his eyes closed tightly, he rolled onto the grass, moaning.

Carl had seen Will in that same position on the couch at Sam's house. He immediately became suspicious of his behavior, assuming he was faking. He leaned back, huffed, having no time for Will's theatrics. "You managed to fake your way out of your dad's house. I don't believe a thing you're doing so give it a rest."

Will continued to hold his head, eyes shut tightly against the day's bright sun. He looked deep inside his thoughts and felt someone else mauling around his skull. He could see long forgotten memories being opened like a book and played out then another chapter began, more memories unfolding, the memories playing over one another, pain, excruciating pain drilling holes in his mind. He attempted to close one memory, but more memories opened faster than he could close. He was sparing with a ghost in his own mind. For the first time, he felt as if he was truly going mad. Fighting for control over his mind, he anticipated where the ghost in his head would go and fought for control. He closed some of the memories, more than were being opened, he was finally beginning to take back his mind. He raced from image to image, shutting down the memories but the ghost in his head began to work faster to unlock long forgotten times.

Memories played out, one over the other, blending, meshing together, all sense of time had long disappeared, he was old, then young, his mother alive one moment, dead the next then alive again. Doors closing and opening, he tried to keep them shut, but the ghost had the key to unlock everything in his mind.

From his fight earlier in the day, Will learnt a few tactics, instead of fighting the memories, he turned to find the ghost. Anticipating where the next door would open, he hid behind the memory hoping it would be the next one. He worked his way towards the ghost, figuring out the pattern, where would the next door open?

Nicole kicked back, her head snapping like a bobblehead on a car's dash. She felt Will grab the memory she was about to open and slammed it shut. He then pushed hard, and Nicole lost control, allowing Will to swing the door into her mind. Intense pain cut through her head. For the first time, she knew the type of pain she was causing Will when she was in his head.

Will ran through her memories, attempting to find his way around. He was new here, never having done this before. He didn't know where to turn, what to do, where to go or how to properly do what she was doing to him. Fumbling his way about, he grabbed at whatever he could, not knowing Nicole had recovered and was right behind him. As he found one of Nicole's doors, he took hold, opened the memory wide and saw the person who was attacking him. She was not what he anticipated. Will wasn't sure what he would find, but this woman was certainly not it. He paused for only a moment to remember her face so that he could find her and make her pay for what she was doing to him. In that brief moment, Nicole saw him hesitate, and she pushed hard, knocking Will from her door making him lose his balance. Seeing him off balance, he was in her mind, she had the power and wanted to make him pay. She used all of her energy and attacked him with fury and vengeance. Will felt something, some force wrap around his entire body. He thought he was only screaming in agony in his own mind, but Carl jumped back as Will let out a high-pitched yell.

On the grass, Will held his head; his breathing was so rapid, Carl wondered if he was dying. He turned Will over, his eyes were closed, but under his eyelids, it looked like snakes swimming beneath them. Carl had heard of REM sleep, but this was beyond any normal eye movement he had ever seen. Will was unconscious, panting, covered in sweat.

Carl grabbed his phone laying on the grass, swiped up and called 911.

Inside Will's mind, Nicole fought for control. She had pushed back into Will's mind. She knew what she was doing, she wanted revenge, not only for Paul but for the girls he killed. Opening the doors, Nicole has seen not only how they were killed but what he did to them afterwards. She felt their fear and pain. It was too much for her; she wanted to make him pay for what he had done to them, and her.

She ripped at anything she could find; more memories sprang up, she saw Sam at his mother's house, making love to her with Will in the next room. She had a moment of sympathy for the boy but cast it aside and kept tearing at Will's mind. More and more, the visual life of Will played out in different times all at once. Will was seeing scenes of his entire life being played out all at the same time. He couldn't focus on any one and Nicole didn't take the time to see the mayhem she was causing. She just kept opening doors, letting the memories loose and running to the next.

Will forced his eyes shut but the flood of images couldn't be stopped.

Images overlaid upon one another, it was like trying to focus on one song as thousands played at once. Memories that he had forgotten, painful ones, ones that he buried long ago, were now being replayed with full clarity. There was no way to stop seeing what was going on inside his head. The pressure, the pain, was too much. Will relented, gave up, hoping the ghost would taste victory and stop. Instead, memories sprang up and flooded his mind until there were just too many to take.

Will rolled around on the grass, his screams had drawn the attention of other visitors to the graveyard. There was now a crowd gathering behind Carl as he attempted to restrain Will before he hurt himself.

Inside, Will had lost the ability to fight back. He dropped to his knees, called out to the ghost and begged for the torment to stop before he went insane.

He still couldn't find the woman who was attacking him, but he heard her voice in his head, "Stop? Stop? Did you stop when those girls asked you to stop? Did you? Why should I?" With that, Nicole blindly reached forward and pulled on as many doors as possible; flooding Will with memories he had long forgotten. Images of himself as a young baby, being held by his mother. Images that normally could never be remembered, Nicole ripped them from his mind and displayed them as if they were occurring at that moment.

Will looked up at his mother, he couldn't recall her this young; she was changing his diaper. How could those memories still be locked away, to be opened and seen again? Nicole opened another door from the past, Will was being breastfed, held by his smiling mother. Unable to comprehend what he was seeing, he collapsed on the grass, his arms falling softly to his side. His breathing slowed, slowed until it stopped. His chest no longer rose and fell. All eye movement stopped.

Carl searched for a pulse in the neck; he wasn't sure where to feel, he had seen them doing this on television all the time. He fumbled about, fingers resting all over the side of his neck. He felt nothing, then tilted Will's head back to give a few rescue breaths, and as he did, the eyelids opened. Both of Will's eyes had ruptured, they were blood red. Carl stopped what he was doing and placed his hands on either side of Will's head and carefully turned his head, so he could face him. There were no pupils, everything in the eyes were gone. His eyes had filled with blood unable to see anything anymore.

Nicole opened her eyes; it was done. He was dead; she tore apart every last remnant of what Will was before she stopped. She wanted to make sure he paid. In the darkness, she reached for the light switch. Looking in the mirror, she saw the toll the fight had taken. The person looking back at her in the mirror wasn't the same person that entered that bathroom only a few minutes earlier. That person was tired, bags under her eyes, she had aged, the fight had changed her.

Splashing water on her face did little to repair the fatigue. Wiping the water from her eyes, she noticed her hair was severely in need of a haircut. It was getting longer than she had it for the past few years but thought it was time for a change. She pulled her hair back into a small ponytail, took in a deep breath and stepped into the hall. Simone stood outside Paul's room with a look of concern and relief. Nicole slowly approached her with a broad smile.

They both entered Paul's room where she noticed a strange younger woman standing over him. The stranger turned to face them as the door closed. Nicole recognized her immediately from the picture Paul kept in his pocket. Her eyes were red and puffy from crying; she took in a deep breath then ran to embrace Nicole. She wrapped both her arms around the younger woman and squeezed hard. The younger woman responded in kind.

"My dad's told me all about you."

Nicole pulled back, looked into Paul's daughter's eyes then hugged her again.

Nicole looked down to see Paul beaming.

Despite everything she had done, Nicole had no regrets.

About The Author

After graduating as a paramedic in 1983 from Fanshawe College in London, Ontario, Perry Prete moved to Windsor, Ontario, and then Brockville, Ontario, where he now continues to work full-time as a paramedic for the county.

He continues to write and operate a pre-hospital medical supply company. With over thirty years of experience as a field paramedic, he draws on his career to bring realism to the calls depicted in his writing.